RACHEL VINCENT

ALPHA

MIRA®

ISBN-13: 978-0-7783-2818-6

Recycling programs for this product may not exist in your area.

ALPHA

Copyright © 2010 by Rachel Vincent

For questions and comments about the quality of this book please contact us at Customer_eCare@Harlequin.ca.

www.MIRABooks.com

Printed in U.S.A.

To everyone at MIRA Books
whose unsung efforts behind the scenes helped
make this, my debut series and first venture into
publishing, the experience of a lifetime.

To all the friends I've made through my writing.
You've kept me sane—or at least convinced me
that I'm not alone in my neuroses.

And finally, to all the Shifters readers
who have stuck it out with Faythe and with me
as we grew and learned. This has been an amazing
journey, and I'm so thankful for everyone
who traveled it with me. I'm not bowing out,
but this is Faythe's last hurrah.
Thanks for helping me send her off in style....

One

"Are you sure about this?" Jace hesitated, one hand gripping a bare branch overhead, the other poised over his zipper. But I could see the truth. He wanted this as badly as I did.

"Absolutely." I pushed my last button through the hole and let my shirt fall to the ground in a patch of mottled sunlight. My skin was already covered in goose bumps, as much from anticipation as from the February cold. "Now shut up and take off your pants."

He shrugged and grinned. "You know I'm always up for some sweaty fun." But the look in his eyes as his gaze roamed south of mine belied his casual zeal. Part bloodlust, part real lust, and all exhilaration —just like me.

"I'm not sure that's quite how I'd describe this." Not that I wasn't looking forward to a little action. It had been *days,* and I was really starting to crave—

"What the hell is this?" Marc growled, an instant before he tore through the brush to my left. Sunlight burst into the woods with his intrusion, spotlighting my exposed bra and Jace's…total nudity. *Damn, that boy's fast!* Fury emanated from Marc like a deep, dark glow, emphasizing his strong, dark features. "You are *not* doing this without me."

Shit. "Marc, this isn't what you think, and we don't have time to explain…" My eyes narrowed as his last few words finally sank in. "Wait…*what?*"

"I said, not…without…me." His brow rose in silent challenge, and all words abandoned me.

I blinked, lost for a moment in the possibilities, then I shook my head to clear it. "But we're not…" I waved one hand back and forth between me and Jace, unable to actually vocalize what he surely thought we were doing. "We're going after Ryan. I caught a whiff of him on my run."

"Vic told me." Yet he was still clearly pissed, even knowing Jace and I hadn't run off for a secret, midday tumble in the…underbrush.

"You didn't tell my dad…?"

Marc had been talking war strategy with my father when I'd come in from my run, and I hadn't told them where we were going because I didn't want my dad to know about Ryan. Not when we could easily take care of the problem ourselves and spare him—and my mother—the additional tension.

He shook his head slowly, as if doubting his own decision. "Ryan's the last thing he should have to deal with right now."

"Yeah." And I was really looking forward to the exercise, to burn off a little stress through good, clean exertion. As opposed to the other, sweatier kind, which we were all currently denying ourselves, to keep Marc and Jace from killing each other.

Whoever said two is better than one was either stupid or crazy. Or heartless.

"I'm coming with you, so get dressed. Now. You're not Shifting."

"Do *not* start ordering her around," Jace growled, and dread pitched deep in my stomach, like nausea with a heartburn upgrade.

Marc snarled, and I saw the instant he lost control of his temper. He lunged for Jace. Jace leaped forward. I threw myself between them.

Both hard bodies slammed into me. Air exploded from my throat. My grunt of pain hardly carried any sound. For just an instant, I couldn't move, crushed between them, confused by the collision of scents and hurting all over. My torso was one giant bruise—I wouldn't have fared much better between two oncoming cars.

I'm not sure which of them moved first, but suddenly I was on the ground, staring up at two concerned, angry faces. "Damn it, Faythe, you're going to get yourself killed," Marc snapped.

I sucked in a painful breath, and my voice came out hoarse. "Evidently that's what it takes to keep you two from killing each other." Though truthfully, while Jace would eagerly defend himself, he had yet to actually attack Marc. The reverse could not be said.

I shoved them away and pushed myself to my feet, glaring at Marc as they both stood with me. "Look, I know this whole thing is my fault…"

"Not *just* yours." Marc glowered at Jace over my shoulder.

"…and I know the timing could not have been worse. And I'm sorrier about both of those than I could possibly explain. But if I have to spend all my time and energy trying to keep the two of you apart, I really am going to get myself killed, and it'll be your fault."

Marc reeled like I'd punched him. But he recovered quickly, with a fresh dose of anger. "You reap what you sow, Faythe. And I'm still going with you."

I crossed my arms over my chest and tried to ignore the fresh chill bumps. "I think you and Jace should stay away from each other until you've cooled off."

"Why? So you two can top off your hunt with a little more…reaping and sowing?"

I closed my eyes, breathing through the acute ache in my chest, which had nothing to do with the midtom collision. Then I made myself look at him. "Do you honestly think I'd do that to you?"

"I think you already have."

He was right, but the barb still stung. I hadn't even come close to earning forgiveness yet, but this was not the time to try. Something always seemed to get in the way. "We're going after Ryan. You're welcome to join us, if you can control your temper."

I'd never seen Marc as bitter or openly antagonistic as he'd been over the past week. His anger was getting in the way of his concentration, his sleeping pattern, and his job, but he couldn't work around it because he couldn't solve the problem—that was up to me—nor could he get away from it. Every time he turned around, Jace and I were there, our very presence reminding him of what had happened.

This wasn't going to get any better until I made a decision, one way or another.

Marc's dark brows dipped low and he stepped closer, so that I had to look up to meet his eyes. "I'm going— on my own terms." He pulled his black T-shirt over his head, and my gaze caught involuntarily on his chest, sculpted by years of enforcer training and scarred by the rogue who'd brought him into my life fifteen years before. I wanted to trace those scars with my fingers, but I wasn't sure I had the right to anymore. He'd barely touched me since he found out about me and Jace.

"You don't outrank me yet," he spat. "So put your shirt on—you're staying on two legs. And this time see if you can keep them together."

I actually staggered backward, floored by the depth of his anger. But not really surprised. I deserved the worst he had to dish out, and he deserved the outlet, especially considering that he couldn't vent where anyone else could hear him. But *damn,* the venom in his voice stung.

Jace growled and stepped forward, but I put a hand on his stomach to stop him.

I wanted to yell at Marc, to fight back, but that would only make the whole thing worse. So I swallowed my anger and stuck to the subject. "Hell, no. I'm faster on four legs." My private run had been cut short by the unauthorized scent in the woods, and I was dying for some exercise in cat form to help clear my head and fight off the bloodlust we'd all been battling for the past couple of weeks. Ever since Ethan died—my brother murdered on our own property.

Marc snatched my shirt from the ground and shoved it at me. "Unless you're planning to kill him, claws and canines won't do you any good this time."

He was right, so I groaned and shoved my arms through the sleeves, then turned my back on them both, already running toward the spot where I'd first caught Ryan's scent. "Catch up with me when you've Shifted."

I wasn't a leader. Not really. Not yet. But my father was training me to replace him as Alpha someday, and an Alpha had to be ready to ask questions and issue orders, both of which were hard to do in cat form.

Normally, an Alpha—even a trainee—wouldn't haul ass through the woods on her own while looking for a known trespasser. Especially in human form, and virtually defenseless against someone with claws and canines. However, this particular trespasser was more than merely known. He was reviled, scorned, and pitied. But he was not feared.

Also, he was my brother.

My pulse raced as I ran and each breath came faster than the last. I tried to exhale it all—to purge my body of the poison I'd been living and breathing since I'd started lying to Marc. That was all over. He knew that I'd slept with Jace—once, in the onslaught of grief for Ethan, while Marc was missing and presumed dead—but the truth had only made things worse. I could apologize, and I had many, many times, but I couldn't tell him it was over. I couldn't tell him I didn't love Jace. Not without lying to him again.

I hated myself for that, but it was a useless hatred. It changed nothing. I loved Marc, but I didn't deserve him. I loved Jace, but I couldn't give up Marc. And no matter what I decided, Marc had made it clear that he couldn't live with Jace anymore. Once the war was over, one of them would have to go. But I didn't want to lose either one.

Lost in my thoughts and ungainly in human form, I tripped over an exposed root and caught myself on a twisted branch, sparing only a moment to regain my balance. Then I was off again, my lungs burning from the cold.

A few steps later, two sleek, dark forms passed me so quickly I couldn't even focus on them. But I could smell them. Marc and Jace, fully Shifted into cat form and embroiled in an impromptu race. Everything was a competition now, whether or not it involved me. Everything was tense, and dangerous, and painful. And I could practically taste Marc's frustration. He could probably have outrun Jace—except he didn't know where they were going. He hadn't been there when I told Jace where I'd smelled Ryan.

By the time I got there, they had him treed, a slim human form clinging to the branches overhead. Ryan was little more than a patchwork of shadows cast by the crisscross of branches, but I could swear I saw those shadows tremble.

Marc had wanted him dead all along for what he'd done to me. For giving me to South American tabby traffickers, who would have sold me to the highest bidder.

"Stand down," I said, and both toms obeyed. Even in his unprecedented state of rage, Marc wouldn't expose the dissention in our ranks to the enemy. And despite my mother's soft spot for her second-born, the rest of us definitely considered Ryan an enemy.

"Get down. Now," I ordered, and after a moment's hesitation, Ryan dropped to the ground in front of me, knees bent, arms spread for balance. I tried not to acknowledge the skill in his dismount. I attributed it to the frequency with which a coward like my black-sheep brother was probably treed.

"Faythe." Ryan nodded in tentative greeting, careful

not to bow his head too low. He wasn't prepared to acknowledge my rank in the Pride. Not yet, anyway. Even though he was no longer a member.

The shadow of a bare branch fell across his face, and in my mind I saw steel bars. He'd shown up under a truce flag of sorts for Ethan's funeral, but there was too much else going on then—I'd hardly given him a second thought. But seeing him here, hiding in the shadows, brought it all back.…

"Give me one good reason I shouldn't let them tear your arms off and watch you bleed out."

"Because Mom would smell my blood the next time she gets within half a mile of here."

I raised both brows, reluctantly impressed. I'd expected him to beg for his life, or at least appeal to our frayed familial bond. But he obviously knew that would do no good. And that even if I were willing to kill someone who posed no immediate threat, I wouldn't hurt our mother, even to punish him. She'd already buried one son, and I would not put her through a second funeral in less than a month.

"What the hell are you doing here? And keep in mind that Shifters can take a lot of pain without actually dying." I'd know.

Ryan had seen me beaten into a mass of blood, lumps, and purple bruises after fighting off the first of the psychotic rapists and murderers he'd helped kidnap me and two other tabbies, including our cousin Abby. All to protect his own ass. For him, that was always the bottom line. Ryan was a Grade-A coward. Just looking at him made me feel sick.

"I need to see her." Our mother, of course. His crutch,

bank, security blanket, and the only member of our family he actually seemed to care about.

"I don't give a shit what you need," I spat, and Marc huffed in agreement.

"Fine. I get that and I don't blame you." Ryan nodded, always eager to placate, to keep from getting his face pounded in. "But she needs to see me."

I rolled my eyes. "Why would she need to see you?"

"For the same reason she needs to see you. Because she's our mother. Don't you think she's been through enough with Ethan?"

"Don't." I swallowed thickly and my hands curled into fists as Jace growled at my side. "You do *not* get to say his name. Ethan was everything you're not. He fought for all of us, over and over. He *died* fighting for an innocent tabby. But you... You sold us out." He dropped a gaze full of guilt, and that only made me angrier. "Look at me," I demanded, my throat aching from holding back the things I wanted to shout at him. The accusations I'd been holding in for months. "Eye contact is the *least* you owe me."

Ryan raised his head, and the misery I saw on his face did nothing to mollify my rage. He didn't know misery. He knew nothing like the pain he'd caused.

"Abby was seventeen years old, and a virgin, and you let them rape her. Sara was getting married, and you let them rape her, then *kill* her. And you let them put their hands all over me. You let them try..."

He flinched, and I couldn't finish. He knew what he'd let them try. And from the way he cringed, I'd say the memories hurt. *Good.* But they couldn't hurt him like they hurt me.

Rachel Vincent

"Don't you dare tell me what Mom needs. She does not need *you*. None of us do."

Ryan sighed and his gaze strengthened, like he was looking for something in my eyes. "I know you don't want to hear this, but she forgave me, Faythe. Why can't you?"

My fist flew before I knew it was going to. His nose crunched, then blood sprayed my shirt and neck. Ryan howled, but the sound ended in a gurgle. His hands flew to cover his face.

Marc purred and rubbed against my ankle. Ryan dropped to his knees, cradling his ruined nose.

"Mom wasn't grabbed, and kicked, and punched, and humiliated," I snapped. "She wasn't thrown around a cage in a filthy basement. She wasn't *touched*. She has the luxury of forgiveness because she doesn't fail to fight them off in her nightmares. Did you know I dream about it, Ryan?" I dropped into a squat in front of him and pulled his head back by his hair until I saw his eyes, already surrounded by rapidly swelling, darkening flesh. "Did you know it happens all over again, every night I sleep alone? Every night I'm too tired to fight off the memories?" I swallowed a sob and forced the next words out. "I needed you then. You were supposed to protect me. But I don't need you now."

My fist slammed into his jaw, and his head hit the tree trunk. His eyes watered, but I couldn't tell if they were tears of regret or pain. And I didn't care.

One of the guys tugged me backward by the hem of my shirt, and I stood, the cold forgotten. "We were family." I kicked, and my boot slammed into his thigh. "You were my big brother."

Ryan's tears fell. He was saying something, but I couldn't hear him. Didn't want to.

"Brothers are supposed to make sure things like that *never happen* to little sisters. It's your *job,* whether you're an enforcer or not. Ethan knew that. Why the hell didn't you?" I kicked again, and Ryan huddled against the base of the tree. He didn't even try to defend himself. Like he wanted to be punished. Like being hit alleviated some of the guilt.

Marc tugged me again, and I stumbled backward, half-shocked to see the blood on my hand. I hadn't realized I still carried that much rage.

Ryan looked up. He wiped blood and tears on the sleeve of his jacket and stood slowly. "I'm so sorry, Faythe. I know it's never gonna be enough, but I am so, so sorry."

Yeah. Tell that to Sara and Abby. "Get out." My eyes burned, and I wanted to rub them. Or close them.

"Faythe…"

"Get out!" I shouted. "And if you come back, I swear I'll wear your canines as earrings."

"Please…" He tried one last time, swiping at the steady trickle of blood from his nose.

"Go!"

Finally Ryan ran. He looked back twice. And I only realized I was crying when I fell to my knees, and Jace licked the hot tears from my face with his warm, rough tongue. They curled around me, both of them sharing their warmth and their comfort, and I dug my fingers into their fur. And for several minutes, I could only cry.

* * *

I sat on the couch in the guesthouse, my fingers still numb from the cold, my face still red from crying.

Marc zipped his pants, and the metallic whisper was loud in the near silence, even from the kitchenette across the room. While Jace finished his Shift, Marc brought me a cold bottle of water; no doubt all the glasses were dirty. Half a minute later, Jace stood, nude from his Shift and in no rush to reach for his clothes.

Marc scowled and tossed him the jeans I'd picked up on our way out of the woods.

Jace watched me in concern as he pulled them on, and the look Marc shot him could have frozen lava. But Jace was unfazed. "I'll get her fixed up. You go get her a clean shirt."

"I am not leaving you alone with her. Here." Where Jace and I had…*connected*. On the living room floor.

Jace rolled brilliant blue eyes. "Like I'm gonna hit on her while she's upset."

"If memory serves, that's when she's most…receptive," Marc spat.

My temper flared and my hands curled into fists, but I kept my mouth shut. He'd survived being cuckolded—I could survive his anger.

Jace stomped into the kitchen and slammed his hands flat on the countertop, staring across the island at Marc. "You can take this out on me if you want, but leave her the hell alone."

"You talk to me like that again, and I'll take this out on your face," Marc growled through clenched teeth.

"Go for it." Jace stood straight and spread his arms, inviting the first blow. He wanted to fight, but he wouldn't start it because he knew that would piss me off.

Marc was *trying* to piss me off. To hurt me like I'd hurt him.

And his tongue turned out to be just as sharp as mine.

"No." I should have been encouraged by the fact that I didn't have to raise my voice to stop them, but in that moment, I was kind of seeing the cup as half-empty. "Unless you want to tell my dad that I beat the snot out of you both, you better lay the hell off." I looked up from the bottle, cold and wet in my hand. "I can't go in there wearing Ryan's blood, and if I borrow a shirt from either one of you, someone's going to ask what happened to my own."

"Fine." Marc nodded toward the front door. "Jace, go get her a clean shirt. She has another one just like it." In fact, I had several button-down black blouses, useful for both work and play.

Jace shrugged. "And what should I say when someone sees me rooting through her drawers, or even just coming out of her room with a shirt?"

"Damn it," Marc swore. No one would question his presence in my room, or his possession of my shirt—in a good month, I lost a couple of articles of clothing in the line of duty, and at least one more to the force of nature that is Marc and his impatience. He slammed one fist into the countertop, then took off for the door without another glance at either of us.

When he was gone, Jace ran water in the sink, then sank onto the couch next to me with a steaming, damp rag. "Do you, um, want to take that off?" He was staring at my bloodstained shirt. "In the most platonic sense of…stripping."

"I shouldn't." Not until Marc was back. But I could hardly stand the scent of Ryan's blood on me. It reminded me of what I'd just done to him, and what he'd let happen to me. So I twisted away from Jace and unbuttoned my blouse.

He gave me space to move, but I felt his gaze on me like a palpable heat, and my heart beat faster.

My hand shook when I dropped the soiled cotton on the floor.

"Here, lean back," Jace whispered, and when I didn't move—when I couldn't, for fear of shattering my fragile self-control—he slid one strong hand behind my neck and cradled my skull, tilting my head back with gentle pressure.

He wiped the back of my jaw with the warm, wet rag, and his pulse whooshed faster with each movement. He closed his eyes, and my heartbeat spiked with panic. There was no platonic touching between me and Jace. Not anymore. And I'd already learned that an ounce of prevention was worth a pound of…Marc's fury and pain.

"I got it." I took the rag from him and perfunctorily cleaned my neck and chest, while he stared at the floor, obviously determined not to watch. To think about something else. When I was done, I dropped the rag on the end table and turned to lean against the couch arm, my legs folded beneath me to keep distance between us.

Jace frowned at me, his intense gaze searching mine. He'd found something else to focus on, and I could already tell I wouldn't like the change of subject. "Do you really dream about it? About being in that basement?"

I stared into my lap, where my fingers tried to twist one another into knots, until Jace's hand closed over them. "You think I'd make that up?"

"You never said anything. Does Marc know?"

I nodded. "How could he not?"

Jace inhaled deeply, and I heard his pulse speed up. "If sleeping alone makes it worse…you don't have to sleep alone." I looked up with one brow raised, but he rushed on. "I'm not asking for anything. I'm just saying…I'm here."

My heart ached, like it was too full to fit in my chest, and I blinked to keep him from seeing that. "Yeah. Until Marc kills you."

"I'd like to see him try."

"I wouldn't."

Footsteps clomped up the stairs, and Jace moved a foot away on the couch. The door swung open and Marc took us both in. He scowled, but made no comment. We hadn't broken the rules—technically.

"Here." He tossed the clean shirt at me and I stood to put it on. "You better hurry. Angela just turned into the driveway."

Two

I jogged across the backyard toward the main house, Marc and Jace on my heels. We burst through the back door, and they passed me when I stopped in the guest bathroom to make sure my shirt was straight and there were no leaves in my hair. I had gotten all the blood off my neck, but I had to wash my hands to get Ryan's scent off my right fist, which was when I discovered I'd split two of my knuckles on his face. Crap.

None of my fellow cats would give it a second thought; they'd assume I'd assaulted the hanging bag without my gloves again. But Angela… She probably wouldn't know what to make of my split knuckles, not to mention the thin white line bisecting my left cheek. At least my sleeve covered the long, zigzag of new scar tissue on my left forearm—that was one less question to answer. Assuming she was bold enough to actually ask.

Her engine growled out front, and my pulse spiked almost painfully. Why was I so nervous? Well, truthfully, everyone was nervous. It isn't every day you meet your dead brother's pregnant girlfriend. A human girlfriend, at that. And she had no idea that we weren't completely human, so a good deal of the ambient tension had to do with hiding our little secret, so she didn't run screaming into the…broad daylight.

The rest of it had to do with the baby. Ethan's baby, whose existence we'd only discovered the day we buried my brother. A tiny piece of him we'd had no reason to hope for. The grandchild my parents never expected.

That baby was a genetic miracle, and we desperately wanted Angela to like us. To want to include us in her child's life.

Yet my own nerves went beyond that. They were a complex mix of jealousy, nostalgia, and relief over my near miss with a tragically mundane life.

Angela would be my first up-close look at anything resembling normalcy since I'd left grad school. The freedom I'd once fought for was now gone—choked out of existence by the iron grip of responsibility—and the life I'd once run from had reclaimed me. I'd made my own choices, and while I had undeniably moved past that escapist phase of my life, there was some tiny part of me that leaned toward panic at the knowledge that I couldn't go back now even if I wanted to.

I stared into the mirror, trying to see myself as she would see me. Tangled hair, scarred cheek, skinned knuckles. My face was too thin, my arms and shoulders too well-defined. And there was a hardness behind my eyes now, difficult to describe, but impossible to miss.

I'd seen and done things that would have put most women my age in a padded room. I'd fought for my life, my freedom, and my family. I'd been kidnapped, beaten, broken, clawed, and stabbed. I'd caught rogues, and killed killers, and I'd watched my brother die. It was hard to believe that less than a year ago, I'd been a student like Angela.

Minus the whole faulty-condom-turned-miracle thing.

My mother appeared in the bathroom doorway, nervously twisting her wedding ring as I tried to finger-comb my hair. "She's here."

"So I heard." I turned away from my identity crisis and smiled, almost amused to see her so flustered. My mom hadn't blinked an eye when she'd faced down a jungle stray in her own basement, but now she looked ready to lose her breakfast. "It'll be fine," I insisted, while doubt rang in my head, soft but insistent. There was no way we'd come off like the average American household. The Addams Family had a better shot.

What if Angela knew something was scary-different about us, and she took off with Ethan's baby? What if she decided not to have it?

"Maybe we shouldn't do this." My mother straightened her freshly pressed blouse, and the high arch of her brows managed to convey both eagerness and dread. "I mean, obviously we should help her financially, but maybe we should…keep our distance. It's not really a good time, with you all leaving tomorrow…."

After months of waiting, lobbying, and fighting on the sidelines, our big day had finally come. Marc, Jace, and I would accompany my father to a meeting of the full Territorial Council, ostensibly for the vote that could reinstate him as council chair—or put Jace's megalo-maniac stepfather, Calvin Malone, in power. But our real reason for going was to present hard-won evidence against Malone as a traitor to our species and hopefully put him out of the running. And completely out of power.

I shoved aside my own doubts and linked my arm through hers to keep her from twisting her own fingers off. "The timing is out of our hands," I said, and she could only nod. "Let's just try not to overwhelm her."

I stepped into the hall, half tugging my mother, and rolled my eyes when I saw Brian, Parker, and Vic peering through the sidelight windows. "Guys. Come on. We're trying *not* to overwhelm her."

Brian shrugged, looking younger than ever, and Vic just frowned and crossed his arms over his chest. "You really think there's any chance of that?"

"If you guys lay off the stares and turn on the charm, yeah." Though privately I had my doubts. "Remember, you're normal, nonfurry ranch hands and good friends of the family." That was close enough to the truth to be believable—if the Lazy S had been a functioning ranch. And if ranch hands were trained to protect their Alpha, patrol their territory, and take down bad guys with badass paw-to-paw combat.

"Brian, go tell my dad she's here," I said, and he took off dutifully toward the office, which was virtually soundproof with the door closed, thanks to solid concrete walls.

"This is so weird." Parker ran one hand through straight salt-and-pepper hair. "Ethan would have been a dad. I can't picture it."

"I can." I steered him away from the door, hoping Angela wouldn't smell the whiskey on his breath. At one o'clock in the afternoon.

My mother ducked into the living room to tweak an arrangement of snacks, and I squeezed in next to Vic to peek out the window. Our guest still sat in her car with the driver's-side door open, digging in her purse for something. But I had the distinct impression that she was stalling.

I couldn't decide who was more nervous—Angela or my mom. Or me.

"Scoot over," Kaci said, and I turned to find the young tabby standing behind me, hazel eyes wide, long brown hair pulled into a thick wavy ponytail at the base of her neck. Kaci didn't look nervous. She looked curious. And skeptical.

Ethan's death had hit her very hard, and she now seemed both fascinated to meet his only remaining link to the world and ambivalent to the woman who'd known a very different side of him. "She looks...normal."

Jace laughed. "You were expecting two heads?"

Kaci only frowned. "How come she's just sitting in her car?"

Marc spoke up from the dining room doorway, making no attempt to look through the window. "I'm sure she's nervous."

And she hadn't even met our brood yet. "Okay, why don't you guys all go sit, so we don't overwhelm her the moment she walks in the door."

Marc's frown mirrored Kaci's, but he herded the thirteen-year-old tabby toward the living room and shot one last irritated glance at me and Jace before stepping through the doorway and out of sight. I'd been nominated for the welcoming committee because I was the only tabby near her age—at least, the only one with flawless English—and Jace got to play because he'd set up the meeting with Angela. He'd dated her twin for a few weeks, back when Ethan and Angela first started going out.

Yes, Jace and Ethan dated twins. Seriously.

Jace stepped closer to me in the deserted hallway, ostensibly to look through the window, and the warmth from his chest leached through the back of my shirt. "You ready?" he asked, but the question felt loaded, like Angela was the last thing on his mind.

Mom was right; the timing could *not* have been worse.

I sighed. "Not even kind of."

He turned me by both shoulders and grinned down at me. "She won't bite. And she's probably the only person within a square mile who can swear to that right now."

"That's part of the problem."

I opened the door, and Angela looked up when we stepped onto the porch. Then she took a deep breath and got out of the car.

She's so young, I thought, taking in her slim form and freckled cheeks. But she was only a year younger than I was, and twenty-two really wasn't that young to be a first-time mother. Even today, most tabbies already had a son or two by Angela's age.

I smiled, and her mouth turned up in a nervous reflection of my own expression. Then she noticed the tom behind me, and her whole face brightened.

"Jace!" She sounded so familiar I had to fight a sharp jolt of jealousy, though I knew she and Jace had never been involved. But I was suddenly irritated by the realization that she knew more about some part of his life than I did. And even more about Ethan's. "I wasn't sure you'd be here."

"Like I'd let you walk into the lion's den all alone," he teased, and that streak of jealousy in me grew stronger as her smile widened. Though Jace and Ethan had rarely ever sat at home on the weekends, I couldn't remember ever actually seeing him interact with someone outside the sphere of our secret existence. He was…different. Relaxed and confident, showing no sign of the power struggle with Marc or the bloodlust we'd all been battling for weeks now.

I was amazed that he could turn all that off and set her at ease. And beneath my jealousy, I was grateful, because none of the rest of us knew Angela well enough to play Virgil, guiding her through the hell our world had become since Ethan's death.

"Don't worry, they're all eager to meet you," Jace said, and I followed him down the steps, hanging back when she hugged him, clinging to him like a life raft in a storm.

"Andrea still asks about you," she said, when he finally pulled away.

Jace stiffened, like he wanted to glance back at me, and pulled one hand through his hair. "How is she?"

"Fine. Surprised." She grinned and ran one hand over her flat stomach, and some vague tension in me eased. She was happy to be pregnant. She didn't resent Ethan's baby, and that made me like her, in spite of her familiar manner with Jace. "She's excited to be an aunt."

So was I.

I'd never expected to be related by blood to a child who wasn't mine. Few toms ever had children, and though Ethan was a great fighter, he wasn't a leader. He would never have been an Alpha, nor would he have settled in a childless human marriage like Michael. So if not for Angela and her baby, we would have nothing left of him but memories.

My eyes watered at the thought of a baby with Ethan's green eyes, and a shock of his black hair.

"Is that her?" Angela asked, and I glanced up, surprised.

"Yeah." Jace waved me forward, and I took the last two steps slowly. "Faythe, this is Angela Raymond. Angie, this is Faythe, Ethan's sister."

"It's so great to meet you." She threw her arms around my neck, and I stumbled back in surprise. But Angela was unfazed, so I patted her back awkwardly. "The guys talked about you all the time," she said, when she finally let go, and her blue-eyed gaze met mine frankly, after a brief, puzzled glance at my scarred left cheek. Obviously they hadn't mentioned that. "I feel like I already know you."

Oh, I doubt that....

But she was so wide-eyed—so earnest, in spite of her nerves—that it was impossible not to smile back at her. Not to like her.

Ethan had considered himself a player. He'd had no trouble lovin' 'n' leavin' girl after girl. Until Angela. And now, seeing her, hearing her, I understood why she'd outlasted the others, and I wondered if, given time, she might have actually won a place in his heart, instead of just his bed.

"Everyone's excited to meet you," Jace said, gesturing toward the front door.

"Everyone?" Her forehead furrowed and she looked at the house as if it might swallow her whole.

"Don't worry." Jace put one hand at her back to guide her forward. "Meeting them is the easy part." He glanced back at me and winked. "Remembering the names might be a bit of a challenge."

I closed Angela's car door, then followed them inside.

The house was silent, but for the whispered breaths and excited heartbeats coming from the living room, which Angela probably couldn't hear. Everyone was listening. Waiting. Eager for the first up-close glimpse.

This was unprecedented. We'd only recently learned that humans and werecats could sire children, and while strays were proof that that *had* happened—to be "infected," a human must already carry a recessive gene donated by a werecat somewhere in the family tree— there were very few cases of toms actually claiming their illegitimate children. And all of those cases were very recent because, before, such pregnancies had been considered impossible.

Ethan's baby would be born human, and the difference between his blood and his mother's would be small enough to avoid detection in the basic newborn tests, as had been happening for decades with potential strays. So my nephew—the baby would almost certainly be a boy—would have no true place in our violent, complicated world until and unless he was one day scratched or bitten by a werecat. And infection was still a capital crime, even between blood relatives, a concept we as a species had only recently been forced to confront.

As Angela stepped through the front door into our house—our Pride's headquarters ever since my father became Alpha—I tried to imagine what we must look like to her. What we must *feel* like. Most humans lacked the appropriate mental compartment in which to file us. They would sense something different about us, but be unable to say what. We might scare her. We might fascinate her. We might never see her again.

That was my mother's worst fear.

Jace led her to the first room on the right, and Angela stopped cold in the doorway. Her smile froze, then faded into uncertainty as her focus skipped from face to face, none of which I could see from the hall.

We were a motley bunch at best—even compared to most other Prides—and we were a lot for a human to take in at once. Especially a newly pregnant college student, whose boyfriend had just died.

This was as hard for her as it was for us.

Sympathy for Angela flooded me, and I gave Jace a little shove. He raised one brow at me but moved over, and I edged past Angela into the living room to make the introductions. To represent my family and try to bridge the gap between worlds.

All the men had stood when we'd entered the room, and every last one of them stared straight at her. I sighed in frustration and rolled my eyes at several of them. *Way to look normal, guys.* I forced a laugh and turned back to her. "Did Ethan tell you we have a big extended family?"

She nodded hesitantly.

"I know it's kind of overwhelming, but everyone really wanted to meet you." Though in retrospect, introducing her to the entire household at once seemed like an extraordinarily *bad* plan.

She nodded again, mute.

I led her to the right and we worked our way around the room. She shook hands, and I made brief introductions and explanations. My fellow enforcers were first.

"Angela, this is Brian, Vic, and Marc. They work for my father."

"On the ranch? Like Jace?" Her eyes lit up; she was pleased to have found some logic to cling to in the sea of confusion we'd tossed her into.

"Um, yeah." They each shook her hand and welcomed her, but Marc eyed Jace as he followed us around the room.

Next came Kaci. "This is my cousin Karli." The identity under which she would attend school, once everything had calmed down. Assuming that ever happened.

"Hi, Karli," Angela said, obviously more at ease with a young girl than with a room full of strange men.

"Hey. So, you're gonna have Ethan's baby?" Kaci said, after a frank, curious glance at Angela's flat belly. "Well, I guess it's your baby, too. But I hope it looks like him, at least a little bit."

Angela smiled. "Me, too." And just like that, she'd won Kaci over.

While we crossed the rug toward Owen, he bent to help Manx up, with Des in her arms. Her hands were carefully arranged beneath the folds of the baby's blankets, so that her fingers—the nails ruined from her recent declawing—wouldn't show. "And this is my brother Owen."

Owen shot her a friendly, lopsided grin, and stuck out one calloused hand for hers, his other arm around Manx. "Pleased to meet you. I'm just sorry Ethan isn't here to make the introductions."

"So am I." Angela shook his hand warmly, then her gaze was drawn to Des's face as he yawned and stretched one chubby arm from beneath his blanket. "And who's this? Ethan didn't mention a nephew."

Owen flushed, but stroked the baby's face with one long finger. "Mercedes is a friend of the family, and this is her son, Desiderio."

"How beautiful!" Angela said, when Manx tilted her bundle forward so her child could be admired.

"Please forgive me for not shaking," she said, and Angela smiled at her exotic accent.

"Don't worry about it. You've got your hands full."

Manx smiled in relief and glanced at Owen, who beamed back at her. She'd been nervous about hiding her hands, no matter how many times he'd assured her that it wouldn't be an issue.

"Dad?" I said, and my father stepped forward in his usual suit, minus the jacket. "This is my father, Greg Sanders." It felt weird not to add his title after the basic introduction, but Angela wouldn't even know what an Alpha was, and telling her—exposing our existence to a human—would only get me brought up on more charges.

She held out her hand and my father shook it formally, studying her face like he'd be tested on it later. "It's so good to finally meet you. I see now why Ethan tried to keep you all to himself."

Angela blushed, and I stared at my father in surprise. Who'd have known he could be charming, when he wasn't barking out orders?

"And this is my mother," I said, as my mom clasped her hands in front of her own perfectly pressed slacks. "Karen Sanders."

Angela took a deep breath, and I almost laughed out loud at the sudden realization that in a room full of large, strange men, she was more nervous to meet my mom than anyone else. What the hell had Ethan told her about our mother? Or was there some sort of ritualistic meet-the-mom nerves I'd been spared by virtue of the fact that Marc—an orphan—was my only long-term relationship?

Angela held out one shaking hand, and Mom took it in both of hers. "I'm so very happy to meet you," my mother said, looking directly into her eyes. "And I want you to know that you—and your child—are always welcome here. We hope you'll bring him to see us often."

I frowned. Mom was a little over the top, but she couldn't help it. She'd been dreaming of grandchildren for years, and this one in particular was such an unexpected blessing.

Angela burst into tears. Her hands flew up to wipe her cheeks, and she sucked in a great, hiccupping breath, trying to stop the flow.

"Oh, come sit," my mother insisted, already guiding Angela toward the couch.

"I'm sorry," she sobbed, blotting beneath her eyes with the tissue my mother plucked from a box on the end table. "This has just all happened so fast, and I was afraid you guys would be mad, or think I was a… But you're so *nice*…." The tears started again. "Thank you."

My mom sank onto the couch next to Angela and wrapped an arm around her shoulders while the rest of us stared, speechless. "We're just so glad you want to involve us in the baby's life."

After a couple of minutes, Angela had herself under control, and my mom fixed her a plate of tiny sandwiches and sliced fruit.

"So, how far along are you?" my mother asked. "And have you seen a doctor yet?"

"Yes, just for the initial visit. He says I'm thirteen weeks along."

My mom's eyes widened. "Three months. Wow. There's so much to do!" I could practically see the gears spinning behind her eyes. But my father was more practical.

"We'd like to help with the cost either way, of course," he began, and Angela's forehead furrowed. "But if you're interested, we have a family physician who would be glad to see you."

Dr. Carver, of course.

"Um, sure," she said. "I'll meet him."

While she and my mother chatted softly, the guys all filled plates, then stood around the room snacking, and almost reverently observing the miracle that Angela and her child represented for us. It was the single most peaceful, optimistic moment we'd experienced since Ethan's death, and I never wanted it to end.

Unfortunately, Angela's introduction into our family felt very much to me like the calm before the inevitable storm. And I could already feel the clouds gathering...

Three

Montana. Again. Because the last visit worked out so well…

I hauled my duffel from the rear floorboard of the rental car and glanced up at the cabin as phantom pain in my side heralded an avalanche of memories. I'd shed blood and spilled blood here. I'd loved Marc and let him go. I'd found Kaci, killed bad guys, and narrowly avoided execution.

That cabin and I had a love-hate relationship, almost as complicated as my history with Marc. But Montana was an appropriate setting for this particular council meeting. Calvin Malone should be ousted where he'd first begun his quest for werecat world domination.

Malone would try to prevent the council—the majority of which harbored no fondness for my Pride—from hearing our evidence, I had no doubt. But I was prepared to shout the list of his crimes from the nearest mountain top, if need be. And to shove the bloody evidence of his guilt down the other Alphas' throats, if it would help.

"You okay?" Jace lifted the duffel strap from my

shoulder. If he could relieve my emotional burden so simply, he would. Jace was no longer as easy to understand as he'd been a month earlier.

"Yeah. I'm good." That was an outright lie, but it was one I clung to. Survival had become a game of bluffing. Of putting on my game face and pretending I wasn't worried. That I didn't have everything in the world riding on this meeting.

But I did.

If Calvin Malone were voted into power, we would have to remove him by force. Otherwise, he would make life hell for the south-central Pride and our allies, because we were everything he hated. Everything that threatened his tunnel vision of werecat society as his own personal autocracy. In Malone's paradise, membership would be by invitation only. Not open to those lacking purebred pedigrees. Inaccessible to those without a Y chromosome, unless they bent to his will.

My temper spiked just thinking about it, and some dark voice deep inside me insisted that if our evidence against him failed, we should simply screw the vote and bring on the pain. We'd been ready—even eager—to fight for weeks,

But Paul Blackwell, the elderly interim head of the Territorial Council, had convinced my father to give peace a chance, as cheesy as it sounded. If we could possibly avert full-out civil war and the inevitable casualties on either side, we owed it to the entire werecat population to try. Even I couldn't argue with that. In theory.

However, in my experience, the concept of peace had a lot in common with the Loch Ness monster—I found both elusive and difficult to believe in. So, I would hope for the best, but prepare for the worst.

Marc popped the trunk, then slammed the driver's-side door and I jumped, startled from my own thoughts. "Jace, run up to the lodge and get the key."

Jace went stiff, and I spoke up before he could growl. "I'll get it." As tired as I was of standing between them, it was safer to play peacekeeper than to break up the fight that would result if I didn't. Safer physically and politically. The whole world would know about me and Jace soon enough—two of Malone's men had figured it out and would surely disseminate the information whenever it would most damage our cause—and I wasn't eager to clue anyone in early via a Marc-Jace death match.

"You can't go by yourself," Marc insisted. "Malone and his men might already be here." And they were gunning for all three of us, after the trespassing/kidnapping/assault crime trifecta we'd pulled off the week before. Not that we'd had any other options.

"Blackwell came down yesterday, so even if Malone's here, he's not alone," I responded. "And he's not going to make trouble just hours before the vote." But the truth was that both Jace and Marc had more to fear from the Appalachian Pride than I did. Malone still needed me alive, but since the council had yet to officially recognize Marc's readmission into our Pride, he technically had no rights within our society. Which meant that his word alone would not stand against his attacker's, should it come down to that.

And Malone was just looking for an excuse to get rid of Jace—his stepson—without witnesses.

"You guys stay and wait for my dad. Please." Our

Alpha had ridden from the airport with Umberto Di Carlo and his men, so they could talk strategy on the way. "I'll be right back." Then, before either of them could argue, I shoved my bare hands into my coat pockets and took off at a brisk walk with them both staring after me.

We could all three have gone together, but frankly, after hours spent on the plane, then in the car with both Jace and Marc and the choking amounts of testosterone they were dumping into the air, I really needed a little time to myself, to clear my head.

To think about my decision. And the fact that I didn't want to choose. Or tell anyone else what was going on. But the expiration date on that option was rapidly approaching, even if Alex Malone and Colin Dean hadn't been telling stories yet.

My father was definitely suspicious. If we weren't in the middle of the biggest series of catastrophes ever to hit the south-central Pride in a single month, he'd have already figured it out. We'd delayed telling him before to keep from adding to his stress level, but now our time was up. I'd planned to tell him on the drive from the airport, but I lost that chance when he rode with Di Carlo instead, so now I'd have to make time to get him alone and try to explain. *Before* he heard from anyone else.

Jace was sure my dad would throw him out. Marc was worried about the same thing. Or rather, he was worried that if Jace got thrown out before I'd come to a decision, my father would pressure me to choose him in Jace's absence, even if that wasn't what I really wanted. Marc didn't want to win by default. He wanted to win for real. Forever.

But my dad wouldn't kick Jace out. Not now. Not with everything else going on. Probably not ever. Jace was a part of our family and, like Marc, he had nowhere else to go.

"Damn, somebody sure did a number on your face," a familiar voice called, drawing me from my thoughts.

My hand flew to my left cheek and my pulse raced so fast my heart felt stressed by the effort. I looked up to see a tall form in the shadow of the cabin ahead. His clothes were a dark blur, but his height and shockingly white hair were unmistakable. As was his voice. Colin Dean.

Damn, damn, damn.

"I was gonna say the same to you." I forced my hand back into my pocket without letting my fingers trace the thin, straight scar running from my left cheekbone to the corner of my mouth. Dean had put it there. He'd carved up my face slowly while I'd stood frozen, afraid to breathe too deeply for fear of pushing the blade farther into my skin. But in the end, he'd gotten the worst of our little exchange—I'd buried the knife in his gut and left him bleeding. But not before Marc had broken his nose and one cheekbone, and Jace had sliced the side of Dean's face wide-open.

Surely his scars were worse than mine.

Dean stepped into the light, and for the first time since we'd met, his face made me smile. His scar was thick and knotty, and unlike mine, he could trace it from the inside with his tongue. His nose had healed straight, but was still kind of swollen, even after a full week and ample time to speed his recovery by Shifting. But the faded yellow bruises around his eyes and the darker one on his cheek only made Dean look scarier and more pissed off than I'd ever seen him.

Maybe my father was right. Maybe we should have killed him.

For a moment, I regretted my decision to come by myself. I'd assumed Malone and his men were staying in the cabin on the other side of the main lodge, where they'd stayed last time, in which case I wouldn't have run into any of them alone.

Either I was wrong, or Dean had come looking for me.

He stalked toward me, and my options raced through my head. I could run, but then he'd chase me, either for fun, or because he truly couldn't control his cat's instinct to pounce on anything resembling prey. Or because he didn't want to control it.

I could stand up to him and fight. But that would be stupid with the vote coming up. I couldn't risk doing anything that would make my father look bad.

I could yell for Marc and Jace, but that would label me even more a coward than running would.

Or I could keep walking and hope Dean had orders not to touch me—surely Malone wouldn't want to get his hands dirty, either, this close to the election.

I walked on, and Dean altered his course to intercept me. "How many stitches did it take to hold your guts in?" I asked, clenching my fists in my coat pockets as he fell into step beside me, like we were old friends.

"Nowhere near what it'll take to sew you back together when I'm done with you."

"That sounds like a threat." My voice came out cool and confident, and I hoped my racing heartbeat didn't ruin the impression. Yes, I was a damn good fighter, but

Dean outweighed me by more than a hundred pounds and had been training at least as long as I had. Probably much longer. And his grudge against me had moved far beyond the desire to see me dead—he wanted me broken and humiliated first. If he wasn't under orders to play nice, we were both going to walk away from this one with new scars. Assuming we walked away at all.

"Caught that, did you?" His shadow stretched past mine on the brown grass crunching beneath our feet. "Sooner or later, you're gonna find yourself alone with me, and I'm gonna find out what it takes to make you scream like the bitch you are."

I shrugged without pulling my fists from my pockets, relieved to see that we were now within sight of the main lodge. "We're alone now. What's stopping you?" Aside from the dozen or so enforcers in the lodge ahead, well within hearing range, should one of us shout.

"Formalities…" Dean growled, stepping in front of me to block my path. "But after the vote, the council's gonna put you in your place, and I'm one of the toms who's gonna keep you there."

I raised both brows in silent challenge, confident now that if he was going to throw a punch, he'd already have done it. "You have no authority over me, and the council can't change that." Even if Malone became council chair, he couldn't reassign me to his own Pride, nor could he make my father hire Dean as one of our enforcers. No council chair had ever even tried anything like that. There was no precedent to support it.

"In case you haven't noticed, things are changing around here, and Cal knows exactly how to purge the impurities your Pride breeds so the rest of us can live clean."

Impurities? Motherfucker was talking about *Marc!*
I pulled my fists from my pockets, but before I could act
on my rash impulse, Dean was talking again.

"Cal has plans, including consequences for little girls
who step beyond their boundaries. And I just might be
one of those consequences."

I laughed out loud. I couldn't help it.

Dean's eyes flashed in anger and suddenly I realized
his fury was completely impotent. He was goading me
because Malone had him on a tight leash, at least for
the moment.

My fists relaxed. I propped my hands on my hips and
looked up at him. "Can I see it?"

He blinked, still scowling. "See what?"

"Your scar." His expression darkened like a sudden
eclipse, and I let my gaze grow cold. "You want to hear
me scream? Give it your best shot. But until then, every
time you take off your shirt, you may as well be handing
out my business card. I shoved my blade deep inside you
and loved *every single inch* of it. When I can't sleep at
night, the memory of you screaming like a little bitch
is my lullaby. And everybody knows exactly what that
scar means—that you got your ass handed to you by a
little girl. Again."

"You fucking bitch..." Dean picked me up by both
arms, and my toes barely brushed the ground. It took
every ounce of self-control I had to let myself hang
there, instead of kicking.

"Do it," I said, staring straight into his eyes. Daring
him. "Hit me. Throw me. Pick a fight, hours before the
vote. I'm sure Malone will understand."

Dean growled. His hands tightened around my arms,
and my fingers twitched when he squeezed a nerve.

"You fucking moron, put her down!"

I couldn't see the speaker—couldn't make myself look away from Dean while he held me like a rag doll—but I'd know Alex Malone's voice anywhere.

"You put a single bruise on her, and my dad will find new ways to skin a cat."

Dean dropped me, but his furious glare never left mine. I landed with my knees bent and barely resisted the urge to rub my arms where he'd held them. "He won't get the chance. Touch me again, and I'll gut you. And I don't need a knife to do it." Thanks to the partial Shift of one arm.

Alex stepped around the Nordic-looking giant and sneered at me, then whirled on Dean. "What the hell is wrong with you?"

Before Dean could answer, movement over his shoulder caught my eye. "Faythe?" Marc called, jogging toward us with Jace on his heels.

"I'm fine," I insisted, as they barreled to a stop on either side of me. "Dean and I were just comparing war wounds. He won. Someone cut him up pretty badly, huh, Colin?"

Dean growled again. "Stay out of my way, bitch. Or I'll make that scratch on your face look like a mercy." He and Alex stomped back toward their cabin.

"What the hell was that?" Marc demanded once they were gone.

I shrugged. "Dean's playing games, so I tried to draw a foul."

Jace frowned. "You wanted him to hit you?"

I tossed my head toward the main lodge, where several forms were now visible in the windows. "With an audience to see him throw the first punch? Hell, yeah. We need every advantage we can get over Malone."

"Well, let's aim for advantages that don't involve any more stitches or bruises for you, okay?" Jace smiled, and Marc scowled, and as had become my habit, I stood between them. Alone, among company. Untouched, and frankly missing the easy physical contact most werecats thrive on.

"Let's just get the key." Marc shoved his hands into his jeans pockets and headed for the lodge. "Your dad's waiting."

Jace and I followed without a word, but that brief, awkward silence couldn't compare to the one that greeted us when Marc pushed open the front door of the lodge. The main room was crowded with toms, and I didn't find a friendly face among them. Milo Mitchell and Wes Gardner—Alphas of the northwest and Great Lakes Prides, respectively—sat opposite each other in worn armchairs, a battered coffee table separating them. Three of their enforcers sat on the matching couch, all glaring at us with identical expressions of disgust.

We'd lost Gardner's favor when we failed to execute Manx for killing his brother Jamey. Traumatized from having been kidnapped, raped, and held prisoner, Manx was on the run and pregnant at the time, and the fact that no other Alpha in the world would have killed a pregnant tabby did little to mollify Wes. He'd felt excluded from the process and had resented my father ever since.

Milo Mitchell's son Kevin was exiled from the south-central Pride around the same time, for sneaking strays into the territory for money. Mitchell's hatred of all things Sanders was cemented when Marc killed Kevin during a fight in the free zone less than a month before the scheduled vote.

I hovered in the doorway, overwhelmed by the waves of hostility crashing over me. Nearly everyone in that room hated me, and some of them hated Marc even more. Jace's real enemies were in his birth Pride, but his stepfather's allies were more than willing to dislike Jace based purely on his association with me and mine.

"You have a lot of nerve showing up here," a new voice growled from my left, and I turned to see Jerald Pierce—Parker's father and Alpha of the Great Plains territory—stalking toward me from the kitchen.

"Thanks, I guess." I shrugged and tried to let the animosity roll off my back, but it's hard to stand tall in the face of pure loathing. Especially when so much of it is coming from a close friend's father. No wonder Parker had opted to stay at the ranch, in the company of a growing collection of bottles. "Though I tend to think of it as a sense of duty and obligation to my Alpha." My father. The strongest, most even-tempered and noble man I'd ever known.

"What about honor?" Pierce demanded. "Aren't you the one always talking about doing the right thing? Where the hell was that sense of honor when you were handing my son over to be slaughtered by a flock of dirty thunderbirds?"

Well, at least it's out in the open now.... Though that did nothing to break the tension in the room.

"Faythe did what she had to do to save an innocent tabby's life," Marc insisted, flushed with anger, but obviously trying to keep his temper in check. "She made a decision only a real leader could have faced, and—"

"Bite your tongue before I rip it out of your mouth!"

Pierce roared, and Marc bristled like a tiger on alert. I moved closer to him, and to my relief—and surprise—Jace stepped up on his other side, ready to defend his Pridemate if necessary, in spite of their personal rivalry. "I always gave you the benefit of the doubt," Pierce spat. "I even defended you when they said a stray could never be as good an enforcer as a Prideborn cat. But then you helped her lead my boy to the slaughter! What the hell is wrong with the bunch of you? How could you hand over a member of your own species to be pecked to death by a bunch of giant buzzards?"

I wanted to argue. To defend myself and my actions. But we'd discussed it with my father and had agreed not to comment on what happened to Lance Pierce. Including the fact that I'd ordered Marc to execute Lance to spare him from being eaten alive by the birds. Malone was sure to declare that a murder, rather than a mercy.

"I guess Cal's right about strays. You're genetically inferior. You didn't give a damn about my son because you're not even the same species. And you!" Pierce turned his dark-eyed fury on me, and I almost took a step back, floored by the depth of his hatred. "You're an abomination. Turning your nose up at your real duty and obligation to hand over one of your own in cold blood. I feel sorry for your father, saddled with such a self-righteous whore for a daughter. Refusing to give him any heirs, yet flaunting two lovers in front of the whole world. You truly have no shame."

I reeled like I'd been slapped. My cheeks flamed. I could actually see bright red patches of skin at the bottom of my field of vision. And the double standard burned like hellflames. If there was an enforcer in the room who'd only been with one woman, then I was Garfield.

"Jerald." Paul Blackwell didn't even raise his voice, but every head in the room turned toward him, and Pierce went silent instantly. The senior Alpha and acting council chair stood in the kitchen doorway, leaning on a worn cane, looking every bit of his seventy-something years. "You'll have a chance to air your grievances, but this is not it."

Pierce nodded angrily, but refused to back down, so I had to step around him to accept the key ring Blackwell held out to me. "Tell your father we vote at seven sharp. If he has any preliminary business, he'll need to present it before that."

The slight arch in Blackwell's brow was so subtle surely no one else noticed it. But I knew what that meant. If we were going to play the ace up our collective sleeve, we'd have to do it soon.

I nodded, clenching the key ring, then turned and marched out the front door with Marc and Jace on my heels.

"If this doesn't work, we are *so* fucked," Jace whispered, as we walked across the grass in a straight line. "They'd string us all up now, if they could. There's no way any of those three are gonna switch sides."

"It'll work," Marc insisted, for once forgetting to growl at his rival. "It has to."

I could only nod, still stunned by Pierce's speech. My hand strayed to the left side of my coat, beneath which I could barely feel a long, straight ridge. Two thunderbird feathers, stained with Lance Pierce's blood. Evidence that Lance had killed the young bird, and that Malone had tried to frame us for the crime, simultaneously weakening our defenses and diverting the aftermath from his own Pride.

Those feathers were the key to our preemptive strike. We hadn't come for the vote. We'd come to prevent it—by charging Calvin Malone with treason.

Four

"We have to tell my dad." I shoved my freezing hands into my coat pockets and sighed. My breath hung on the air, a thin white cloud I walked through with my next step.

"That Jerald Pierce has lost his fucking mind?" Jace shrugged on my left, always a few inches closer to me than Marc would let himself be. "The sooner, the better. Telling Parker will be the hard part."

"He's already expecting it," I said, thinking of his distraught drinking binge.

Malone's cabin was in sight up ahead, and I wondered if any more of his psychotic henchmen were ready to rumble. After being called a whore in front of half of the Territorial Council, a good fight might be just what I needed to purge some seriously unhealthy resentment and aggression.

But everything looked quiet as we approached. Pity.

"But I wasn't talking about Pierce." Damn it, they were going to make me say it. "We have to tell my dad about us. This." I stopped walking and pulled my hands from my pockets to make a gesture encompassing all three of us. "Whatever this is. Now."

"There is no us," Marc said, his voice low and heavy. He met my gaze frankly and left two feet of cold, empty space between his body and mine. "There's you and me, or there's you and him." He waved one hand toward Jace, and I flinched.

"I know." I sighed. And after Pierce's public broadcast, I was hyperaware that if I didn't make a decision soon, either Marc or Jace would take the choice out of my hands. "But my point is that Pierce just told Blackwell—and the whole world—exactly what's going on." And that came as a surprise, because we'd fully expected our enemies to keep the secret until revealing it would do us the most damage. Which should have given us time to break the news first. "And if my dad finds out from anyone other than us—other than *me*—well…I can't do that to him."

Dealing with my catastrophic love life was the last thing he needed at the moment, but learning about it in front of the entire council would be much, much worse.

"So we'll tell him." Jace shrugged again. He'd only agreed to keep our relationship quiet out of respect for Marc. Marc was the one really suffering, and that would only get worse once everyone knew he'd been cuckolded.

"No, I'll tell him." I couldn't drag Marc in front of my father and announce that I'd cheated on him. And couldn't let Jace see how strongly my father disapproved of him at my side. That wouldn't be fair to either of them. I would take the fallout alone. "I just need you guys to keep everyone else out of the way for a few minutes so I can tell him in private."

Marc looked like he wanted to throw up. I reached out for him, but he backed away. "You want me to entertain our allies so you can tell your dad you're not sure you want me anymore?" Pain swam in his golden brown eyes, and when I couldn't figure out what to say to make it better, he shook his head slowly and took off across the cold dead grass toward our cabin.

I ached to go after him, but he wanted to be alone, and I understood why.

"He'll be okay." Jace tried to pull me close, but I stepped out of his reach, apologizing with my eyes. If I couldn't touch Marc, I couldn't touch him, even for innocent comfort. Both because that wouldn't be fair to Marc, and because where comfort was concerned, there didn't seem to be much innocence left between me and Jace.

"I'm not sure any of us will be," I whispered, as we passed Malone's lodgings.

The rental van was parked in front of our cabin, with Umberto Di Carlo and my father in the front seats. As we approached, the sliding door opened and Mateo Di Carlo got out to give me a hug, while two of his fellow enforcers nodded in greeting.

"Hey, Faythe, how are you holding up?"

"I'm fine, Teo. Thanks." People asked me that all the time now, and Jace got the same questions. My brother Ethan—Jace's lifelong best friend—was only three weeks in the ground, and we'd seen so much tragedy and disaster since his death that we'd had to put true mourning on hold. But his absence still snuck up on me at night, when I was lonely and needed someone to talk to. In many ways, Ethan had been the soul of our family, much as my mother was the heart, and his death had seared a hole through my own chest. Sometimes I thought we'd never truly recover, as a family or as a Pride.

"Did Marc come through here?" I asked, as my father rounded the front of the van.

"I thought he was with you." He took the key I offered while the guys helped Bert Di Carlo with the luggage.

"He was. He just…needed some time to himself. He'll be back soon."

He raised one graying eyebrow, then nodded and unlocked the front door. I followed him into the living room, glancing around at the familiar worn furniture and outdated kitchen appliances. It looked about the same as it had when we'd left—was it really just three months ago?—and without my werecat's nose, I couldn't even smell the residual blood.

Ethan's blood. My brother had been gored here, defending me and Kaci. And now he was gone. For a moment I got lost in the memory, and in the pain of my own loss. So much had changed in so short a time. Very little of it for the better.

"Faythe?" My father frowned at me as the guys trooped in with our luggage. "Quarters will be a little cramped, since we're doubling up." Last time, only four territories had been represented; this time, all ten Alphas were coming, with enforcer entourages. "I'm putting you, Marc, and Jace in the far bedroom, but I'm guessing Jace won't mind taking the couch, if you think that would be…more prudent."

"Yeah, about that…" My hands twisted together, in spite of my own best efforts to keep them still. To remain calm. Then I forged ahead before I could back out. "Dad, I need to talk to you." I half whispered, hoping the others wouldn't hear. Though they'd find out soon enough, anyway. "In private."

Jace glanced at me on his way to the first bedroom, carrying four suitcases at once. My father took one look at my face and nodded. "Outside?"

"Sure." I hunched into my coat and followed him back into the February cold, so much sharper and bitterer than it had been in November.

My dad clomped down the steps in hiking boots and jeans. It was too cold for his traditional suit and dress shoes, though he'd probably change before heading to the main lodge. "What's wrong, kitten?" He slid one strong arm around my shoulders, and I leaned into him as we walked, treasuring the voluntary physical contact after spending most of the past week virtually untouched.

But I waited until we were on the edge of the tree line—out of casual earshot—to answer, trying to come up with an acceptable opening line while we walked. When my dad finally stopped and faced me, I made myself meet his gaze. Long gone were the days when I would stare at the ground and whisper confessions like a naughty little girl, even if that's exactly what I felt like. I'd made a very adult mistake—which necessitated a very adult decision I had yet to make.

"Faythe…?" My father prodded, and I could read growing concern in his crinkled forehead and the tense line of his jaw. He even seemed to have more silver in the gray streaks at his temples. "Is this about Marc?"

"Yeah. Um, things have gotten a little complicated

between me and Marc." I crossed my arms over my chest to hold my coat closed. "And Jace…"

"Jace?" My dad blinked, and I saw the exact moment understanding surfaced behind his eyes. He closed them, and his next exhale was long and very, very heavy. He glanced at the cabin, then motioned for me to follow him into the woods, where he stopped before we lost sight of the van. "How long?"

"Since the day Ethan…" I leaned with my palm on a bare tree trunk. I couldn't finish that sentence. "But I'm not… We're not… I don't think we need to get into details here, Daddy, but Jace and I…*connected,* and it's not… Okay, it *is* physical, to some extent, but it's more than that. A lot more."

He sighed again and looked at me with his poker face in place, and something in my chest tightened. I desperately wanted to be able to read his reaction. "And Marc knows?"

"Yeah." I took a deep breath, preparing to say the worst part. "As does half the council."

"What?" His poker face collapsed beneath bold lines of anger and bewilderment.

"Dad, we were going to tell you when things got a little calmer and we'd had a chance to sort it all out. But when we went to the lodge to pick up the key, Jerald Pierce called me a whore in front of half the council, so I think it's safe to say that this particular cat is out of the bag. And they're probably going to try to use it against us."

"How on earth did Jerald find out?" my father demanded softly, but I knew what he was really asking: How the hell can the entire opposing half of the Territorial Council know something so intimate about three of his enforcers, when he didn't know?

"Alex Malone figured it out last week, while Dean was using my face for a cutting board. Then Dean told Marc. And evidently anyone else who would listen. But I wanted you to hear it from me. I'm sorry I didn't tell you earlier. We didn't want to give you one more thing to worry about."

My father glanced at the forest floor, then sank onto a thick, dry fallen log. "How is Marc?"

I closed my eyes against the burn of fresh tears. "He's pissed, and hurt, and about a dozen other complicated, volatile emotions he has every right to feel. He's fighting his instinct to kill Jace, and he's not exactly happy with me, either. Though for the record, I'm not even sure he *could* kill Jace. He says I have to choose. Soon."

"He's right. This could get ugly, Faythe. Marc's thought of you as his since you were sixteen years old, and temporarily losing you to the human world was hard enough for him. But to another tom? One who's shown some serious grit lately? I'm guessing he's juggling a lot of pain and humiliation, and coming from a potential Alpha, those are both likely to look a lot like anger."

"I'd call it more of an encompassing, blinding rage." I swiped one sleeve across my eyes and sat next to him. The bark was cold and rough, even through my jeans, but the trees blocked most of the frigid wind.

"And do you understand why?" My father's voice was soft, his gaze calmly searching.

The answer seemed obvious, but the quiet intensity with which he asked told me that this was important enough for me to dig deeper than my impulse answer. I was the first potential Alpha in history who didn't have a personal understanding of the tomcat's position in our world, and how tenuous that status really was.

"Because this is about more than me hurting him. More than our relationship." *Shit*. My heart crumpled as the system of dots began to connect in my head, illustrating for me the complicated connections and hierarchies that defined a tomcat's rank within our world. "I've damaged his status. They already see him as an outsider, as inherently weaker. Lesser. They'll see this as me rejecting Marc on some level, and if he's not good enough for me, why would he be good enough for them?" My father nodded, and I hated myself a little more.

I'd insulted Marc personally and politically. I'd stabbed him in the back and in the heart at the same time. And considering how very public our troubles were about to become, I now considered myself lucky he was even speaking to me.

"Is this going to hurt us, politically?"

"You're not on trial this time, Faythe."

But we both knew I was. We all were. Everything a Pride cat does reflects on his Alpha, and all of it was fair game during the vote. Which is what we'd been counting on, with respect to the bloodstained feathers still in my inside jacket pocket.

Unfortunately, that sword sliced both ways.

"Are you mad at me? Or disappointed?" Somehow, that mattered more to me than the collective opinion of the entire council.

My father took off his glasses to polish them on the tail of the shirt showing through his open coat. "I would have been both, if this were just a game. If you were trying to make Marc jealous, or rebelling out of boredom. But if this is really more than that...I don't see how I could be mad without calling myself a hypocrite. You can't help who you love, Faythe. No one can."

I blinked, confused. "You mean Mom...?"

He put his glasses back on, and a wistful smile stole over his lips. "She was engaged to Bert Di Carlo first. But then I came to the territory to enforce for your grandfather the summer after my freshman year in college, and we both fell, hard and fast."

I sat stunned into silence. I knew my parents were still crazy in love—how else could any marriage last so long?—but I'd had no idea there had ever been such complications in their relationship. "How have I never heard this?"

"Why open old wounds? The past is the past, and it worked out for the best for all of us, in the end."

"Was it hard?"

My dad shifted on the log to face me, and I could see the pain on his face, still very real even three decades later. "I'm not going to lie to you, Faythe. Bert didn't speak to either of us for two years."

"But now..."

"Now he's one of my best friends and biggest supporters."

And if it worked out for them, it could work out for us, right? No matter who I chose. Except... "Do you think he would have gotten over it if he hadn't found Mrs. Di Carlo?" I fiddled with the zipper tab at the hem of my coat. "If he hadn't fallen in love with someone else?"

"I honestly don't know. He might not have. New love can help heal some pretty big wounds."

Jace and I knew that better than most. But love could also open wounds. Big, gaping, gory ones.

"I don't know what to do." The ache in my chest was as strong as ever, and it deepened at the thought of letting either of them go. "I know I'm too old to be coming to you with boy trouble, but I'm lost, and I'm pretty sure that whatever I decide, I'm only going to make things worse. But Jace loves me, Dad. For real."

That time, his bittersweet smile was equal parts angst and sympathy. "First of all, you're never too old to ask your father for advice."

I forced a smile with tears still standing in my eyes.

"And second, I have no doubt that Jace loves you. He's been watching you like you hung the moon from the day you came back to the ranch. I just didn't realize he'd gone beyond staring. I didn't think he *would,* after Marc got ahold of him last time."

"Jace is changing. He's…challenging Marc, and not just over me."

He nodded slowly, staring into the branches as if he were seeing something else. "I saw that, too. Ever since Ethan… I just hadn't put two and two together."

I swallowed thickly and bark cut into my palm when I gripped the log beneath me. "I think he could be an Alpha. He could be a *good* Alpha, Dad."

He nodded hesitantly. "Maybe so, with some training aimed at leadership. But that's not the most important question right now. What I need to know is, do you love him?"

More tears came, and this time I let them fall, hot on my frozen cheeks. "Yeah." I blinked, and my father's face blurred. "I don't want to love him—this would be *so* much simpler if I didn't. But I do. He's funny, and passionate, and strong, and he believes in me more than I even believe in myself. When he looks at me, I feel like I could take on the whole world and come out standing tall. I like myself better when I'm with him, because of how he sees me. He makes me feel beautiful and powerful, like I'm the most important thing in the world, and I don't know how to walk away from that. I don't know how to walk away from *him*."

Jace was like a drug, steadily, stealthily subverting my willpower. And there was *serious* heat between us. The kind that can knock down buildings or make a person spontaneously combust.

My father looked stunned, and it actually took him a moment to recover from my discourse on new love. "And you still love Marc?"

"More than I can even explain. He's my rock—strong and steady, and ready for anything. He knows what I need before I know it, and he pushes me to work harder, and look deeper, and be better. He challenges me, and infuriates me, and he lights me on fire, deep in my soul. And he has never, ever let me down. Sometimes it feels like he's the only thing keeping my heart beating. I love him so much that it feels like I'm dying a little bit every day that he won't smile at me. Or touch me. Not even a hug. He keeps this distance between us now. And Jace has to do the same, because they have this weird, fragile truce that isn't quite working, but I know better than to make them break. But this truce is going to break *me*."

The tears fell faster, and a truly pathetic sob followed. "I love them both, and they both love me, but neither of them will even hold my hand, and I'm more alone now

than I've ever been in my life, and it's all my own fault."
I sniffled, my nose running from the cold and from
the tears. "It's not supposed to be like this. Love isn't
supposed to break your heart. Or anyone else's. There
aren't supposed to be two of them. How did this even
happen? I mean, I *know* how this happened, but I can't
make any sense of it. Even if I hadn't…*connected* with
Jace the night Ethan died, this all would have surfaced
eventually, and I can't think of any less painful way it
could have played out."

He pulled me close, one arm around my back, and I
put my head on his shoulder like I hadn't done since I
was a child. "Faythe, your heart doesn't answer to your
brain. And neither do theirs. If that were the case, do you
think Marc would still be waiting for your answer?"

"Of course not. If his head were in charge, he'd have
kicked me to the curb years ago." I sobbed again, and
this time my father chuckled. "What's so funny?" I demanded, tilting my head when my cheek got his coat
wet.

"You didn't cry when Kevin Mitchell broke your arm,
or when you got stabbed in the hip the last time we were
here. But boy troubles are still enough to reduce you to
tears."

"I think this runs a little deeper than 'boy troubles,'
Daddy."

"Yet I'm reminded of your freshman year in high
school, when you sat in your room crying over…what
was his name? Chad Baker?"

"How on earth do you remember that?"

"You're the only daughter I have, Faythe. I remember
everyone who's ever hurt you."

I pulled away to stare at him in awe, still wiping

sloppy tears from my increasingly cold-numbed cheeks. He was serious.

"Anyway, on the bright side, you do have one advantage most other tabbies don't."

"I do?" I blinked, thoroughly at a loss.

"This doesn't have to be a political decision. In fact, it shouldn't be. You don't have to marry an Alpha, Faythe. You're going to *be* an Alpha. I have no doubt in my mind that by the time I'm ready to retire, you'll be ready, no matter who you choose. So you have to follow your heart on this one. You owe that to yourself, and to both of them."

"That's what Marc said."

My father's eyes widened, and I saw unmistakable respect in his small smile. "He did?" I nodded. "Then he must really mean it, because though I see great potential in Jace, right now Marc's better prepared to help you run this Pride."

"I know." My brain was whirring, while my heart only beat sluggishly in protest. "But I don't need to run it right now. Right? And in a few years, that could change?"

"Of course. That's why the only advice I can give you is this…" He sat up straight and twisted on the log to face me, his gaze boring into mine. "Don't confuse the issue by trying to figure out who loves you the most, or who needs you the most. In the end, it only comes down to one thing: choosing the one you can't live without."

Five

"How'd it go?" Jace whispered, standing next to me at the counter as I poured Coke into a glass of ice. The cabin was crowded now, but the kitchen was empty. Still, werecats have amazing hearing, even in human form.

"He's not mad." I lifted the glass for a sip, and soda fizz sprayed my nose. "I thought he'd be furious, but he... He said you can't help who you love." I looked up at Jace, and his cobalt gaze seemed to burn right through me. "It turns out my mom used to be engaged to Bert Di Carlo. I think... Jace, I think he really understands."

Jace smiled, and his whole face lit up. "Should I go say something? Make some sort of formal declaration?" He leaned closer to whisper into my hair. "Or thank him for not ripping my lungs out through my throat for sleeping with his daughter?"

I grinned. I couldn't help it. I hadn't seen him look truly happy for more than a minute at a time since Ethan died, and I wanted so badly to make him happy. To keep him smiling. When Jace smiled, I felt warm inside. He took the edge off the winter-in-the-mountains chill. "I think that would be a little awkward right now. He's telling them."

I nodded toward the living room, where my dad sat with Di Carlo and all three of his enforcers. As humiliating as it was for me—and even more so for Marc—my dad's allies needed to know what was going on, since it would probably be used against us in the vote. Full disclosure to our allies—that was one of the things my father offered, but Malone did not. Surely once *we'd* disclosed Malone's crimes, those Alphas who didn't already know about them—we were pretty sure Wes Gardner and Nick Davidson were completely in the dark—would jump ship. How could they vote for a traitor and a murderer?

"I want to kiss you." Jace's whisper pulled me from my thoughts and I glanced up to find his eyes blazing with raw need. "Just because Marc won't touch you doesn't mean I shouldn't. Right? I don't have that kind of self-control, and honestly, I don't see the point in it. Are you supposed to be impressed by how long we can go without touching you? 'Cause if that's the game we're playing, I think I'd rather lose."

I almost melted from relief at his declaration, even with the wash of guilt that followed it. I was tired of being untouched. Alone in a room full of people. How was I supposed to choose who I wanted to spend the rest of my life with, if I couldn't be alone with either of them, allowed to feel anything that wasn't pain and regret? How was denying everything that felt good about love supposed to help me make my choice?

Jace saw my indecision and tugged me into the hall, out of view from the living room. He pressed me against the wood-paneled wall, and my hands found his chest on their own, before I even realized what I was doing.

"It's not wrong, Faythe," he whispered, and my heart ached from wanting so badly to believe him. "This is what we're supposed to be doing. Exploring our relationship. Helping you choose." He ran his hands lightly over my arms, raising chill bumps the length of my body.

"You think my decision should be based on who kisses best?" I barely breathed the words, my eyes closed, trying to resist what felt so wrong, yet so right.

"We both know it's about more than that, but it's physical, too, and I don't want you to forget what I feel like." Jace leaned into me, sliding one knee between mine, and his skin was hot, even through our clothing. "What I taste like… But if this is a contest, that makes you the judge." One side of his perfect mouth turned up in a wicked grin. "So how 'bout it? Who's better?"

"Mmmm…" I purred as he rubbed his cheek along my temple. "It's been a while. I'm not sure I remember."

His breath brushed my cheek from centimeters away. "Let me remind you. Let me kiss you, Faythe." His voice was low and gravelly, almost broken with need for me, and I was overwhelmed by the power of that need.

A kiss wasn't all he wanted; I could feel that much with him pressed against me. But it was a damn good start.

"I'm going to kiss you," he said, when I didn't answer.

Yes… No sound came out, but he heard me, anyway.

Jace's lips met mine, and I tilted my head up to meet him. My mouth opened, and the kiss deepened. He was hungry for me, and I was half-starved from the recent famine. His lips were hot, his hands warm on my hips, even through my clothes. My arms slid around his back, feeling the play of muscles with each minute movement.

His tongue dipped into my mouth, and suddenly I ached in other, more sensitive places. We were making out in the hall, in full view, should anyone walk in. The thrill of possible discovery was unmitigated by the fact that everyone knew. That we were no longer stealing hidden comfort kisses in the throes of bitter pain and chaos. If anything, I wanted him more now. And he clearly wanted me....

The screen door squealed open from the kitchen. I jerked back from Jace and smacked my head on the wall. But he wasn't interested in stopping and I wasn't fast enough. Marc stood in the doorway, hands fisted at his sides, face lined in pain.

Jace stepped back and I straightened my shirt, but the damage was done.

Marc had only seen me with Jace once, in my bedroom, when I'd first returned to the ranch. It wasn't real back then. Because I hadn't taken Jace seriously, and Marc and I weren't even together at the time. But Marc had ripped my door from its hinges and broken through the Sheetrock with Jace's head.

"Don't stop on my account," he snapped, jaw bulging furiously. "Hell, why don't we sell tickets?" He stopped when intrusive silence descended from the living room. Marc scrubbed his face with both hands, then crossed his arms over his chest and stared at the floor, clearly trying to get control of his temper.

"Marc..."

"No." He looked up, flames raging behind his eyes. "Outside, if you want to talk."

I nodded and headed for the kitchen, grateful that he hadn't just stormed out again. Jace started to follow me, and Marc turned on him, growling, pulling one fist back.

"Stop!" I shouted. My father appeared in the doorway, tense and angry. Jace practically buzzed with fury. I sucked in a deep breath and grabbed Marc's arm, pushing it down steadily while I stared straight into his eyes. I begged him silently to back off, fully aware that if he wasn't willing to, I couldn't make him.

"Faythe..." My father's warning held little of the sympathy he'd shown earlier. He wouldn't judge me, but he *would* preserve order. He had to. And so did I. "If you can't handle this, *I* will."

"It's okay. I got it." I let go of Marc's fist and it stayed down, though his eyes still flashed with anger and an underlying personal agony. I gestured for Marc to head on out. Jace tried to follow again, and this time I stepped into his path. "Jace, give us a minute."

"Hell, no!" He was tense all over, and I could feel fury radiating like heat from a bonfire. "You shouldn't be alone with him when he's like this."

My dad growled in warning, and I glared at Jace. "Don't tell me where I shouldn't be. Stay here. I need to talk to Marc."

He scowled, but nodded. I shot an apologetic glance at my father, then ran out the back door after Marc. But the backyard was empty. I raced down the steps, adrenaline flooding my veins, demanding an immediate search.

"Over here," Marc said, and I whirled around to find

him leaning against the shed near the tree line. I jogged across the yard and into the shed while he held the door open for me. He yanked the pull chain on the light, then leaned against the closed door, and I held up the wall next to him, giving him the two feet of distance he seemed to prefer.

I pushed hair behind my ears, wishing he'd look at me. Wishing he'd touch me, and show me that he could still feel something for me other than anger, even if that something else was buried way down deep.

But instead, he stuffed his hands into his pockets, reinforcing the physical and emotional distance he was building. He blinked into the glare from the naked bulb, and his face was blank. Completely unreadable.

"You were really going to hurt him." I'd read that much in his posture. And then Jace would have hurt him back, and the situation would have been unrecoverable.

He rolled his eyes and let his head fall against the wood plank wall at his back. "Do you blame me?"

I sighed. He had every right to be pissed, but I had to think about the good of the Pride. "If this war really happens, we're going to need him, and you know it."

"Maybe you both should have thought of that before you let him shove his tongue down your throat in front of—" Marc's voice broke beneath obvious anguish, and my heart suddenly felt like it weighed ten pounds. "Why are you doing this to me, Faythe? Am I not suffering enough, knowing he's been inside you? Is the floor show just to give me a visual? To make sure I know exactly how much you like it…?"

"No!" I took a deep breath, trying to compose my thoughts. "Marc, I'm not trying to hurt you. I swear. I just… You say I have to choose, but I don't know how to do that if you won't come near me, and you won't let him near me, either. You won't touch me, Marc. Not a hug. Not a kiss. You won't even sit less than two feet from me."

"And your solution is to let *him* grope you in plain sight?"

"I just wanted to know I wasn't alone." I closed my eyes, grasping for an explanation he'd understand. "I know how he feels. He wants to *show* me how he feels about me, and you don't. You *won't*. I miss you, and missing you is so much harder when I can still see you, and hear you, and smell you, but you won't touch me. You hardly ever even look at me unless you're too pissed off to avoid it, and I can't tell if you still want me, or if you just want to make me pay for what I did."

"You slept with someone else!" Marc whirled around and punched the wall of the shed, and his knuckles came away bloody. "Hell, yeah, I want you to pay! I want you both to pay. How am I supposed to look at you after you've been with him? Knowing you still want to be with him? I'm in the right here, Faythe. *You* screwed up—you screwed *him*—and *I'm* paying for it."

"I'm sorry…"

"Sorry doesn't mean anything! Not when you're still with him. It's not just that you cheated—it's that he's still here, and you're still with him. It just goes on and on, and it *hurts* every single time I see you with him. I hate it that he makes you smile, and that there's nothing I can do to stop this. I can't think straight, and every-thing hurts, and nothing makes sense anymore. You're shredding my heart with one hand and stroking his ego with the other. And it's killing me, Faythe. You're killing me. And it's only going to get worse, now that everyone knows."

I swiped tears from my cheeks with cold, shaking fingers. "What do you want me to do?"

"I want you to be sorry enough to tell him to go get his thrills on top of someone else's girlfriend. I want you to swear I'm the only one you want, and the only one you'll *ever* want, and that you'll never even look at anyone else again. I want you to want me, Faythe. As much as I want you."

"I do want you. I never stopped wanting you." I couldn't hold back the tears, and my words were halting half sobs. "This isn't about you.…"

"Well, it should be!" he shouted, and I flinched. "Everything I do is about you, and I want the reverse to be true, too." I wiped more tears, my throat aching with words that would only make this worse. "What, you need a reminder? That's what he was doing, right? And now you smell like him. You probably taste like him. You should taste like *me*.…"

He was on me before I could even catch my breath, his mouth bruising mine, and after that, breathing didn't seem so important. Marc pressed me into the wall of the shed, his hands on either side of my shoulders. He kissed me like it had been years, rather than days. Like he was reminding us both.

My body responded without consulting my brain, and I clutched at him, pulling him closer. I'd missed him so much.

His lips trailed down my neck and his hands wandered beneath my shirt, claiming. Demanding. He pulled away just long enough to tug my tee over my head. My shirt hit the dusty shed floor, and my bra landed on top of it an instant later.

His mouth fed from mine, his tongue slid between my lips as his hands explored territory I'd thought abandoned. Then he dropped into a squat, leaving my mouth cold and empty, and lifted first my right foot, then my left, to pull my boots off. He dropped a trail of hot kisses down my stomach. I gasped when he tugged my jeans button free, but Marc was silent. Eager, but still angry.

I almost lost my balance when he shoved my pants and underwear down with both hands, then tugged them free and slid them across the floor with one foot. He unbuttoned his own pants and pushed them halfway down, then lifted me and held me against the cold wall with his own body.

He slid inside me completely with one stroke, and I had to wrap my arms around his neck for balance. This was not gentle, tender sex. This was desperate need and scorching lust, part revenge, part passion. This was him reclaiming what he thought he'd lost and giving what he thought I'd asked for.

Every thrust was fast and hard. Every stroke was deep and long. Friction burned between us, and my pleasure built too fast to be savored, too hot to be held. By the time he shuddered against me, within me, slamming me into the wall over and over, shaking the entire shed with our fierce union, my own intense, tight coil of pleasure had eclipsed all sight, smell, and sound that wasn't Marc.

He collapsed against me, his shirt damp with my sweat and his. I clung to him, still throbbing around him, breathing hard as my heart pounded, stunned, and finally hopeful.

Then, without a word, he lifted me and stepped back, withdrawing in every sense of the word. He set my bare feet on the dirty floor and zipped his pants up. I stood there naked and in shock, staring after him as he shoved the door open and let in a frigid draft. "Maybe now you'll remember."

Then he was gone, and the world was cold.

I got dressed slowly, all alone, reeling. I could still feel echoes of him, deep inside. I could still smell him on my skin, taste him on my lips. But I'd never felt more alone in my life. Abandoned. Dismissed.

My shirt and jeans were covered in dust. I brushed them off as best I could, but still looked like I'd rolled in it. Was that what he wanted? That I smell like him and look like we'd just rolled all over the ground? Had I been marked? Reclaimed, then left to wonder what the hell just happened?

Stunned, I crossed the cold yard, plodded up the steps, and opened the kitchen door slowly, to keep it from creaking. I needn't have bothered. Marc wasn't there. But Jace was.

"What the hell happened?" he demanded in a whisper, as voices floated in from the living room—the others still discussing the upcoming vote.

"I…" I brushed past him, headed for the soda I'd poured half an hour earlier. I gulped from the glass, trying to figure out what to tell him, and nearly choked when a melting sliver of ice wedged in my throat.

"You smell like him, he smells like you, and you're

wearing half the damn mountain on your clothes," Jace hissed. "I guess I know what happened."

"I'm not sure *I* know what happened...." The glass was slick in my grip, so I set it down, still trying to gather my thoughts. "But I think I just got a dose of my own medicine."

Jace scowled. "I'd say we both did. Marc's back in the game."

I drained my glass and poured a refill. "I'll be right back. I need a shower." But the floor creaked when I stepped into the hall, and Marc heard it. He'd probably been listening for it.

"You two boycotting the meeting, or are you gonna get in on this?" he called.

I groaned on the inside. Marc was going to make me pay. He was going to humiliate me, like I'd humiliated him, by making me show up for an important strategy meeting smelling like him and covered in the dirt they'd assume he'd rolled me in. Everyone would know what we'd done, if they didn't already.

He was making a statement. Staking his claim. And Jace and I would have to live with it.

But with any luck, if I let him have his moment—let him publicly air his grievance—he'd be able to work past some of his anger. *Please let him work past some of his anger....*

"Faythe?" my father called, clearly oblivious to the game Marc was playing—so far.

"Yeah. I'm coming." Dialing up my courage, I brushed more dirt from my clothes with my free hand, then marched back through the kitchen and into the living room with my head high. Or at least not drooping. Jace followed me and took up a post in the doorway, looking angrier than I'd ever seen him.

Marc sat on the arm of the couch, watching me, apparently at peace with the world, at least for the moment.

I leaned against the wall, sipping from my glass, trying to ignore the stares as they roamed down from my hair—evidently disheveled—over my shirt and pants, taking in the smudges I couldn't get out without detergent. "Okay, as much fun as this awkward silence is…" I had to force my hand to relax around my glass before it cracked. "What's the plan?"

My father cleared his throat, mercifully drawing the collective focus from me and setting us all back on track as only he could. "The vote takes place in an hour and a half. When they ask for prevailing business, I'll make the formal charge against Malone, then we'll present our evidence. Faythe?" My father turned to me, and for once, I was glad I couldn't read his expression.

"Yeah." I set my glass on the coffee table and lifted my coat from the back of an armchair. From the inside pocket, I pulled a clear, gallon-size freezer bag—the only size big enough to hold two fourteen-inch-long thunderbird feathers—and held it up for everyone to see.

The south-central cats had all seen it, of course, but Di Carlo's men had not. They gathered around for a closer look when I laid the bag down on the coffee table. "Can we open it?" Teo Di Carlo asked, and my father nodded.

"Just for a minute, though. The blood's already dry, and the scent is only going to fade with time and exposure to air." And we needed everyone at the vote to be able to tell without a doubt whose blood stained that feather.

Teo carefully pulled open the seal and held the bag to his nose. His eyes brightened as he inhaled. "That's definitely Lance Pierce."

"I can smell it from here," one of his fellow enforcers added, from the other end of the couch.

"There's no doubt about it, Greg," Bert Di Carlo said, his voice rumbling throughout the room. "Now, whether or not Malone's allies will accept the obvious conclusion… That remains to be seen."

And that's what we were most worried about. Michael—my oldest brother was an attorney in the human world—had warned us that our evidence was circumstantial at best. It only proved that Lance Pierce had bled on a thunderbird feather, not that he'd killed the bird. Or that the feather had even been attached to a bird when it was bled on. But since the werecat legal system didn't mirror the human one, we were hoping it would be enough. I'd been tried for murder with less evidence.

Of course, I'd been found innocent of that particular charge.…

"Bert, would you mind going to fill Rick and Ed in?" My father asked. "Then we can all meet at the main lodge in half an hour." My uncle Rick Wade and Ed Taylor—Alphas of the East Coast Pride and the Midwest Pride, respectively—were sharing a cabin on the other side of the main lodge.

Di Carlo nodded and rose, motioning for Teo to join him. On their way out the door, they let in a frigid draft and a glimpse of the rapidly darkening winter sky, and seconds later their footsteps faded into the distance.

"Everyone get ready," my father said, then he disappeared into his room to change into his suit.

Marc followed me into the bedroom we were supposed to share with Jace and snatched Jace's duffel from the floor. Before Jace could protest, Marc tossed the bag to him. "You've got the first shower. Take your time."

Jace bristled, but I only shook my head. "Please, Jace. I'm tired of fighting with my own Pridemates. Let's just save it for the real fight, okay?"

Jace spun without a word and stomped off toward the only bathroom.

I set my bag on the dresser and unzipped it, and was digging for clean clothes when Marc crossed the room and closed the door. "You can change and brush your hair, but don't you dare take a shower."

"Don't tell me what to do." I turned to find his hard gaze trained on me, his forehead furrowed.

"You owe me. Everyone knows you slept with Jace, and Dean will tell anyone who'll listen that it's because I couldn't keep you interested. You've turned me into a walking joke, and the least you can do is make sure everyone knows I'm not out of the game yet."

"This isn't a game, Marc." Why did they both keep referring to it as such?

"The three of us, all tangled up in knots? Hell, no, it's not a game. It's my fucking train wreck of a life. But you walking around smelling like we just had a roll in the shed? That's just more of you lying in the bed you've made. With me, this time."

I sighed and sank onto the side of the bed, holding my change of clothes. "Fine, if it'll make you happy."

He snatched his own change of clothes from the dresser and left the room, slamming the door.

Jace came back a few minutes later, as I was pulling a clean shirt over my head. He stopped cold in the doorway, his hair dripping on his shoulders. "Aren't you going to shower?"

"I can't."

"The hell you can't. He's doing this on purpose. Punishing us both."

I sat on the end of the bed and grabbed my left boot. "Don't you think we deserve it? We humiliated him, and this is just the beginning. What do you think everyone's going to be saying behind his back? It's not going to kill either of us for me to walk around smelling like him for a couple of hours."

Except that I hated being marked, and Marc damn well knew it. Which was the whole point.

I zipped up my boots and Jace dropped his duffel on the floor and stomped out of the room.

Great. This must be the episode where Faythe can't make anyone *happy.* Fortunately, my plans for Calvin Malone had nothing to do with his happiness.

Clad in jeans, boots, and a plain, snug black long-sleeved tee, I grabbed my jacket in the living room, and we headed toward the main lodge as a group. I expected both of the guys to give me the proverbial cold shoulder, but to my surprise, they took up positions on either side of me, only pausing briefly to glare at each other. Not a promising start to the evening. But surely once they had a mutual enemy to focus on, the personal rivalry would fade for a little while.

The cabin Malone and Mitchell shared was dark when we passed it, and when we got to the main lodge, I realized we were the last to arrive. One of Paul Blackwell's men met us at the door and led us to the formal dining room at the back of the lodge, where I'd stood trial for my life three months earlier. The room was long, and it normally appeared even larger than it was, thanks to an entire wall of windows. But it felt small and cramped, packed with ten Alphas and a grand total of thirty-six enforcers. I'd never felt such a concentration of testosterone and hostility.

And I was the only woman in the room.

The three solid walls of the room were lined in folding metal chairs, most already occupied with beefy toms. The table in the center sat ten, and nine of those spots were filled with the other Alphas.

An odd hush descended as I entered the room followed by Marc and Jace, and I fought the urge to drop my eyes, which got easier when I realized they weren't focused on Marc's scent still clinging to me—they hadn't had a chance to smell me yet. This was the first time about half the men in the room had seen me since Colin Dean sliced my face up.

Most of them didn't know what had happened to me. I'd declined to answer the few who'd had the nerve to ask, and Dean didn't seem to be advertising that little bit of trivia, probably because his scar was bigger than mine. But I'd obviously been cut on purpose—accidental cuts aren't that straight or even.

I stared back boldly, silently daring someone to comment, and only when the return glances went to Colin Dean did I realize which direction the prevailing rumor winds were blowing. They may not have put all the pieces together yet, but our similar scars were too much of a coincidence to be unrelated.

Paul Blackwell stood at the head of the table, his cane

hooked over the arm of his chair. Malone sat to his left, and the seat opposite had been reserved for my father.

My dad took his place and Blackwell cleared his throat, signaling for the last of the stragglers to find a seat. But when I looked for a chair, I saw that there were only two available. One between Alex Malone and Colin Dean, and the other on Alex's other side. They had set us up, insuring that I'd have to sit with one of them instead of with either Jace or Marc. Marc had already taken the seat between Dean and the wall, and when I smiled to thank him for taking that option out of the mix he returned my smile with a tight one of his own.

I deliberately took the chair between Alex and Dean, to show them I couldn't be intimidated. Both men looked perversely pleased by my choice.

When I sat, Blackwell spoke. "Before we begin, is there any prevailing business?" He knew what we were up to. He'd been at the ranch when we were attacked by the thunderbirds, and he'd launched the initial investigation into Malone's involvement. But he remained officially neutral, which he considered the only appropriate course of action for the council chair. At least until we'd formally presented our case.

"I have one bit of business," my father said, and I treasured the look of surprise on Calvin Malone's face, brief though it was.

"Go ahead, Greg," Blackwell said.

My father stood and straightened his suit jacket. "I charge Councilman Calvin Malone with treason against this organization and its members."

Six

"What?" Alex Malone popped up from his seat like a jack-in-the-box, and his surprised, angry gesture came within inches of smashing my nose. But at a single glance from his Alpha, he dropped into his chair, fuming in silence. His gaze was glued to the table, where my dad now stared down at his, both Alphas impeccably composed, while the level of tension in the room rose quickly enough to make the rest of us sweat. Literally.

Malone leaned back in his chair, arms crossed over his chest. "Now, Greg, I hardly think that my questioning of your authority qualifies as treason."

"No. But inciting war with another Shifter species does. Especially when that war is intended to hide your Pride's guilt and cripple my Pride's resources."

"Greg, these are very serious charges," Milo Mitchell said, from his seat next to Malone. Like we were unaware.

"Accompanied by very few details," Nick Davidson added. "I assume you can provide both specifics and evidence?"

"Of course." My father nodded, and this time,

Malone's slow blink was the only indication of his surprise. He didn't know about the feathers. "I believe you all know that, last week, my Pride was attacked by a Flight of thunderbirds from a nest in New Mexico. Evidently they winter in the werecat free zone just to the west of my territory. We were hosting several guests at the time—" no need to mention that our "guests" were helping us plot an attack against Malone's Pride in retaliation for my brother's murder "—and between us, we lost two enforcers and sustained multiple serious injuries. But we also captured a prisoner, who told us that his Flight was attacking to avenge the death of one of their own—whom they believed we murdered."

"And how exactly does this make Calvin Malone guilty of treason?" Mitchell demanded, while Malone sat silently beside him, apparently unfazed by our allegations.

"We have evidence that the thunderbird in question was killed not by one of my enforcers, but by one of his. But Calvin blamed the murder on us, inciting the thunderbirds to attack and cripple my Pride, while sparing his own."

"The thunderbirds told you this?" Nick Davidson leaned forward, propping both elbows on the table. He looked considerably older than forty-two, but then, he'd had a rough few years. He'd lost his wife to cancer and was left to raise their seven children—including one small daughter—alone.

"Not initially." My father frowned and his focus returned to Malone, who stared back as if none of this bothered him. "Brett Malone told us. Right after he asked for sanctuary. Less than an hour before he died."

The room went completely silent. I think most of us stopped breathing. Even Paul Blackwell looked shocked, his wrinkled hands clutching the arms of his chair like he might fall over without it. He'd known we would accuse Malone of treason, but evidently hadn't foreseen the blatant implication of murder.

Calvin Malone rose, brown eyes blazing. He leaned with both palms flat on the table, glaring at my father as if bold eye contact would be enough to intimidate him. "Are you saying there was something suspicious about my son's death?"

My father stood firm, unruffled. "I'm stating facts. The conclusions you draw are your own."

"Brett died during a training accident." Milo Mitchell leaned forward in his chair, but was obviously unwilling to draw any more attention to himself by standing. "His death has been very hard on his family, and it is reprehensible of you to slander the dead, Greg."

"I'm not slandering him, Milo." My father returned his gaze boldly, and Mitchell looked away. "I have immense respect for Brett Malone. It takes a great deal of courage to stand up for what's right, especially when that means standing against one's own father."

"Brett had nothing to fear from me!" Malone roared from across the table, and I couldn't resist a tiny grin of satisfaction at seeing him lose his temper. Especially when Alex flinched on my right. He sat so stiff and tense that I was half convinced he'd explode if I poked him.

"And he had no plans to defect," the Appalachian Alpha continued, softer now, but with no less vehemence. "Unless you have some evidence suggesting otherwise, I strongly suggest that you let my son rest in peace and move on with the more relevant parts of this discussion. Assuming there are any."

Malone started to sit, then froze when my father turned toward the far end of the room, where Marc, Jace, and I sat interspersed with the Appalachian enforcers. "In fact, I do have some rather suggestive evidence." My father smiled at me briefly, then nodded at Marc.

Marc stood and reached into the inside pocket of his coat as he crossed the room. All eyes were on him—more than half the gazes openly hostile—as he handed several folded sheets of paper to my dad.

"What's that?" Milo Mitchell demanded, without acknowledging Marc. We'd been expecting some static over his unofficial reinstatement into the Pride, but so far no one had said a word. Neither had Malone even mentioned the covert ops we'd unleashed on his Pride, in spite of the fact that several of his men had been seriously injured.

My theory on his silence was that Malone was planning to throw consequences at us full force, once he had the power to overrule any objections. Which was one of the more critical reasons we had to keep him from being voted in as council chair.

"Calvin, when did Brett die?" my dad said, without answering Mitchell's question or unfolding the papers. "Time and date, please."

"This is completely inappropriate," Malone insisted, as a vein in his temple throbbed visibly. "I'm not going to let you turn my son's tragic death into the center ring of whatever circus you're directing. We're here to vote."

"I don't think we can afford to gloss over such serious accusations. And I would think you'd be eager to defend yourself."

"There's nothing to defend. I've done nothing wrong."

My father raised one brow, still eyeing Malone steadily. "Then answer the question. When did Brett die?"

Malone sank stiffly into his chair, still pushed back from the table, and when Blackwell didn't object to the question, he had no choice but to answer. "Last Monday night."

"What time of day?" My dad slowly unfolded the first piece of paper, focused on it now, rather than Malone, as if the other Alpha was no longer worthy of his full attention.

"Afternoon. I don't remember the exact time. It was a very traumatic day."

"I'm sure your wife was traumatized, as well, but she remembers the time. According to Patricia, Brett died at around 3:45 p.m."

Malone nodded slowly, eyes narrowed in barely contained fury. "That sounds about right. What's your point?"

My dad laid the first sheet of paper faceup on the table and pushed it toward Malone. "This is a printout of the recent activity on Jace Hammond's cell phone. My daughter borrowed it last Monday afternoon, in front of multiple witnesses. The highlighted line shows a call she made at 2:49 p.m. the day your son died. Do you recognize the number she called?"

Malone looked like he wanted to say no. To say he didn't recognize his own son's phone number. But he knew we could prove whose number it was, so finally he nodded. "It's Brett's. So what? She called him, and he probably hung up as soon as he heard her voice."

"Look again," I said, then rushed on before anyone could tell me to shut up. "That call lasted seventeen minutes, and I'm more than willing to testify about what he told me."

"You don't have the floor," Mitchell snapped, eyes flashing. "And hearsay testimony is inadmissible."

One of the few parallels to the human legal system. Which we all already knew. But Mitchell was ill informed.

I stood and addressed Paul Blackwell, trying not to be completely creeped out by the fact that I'd just left both Alex Malone and Colin Dean at my back, where I couldn't watch them. "Councilman, if I may?" I said, in my best, most respectful voice. Who says I never learn?

Blackwell gave me a short, reluctant nod, and I squashed my brief urge to grin in triumph before redirecting both my gaze and my comments to Milo Mitchell, whose son Kevin had broken my arm and tried to kill me, Marc, Jace, and Dr. Carver earlier that same month.

"Hearsay isn't admissible during a trial, but as Councilman Malone has already pointed out, he's not on trial. We're simply offering evidence as a basis for the charge we're leveling against him. We have every right to present both the charge and the evidence, and I can cite multiple precedents, if you'd like."

I'd worked with Michael for eight straight hours, memorizing cases and learning how the council's ruling in each one supported our strategy. And silently I dared Mitchell to challenge my knowledge. To give me

a chance to show off and to make a fool of him. That's
the least he deserved after conspiring with Malone to tag
strays in the free zone, a plot that had nearly cost Marc
his life, and had convinced most of the strays that there
could be no peace between them and the Pride cats.

But Mitchell must have seen the truth in my eyes,
or in my confident bearing—which I'd also worked on
with Michael. Apparently there's a difference between
confident and cocky. Who knew?

Either way, Mitchell only shook his head. "That won't
be necessary."

That time I resisted a smile in favor of a small nod,
the most noncommittal response, and one most Alphas
perfected quickly. Then I turned back to Blackwell.
"Will the council hear my testimony?"

Blackwell hesitated, but to his credit, he didn't glance
around for input from his fellow Alphas. He only had a
matter of minutes left as the council chair, and he wasn't
going to waste it. "Yes. Briefly."

"Thank you," I said, and though my father dared
not actually smile under such grave circumstances, I
saw approval in his brief, encouraging nod. "The day
the thunderbirds attacked my Pride, I personally in-
terrogated the prisoner twice, and based on information from him, it became clear to me that Councilman
Malone manipulated the Flight into attacking us. He
lied to them about who was responsible for the death
of their thunderbird."

Anyone else would have minced words. Called
Malone misleading, rather than a liar. But I rarely got
the chance to tell the truth when it really mattered, and,
like Blackwell, I wasn't going to waste it.

"That is not—" Malone started, but Di Carlo cut

him off with a single, gruff noise from the back of his throat. It wasn't quite a growl—that would have been considered an open declaration of hostility—but it was enough to shut him up.

"Faythe has the floor. Let her speak."

I could have kissed Di Carlo.

"I told both my Alpha and Councilman Blackwell what I suspected, but they both said we couldn't act without evidence. So I called Brett, because he had access to information we needed, and frankly, he owed me a big one." I'd saved his life only a quarter of a mile from where we sat, when a stray gored him and Colin Dean was too chickenshit to go help him without wasting time Shifting.

Blackwell nodded. "Go on."

"Brett didn't want to do it at first, Councilman Malone." I shot Malone a wide-eyed, earnest look, knowing it would piss him off for me to address him directly. But there was nothing he could do about it. And I was telling the truth. "He wanted to stay loyal to his birth Pride, but he knew what you were doing was wrong. He asked for sanctuary, and my father offered him not only a place to stay, but a job as an enforcer. Brett agreed. He was a good man, Councilman, and we've all lost something with his death."

Malone tried desperately to hide his rage, but it couldn't be contained. His face flushed so red I was afraid the capillaries in his nose would burst. He clenched the arms of his chair so tightly the wood groaned, drawing all eyes his way.

In that moment, revenge, even in such a small, brief dose, was sweeter than my mother's sun tea. And so much more refreshing...

"What did he say?" Nick Davidson asked, when I paused a little too long to enjoy Malone's reaction.

"He said that he and several of his fellow enforcers were in the free zone in New Mexico..." I paused, and my uncle interrupted with a leading question, as planned.

"Wait, what were they doing in New Mexico?"

I shrugged and gave the entire council a wide-eyed look of confusion. "You'd have to ask Councilman Malone that. All I know is that that particular part of New Mexico is within miles of our western border, and several hundred miles from the Appalachian territory."

I paused for a few more seconds, to let that sink in. Yes, I was being heavy-handed and obvious, but sometimes that's the only way to feed information to a group of Alphas. In large numbers, they don't seem to be able to grasp subtlety.

"Anyway, he said he and his fellow enforcers were in New Mexico, and one of them killed a thunderbird in a dispute over a kill. They called in their Alpha, and when the thunderbirds came looking for their Flight-mate, Brett said his father, Councilman Malone, told the birds that one of the south-central Pride cats had made the kill. Brett said his dad worked out a deal. In exchange for information about where to find our ranch, the birds had to promise to bring the tabbies to him—to keep them out of harm's way, of course—before the real bloodshed began."

I paused again to let that sink in and to judge the reactions. Our allies had already known what was coming, of course, and Blackwell'd had a good idea.

But Malone's allies' reactions ranged from confusion

and disbelief—from Nick Davidson—to utter outrage from both Milo Mitchell and Jerald Pierce.

"Who did Brett say really killed the thunderbird?" Di Carlo asked, right on cue. All that rehearsal had paid off.

This time my hesitation was real. I felt bad for the Pierces—for Parker most of all, even though he wasn't there—and was far from comfortable with my decision to turn Lance Pierce over to the thunderbirds knowing he'd die. But I'd had no choice. The thunderbirds had been holding Kaci, and they would have killed her without hesitation if I hadn't come through with what they wanted.

I would have traded almost anyone's life for Kaci's. Even my own. And Lance *was* guilty.

"It was Lance Pierce," I said finally, watching Councilman Pierce in my peripheral vision.

Sure enough, he leaped to his feet, eyes red and damp, face flaming with fury. "You have no proof of that! None!"

That part was unscripted, obviously, but not unanticipated, and it played right into our hands.

"Councilman Pierce, I'm truly sorry to have to tell you this, but we do have proof." With that, I pulled the clear plastic bag from my inner jacket pocket and stepped forward to set it on the table, where Pierce stared at it like it was a grenade I'd just pulled the pin from. "This is the evidence Brett offered in exchange for sanctuary. Unfortunately, he died less than an hour after we spoke to him, before he had a chance to retrieve it or leave the territory. So we had to go in and get it ourselves."

There. I'd just admitted to trespassing, but that was a

calculated risk we'd already decided on. There was no way around admitting where we got the feather, and if our plan worked, Malone would never be in the position to do anything about it.

Pierce stared at the bag and reached out for it twice. Yet both times, he pulled his hand back as if the plastic had shocked him. He couldn't do it. But Nick Davidson could. He picked up the bag and opened it, then sniffed carefully at the contents.

His eyes widened, and he glanced solemnly at Pierce. Then he nodded, and Pierce's face crumbled. "No…"

Having presented my testimony and evidence, I went back to my seat, sparing a single raised eyebrow at Colin Dean, who looked like he wanted to rip my head from my shoulders.

Davidson passed the bag down, and one by one, the Alphas smelled the feather. All of them, including Malone, who already knew what he'd find, and my father and Di Carlo, who'd already smelled it.

"Calvin, this is pretty convincing evidence," Blackwell said, when the feather landed on the table in front of him after making a complete circuit. "More than enough to warrant a trial. I'm afraid we're going to have to postpone the vote…."

"No." Malone stood again, jawline firm, hands steady on the surface of the table. "This is completely circumstantial. It proves nothing. We don't know how or when Lance's blood got on this feather, or even whose feather this is. For all we know, the thunderbirds could have dipped it in Lance's blood after they killed him. We have a responsibility to uphold justice, and this is not justice. My word holds just as much weight as hers."

Malone paused to shoot me a calm, cold glance.

"More, considering that I represent an entire Pride and I've never been convicted of a crime, neither of which can be said about Faythe Sanders. And my sworn word is that none of this is true. I never met with a thunderbird, nor did I sell out one of my fellow Alphas and his men. I don't know where they really got this feather, but I suspect it was soaked in Lance Pierce's blood when a Flight of thunderbirds slaughtered him for a crime he didn't commit, which they could never have done if she—" the look he shot at me that time could have burned right through me "—hadn't handed him over as a scapegoat. But regardless, we can't in good conscience accuse an upstanding enforcer—a *dead* enforcer, who can't be here to defend himself—of murder. I won't do it, and I'll be sorely disappointed in any of you who fall for such an obvious attempt to railroad this council and postpone the vote we all came here for."

Blackwell stood, leaning on his cane. "Calvin, you can't deny that this evidence carries some weight."

"Some, yes," Malone nodded gravely. "But not enough. It's circumstantial evidence at best, presented by a girl of questionable morals who's already been convicted of a capital crime. We cannot afford to take her word at face value, and the only way to verify it is with testimony from the thunderbird I supposedly dealt with."

My temper flared over the "questionable morals" dig, but I couldn't fight that one without making a fool of myself and further humiliating Marc. And there was a bigger issue at stake.

The thunderbirds could only be contacted in person, and even if we had that kind of time to spare, I had no reason to believe the birds would actually testify. They didn't give a damn about our political turmoil, or any werecat injustices that didn't directly affect them.

There had to be someone else who could back me up. Someone whose word the council would have to accept. But my father hadn't actually heard what Brett said over the phone. The only ones who had were Marc and Jace, and Malone would no more accept their testimony than mine. He'd remind everyone that the council had yet to recognize Marc as a Pride cat since his return, and if I brought Jace before them, Malone would call him biased and have the perfect excuse to call me a whore in front of the entire assemblage.

"If what Ms. Sanders says is true, surely she can present this thunderbird for us to question. Right?" Malone looked at me expectantly, and to my complete outrage, I realized that people were listening to him. A couple of the Alphas—Davidson and Gardner—seemed unsure of what to believe, but Mitchell and Pierce aimed incensed glares my way.

I was at a complete loss for words. If I admitted that the thunderbirds probably wouldn't testify, we could kiss the case against Malone goodbye. But if I promised them something I couldn't deliver, I'd be blowing another huge hole in my own credibility. So I said the only thing that felt true beneath so many restrictions. "I can try."

"Good." Malone gave a perfunctory nod. "We look forward to that testimony, at the earliest possibly occasion. But in the meantime, I see no reason to put off the vote based on unconfirmed, unsubstantiated, circumstantial evidence against an Alpha who doesn't have a single blemish on his record."

"But…" I stammered, my hands already going cold

from shock. In all our strategizing, we'd never thought Malone would be able to just ignore our charges and carry on. And our evidence wasn't uncorroborated. But Marc and Jace weren't suitable witnesses, and no one else had heard Brett's phone call, or Lance's confession.

Except Kaci...

No. I couldn't drag her into this. She was already terrified of the council in general, and Malone in particular, and there was no way they'd let me sit with her while she testified. They probably wouldn't even let me be in the same room. And on her own, she was too easy to intimidate.

I couldn't sacrifice her mental and emotional health, even for this.

I shot a frustrated, helpless glance at my father, wondering if he knew what I was thinking, and he turned to Blackwell.

"Paul, I can personally testify that our prisoner told us that a member of our own species blamed the thunderbird death on our Pride."

"Yes, but did he actually name this informant?" Blackwell asked, looking both hopeful and grim.

"No, but the Flight later confirmed Malone's identity to Faythe."

Blackwell frowned, and his forehead crinkled. And I knew what was coming before his mouth even opened. "I'm sorry, but he's right. If you're basing your charges on circumstantial evidence and uncorroborated secondhand information, we need to have this evidence and hearsay authenticated before it can be accepted." Blackwell's scowl deepened, as if the words tasted bad in his mouth. However, he would follow the letter of the law. It was his crutch in the face of uncertain moral terrain, but it crippled him in the field of justice. "We have no choice but to proceed with the vote as scheduled."

Seven

I stood slowly, fear and anger warring inside me. I couldn't make my hands unclench at my sides, but my voice and my face were under control. Even-tempered and respectful, at least from the outside. "Councilman Blackwell, please reconsider."

"You no longer have the floor!" Mitchell snapped, glaring at me from across the room.

"Neither do you." When the first unruly tendril of my temper began to uncoil, I grasped at it desperately, trying to keep it in check. To keep my mouth from digging a hole my father couldn't climb out of. I turned back to Blackwell, ignoring the complete outrage written in every line on Mitchell's face. "Councilman, you know these charges have merit. You were there when the thunderbirds attacked. You know we're telling the truth."

Blackwell's gaze hardened beneath wiry gray eyebrows, and I realized I'd made a mistake, reasonable though my presentation was. I'd questioned his judgment in front of the entire council.

"What I know," Blackwell said, his creaky voice

steadier than I'd heard it in years, "is that you've had your say and I've made my decision. This council is not unmoved by impassioned pleas, but neither is it governed by them. If we don't abide by our own rules, we will fall into chaos. Little better than the lawless warlords to our south. When you bring eyewitness testimony, we will hear it, and we'll decide then whether or not to try Councilman Malone on the charges your Pride has brought forth. Do you understand?"

I understood. I also understood what Blackwell was *not* saying—that he was sacrificing truth and justice to preserve order in a legal system he would no longer be in the position to enforce. For all his ideals, Blackwell was about to lose his position of authority, and if Malone was voted in with enough support, he would be able to completely restructure the council.

By the time we came back with a thunderbird to testify—assuming that ever happened—Malone might simply refuse to hear the testimony. If he retained the support of all of his current allies, his power would be virtually limitless. He'd be more of a dictator than a council chair.

Especially if Blackwell insisted on remaining neutral. By refusing to accept our evidence, he was creating the very monster he was trying to destroy. How could he not see that?

But for the moment, there was nothing I could do. Nothing any of us could do, without declaring war right then and there. And that would have been beyond foolish. We were outnumbered by our enemies, and most of our troops were hundreds of miles away, at the ranch.

My father watched me intently, but sent me no signal. No silent instructions for my next move. He was as frustrated as I was. Maybe more so. So I could only nod and return to my seat, in spite of every impulse urging me to keep talking until they all saw reason.

On my left, Colin Dean spread his legs to take up as much room as possible in his folding chair. His thigh met mine, and I wanted to reopen his newly healed scar with my bare fingernails.

I started to scoot away from him, then realized that would mean scooting closer to Alex Malone, who'd been directly involved in Ethan's death, his own brother's murder, and the new scar bisecting my cheek. So I could only sit there, fuming and grinding my teeth, trying to ignore the unwelcome warmth leaching into my leg from Dean's as Councilman Blackwell called for the official vote.

It would be an open, vocal vote, for something this big. Each Alpha's decision would go down on record. We might have actually pulled it off, if they'd used closed ballots. If the weaker of Malone's allies—Nick Davidson seemed less than solidly on board—didn't have to face him during the procedure, or admit that they'd switched sides.

Or if Blackwell had voted. But he stuck to his guns, shaky though his aim was.

One by one, they went around the table, and each Alpha said a name. My father and Malone were excluded, and Blackwell removed himself from the proceedings.

The vote started with Milo Mitchell, whose son Kevin had been exiled by my father, then killed by Marc. "My vote goes to Calvin Malone." No surprise there.

Next came Umberto Di Carlo, across the table from Mitchell. "I support Greg Sanders."

Then Jerald Pierce, who had two sons—Parker and Holden—in the south-central Pride, and had just lost his oldest, Lance, to the thunderbird justice system. "Malone." I wanted to shake him and ask how he could side with one son over the others. Especially considering that Lance's cowardice had cost two other lives, and almost cost many more.

After Pierce came my uncle Rick Wade, my mother's brother. "Greg Sanders has my vote, and my unyielding support." I wanted to cry.

Wes Gardner, whose brother Jamey had been killed in our territory by Manx, voted with a single word. "Malone."

Aaron Taylor, whose daughter we'd saved from being kidnapped and sold in the Amazon, showed his loyalty by voting for my father.

And finally came Nick Davidson, and for a moment, I thought he'd falter. I thought he was seeing the light at the last minute. Then he closed his eyes and sighed. And said, "Calvin Malone."

And just like that, justice died without so much as a whimper of pain. Four votes to three. If Blackwell had voted, he could have forced a tie and bought us time. But he went with his conscience, and as inconvenient as that turned out for the south-central Pride, a part of me respected him for sticking to his guns, regardless of the consequences.

Yet there was another part of me that wanted to choke him where he stood.

And suddenly I understood something my father had been trying to teach me for almost a year: sometimes you have to do the wrong thing for the right reason in order to truly make a difference.

I'd come close to understanding that with Lance Pierce, when we'd had to turn him over to save Kaci. But in a span of ten minutes, by simply refusing to act, Paul Blackwell had driven home a point my father hadn't been able to make me see in all my time as an enforcer.

The world isn't black and white, good or bad. The battles that make a real difference are fought in the murky area in between, where the greater good requires brutal sacrifice. Where both the means and the ends are just shadows in a featureless gray landscape.

And that was the death of my idealism.

Jace followed Marc out the front door by less than a second, and they glanced around in unison, both looking for me. Temporarily united in their common concern. They found me leaning against the wall to the left of the front porch, and their identical expressions of relief would have been funny, if we hadn't just seen justice strangled by the steel-gloved fist of oppression.

Melodramatic? Maybe. But also accurate. Calvin Malone couldn't even define integrity, much less uphold it.

"You okay?" Jace jogged down the steps first, but neither made any move to touch me, so we stood there like the first three kids at a junior high dance, unsure who should make the first move.

"No. That did *not* just happen." I sniffled in the cold.

Jace shoved both hands into his pockets, probably to keep from reaching for me. We all needed someone to either hold or punch, but neither of them would cause any more trouble, after what we'd just witnessed. "No one's less thrilled about seeing Calvin in charge than I am."

"Don't bet on that," Marc mumbled, leaning against the cabin wall beside me, only a few inches away this time. "His first act as council chair will be finding a way to get rid of me."

"That won't be easy." Jace sat on the top step, facing us. "This is a pretty damn hostile takeover, and he's gonna have Faythe's dad, her uncle, Bert Di Carlo, and Aaron Taylor fighting him every step of the way. Which means that for even a simple majority—that vital six out of ten votes—he's gonna need Blackwell."

Marc kicked a pinecone across the dead grass. "Paul Blackwell isn't going to lift a finger to keep me here, even knowing what Malone tried to do to us."

"Yes, he will," I insisted, grasping for the silver lining surely edging the storm cloud that had just rolled over us. "Blackwell may not be openminded or progressive, but if Malone forgets to cross one single *T,* the old man will vote against him. In fact, I bet Blackwell will be *looking* for legitimate reasons to go anti-Malone."

Marc shrugged. "So Malone will do what he always does—hide his personal agenda within some technically valid, if morally repugnant, new proposition. Either way, he's going to make our lives hell."

"I know." There was no way around that. And I'd be next on his list of lives to ruin. Experience had already shown us that Malone was willing to do anything to marry off as many of his sons as possible into Prides where they could later become Alphas, thus putting a considerable piece of the territorial pie under his own paw. He'd already mentally paired me with Alex, his oldest son, now that Brett was dead. And I had no doubt that he'd use our trespass onto his territory to get rid of Marc and try to blackmail me into a position that would better benefit him.

Jace would be harder to dispose of. He was neither a stray nor a shrew, and he wasn't technically guilty of trespassing, because he'd been invited by his mother, to mourn his brother's death with the rest of the family.

But we all knew Malone would kill Jace if the opportunity presented itself. After killing his own first-born son, taking out the stepson he'd never liked in the first place wouldn't even faze him. Especially if it could be written off as self-defense, or somehow otherwise justifiable.

Jace sighed, and his warm puff of breath was visible in the glow from the porch light. "There has to be a way around this. We're screwed so long as Cal's in charge."

"So let's get him fired," I whispered, to guard against eavesdroppers. I pushed myself away from the wall, clinging to the only bit of hope I could see on the horizon, far-fetched though it was. "Let's go back to the Flight and snag a witness. Now, before Malone has a chance to come up with some reason to outlaw thunderbird testimony. We already know Blackwell's not going to support him on that one."

"But do we really want to squander our best asset on testimony?" Marc asked, his voice as soft as mine.

The thunderbirds owed me a favor for saving the life of one of their young when Lance Pierce took her hostage in a last-ditch effort to save himself. And they were eager to remove themselves from my debt. But we'd been saving that favor, planning to ask for their services as air support in our inevitable, imminent war against

Malone. The thunderbirds were ferocious adversaries, and we had yet to come up with a way to defend against attacks from on high, short of shooting them out of the sky. But if we called in my favor for testimony instead, we'd lose our only real advantage against the Appalachian Pride and its allies.

"I don't know…" Jace began. "If the testimony works and Cal gets tossed out, we won't need to fight, right?"

"We will if he decides to take his position back by force," Marc said. "We already know he's been stockpiling both enforcers and allies, so we have to be prepared to defend against the backlash."

I thought for a moment, pulling a tissue from my pocket to wipe my dripping nose. "So, if we're going to fight anyway, asking one of the thunderbirds to testify is pointless. Especially if it means giving them up as allies in battle."

"Exactly." Marc nodded firmly, still speaking in a whisper. "The way I see it, we gave peace a chance, and peace screwed us over. It's time to get serious. Time to avenge Ethan—" Malone had sent the contingent that killed Ethan and tried to take Kaci "—and put an end to Malone's tyranny permanently."

"And for that we need to officially enlist our special forces." I nodded, pleased with the direction our discussion had taken. "We can leave tonight and be there first thing in the morning."

"Where you going?" Colin Dean stepped around the corner of the cabin, and I froze. My enthusiasm for the road trip/assignment flared into a blaze of anger in my chest that eerily mimicked vicious heartburn. "Romantic getaway to ease the sting of total failure? Just the three of you, or are you hoping to add a fourth? Rumor has it you're pretty hard to keep satisfied. Right, Marc?"

Marc snarled and lunged for Dean. I grabbed him from behind as Jace stepped in front of Dean to protect him from Marc, and Marc from assault charges.

"Marc, stop!" I shouted, digging my heels into the frozen ground to hold him back. "He's not worth it!"

Dean only laughed, inches from Jace's chest, because he refused to back down, either to avoid admitting he was in any danger, or because he wanted to fight Marc—so long as Marc took the first swing.

Unless someone was seriously injured, occasional one-on-one brawls were typically overlooked by those in charge. Sometimes tempers had to be vented to avoid later, more vicious explosions, and honestly, sometimes horsing around just got out of hand. But Marc couldn't afford to give Malone any reason to kick him out. And Dean damn well knew it.

"What, you'll share with Jace but not with me?" Dean raised one taunting eyebrow at Marc. "What happened to 'the more, the merrier'?"

"I should have cut your tongue out when I had the chance," Jace growled, glaring up at Dean from inches away.

"Yeah." Dean nodded, grinning. "You should have. Then neither one of you would have to hear how hard her nipple got when I traced it with the tip of my blade. I'm sure she was just cold. It probably had nothing to do with the fact that she liked having my hands on her. Not to mention my knife." He glanced at me, and my fingers twitched around Marc's arm as I briefly considered letting him go. I *really* wanted to see Dean's face broken again. Or maybe his neck…

"Isn't that right? You could have stopped me anytime you wanted, which either means you were too proud to beg, or you liked it." Dean's focus shifted to Jace again as Marc's arm tensed beneath my hands and I remembered that we couldn't afford to take the bait. "You could have stopped it, too, but you let me cut her. What kind of man lets the love of his life get carved up like a fucking turkey while he watches?"

Jace's fists clenched at his sides, but he kept his mouth shut. I didn't have that much self-control.

"If you ever come near me with a knife again, I *will* kill you." My voice was calm, and clear, and soft, revealing none of my hidden panic at the memory of Dean wielding a blade, yet all of my cold determination to see him dead. I was kind of impressed, and so was Marc. I could tell because he relaxed a bit beneath my grip.

Dean's eyes narrowed. "The rules are changing, and you're in for a very rude awakening, little puss. I hope you do resist. I hope you have to be broken like a wild horse. And by the time I'm done with you, you're going to wish I'd slit your throat, instead of your cheek." He glanced at the window over our heads, smiled coldly, and turned to walk off toward his own cabin, as if he hadn't a fear in the world.

"If I accomplish nothing else in my life, I *will* see that bastard bleed out," Marc breathed.

"He's mine," I insisted, as Jace fell in at my side to watch Dean go.

The front door opened on my left, and my father emerged, followed by Di Carlo and his enforcers. "What happened?"

"Just a little fraternizing with the enemy," Jace said. "Nothing we can't handle."

"Dean's trying to bait us into a fight." I tucked my arm into my father's. At least I could accept his comfort without pissing anyone off or making anyone jealous. "What's up with Malone?" After the official vote, the Alphas had kicked the enforcers out so the new chair could meet with his council for the first time ever. "Is he already plotting to take over the world?"

"One Pride at a time." My father sighed as we turned toward our cabin, the path lit only by cold, white moonlight. "He came prepared with a list of ideas to 'restructure' things."

"Steal from the poor to feed the rich?" Marc asked from my right, and I could practically taste Jace's frustration at having lost a place at my side.

"Something like that." My dad rubbed his forehead with his free hand and lowered his voice. "If his new proposals pass, this is going to get unpleasant very quickly."

"We were just thinking the same thing." I glanced from Marc to Jace, and they both nodded for me to continue. "We think it's time to call in the reserves. If we leave first thing in the morning, we can be in New Mexico by tomorrow night."

My father stopped and faced us, and Di Carlo and his enforcers fanned out around us all. "You think we should strike here? On the mountain?"

I shrugged, trying to look more confident than I felt. "It's neutral territory, so Malone doesn't have home field advantage. And if you call in our men while we're gone, they could be here by the time we get back with the birds, which means we'll have Malone vastly outnumbered. It could all be over relatively quickly and easily."

Assuming he didn't catch wind of what we were doing and bring more of his own men.

My father considered for a moment, then looked to Di Carlo for an opinion. "We've never fought on a large scale in neutral territory." So far, war had always come in the form of a territorial invasion. "If this maneuver didn't occur to us, it probably won't occur to him."

I nodded, eagerness creeping up from my toes to tingle in the rest of my body. "And if we don't make a move soon, we're going to lose the opportunity. Malone'll do everything possible to handicap us, starting with exiling Marc." One of our very best fighters. "Again." Or worse.

Di Carlo frowned. "I agree, but are we really ready to go to war this soon?"

"We've been ready," Jace said. "We just need to call in a little favor and get the rest of our men in place." Only a few enforcers apiece had accompanied the Alphas to the cabin complex.

"I don't see that we have any choice," my father said. "Calvin's already talking about supplementing the council chair's budget, for operating costs. I have no doubt he'll spend that money hiring more enforcers. Add his allies' troops to that, and our chances of a victory decrease with every day that we give them to prepare."

Di Carlo finally nodded. "But we need to make sure Aaron and Rick are on board before you three head for New Mexico. Unfortunately, we won't have time to discuss it all tonight. We reconvene in fifteen minutes."

"How about over lunch tomorrow, in our cabin?" my father asked.

Di Carlo thought for a moment, then nodded again.

"I'll pass it along, and hopefully you three can leave that afternoon."

My father glanced from me to Marc, then to Jace. "I'll fly Vic and Brian out to replace you."

I couldn't resist a smile. It was finally happening. Malone was going to pay, and a mere pound of flesh would not suffice. Justice demanded all one hundred eighty pounds of him, laid out cold and dead for the earth to reclaim.

Eight

"I'd call him crazy, if he weren't so well organized." My uncle Rick Wade leaned back in the ratty armchair, his furrowed forehead reflecting the disappointment on every other face in the room. Including my own, no doubt. "Malone knew he was going to win, and he came prepared. Some of his proposals are obviously dictatorial, but they've been phrased very carefully, so they're hard to reasonably object to."

"Yeah, he's good at maintaining the illusion of integrity. It's like an evil superpower." I flipped up the chipped, stainless-steel lever on the kitchen faucet, and water poured into the huge pot. It would take forever to boil on the outdated electric stove, but spaghetti was the easiest meal we knew how to cook in large quantities, and we had extra mouths to feed—my uncle and Aaron Taylor, plus Vic and Brian, who had flown in that morning to replace me, Jace, and Marc, under the assumption we'd be leaving soon for New Mexico.

At the stove, Marc stirred two skillets of ground beef. He was stiff and still irritated because I'd spent the night on the couch, rather than sleep between him and Jace, or try to convince one of them to take the couch.

Jace looked up from the slices of French bread he was buttering and gave me a small smile. At the moment, anything that pissed Marc off made him happy—Jace was still mad about me wearing *eau de Marc* the night before.

"And you don't think recruiting testimony from the thunderbirds would do any good?" my uncle asked, looking less than convinced.

"I think we've moved beyond political solutions, Rick," my father said from the chair opposite his brother-in-law. "We always knew it would come to this."

"And it's about damn time," Umberto Di Carlo rumbled from somewhere beyond my line of sight. "I was tired of playing nice, anyway. Everyone knows Cal ordered the maneuver that got Ethan killed and *we* know he's responsible for the thunderbird attack that killed Charley Eames and Jake Taylor—"

Aaron Taylor blinked at the mention of his dead son, and I looked away from his pain, because it resurrected my own.

"—and almost cost us Kaci," Di Carlo continued. And that was without even mentioning the strays he'd had tagged and/or murdered in the free zone, which had almost gotten Marc killed. "It's time he pays for all of that. I say let's quit dragging our feet and make it a real consequence. One he can't live with."

"I couldn't agree more." My father's comment was so soft I almost missed it, and when I glanced up, I saw him staring at the coffee table, his hands templed beneath his chin. He was eager for justice, but no Alpha in his right mind would ask for war without considering the consequences. The possible losses.

"I want to see him pay for Jake's death. But before we jump into anything, I need to know that we're all on the same page," Aaron Taylor said, as I turned off the water and hauled the half-filled pot out of the sink. "We're talking about *war*. About attacking another Alpha and his allies…"

"We're talking about killing Calvin Malone." I left the pot on the counter and crossed the kitchen to the doorway, where I could see the whole room. The Alphas had grouped around the coffee table, and Di Carlo's enforcers lined the far wall. "We're talking about removing him from power by removing him from *life*. That's what he deserves, and that's the only permanent solution to the growing problem he represents."

Taylor leaned forward in his chair, eyeing first me, then his fellow Alphas. "Yes, but full-scale war? If Jake's death has taught me anything, it's that we can't afford to lose that many toms."

"Neither can we afford to leave Malone in charge," my father pointed out in his quiet, reasonable tone. "The loss of both lives and liberty would be devastating."

"Yes, but why not target only Malone?" my uncle asked from the couch.

I picked up an open box of spaghetti from the counter. "We could do it that way, and personally I'd love to be there when Malone takes his last breath. But that's only postponing the inevitable. What do you think the Appalachian Pride and its allies will do if we assassinate their leader? What would *we* do, if they killed one of *you?*"

Uncle Rick sighed. "Full-scale war. But we can't turn back from that, once it starts."

"Of course not." My father dropped his hands and sat straighter, drawing all attention his way while I set the pot on the stove and turned the burner on high. "That's the point. The direction the council is headed is unacceptable, and it's going to take something drastic to set it straight again."

"I agree." Uncle Rick's shoulders slumped beneath the burden of responsibility they must all have been feeling. "All I'm saying is that, after this, it'll never be the same. The council may never be truly united again."

"It hasn't been for quite some time," Di Carlo pointed out. "And our failure to act won't change that. If we start a war to get rid of Malone, we may destroy the council in the process. But if we let things continue, he'll restructure the council to suit his own needs, effectively destroying it himself."

"He's already started that," Taylor interjected, and his heavy gaze landed on me with particular weight.

"Whoa, what does that mean?" I glanced at the pot of water, then decided that food could wait. The council had met until late the night before and reconvened early in the morning, without enforcers once again. Evidently the rest of us had missed more than just the design of Malone's new stationery.

My father took his glasses off to polish the lenses, and only once he had them back in place did he meet my gaze. "Calvin had an entire list of policy changes ready to go before the vote, and since then, he's been introducing one after another. So far, about a third of them have passed, and each time, Paul Blackwell has been the swing vote."

Dread clenched my stomach like an iron vise.

Unfortunately, even with the new unspoken hostility between them, Blackwell and Malone still shared a few ideological tenets, such as the belief that strays had no place within a Pride, and that a tabby's primary responsibility is to provide her territory with its next generation. So if Blackwell could be counted upon to vote his conscience—and history had already proved that he would—he would have to support Malone in most policy changes intended to hurt me and/or Marc.

Shit. "What's passed so far?"

"New Alphas must be approved by a simple majority of the council before they will be officially recognized," my uncle said, his frown deepening until I thought his face would collapse in on itself.

That one could be aimed at either me or Marc, and would no doubt apply to Jace, too, if his father had any idea how much of a threat Jace had become. "Wow, they're planning way ahead. What else passed?"

My uncle sighed. "All Prides must pay a monthly stipend to a discretionary fund that will be used to finance council business."

"What kind of business?" Marc asked, as he drained the first skillet of beef.

"Establishing a new, permanent council headquarters, hiring new enforcers as needed…"

Anger burned in the back of my throat, where a growl itched to form. "For which Pride? Malone's, I assume? We're supposed to pay for him to hire new thugs? No way in he—"

"Not for him," my father interjected, before I could complete the planned profanity. "Enforcers for the council at large, to handle any issue that involves more than one Pride. They'll be like state troopers, to our city police."

"That one's a direct shot at your dad," Uncle Rick added. "For handling the Manx issue on his own instead of turning it over to the council."

It took real effort to make my pulse stop racing, and to keep my teeth from Shifting out of fury. "Is that it?" If those were the laws that passed with Blackwell's vote, I could only imagine what kind of horrible proposals he'd actually found objection to.

"Those are the most threatening so far." Di Carlo ran one hand through hair still thick and dark in his late fifties. "But we're supposed to debate one more this afternoon...." He glanced at his fellow Alphas, none of whom seemed inclined to complete Di Carlo's aborted sentence.

Every hair on my body stood straight up. "What? What's the new proposal?"

Finally my father sighed and leaned forward with his elbows on his knees, looking more pessimistic and frustrated than I'd seen him in a very long time. At least when Ethan died, he'd gotten angry. I'd much rather see him angry than discouraged. "Faythe... His new proposal says that no woman can serve as an enforcer until she's given birth to a daughter."

Noooo...

My uncle took one look at the horror surely clear on my face and rushed to explain. "Originally the policy said that no women should be allowed to serve, period, but Blackwell balked at that, so Malone tacked on the daughter codicil. And it looks like Blackwell's going to support that one, too."

Of course he was. He'd always believed that I was better suited to a diaper bag than a pair of handcuffs.

"The problem is that there's no good way to protest that one," Di Carlo said. "If we want to survive as a species, we *do* need…" His voice trailed off, but we all knew how that sentence should have ended.

I'd grown up knowing one great, pervasive truth, and had discovered another since I started working for my father. The first was that in order to survive, the south-central Pride needed me to give them children. Because of a genetic inconvenience, there were usually four to six boys born before each daughter, and like most tabbies, I was the only girl in my family. The vacancy of my womb meant the end of my family tree and extinction for my Pride. There was no way around that.

The second—equally important—was that I wanted to serve as an enforcer, and some day as an Alpha. I had yet to come up with a compromise between my own personal rock and hard place, and until I did, the council—especially now that Malone was leading it—would use that against me.

It's not that I was opposed to the idea of having children. I never had been. However, if, when, and with whom were *my* decisions to make, and no one had the right to take those choices from me. But Malone had obviously found a new way to try.

I blinked, but the room refused to come back into focus. My blood raced so quickly the whole cabin seemed to spin. I glanced at my father, desperately wishing he would tell me I'd heard wrong. That Malone wasn't trying to get me fired and sentence me to serial childbirth, all in one fell swoop.

But he couldn't.

I dumped the dry noodles into the pot, struggling to control my temper, then turned to face the rest of the room again.

"So we're agreed? Malone must die."

The cabin got quiet after lunch. The Alphas had gone to the main lodge to try to keep the most sexist policy proposal ever written from becoming official Pride law, and I could do nothing but wait for the outcome. And ponder my future. And wash the dishes.

Teo and Vic had volunteered to make one of their mother's recipes for dinner. Teo went to town for supplies and Vic had insisted on going with him, ostensibly to make sure his older brother didn't mess anything up.

But the truth was that he didn't want to be near me and Jace. He was taking our relationship almost as hard as Marc was, and had barely said a civil word to either of us since we'd gone public. I think he was even a little mad at Marc for not pressuring me harder for a decision. Or killing Jace.

Jace had offered to help with the dishes, but I sent him into the living room for a tense, overtly hostile game of cards with Marc and my cousin Lucas, who tried to keep the peace. I needed time alone to think, and I wasn't up to watching Marc watch me and Jace, waiting for our hands to touch accidentally on purpose in the soapy water.

I'd just set the last plate in the dish drainer when the rumble of an engine drew my gaze to the front window. I expected to see Vic and Teo Di Carlo returning in the rental van, but instead, I saw a gray sedan passing slowly on the narrow gravel road that ran across the cabin complex.

The car was unfamiliar, but there was no mistaking Colin Dean's shock of white-blond hair in the driver's seat. There was second man in the front passenger seat and a third in the back, both facing away from me. But as they drove directly in front of our cabin, Dean gestured toward it, and the other toms turned to look. And my heart literally skipped a beat.

I knew them both. The big guy up front was Gary Rogers, whom I still half thought of as Deep Throat. I'd broken his arm to get him to talk, in the woods behind Malone's property when we'd snuck in to get Lance Pierce. And the tom directly behind him was Jess... something or other. Jess had pinned, then groped, me, and Marc had bitten off the offending thumb and left him to bleed next to the grave they'd dug for Jace.

What the hell were they doing in Montana? Even if Malone thought he needed extra security, those two would surely have been his last choice, after failing to stop me and Marc from rescuing Jace and taking Lance. Which only left one possible reason for their presence: they were witnesses.

"Guys!" I twisted the faucet too hard and it creaked beneath my grip until I loosened it.

Marc put his cards down, and they all three looked up as I crossed the kitchen into the living room. "Dean just drove onto the complex with Gary Rogers and Jess what's-his-name. I think Malone's going to charge us. Soon."

"That figures." Jace frowned but didn't look particularly worried.

"Well, it's not like we didn't see it coming." Marc

scooped up the rest of the cards and tapped them into a neat stack in preparation to shuffle. "We'll tell your dad when he gets back, but if we go through with the attack, some stupid trespassing and assault charge is going to be a pretty moot point, right? It's not like Malone's going to be around to oversee a trial."

But I couldn't shake the unease eating away at my insides. Halfway through their next hand, I got up to pace.

"Faythe…" Jace laid his cards down and joined me at the window, and I could feel Marc's gaze on us. "So what if he charges us? It's not going to make any difference in the end. Come on, you're gonna drive yourself nuts staring out the window."

"Us, too," Lucas quipped, already dealing me in. "Come help me teach these two a lesson." Because I couldn't play spades partners with either Marc or Jace.

"I'm sorry." I sank onto the couch and picked up my cards, organizing them by suit on autopilot. "I just don't understand why he'd fly Jess and Gary all the way up here just to make formal charges. They don't need witnesses for that."

"Maybe the council made him do it, after they refused to consider our charges against him without witnesses. I can totally see Blackwell making him prove he's willing to play by his own rules."

"Yeah, I guess. But this still feels like overkill. Even when I was up for murder and infection, they only sent a letter, and they don't have us on anything near that serious." Because neither trespassing nor assault were capital crimes.

Lucas shrugged. "Unless he's planning to charge you as accessories to Lance's murder."

"No way." But despite my protest, that was a distinct possibility. "First of all, Lance wasn't murdered—he was executed." And no one but me, Marc, Jace, and Kaci knew that the thunderbirds hadn't been the ones to actually kill him. "Second, neither Jess nor Gary even saw us take Lance, much less saw him die." We'd left them bound in the woods when we moved on to complete our assignment.

"Well, unless you want to go down there and ask Malone what he's up to, there's nothing we can do but wait." Marc scowled at the comforting hand Jace put on my shoulder. "And play cards. Your bid."

I tried to pay attention, and after winning two hands of spades in a row, I finally began to relax—until the first set of footsteps pounded up the front porch steps. Followed quickly by several more.

We'd heard no car engine, which ruled out Vic and Teo, and my father and his allies didn't move so quickly or stomp so hard—unless something was wrong.

We stood in unison. Cards fluttered to the floor. The breakfast table chair behind Marc fell over to clatter on the hardwood. The front door flew open, and I nearly choked on surprise, then raw terror.

Alex Malone stood in the doorway, aiming a gun at my chest. Colin Dean stood at his back, along with several more enforcers I barely recognized. None of them had been on the compound during the vote the night before. Malone had brought in reinforcements.

"Whoa…" Marc started to step in front of me, then froze when Alex clicked off the gun's safety.

"Don't move." Alex stepped into the living room, and his men fanned out behind him, all holding pistols.

"Since when do we carry guns?" Jace asked, his voice calm and low. Other than the occasional tranquilizer gun for rogues who couldn't be reasoned with, most Shifters eschewed firearms because of a deep-seated fear of being shot by hunters, as well as the generally accepted belief that when gifted with claws, canines, and supernatural senses, guns were an unfair advantage. Thus carrying them was dishonorable.

Clearly Malone and his men were unbothered by that pesky sense of honor.

"Since the council approved them for the use of the new inter-Pride task force ten minutes ago." Dean pointed his pistol at me when Alex adjusted his aim toward Jace.

"You brought them with you…" I whispered, stunned by their brutal preparedness and our deplorable lack of foresight. A chasm of fear opened deep inside me, big enough to swallow me whole.

Dean shrugged and shot me a cocky grin. "We came prepared."

I couldn't help wondering what else they'd come prepared for.…

"You're being taken into custody on charges of trespassing, kidnapping, murder, and treason. Walk slowly toward the wall and put your hands behind your back," Dean said to the room in general.

"Or what?" Jace demanded. "You'll shoot us, in front of all these witnesses?"

Dean sneered. "If you put up a fight, we're authorized to shoot to wound. So keep that in mind before you start swinging."

"This is because of the knife, right?" I stared pointedly at the thick scar bisecting his left cheek. "You can't be trusted to hold on to your own blade, so they gave you a gun. What makes you think you're any better with that?"

"We'll find out if you don't put that tight little ass against the wall."

Marc growled. "You touch her and I'll—"

"You'll what?" Dean demanded. "Bleed all over the floor? Because that's exactly what's going to happen if you so much as twitch. Now all of you, up against the wall. Three feet apart."

"What the hell did *I* do?" Lucas crossed thick arms over his broad chest, towering over everyone in the room, including Dean.

"We're not here for you." Alex prodded Jace with the barrel of his gun until his half brother stepped reluctantly toward the long back wall. "But you're not going to get in the way, either. Up against the paneling, or I'll put a hole in your foot."

Lucas growled, but complied. None of us could fight with a gunshot wound, and we couldn't afford the time to heal one. Better to escape custody later, than to get shot resisting it.

Marc went next, turning his face toward me as some nameless enforcer shoved him chest-first into the wall. He had to tuck his gun into the back of his pants to cuff Marc, but two of the three spare goons at his back had Marc in their sights, just in case.

"You're next, princess." Dean stepped close enough to see down my shirt, but I refused to budge. I would not be handcuffed and dragged out of our own cabin like some kind of criminal. "That's it. Fight. Make me get rough. I'm just looking for an excuse."

"Faythe, just do it," Jace warned, and I could hear the pain in his voice, from what it cost him to say that.

"Is that what you said to get in her pants?" Dean asked, but he was watching me, not Jace, and he stepped closer to whisper the next part, his gun bruising my sternum, his breath sour in my face. "Is that all it takes? One good, hard order?"

"Fuck off," I whispered through clenched teeth. My hands curled into fists so tight my fingernails cut into my palms. I concentrated on that minute pain to keep my focus. To keep from getting so mad my face Shifted. If that happened, I had no doubt Dean would shoot me. He wouldn't even hesitate.

"Up against the wall. Now."

"Faythe, it'll be okay," Marc said through gritted teeth.

"Oh, no, it won't. Not for any of you." Dean laughed, still staring down at me. "But *I* might make out all right. Now move."

When I didn't, he grabbed my arm hard enough to bruise and physically turned me, but I didn't walk until he shoved the barrel of his gun into my back. I stopped at the wall, and when I glanced at Marc—my teeth clenched in impotent fury—Dean shoved me from behind, smashing the side of my face into the paneling hard enough to stun me.

I blinked, and the room stopped spinning, but not before he'd pulled my arms behind my back. "Shouldn't you Mirandize us or something?"

"You mean tell you your rights?" Dean chuckled again. "You no longer have any rights. And you better keep that in mind before you go running your mouth." Cold metal closed around my left wrist, then my right, and he clicked the cuffs too tight on purpose. "Find their phones."

"On the end table," Jace said, before Alex could pat him down.

"Front pocket," Marc said, obviously hoping to avoid that same process. The nameless goon made a face as he reached around Marc to slide the slim phone out with two fingers.

"What about yours, princess?" Dean whispered into my ear. "Where are you hiding the goods?" He slid his free hand slowly down my side, but I could tell from Marc's look of absolute hatred that Dean was watching for his reaction, as well as mine.

"Te voy a madrear!"

"It's in the front bedroom," I said, trying to pull away from Dean's hand, but his gun poked into my ribs from behind, holding me still.

"How do I know you're telling the truth?" Dean's hand slid over my left hip and around the front of my jeans, barely brushing my empty pocket before dipping way too low for standard searching procedures.

This time, Jace's growl echoed Marc's, and plastic clicked softly as someone turned off his gun's safety.

"It's true, so either shoot me or get the fuck off me!" I shouted, holding back angry tears by sheer will.

"You should calm down," Dean warned, his breath brushing my ear. "You're getting your lovers all riled up, and that just can't end well."

"Dean." Alex Malone stepped into my field of vision. "Does she have the phone or not?"

"Not on her," Dean snapped.

Hmm... Dissention among the ranks?

"Then keep your hands to yourself."

Dean took a step back, but didn't dislodge his gun from my spine. "Let's go."

Alex nodded, and at his signal, the thug behind Marc turned him by one arm and shoved him forward, then marched him toward the front door. Jace was next, and Dean signaled the remaining "task force" members to follow him. The last one released Lucas, then jogged after the others.

On my way out the door, Dean's gun digging into my rib cage, I twisted to see Lucas staring after us in total shock. In spite of his size and considerable enforcer experience, he was just as defenseless as the rest of us. The guns were a game changer. "Get my dad," I said, as Dean shoved me down the first step.

Lucas nodded.

"Yeah, like that's going to help." Dean tightened his grip on my arm and leaned to whisper in my ear, as I stared after Marc and Jace in the rapidly fading daylight. "Daddy can't take a shit anymore without asking Cal for permission, and he sure as hell can't get you out of this mess. I'm your personal warden. And if you take one step out of line, you'll never look in another mirror without crying."

Nine

My dad stepped into the empty living room of the main lodge from the hall just as Dean shoved me through the front door, and it took my Alpha a couple of seconds to process what he saw. Nothing like this had ever happened before in the American Prides.

"Dad?" I was afraid that if I pulled away from Dean, he'd shoot me, and even a nonlethal gunshot wound would make my father lose his temper. Which might get him shot, too.

My father blinked, and when his focus readjusted, his expression went dark, his green eyes glittering with fury. "Get your hands off my daughter before I break them off." His voice was as deep as I'd ever heard it, rolling with rage like thunder across the sky. He knew what Dean had done to me, and what I'd done to him in return. And that Dean would be itching for revenge.

"Now, Greg, that would be a pretty stupid move." Calvin Malone leaned against the kitchen doorway, looking infuriatingly smug. He glanced from me to my dad and back, as if he wasn't sure which sight pleased him more: me handcuffed and held at gunpoint, or my

Alpha's powerless fury. "There's no reason for this to get violent."

"I see a number of reasons for violence." My father took several steps toward me, and Dean shoved the pistol harder into my back. "Let her go, or I'll rip your throat out where you stand."

"Dad, stop! He has a gun."

My father froze in the middle of the floor, as the other Alphas filed in from the hall. He sniffed the air, and his eyes darkened when he picked up the scents of metal and oil.

"Who has a gun? What the hell is this?" my uncle demanded, automatically taking up a position at his brother-in-law's side.

"Alex Malone and Colin Dean and a bunch of other goons just marched into our cabin with guns and hand-cuffed us." I tried to melt Malone alive with the power of my hatred, but he only watched me, apparently content to let me have my say for the moment. "Where the hell are Marc and Jace?"

"Your men are fine. They're being held in cages in the storage shed out back. We only have one extra room inside, and they both agreed that you should have it. I'd think you'd be grateful for their generosity."

"You can't leave them out there. It's ten degrees! They'll freeze!"

Malone rolled his eyes. "They're sheltered from the wind, and if they get cold, they can always Shift. Our ancestors never had electric heat."

"No, they had cooking fires," my father snapped.

"Um, I'm still missing some vital bit of information here," Uncle Rick said, his anger almost overshadowed by the confusion written in every line of his brow. "Can someone give us the short version?"

My father crossed thick arms over his suit jacket. "Dean is holding my daughter at gunpoint, evidently handcuffed," he answered, as Taylor and Di Carlo took up positions between my Alpha and my uncle, drawing a very obvious line in the proverbial sand. "And if he doesn't let her go *right now,* this is going to get very ugly." His voice deepened into a noticeably feline growl on the end, and I realized that some part of his throat had Shifted. And didn't his pupils look a little… vertical?

"Okay, let's all just calm down," Blackwell said, and I looked up to find the old man leaning on his cane. And if I wasn't imagining it, the web of wrinkles on his face looked deeper than ever. He looked…exhausted. "Everyone have a seat and I'm sure we can get to the bottom of this."

"Do I get to sit, or do I have to stand here with this pistol poking a permanent dent in my spine?"

"Of course you may sit." Blackwell made his way slowly toward one of several armchairs and motioned for me to take the one on his left.

Malone scowled at having his authority subverted and set his mug on the nearest end table, rushing to get back into the game. "Dean, put the gun away. I don't think she's going to try anything in a roomful of toms."

Dean hesitated, and only removed the pistol from my kidney when Malone gave him a second warning. "Fine. But I hope I'm not the only one who remembers that she once tried to eat my face off in front of a room full of Alphas."

"Oh, please, that was for show!" I turned on him the

minute I heard the gun safety click into place. "To scare you into telling the truth." I forced a smug smile, all for him. "And it worked even better than planned...."

Dean wanted to say something. Or hit me. That much was obvious. But he couldn't hit a girl incapacitated by handcuffs. At least, not in a room full of witnesses. Though in that moment, I wished with every fiber of my being that he would, so they could all see what a monster he really was.

Blackwell cleared his throat pointedly. "Ms. Sanders, if you don't mind?" I nodded curtly and made my way—awkwardly, with my hands still bound behind me—to the couch he indicated, while most of the other Alphas found seats. But my father and his three allies remained standing, in obvious and silent protest.

Councilman Blackwell propped his cane on the side of his chair and turned to Malone. "Calvin, what on earth is going on?"

But before Malone could speak, Lucas burst through the front door and jogged several steps into the room. "Uncle Greg, they took Faythe and..." My cousin trailed into silence as he took in the rest of the room, including me, handcuffed on the couch. "Oh, I guess you figured that out already."

"Welcome to the party, son." Uncle Rick shot him a wry smile.

"Sorry..." Lucas retreated to one corner of the room to watch with the other enforcers.

Malone retrieved his mug from an end table and took a sip, clearly savoring both the moment and the attention. "Marc Ramos and Faythe are being held on charges of trespassing, assault, kidnapping, and accessory to murder. I'm charging Jace Hammond with all the same crimes, except for trespassing. Faythe will stay here until the start of her trial, then she'll be swiftly tried and sentenced, if that proves necessary."

"You have no right to hold her," my father growled. "There's no precedent for this."

"Nor is there any policy forbidding it. Not that that matters anymore. You might recall that a vote this morning gave the council the authority to hold dangerous criminals until they can be tried and sentenced. I believe it passed by a six-to-four margin."

My father and his allies were the dissenting votes, obviously. At lunch, my dad had said they'd objected to the vague language.

"The operative word there is *dangerous,* Calvin. Faythe isn't dangerous."

Malone nearly spit coffee all over his white button-down shirt. "A show of hands if you believe that!"

No hands were raised, and I wasn't sure whether to be frustrated or extraordinarily pleased.

"Dean…" Malone gestured for his new golden boy to take the floor.

"Councilman Sanders, your daughter threatened to gut me. Without a knife." Dean's faux look of concern could barely conceal his glee at finally getting to deliver a line he'd obviously been waiting for. "Alex was there—he'll vouch for that."

I followed Dean's gesture to see that Alex Malone had slipped into the room at some point and was now watching me in obvious anticipation.

And suddenly I felt like the world's biggest idiot. Again.

"They set me up!" I stood from the low couch—not a simple feat without the use of my hands—and my father gestured subtly for me to sit before someone mistook my sudden motion for another sign of aggression. It took every bit of self-control I had left to make myself drop back onto the couch, but I did it without compromising the indignation I hoped still shone on my face. I glared at Dean, and silently tamped down the urge to let my teeth Shift. "You goaded me on purpose, trying to get me to lose my temper!" Of course, I'd been doing the same thing, so I was really less upset about being set up than about the fact that his ruse had succeeded where mine had failed. "And you've been threatening me ever since I got here!"

Dean met my gaze, completely deadpan. "I have no idea what you're talking about."

"Let's get back to the real issue here," Malone said, wisely drawing attention from Dean before the bastard's bad acting could undo the damage he'd already done to my case. "And that's the fact that Ms. Sanders threatened to use her ability to partially Shift—a skill she was supposed to be teaching the rest of the enforcers, to better equip the entire community—to torture and kill one of my enforcers."

"That's not how it happened!" I insisted, as sudden heat scalded my cheeks. Most of Malone's allies wouldn't believe me, no matter what I said, and those who did were eager to see me fry, whether I was guilty or not.

"You know she didn't mean that," my uncle insisted. "She was upset, and it sounds to me like he was goading her."

"Oh, she meant it." The authentic ring of certainty in Dean's voice drew my focus just in time to see him lift his shirt, exposing the thick, two-inch scar from when

I'd stabbed him with his own knife. "She's looking to finish what she started."

A universal gasp echoed across the room, and I ground my teeth together so hard my jaw ached. To my knowledge, other than Malone, my dad was the only other Alpha who'd already known about Dean's mishap with the knife, and he'd never actually seen the scar. I have to admit, it looked pretty bad. At a week old, even with a werecat's accelerated healing—and I shuddered to think how many times he'd had to Shift to get to that point—the scar tissue was still thick and pink and scary.

"That's why you cut her face?" Blackwell asked, apparently as horrified as everyone else.

"No! It was the other way around," I shouted. *Like Dean could even stand up after taking a knife to the gut!* "He cut up my face and threatened to keep going. I just…" But I let the sentence trail off, for fear of incriminating myself. "He's been out to get me since Councilman Blackwell fired him three months ago."

"This is not the time to get into the specifics," Malone insisted, conveniently cutting off my explanation, rather than Dean's exhibition. "She'll have a chance to tell her side during the trial."

"What? You're afraid that they'll believe the truth if they hear it?" But no one was listening to me. No one who had the power to get me out of my cuffs, anyway. They were all still staring at Dean's scar.

"Calvin, logistically speaking, this makes no sense," my dad insisted, and I could have rejoiced at the reintroduction of logic into the most insane discussion I'd ever tried to follow. "We only have the cabins for three more days, and extending for any length of time would be prohibitively expensive, in both time and money."

Malone stood with his mug, heading toward the kitchen. "You're absolutely right. The only reasonable solution is to hold a very expedient hearing."

"How expedient?" I demanded, already dreading the answer.

The new council chair turned to face me fully, coffeepot in one hand. "Tomorrow."

"No!" my father shouted, and I stared as he closed his eyes, probably counting silently. When he opened them, he was calm and in control again, though I couldn't fathom how he'd managed it. I was seeing the room through a thin film of red rage. "Absolutely not. How are we supposed to prepare a defense in twelve hours?"

"Oh, I can't see how that'll be much of a problem. All Faythe has to do is tell the truth, and anyone you could possibly call as a witness is already here."

My jaw clenched painfully. Of the possible witnesses, the only ones likely to tell the truth were Marc and Jace, whose testimony would probably be considered biased and self-serving—since they were up on the same charges—thus inadmissible.

"But I think you're missing the big picture here," Malone continued, his back to us all now, while he poured his coffee. "A speedy trial will benefit everyone. The council is already convened, and our cabins are paid for. We'll be saving the cost of additional travel and lodging, not to mention the time away from work and our families." Finally he turned to face the room, holding a mug of black coffee. "And really, who here wants to squander time and money, when we could wrap this whole mess up tomorrow with minimal inconvenience."

I had to admit he'd given a pretty good speech. Even the Alphas who would have been perfectly willing to give me time to prepare were not going to admit to wanting to "squander" their time and money.

"This 'whole mess' you're talking about is my life!" My hands curled into fists at my back and suddenly I realized the decision to use cuffs was very deliberate. While I could cut through duct tape or rope by partially Shifting one hand, I wasn't strong enough to break through steel. "Somehow I doubt you'd be in such a rush for justice if it were one of your own men sitting here."

Malone raised one brow and half smiled. "Ms. Sanders, are you suggesting that the council chair is biased?"

Yes. That's precisely what I was suggesting, but I knew better than to admit it. Instead, I watched my father, studying his composure and trying to borrow some of it for myself.

Calm and steady was the only way to address a room full of Alphas, half of which were just looking for an excuse to maim me or pick a fight with my dad. And as badly as I wanted to fight—was literally itching to Shift and slash someone—even I had to admit that this was not the time to start a war. Not with me in handcuffs, our two best fighters locked up in the storage shed, and most of the rest of our men scattered in various Prides all over the country.

I took a long, slow breath. "I'm just saying that rushing through something this important seems... unwise."

Malone actually smiled, glancing around the room at his allies to see if they shared his amusement. "Thank you for your concern. I'm sure we're all very interested in *your* assessment of what constitutes wisdom."

Prick. I felt my face flush even hotter than before.

"Now, Dean, if you'll show Ms. Sanders to her room…"

Colin stood, but I refused, so he hauled me up by one arm.

"Stop." My dad stepped directly into Malone's path. "I will not leave her here alone."

"Of course not!" Malone took another sip from his mug, overworking the whole you're-not-important-enough-to-ruffle-my-feathers routine. "She'll be under armed guard." He gestured toward Dean, whose hand tightened around my arm, and my blood ran cold.

No way in hell was I going to be *under* Dean, in any sense of the world, armed or not.

"That's a blatant conflict of interest!" I insisted, twisting in Dean's grip to glare at Malone. Calm and steady would only go so far, and a controlled facade would not keep me from being harassed—or worse—while I was held handcuffed by a psychopath with a pistol in one hand and a misogynistic chip on his shoulder. "I'm on trial in part for stabbing Dean, and you want to hand him a gun and the key to my room? Maybe you'd also like to tie me up, strip me, and paint a big red target on my chest!"

"Are you suggesting one of the council's task force members can't remain impartial and in control of his temper?"

"I'm flat out *saying* it!" I jerked my arm from Dean's grip and before Malone could protest, I turned to Blackwell, the de facto swing vote in everything important. "Look, Councilman Blackwell, the truth is that I stabbed Dean with his own knife to keep him from carving his initials into my chest."

A couple of the enforcers actually gasped—either because they believed me or because they were impressed that I'd tell such a bold lie in a room full of Alphas. Blackwell actually flinched, so I pressed on, turning to address my next statement to the entire room.

"You have two choices about what to believe. You can either believe that he cut me and I was defending myself, which proves that Colin Dean shouldn't be allowed anywhere near either women or weapons…"

Dean started to grab my arm again, but I stumbled away from him and toward my uncle, who steadied me, even as I rushed on, the words tumbling from my mouth almost too quickly to be understood. "Or you can believe that after I stabbed him for no good reason, he had the strength not only to remain standing, but to remove the knife from his chest, hold me down, and slash my cheek in return. Personally, I think that explanation defies logic, but if you choose to believe that version, then the scar on my cheek can't be anything other than cold-blooded revenge on Dean's part. What's to stop him from doing it again, if you leave me alone with him? It'll be even easier this time, since I can't defend myself."

Silence blanketed the room as my last word faded. My dad's allies looked incensed. Blackwell looked convinced. And even a couple of Malone's allies looked… confused. Which was as much as I could hope for, under the circumstances.

"That's ridiculous…" Malone started, but Blackwell

planted his cane firmly on the floor and stood, cutting Malone off.

"She's right," he declared. "Until we have a verdict, I don't think Ms. Sanders and Mr. Dean should be anywhere near each other. Calvin, assign someone else to guard her, or I'll keep us here in a locked vote all night long, to make sure she's safe."

Ten

"Do we really need these cuffs?" I rotated my hands, trying to relieve the ache in my wrists and the pins and needles in my fingers, but only wound up straining my shoulders. "Dean put them on too tight, and my hands are going numb."

Alex didn't even look at me.

I sat on the end of the twin bed on the right, trying to control my temper with Zen-like concentration on the faded, country plaid bedspread beneath me. Unfortunately, I didn't find country decor relaxing. In fact, it had a nails-on-chalkboard kind of effect on me. As did Alex Malone, my full-time jailer.

Alex sat in a straight-back chair to the right of the door, arms crossed over his chest, glancing my way every few seconds to make sure I hadn't so much as blinked since the last time he'd looked. Occasionally he'd squirm in his chair, searching for a comfortable position, which wasn't going to happen with that gun tucked into the back of his jeans.

I'd lobbied to get rid of the gun, insisting that the weapon and handcuffs together constituted gross overkill. I was hoping Malone would be reluctant to admit that I warranted so much precaution. Instead, he'd asked if I was willing to swear I wouldn't try to escape from an unarmed guard.

Foiled, by my own unwillingness to tell a bald-faced lie...

Sometimes it doesn't pay to be the good guy. And the worst part was that I was too pissed off to enjoy the triumph of finally being acknowledged as a serious threat by the enemy. The risk of being shot kind of sucked the joy right out of the occasion.

But on the bright side—okay, the less-than-pure-gloom side—Malone would never be able to cite inherent female weakness as the reason women shouldn't be allowed as enforcers. Not after the fuss he was making over my detention.

"Hey, asshole, what's your dad going to say when I sustain permanent nerve damage on your watch?" I demanded, still trying to ease the ache in my arms.

Finally Alex's cold gaze met mine. "He's gonna say, 'Good thing we don't need her for her hands.'"

Whatever. That threat had long since ceased scaring me. "Wow. You guys are like a broken record. Don't you ever get tired of the whole 'knock 'em out and drag 'em back to the cave' routine? 'Cause I swear, Cro-Magnons were more subtle."

Alex didn't respond, but the answer was clear. He never got tired of it, because it was all he knew. Probably all his father ever talked about or planned for.

Our system of government was pretty twisted. Alphas were traditionally male, yet territories pass not from father to son, but from mother to daughter, and the only way to become an Alpha of one of those territories is to marry the tabby born into it.

Unfortunately, the strength of the entire system depends on each individual tabby choosing the right man to run her territory—regardless of how she feels about him personally. Sometimes a tabby is fortunate enough to love a well-qualified man. Sometimes love comes several years into a marriage, when they have both Pride members and children in common. Sometimes love never comes. But the worst-case scenario is when a tabby marries for love, but her chosen mate is not strong enough to lead their Pride.

Some people think that's what happened with Jace's parents. That Jason Hammond was too weak, and that's why he died less than four years into their marriage, leaving his wife vulnerable to the advances of a ruthless, power-hungry wannabe-despot like Calvin Malone.

"When did this whole thing start, anyway? This whole 'rule the women, rule the world' plot?" I scooted awkwardly to the corner of the bed closest to Alex, trying to draw his attention, but all I got out of him was another fleeting glance. "It was with Manx, wasn't it?"

Before she showed up, there were no "extra" tabbies, and my cousin Abby and I were the only eligible but unspoken-for female cats in the country. Abby was still in high school, and I'd already turned down Brett Malone's proposal years before, so Malone's ambition was temporarily stymied by circumstance.

Then came Manx.

"Your dad saw her as his golden ticket, right?" Manx was unclaimed and vulnerable, by virtue of being both pregnant and wanted for murder. Perfect prey for

Malone. "Suddenly there's an extra woman in the mix, and by divine rights—or pure, unadulterated gluttony—she must be his, in one fashion or another, right?" Fortunately, he was willing to live vicariously through his sons. Otherwise, the ick factor would be too much to contemplate. "And then along came Kaci."

Kaci was initially ill-nourished from months spent on her own, confused from having no previous knowledge of her own species, and traumatized over having accidentally killed her mother and sister during her first Shift.

And by that point Malone must have heard the choir singing his name. After her trial and the loss of her claws, Manx was defenseless and desperate to protect her infant son. Kaci was young and terrified enough to be manipulated into compliance.

"Your dad's two for three, right?" But still Alex refused to acknowledge me. "Which means it all comes down to me."

I was the thorn in Malone's paw. The fatal flaw in his plan. I couldn't be threatened, manipulated, or coerced into obedience, and I could hold my own in a fair fight. And I was willing to fight not just for myself, but to protect both Manx and Kaci, as well. I was everything Malone hated in a woman—not to mention everything he feared—and he was determined to either break me or kill me.

But I had news for him. Alex Malone wasn't up to the challenge—either part of it. However, hopefully he was up to helping me get out of my latest prison cell. Or at least the cuffs.

"So…how old were you when you decided to pursue professional ass-wipe status?"

That time Alex's head swiveled and he favored me with an eye roll. "Insulting me isn't going to make me talk to you."

Yet I'd just heard his voice…

"I'd think you'd *want* to talk to me. Aren't you supposed to be seducing me, or something? Greasing the wheels on the way to our dreaded nuptials?" I glanced around the room, cataloging potential weapons out of habit. There was nothing I could wield without the use of my hands. "Or has your dad changed his mind about that?"

Alex sneered. "My father never changes his mind."

"Oh, that's right. Your dad's the sort who'll bang his head into a brick wall over and over, convinced the wall will eventually collapse. But it isn't the bricks that are going to cave in, Alex. Fortunately, you seem to have avoided that particular character flaw—you're messed up in an entirely different way."

He rolled his eyes, but I could tell I was irritating him. "That's not going to get you out of here. And I'm not messed up."

"Right. So, I'm curious—is it hard to walk upright with no backbone?"

Alex looked ready to breathe fire, and I wanted to laugh. He was so easy to piss off! Of course, he was only eighteen; surely his temper would even out with experience. Unless he got in my way again, and I had to kill him. "Did anyone ever tell you you're a raging bitch?"

"That *does* sound familiar." I forced my fingers to flex, desperate to regain some feeling in them. "But my point stands. Either you're a moron who's never had an original thought, or you're a coward, too afraid to say what you're thinking."

Alex frowned. "What is it you think I'm thinking?"

"That you don't really want to marry me. I think that's your dad's big plan, but you're not so wild about it." I shrugged. "I mean, I'm a bitch. This has been thoroughly established. What kind of man wants to marry a raging bitch?"

"The kind who wants to be Alpha." Alex plodded toward the dresser and half sat on it, staring at his hands like they held some answer his brain did not.

"Yeah, well, I'm starting to think that job's not all it's cracked up to be."

"Not the way your dad does it," he said, and the sneer was back, along with those cold, hard eyes. "But the benefits package sounds pretty damn good." His suggestive leer was unpracticed at best, and I couldn't resist another eye roll.

"Why is it that every conversation I have with a tomcat winds up being about sex?" I tried to scoot back on the bed and almost fell over without my hands for balance. "And seriously, if that's all you're looking to get out of this, I gotta tell you, there are easier ways to get laid. You should just tell your dad to go to hell. If there's one thing I'm absolutely sure of, it's that you don't have to live your life to please your parents. Or anyone else. It's your life." For however long it lasts.

"So, what, are we bonding now?" Alex crossed his arms over his chest, still leaning against the dresser, and in the mirror, I could see the gun tucked into the back of his waistband.

"Hell, no." I scowled. "You're still the bad guy and

I still want to spill your blood all over this crappy carpet." Being young and naive didn't absolve him of past crimes. I hadn't forgotten that in addition to killing his own brother, Alex was the one who'd told Dean to cut me. "But we'd be a lot closer to neutral tolerance if you'd take these damn cuffs off. My hands are seriously messed up from lack of circulation."

Alex hesitated, glancing at the door as if his father could see him through the hollow wood panel. "You promise not to try anything?"

I arched both brows at him. "You know I can't do that. We've kind of got a mortal-enemy thing going on here." I shrugged and tried on a cocky grin of my own. "But I promise not to try anything right now, and if I make a break for it later, you can totally try to stop me."

To my surprise, Alex chuckled. "I'm gonna hold you to that." He pushed away from the dresser and crossed the room to sit on the bed behind me, digging in his pocket for the handcuff key. "FYI, I have one hand on my gun."

I rolled my eyes on the inside, but I could play my part. I could play *him*. "That's what all the boys say."

He laughed again, and his hand brushed one of my wrists. It might also have touched my palm, but I couldn't feel anything below the cuffs. A moment later, something metallic clicked, and my left hand was free. I tried to flex my fingers again, but they wouldn't move, and when I held my hand up, it had a definite blue tint to it.

"Your hands are freezing," Alex said, while I waited for the next click. "Dean's an abusive bastard."

"You're preachin' to the choir on that one," I said,

but still there was no second click. Instead, my right hand was tugged to the side and I felt warm, damp breath against my neck and something solid against my back.

"This isn't so bad…" Alex whispered, and I froze. "You're not always a bitch. You're kind of funny when you wanna be."

"Yeah. I'm a funny bitch." My pulse raced and my face flushed. The bastard was hitting on me! While I was still half-cuffed! *Who's manipulating whom here? Juvenile little prick!* "Can you open the other cuff now?"

Alex leaned back slowly, tugging on my right arm again while I opened and closed my left fist in my lap. In my current state, I couldn't even throw a decent punch.

"I'm not like Dean, you know," he whispered, and my skin crawled.

Finally the last cuff clicked open, and I started to pull my hand into my lap, but Alex stopped me with one hand around my biceps. "I'm serious." He leaned close again, and his breath on my neck raised chill bumps all over my skin. Not the good kind. The creeped-out kind. "We're gonna be stuck together, but we could make the best of this."

I took a couple of deep breaths, trying to control my temper and think logically. He still had a gun and he was behind me, where I wouldn't see him draw it. "No, Alex. That's not going to happen." I was almost proud of how calm I sounded, even if my voice was bordering on a growl.

"Oh, it's gonna happen, but that doesn't have to be

a bad thing. You're hot, and I'm not exactly a dog. We could both do worse."

What was he, drunk? Delusional, more likely. "You're a murderer." My pitch dropped steadily until my voice was too deep to pass for a human woman's. "You're your father's lapdog, and a repugnant little bastard." I twisted to face him then, relieved only in retrospect to see that he hadn't pulled the gun, because I was too pissed to have stopped, even if he had. "And I'll tell you something else—I'm already tired of you assholes waving guns at me, so either get your fucking hands off me or shoot me. Those are your options. And if we fight, only one of us is going to walk away so you'd better shoot to kill. How do you think your daddy's going to like that?"

Alex swallowed thickly, and an instant later his expression hardened and his eyes narrowed. "You *are* a bitch."

"Like that's a newsflash."

He glared at me like a spoiled child. "I should put those cuffs right back on."

"You're welcome to try." But he'd have to use both hands for that, and if I got a chance to go for his gun, I wouldn't hesitate to shoot him in the leg. Which was part of the difference between me and him—I wasn't afraid to finish what I started. "But if you're not going to, then get the hell off my bed."

"You'll be singing a different song once they take your claws. What are you going to do then? Talk people to death?"

"Maybe I'll arm myself," I snapped trying to hide the horror slowly building inside me. I could *not* lose my claws. I flexed my fingers, glad that they were growing useful again. I would not live my life at his mercy, or anyone else's. "Guns seem to be all the rage lately for the desperate and gutless."

Alex tried to grab my arm again, but I jerked away as the door opened behind me. I whirled to find my father standing in the doorway carrying two steaming mugs. His face was flushed from the cold. "What's going on?"

"Nothing." I inhaled deeply and noted that he smelled like pine and wood smoke, and suddenly I craved the outdoors, though I'd been there only an hour before. "Alex was just being an asshole, but I think the moment's passed. Right, Alex?"

He stood and marched past me to the door, hesitating as my father stepped aside to let him pass. "You get fifteen minutes alone with her, and there'll be a guard posted outside the window."

"Wow. This place is a regular San Quentin," I snapped, reveling in my own sarcasm.

Alex looked up at my father from inches away. "Your daughter has a real attitude problem."

My father laughed, a hearty guffaw, if I ever heard one, and Alex was noticeably startled. "You should have seen her as a teenager."

I couldn't resist a grin as he closed the door in Alex's face.

"How are they?" I scooted back on the mattress until my spine hit the headboard, and my father handed me the blue mug. I sipped from it, expecting coffee, but found rich, sweet hot chocolate instead. Comfort food. The scent of coffee from the other mug had disguised it. "Thanks." I raised my mug and he nodded, then I turned my thoughts back to the issue at hand.

"They're cold, but surviving." He settled onto the edge of the extra twin bed, cradling his own mug. "Marc has a split lip and Jace has a lump on the back of his head. Seems they both balked at the idea of being caged, until they found out it was either them or you. Malone's completely unwilling to house the three of you together, or you with either of them. Not that I blame him."

"I'm surprised he'd let them stay together. Maybe he thinks they'll kill each other."

My father sipped from his mug, and I almost missed the tiny tremor in his hand. He was very, very upset. "They're in separate pens. Cat transport cages, like a zoo might use. Steel frame with steel-mesh sides. They can't stick more than a finger out through the sides, and they can't break out."

Suddenly I felt like I'd lose my lunch all over the bed. "Can they stand up?"

He set his mug on the bedside table. "Not in human form." My father's frown spoke almost as clearly as the hands he clasped in his lap. He was more worried than angry, and that was not good. He needed to get mad. We'd all have to be thoroughly pissed to get through this.

"We have to…"

"I know." He lowered his voice to a barely audible whisper and crossed the rug to sit on the edge of my bed. We were alone, but I had no doubt several sets of ears were listening from the too-quiet main room. "The pens are chained closed, but only secured with a standard padlock. Once we get rid of the guard, we can get them out, given a household hammer and a few uninterrupted minutes."

My brain raced. "Any chance one of Di Carlo's men can get to them?" I was already tired of whispering.

"Possibly. But we have to do it sometime tonight, because they're going to try you in the morning. And we have to free all three of you at about the same time, because once they discover any of you missing, we're either going to have to run or fight. And, kitten, I've never run from anything in my life, and I don't plan to start now."

A tingle of anticipation raced through me at his words. I was ready. I'd *been* ready. And there was something oddly heartwarming about planning a war over cocoa with my father. But...

"Not that I disagree, but what about the rest of our men?" My next words hardly carried any sound. "And our new recruits." The thunderbirds, of course.

My dad shrugged, his brow drawn into a tense frown. "There's no time. Even if we called now, they'd never make it in the next few hours. And we have no way to get in touch with the birds quickly."

Damn. I stood and started to pace. I felt like I was about to crawl out of my skin, though I'd only been locked up for an hour, and the thought of the impending fight didn't help. "Dad, we need air support, now more than ever. Malone called in reinforcements."

"I know." He stood and crossed the room to lean against the dresser beside me. "Officially, they're all either witnesses against you—" Jess and Gary, clearly "—or enforcers to replace the men he reassigned as the inter-Pride task force. But what that really means is that Malone now has more than twice the number of toms at his back that any of the rest of us have, and when you factor in his allies and their men, we're decidedly outnumbered."

A grim prospect at best.

"But we don't have any choice, do we?" I looked up at my father, childishly hoping—just for a moment—that he'd call me silly and promise that everything would be okay. But the time for such promises was long gone, and my father had never been one to sugarcoat the truth, a fact I grew more thankful for with each passing day.

He shook his head and put one arm around me, in lieu of empty promises. "Not unless you want to go to trial. Again."

"Not an option." I didn't stand a chance of an acquittal this time, because I'd actually done everything I was accused of—albeit to save Kaci's life—and even if I was willing to lie about it, no one would believe me. And even if I was willing to go down for playing the part Malone had forced upon me, I would never put Marc and Jace through the same thing.

They wouldn't be declawed. They'd be executed. Especially once everyone found out that Marc was the one who actually killed Lance Pierce. Something told me that the mercy-killing aspect wouldn't draw much mercy for him.

I sighed and leaned into my father, laying my head on his shoulder. "Alex says they're going to take my claws."

"I know." His arm tightened around me, and I wanted to tuck his suit jacket around me, too. When I was a kid, I'd been pretty sure it was better than Kevlar at deflecting bullets—both lead-based and verbal. "Paul Blackwell says Malone's been lobbying for his support all afternoon."

"Did he get it?"

"No." My father sighed and dropped his voice even lower for the rest of his reply. "But we won't get it either when we attack. He'll stand apart and hold his men back."

I sat up to look at him, and the dresser creaked beneath me. "He said that?"

"I didn't ask. If he finds out what we're planning, he'll feel honor-bound to tell Malone, to try to avert war."

My hands clenched around the edge of the dresser. I could barely contain my frustration. "So…what's the plan?" I whispered.

He stood, and I followed him away from the door. "There's only one guard at the shed, and one outside your window. Brian will take care of the one at the shed, and once he has Marc and Jace out, they'll take out your guard and get you out through the window."

"Then we go for the guns, right?"

My father smiled, proud. "Exactly. Only the toms working as guards are carrying, and it'll be hard to get rid of those, but we can even the playing field a bit by disposing of the stockpile."

My stomach churned again. "We're sure there's a stockpile?"

"Virtually certain. And that's your job. Get Alex to talk. Find out where the guns are and how many they have, then knock him out and disarm him when Marc and Jace come for you."

"Get Alex to talk…" I frowned. "That might have been easier before I told him where he could shove his own pistol."

My dad chuckled and I was relieved that he could see

the humor in the situation. "You could talk the green off grass, Faythe. And this time, we're counting on that."

Wonderful. But at least that was an assignment I was well trained for.

My father glanced at his watch, and I knew our mostly private visit was about up. But before he left— or Alex returned... "Hey, Dad, we should probably call Dr. Carver. No matter how this thing ends, we're gonna need him."

He smiled and slid both hands into his slacks pockets. "He'll be here first thing in the morning, I just hope that's soon enough."

But it wouldn't be, for some people. You can't have a war without casualties, and my heart ached just thinking about who we might lose on our side. Malone might hire cannon fodder to stand between him and danger, but we didn't. Every member of our Pride was valued, every enforcer hand-selected and loved like a son or a brother. We were family in the truest sense of the word, if not in the literal sense, and I couldn't stand the thought of losing anyone. Not with Ethan's death still fresh in my memory.

My dad's arm slid around me again, before I even realized he'd been watching me. "What are you thinking?"

My sigh that time was half sob, in spite of my best effort to keep my emotions at bay. "If I could, I'd take the guys out of this whole thing—no one else should have to die because of Malone's megalomania. But they're just as willing to fight for this as I am, and I have no right to tell them they can't. Or shouldn't. Even if it means we lose someone else."

My father's sigh was heavy and long, and when he

finally spoke, his voice was thick, like he was holding back more than he was actually saying. "Spoken like a true leader."

Eleven

"No..." I started to argue that I wasn't a leader, but stopped when the bedroom door swung open. Alex stood in the doorway, holding a bowl of stew and a thermos.

"I'll let you eat," my dad said, already moving toward the hall. As the door closed, he shot me a sympathetic, encouraging smile, and I swallowed my panic long enough to nod in return. Compared to Marc and Jace's lodgings, I was practically being pampered, and I could and would carry out my assignment, even if my skin crawled just from the knowledge that I wasn't free to leave whenever I wanted.

"Here." Alex set the bowl and thermos on the nightstand, but I waited until he retreated to his chair before I crossed the room toward my dinner.

I sank onto the bed and lifted the bowl, relieved to realize I could feel the warmth in my hands. Feeling had returned to my fingers. And the stew smelled pretty damn good.

Alex watched as I scooped up a spoonful of beef and carrots—hours before starting a war was not a good time to begin a hunger strike—and I briefly considered trying to charm him into talking about the guns. He was barely out of high school—too young to have much real experience with women, and just arrogant enough to believe I might actually have a change of heart, once I'd spent a little time with the sex magnet he surely thought he was.

But then I realized that the thought of touching him made me sick to my stomach, and I wasn't that good an actress.

Okay, back to the old tried-and-true: piss him off until he says what I need to hear.

When he noticed me looking, Alex put on his game face—an almost believable expression of regret. He was still trying to win me over. Idiot.

"You know, I get why you hate me, me being your jailer, and all."

I shook my head. "You're just doing your job. I hate you because of Ethan."

He frowned while I chewed. "I didn't kill your brother."

I swallowed my first bite, another spoonful halfway to my mouth. "You were in charge of the group that came for Kaci—which just proves your dad's an idiot. A leader is responsible for his men's actions, and you let one of them kill Ethan. That makes it your fault." As well as his father's.

Alex's pale brown eyebrows drew together. "How was I supposed to know Gibson was gonna pounce?"

I dropped my spoon back into the bowl, pissed now, even beyond the scope of my intended manipulation. "It's your duty to know how the men under you are going to react in any given situation. If you don't know them, how are you supposed to lead them? You should never have taken…Gibson?" I asked, and he nodded, anger and shame clearly at war on his face. "You should never have taken Gibson on that assignment. Ethan was no threat to him—didn't even know he was there— and Gibson killed him, anyway. You were going after a thirteen-year-old girl! What if he'd attacked Kaci instead?"

Alex bristled, and I was almost surprised to see him show a little backbone. "Look, I didn't ask for that assignment, and I didn't pick the men. So you can't hate me for something I didn't even do."

"Grow up, Alex." I set down the bowl and grabbed the thermos. "A real leader wouldn't make excuses. He'd just make sure something like that never happens again." I gulped from the thermos, but cold water couldn't put out the flames of rage burning deep within me. "But you're not a leader, and the men under you know it. And so does your dad. He's only trying to put you in my bed because he knows he can manipulate you, and that'll give him control of two territories."

"He doesn't manipulate me. He's my dad." Alex spoke through clenched teeth, and his growing anger fed my own.

I scooped another bite from the bowl, watching him over my spoon. "He was Brett's dad, too, right? Yet he manipulated you into killing your own brother." His eyes widened and he glanced at the closed door, clearly thinking of all the ears listening in from the other room. "I'm not seeing a strong father-son relationship here, Alex. You two make Anakin and Luke look like Andy and Opie."

He dropped his head again, staring at the carpet as he spoke. "Brett fell out of a tree."

"Right. And you're the only one who saw it happen, right? Everyone knows what you did, and they know your dad made you do it because Brett had decided to come play for the good guys."

"You think you're one of the good guys?" Alex stood, gesturing angrily now. "You handed Lance over to the thunderbirds. You chose another *species* over one of your own kind!"

"I did what I had to do to save Kaci. And we both know Lance was guilty. But I let you and Dean live, even after you tried to kill Jace and make a jack-o'-lantern out of my face. Would a bad guy do that?"

"Only a moron would do that," Alex retorted, and before I could argue—which I was itching to do with my fists—he rushed on. "You're a hypocrite, Faythe. You talk about honor and mercy, yet you're willing to let your whole species die out just because you're a frigid bitch. That's not honor—it's extinction. It's slow-motion genocide."

My hand went slack around my spoon. I couldn't get past his accusations. Was that what everyone thought of me? That I wanted to flush my entire species down the evolutionary toilet? No wonder so many of them hated me. But they were wrong. About everything.

I dropped my bowl on the nightstand, and broth splashed onto the wood. "You are so full of shit, you reek from a mile away. And so does your dad, if that's the kind of bull he's been feeding you. You can't blame an entire species' propagation problems on one woman wanting to have a life of her own before she's ready to create several more. And frankly, the longer I listen to your bullshit, the less I want to have children, for fear they'll turn out like you! Maybe our species wasn't meant to survive. Did you ever think of that? Maybe there's a reason we have so few women, and maybe that reason is because assholes like you and your father, and his pathetic, ass-kiss followers, don't deserve to be here, much less to warp an entire new generation of toy soldiers and broken-spirited baby machines."

I knew I'd said too much—knew everyone in the front room could hear me, and that I might have just made all new enemies. But I couldn't stop. The truth burned white-hot inside me, demanding to be spoken.

"You're not afraid the other tabbies will start thinking like me. You're afraid they'll start thinking, period! You wouldn't know what do to with a woman who has ideas of her own, and your vacant, slack-jawed stare right now proves it." I paused for a deep breath and stood. "And by the way, refusing to sleep with you doesn't mean a girl's frigid. It means she has standards."

I sank onto the bed again, floating with satisfaction and more nourished by the truth I'd spoken than by the soup he'd brought. I'd probably pay for everything I'd said later, but I didn't regret a word of it. Malone and his allies needed a dose of honesty, and they needed to know who they were really dealing with. And now they knew.

Alex fumed. His face flushed purple with anger and humiliation, and he kept glancing at the closed door, hyperaware that the living room had gone completely silent when I started my tirade. "You know, you're only making things harder for yourself, running your mouth off like that. Soon you're gonna be missing your claws and in serious need of a friend, and I'll look pretty damn good next to the alternative."

"The alternative?" I asked, and a flash of genuine

irritation and jealousy passed over his face. Dread settled through me as his meaning sank in. "You mean Dean?"

"Yeah." Alex sank onto the spare twin bed and met my gaze from three feet away, lowering his voice so he wouldn't be heard from the living room. "Marc and Jace aren't going to last long, now that things have changed. We both know that. And if I can't make you see reason by the time they're both gone, my dad's going to give Dean a shot with you. Would you really rather deal with him than with me?" His gaze strayed to the scar on my left cheek. "After what he did to your face? At least I'd never hurt you."

It took every bit of self-control I had left to keep from shouting, and I made no effort to lower my voice. "And I'm supposed to believe that because I've magically forgotten how I got my pretty new scar? You told him to cut me, Alex. This was *your* bright idea, and that's not the kind of thing a girl can just forgive and forget."

"It was just a threat!" His voice was a mere suggestion of sound now, and even I barely heard him. "How was I supposed to know you'd actually make him do it?"

"Alphas don't make empty threats, Alex. They say what they mean, and they follow through. Good Alphas, anyway. Your father obviously doesn't qualify, considering he's keeping you under his thumb with nothing more than a series of idle threats."

"They're not idle," he whispered. "He's very serious about getting rid of Marc and Jace."

"Oh, I don't doubt that. But he'd no sooner try to put Dean in charge of the south-central territory than he'd let Marc run it. Your dad can't control Colin Dean, and

he knows it. But at least Dean has the balls to get the
job done. You... I don't think you have it in you."

"What the hell are you talking about?"

"Your dad wants grandchildren, and I'm *never* going
to willingly sleep with you." I said it nice and loud, careful to enunciate, so everyone in the other room would
hear. "Do the math. What's the only way you're ever
going to get me pregnant?"

"No." He shook his head, eyes wide, though he still
whispered. "It won't be like that. You'll come around,
once Marc and Jace are gone. You won't have claws, or
anyone left to protect you. My dad says you'll need me,
and need can make a woman see reason."

And suddenly I was reminded of how very young
and naive he was.

"Your dad's a raging idiot," I spat, contempt dripping
from my voice. "I will fight you. Every single time. You
will not tame me. You will not break me. I will make
your life a living hell, and if I get a chance to kill you,
I'll take it. And frankly, I don't think you can beat me in
a fair fight. But even if you can, are you really prepared
to do what your dad wants? Over and over again?"

Alex looked sick, like he was about to puke all over
the floor. I breathed a silent sigh of relief that I'd read
him correctly. If he were more like Dean, that approach
would have failed spectacularly.

"You may be young and stupid, but you're not a monster, Alex. And if your father had a single brain cell in
that overinflated skull of his, he'd know that when the
time comes, you'll be no use to him. Hell, I wouldn't be
surprised if he cuts you loose altogether. Then where
will you go?"

His Adam's apple bobbed like he was trying to

swallow rage that had no other outlet. And when he finally spoke, I could barely hear him. "I'm not Brett. You're not gonna talk me into defecting."

I laughed out loud and was thrilled to see him flinch. "My father wouldn't take you. We have standards in the south-central Pride. Cowards need not apply."

"I'm not a coward." There was that anger again. It was a quiet fury this time, bubbling beneath the surface.

"Right. That's why you have a pistol tucked into the back of your pants. A gun can make even the most worthless coward feel powerful, can't it? But what that gun really means is that you don't fight well enough to go without it."

"You don't know what you're talking about."

I rolled my eyes. "I know this—you're not going to surprise us with those guns again. Hunting is big in Texas, Alex. Did you really think we'd be impressed by a couple of stupid pistols?"

I made myself inhale steadily, afraid that if I held my breath, he'd see how important his answer was. That the entire argument had been a lead-in to the gun issue.

Fortunately, Alex was too mad to question the hopefully subtle change in subject. "A *couple* of stupid pistols?" His face was turning red again. "It's not just a couple. It's twenty—more than enough to protect and defend. And they weren't easy to get ahold of, without all the background checks and paperwork."

A sick feeling twisted in my gut and my smug satisfaction began to fade. Malone had twenty guns? Shit. How long had he been planning this? How on earth were we supposed to get rid of that many before the fight? And what the hell were we supposed to do with them?

"Twenty? Talk about overkill… Or does your dad

have twenty enforcers now? With that overinflated ego, he probably thinks he needs that kind of entourage."

Alex frowned. He didn't like it when I insulted his father, which made that my new favorite hobby. "The guns are for the new task force."

"And you're on this task force?"

"Handpicked a month ago."

Before there even *was* a task force. I pulled my knees up to my chest and wrapped my arms around them, noting that conversation had resumed in the living room. They were no longer listening. "Are there actually twenty members?" That feeling of dread grew darker. This task force was a very bad idea.

"Not yet, but there will be. My dad has his eye on several toms from other Prides, to keep things fair."

Or at least to keep things *looking* fair.

"Are you telling me that your dad is passing out handguns to a bunch of power-hungry rookies who've never even held one before?"

Alex frowned. "That would be stupid. We've been training for weeks now, and most of us are pretty good shots." He hesitated, then added, "I'm better than Dean."

I couldn't decide whether I wanted to hit him or hold his hand and walk him back to preschool. Alex was just a kid. He was an impressionable teenager whose sense of right and wrong had been forever warped by a power-hungry father. Unfortunately, he was also an *armed* teenager who could throw a full-grown man into the next room.

"You guys didn't bring all those guns here, did you?" I said, when a more subtle way to ask the question didn't present itself.

His eyes narrowed. "What, you thinkin' of grabbing one, now that you know what you're up against?" I started to deny it, then decided to let him think whatever he wanted. "Not gonna happen. We only brought half, and half of *those* are locked up safe and sound. You'll never get your hands on any of them."

I shrugged, trying to look casual. "I wouldn't even try. I don't even know how to hold one."

"That's just one more reason you should rethink this whole 'ice bitch' routine. Your mouth isn't going to protect you from a 9 mm slug, and it won't save your claws, either. The best thing you can do for yourself now is to shut up and start playing nice, because burning bridges is only going to leave you stranded all alone."

Better alone than with Alex. Or Dean. And what kind of bullshit metaphor was that, anyway?

Alex mistook my silence for capitulation—or at least serious contemplation—and for several minutes, neither of us spoke. Then, finally, he sighed. "Are you gonna eat that?" He gestured toward the half-empty bowl of now-cold stew on the nightstand.

"No. Go for it."

Instead of getting up and walking around the bed, he leaned over me with one hand on the mattress, careful to make sure his chest brushed mine as he reached for the bowl. The arrogant prick.

As he stretched, the tail of his shirt came up, exposing the butt of the gun sticking out of his waistband.

I hesitated less than a second. It wasn't in the plan. I was supposed to wait for the jailbreak, not execute it myself. But life rarely dangles opportunity quite so close to my grasping hands, and I wasn't going to pass this one up.

I snatched the gun. Alex sat up, grabbing for it. I clicked off the safety, as I'd seen him do earlier. Alex froze.

"Faythe…"

I swung the gun, hard. The grip slammed into his temple. Alex collapsed on top of me, out cold, a lump already forming on the side of his head.

"I only said you could *try* to stop me."

Twelve

I rolled Alex off of me and onto the edge of the bed, then pulled his handcuffs from his pocket and secured his arms behind his back. The cuff key went into my front pocket, as I glanced around the room for something with which to tie his ankles. The dresser, chest of drawers, and the closet were all empty, except for a few bent metal hangers on the floor of the closet. The only thing even remotely ropelike was the telephone wire.

Kneeling between the twin beds, I pulled the nightstand away from the wall and disconnected the wire from the jack, then from the phone, and used it to tie Alex's ankles together.

With no duct tape and nothing to use as a gag, I tore the sleeve off his black winter T-shirt, then cursed myself for already having cuffed him. Marc made ripping material look easy, and I'd popped the shoulder stitches just fine, but it took me two tries to get the sleeve torn open along the length of his arm.

I wadded up the loose material and shoved it into his mouth, in lieu of a better gag, then pushed him beneath the bed. If someone looked for more than a second they'd find him—especially if he woke up and struggled—but at a glance, the room would look empty, once I was gone.

The plan had been for Marc and Jace to take care of the guard outside my window, but they obviously weren't free yet, which was the biggest inconvenience in my impromptu prison break. Well, that, and the fact that I wasn't wearing a coat, which meant I was gonna freeze my ass off outside.

I knelt at the head of the left-hand bed to peer out the window, but saw no sign of my guard, or of anyone else. My room faced the side yard—on the first floor, thankfully—and it was cold enough that everyone with an ounce of sense had gone inside. In fact, I could hear the muted crackle-roar of a fire from the main room down the hall, along with the buzz of conversation that would hopefully disguise the few sounds of my escape.

The view from the second bed was the same, which meant my guard had either left his post or was standing right beside one of the windows where I couldn't see him, waiting to bash me over the head and turn me in.

To test the theory, I took a deep, calming breath and unlocked the window, then pulled it open a couple of inches and gasped at the stinging cold. If the guard showed up, I'd say I wanted some fresh air.

But no one came, so I opened it a little more and stuck my head out. The yard was empty.

It was probably a trap. What were the chances that I happened to make my escape during the guard's only bathroom break?

"Where the hell do you think you're going?"

I turned toward the unfamiliar voice and smacked the back of my head on the bottom of the windowsill. "Shit!"

Rubbing my scalp, I watched the guard jog toward me, carrying a travel mug steaming through the vent hole. One of Malone's men. I knew him by sight—he'd been there when we were "arrested"—but his name wouldn't come.

Terry? Tommy? *Something with a* T…

My pulse raced, and I struggled to control it. Not that he could hear very well with that thick hood on, surely.

Teddy! It came to me suddenly as he stomped closer, unzipping his jacket to show me the gun tucked into the front of his waistband. The idiot should have kept it ready.

"Ted, right?" I conjured up a smile, wondering how much he knew about me. How dangerous I was considered by toms I'd had no personal contact with.

His brows rose, then his dark eyes narrowed in the light spilling from the window over my head. He seemed both surprised and suspicious that I knew his name. "This ain't a drive-through window. Get back in there."

"Is that coffee?" My brain whirred, scrambling for the right words, a plausible explanation. "Could I possibly convince you to get me a cup? Alex is pretty stuck on this bread-and-water routine."

"I'm not your fucking gopher." He craned his neck, trying to look around me through the window. "Where is Alex, anyway?"

"Bathroom. They stuck some bull neck right outside the door." I leaned farther out the window and eyed his mug. "Can I just have a sip of yours, then?"

Teddy hesitated, glancing from me to his insulated cup, then back. I rolled my eyes. "You must be the only tom in this complex who's afraid of my germs. Everyone else seems pretty damned eager to catch anything I'm giving out. Which means you're either a big scaredy-cat, or you're really stingy with your coffee." Or he wasn't into girls. I shrugged and started to duck back into the room. "Fine. Keep your damn coffee."

"Here." He shoved the cup toward me, like most toms, eager to defend his manhood. "I hope you like it black."

I grinned. "So long as it's hot." I swear, calling them "scared" works just as well as playing the boob card. Almost. So just for good measure, I gave him a nice, long look as I leaned halfway out the window again.

While he stared down my shirt, I reached for the coffee—and grabbed his wrist instead.

I pulled, hard. He grunted and flew toward me. Coffee sloshed. His face smooshed into the window over my head. I tugged his gun from his waistband.

"Whoa…" Ted dropped the coffee and started to back away.

"Don't move," I ordered.

He froze. "You don't even know how to use that."

"My dad learned to shoot in college, and he taught us all the basics." A little truth with every lie is like salt on potatoes—it just goes down better that way. I raised one brow when he frowned in disbelief. "What? You thought you guys were the only ones shooting up paper deer? Think again."

"You're lying…"

I smiled. "What if I'm not?"

"They'll bust in the minute they hear gunfire."

I shrugged. "Yeah, but you'll still be shot. As will the

next fifteen people who come through that door. You want that on your head?"

"You're not gonna kill 'em."

"No, but I will shoot them. What's Malone going to say when he finds out where I got the gun?"

Teddy hesitated, evidently trying to shoot fireballs from his eyes. "You're a bitch."

"Yeah, I'm thinking of having that put on some business cards. Now turn around and take a step back. You shout, and I'll put a bullet through your shoulder."

He didn't move until I flicked off the safety, glad I'd seen both Dean and Alex do that earlier. And even more glad that they were evidently all carrying the same model gun. "Shit." Teddy turned slowly, arms out at his sides.

"Put your hands behind your back."

Teddy huffed. "You can't tie my hands and hold that gun at the same time." The tension in his hands and neck said he was about to try something stupid.

"You're right about that." I flicked the safety back on and leaned farther out the window, then swung the gun as hard as I could. The butt slammed into the back of his head. Ted crumpled to the ground like a marionette with its strings cut.

I climbed out the window, already shivering violently, and when I was sure Ted was still breathing—thanks to the white puffs of air floating in front of his face—I rolled him onto his stomach and dug his handcuffs from his pocket. Then I took perverse pleasure in restraining him with his own cuffs. That's like being shot with your own gun or stabbed with your own knife. Insult to injury.

I liked the irony.

Teddy's eyes fluttered, and he moaned, already waking up. It was hard to get in a good swing when you're hanging out a window.

Since I didn't have any other way to keep him quiet, I kicked him in the back of the skull, and his head rolled to the left. He was out cold that time. And only once my adrenaline rush began to fade did I realize I'd cuffed him before taking off his coat. Again. And a quick search revealed that he didn't have the keys on him. I was getting too cuff-happy for my own good. Fortunately, I was also free, armed with two guns I didn't know how to use, and filled with the satisfaction of having single-handedly disarmed and disabled two members of Malone's "elite" task force.

And I was freezing my ass off.

I double-checked the safety on the new pistol, then slid the barrel into the front waistband of my jeans—uncomfortably aware that I was now the meat in a two-handgun sandwich—then glanced around to get my bearings. My room was on the side of the lodge; the front was to my left and the back was to my right.

I edged along slowly with my back to the wall, while a clock ticked softly in my head. It wouldn't take long for them to realize I was gone, and I had to free Marc and Jace before that happened. But when I rounded the back corner of the lodge, I discovered via the light and noise pouring from an uncovered kitchen window that I would be in plain sight during my dash across the yard toward the shed where they were being held.

Fortunately, the shed entrance was on the left-hand wall, so the guard hadn't yet seen me. But a straight-forward approach would never work. Even in the dark, when I refused to identify myself, he'd either shoot or shout for backup.

Frustrated and half-frozen, I backtracked quickly, then dashed across the side yard, heading for the woods as quietly as possible. Under the cover of trees, I stopped to Shift my eyes. Light from the cabin didn't reach the tree line, and in my clumsy two-legged form, with inadequate human vision, I'd never make it to the shed without stumbling and giving myself away.

Now better prepared, I picked my way through the underbrush, aiming for piles of pine needles rather than crunchy fallen leaves, until I saw the shed directly ahead. And the tom on duty, too dark to identify from such a distance.

I could tell from his carriage and bearing that I didn't know him. However, the chances of him not knowing me were slim to none, so the "Hey, I got lost in the woods" routine probably wouldn't work.

But then again… He couldn't see as well as I could in the dark, and our sense of smell is nowhere near as good in human form as in cat form. And he wouldn't be expecting Malone's most infamous prisoner—whom he didn't know had escaped—to come tripping out of the woods.

Maybe if I go for the Oscar…

In the absence of a good plan, any plan will work. I moved Teddy's gun from the front of my waistband to the back, next to Alex's. My heart was racing, but that was good—a natural physiological response from a damsel in true distress. After a single moment's hesitation, I took a deep breath and stumbled out of the woods.

I tripped on purpose, breathing hard, and glanced

over my shoulder at the trees I could see much better than could the guard. Half sobbing I pushed myself to my feet and stumbled a few steps farther.

"Hey!" the guard called, and I flinched over his volume. "What are you…?"

"Oh, thank goodness!" I gasped, obviously winded from my race through the woods. Hopefully he wouldn't stop to wonder why he hadn't heard me coming. "There's something out there. Chasing me…" I jogged toward him, half twisted to point at the woods—and to keep my face averted. I panted and heaved, like I could hardly breathe. "Something big. I heard it. Huffing. Growling."

He glanced over my shoulder, his hand going to his waistband in an automatic, natural gesture, and I had a moment to wonder if I'd found the one tom who was truly good with his gun.

"Run!" I gasped. "It's right behind me."

"I don't hear any…"

When he didn't move, I let myself collide with him, collapsing into his arms like beauty running from the beast. That way he was too busy holding me up to go for his gun. But I wasn't. When he stood me up, I grabbed the 9 mm from his waistband—my third capture in half an hour. Not bad for a girl, huh?

"What the…"

"Shut up and face the shed." I shoved him around by one shoulder. "You even look like you're gonna move, and I'll shoot you through the thigh."

"Look, I don't have any cash, and you have no idea what you've stumbled into."

I laughed softly. He still didn't recognize me. "Oh, I have a pretty good idea. I also have a pretty good idea what Malone's going to do to you when he finds out what happened to your gun."

"Faythe?" The guard started to turn, but stopped when I shoved the barrel of the gun into his back.

"One more word, and you'll be fighting blood loss and hypothermia. Got it?" He nodded silently, and I had to work to keep my teeth from chattering. "Good. Take off your coat. Slowly."

The guard slid first one arm, then the other, from his sleeves.

"Drop it, then kick it backward. And keep in mind that if you can take it off one arm at a time, I can put it on the same way. The gun's still aimed at your back."

"You're not gonna shoot me." He let the jacket fall, then slid it backward with his right foot.

"Haven't you heard what a crazy bitch I am?"

After that, he had nothing else to say while I bent for the coat and put it on one arm at a time, doing my best to keep the gun aimed, just as I'd promised. "Now, open the door."

"It's locked," he said, and a glance at the shed confirmed that.

"Unlock it. And drop your handcuffs."

He dug his cuffs from one pocket and dropped them on the ground at his feet, then pulled a key from the other. "Malone's going to have your head for this," he said as he twisted the key in the lock, his fingers already red and stiff from the cold.

"Yeah, what's he going to do, kill me twice?" Of course, death wasn't what I really had to fear from Malone and his men, but nothing I did or didn't do was going to change what they wanted from me.

A second later, he pulled the padlock from the shed door.

"Okay, open it and step inside. And don't touch a motherfucking thing."

The guard opened the door and stepped in. I followed, only pausing long enough to pull the door closed behind me. The dim light bulb dangling from the ceiling was a shock after the dark of the woods, and I stood for a moment to let my cat eyes adjust. But before they could, I heard shuffling from directly ahead.

"Faythe?"

Marc. And Jace was in the cage beside him.

I forced my eyes open wider and smiled. "Surprise."

Thirteen

My blood boiled, in spite of the below-freezing temperature, at the sight of Marc and Jace locked up in five-foot-tall animal cages. Like me, they'd been marched out of our cabin without coats, and in separate cages, they couldn't even huddle together for warmth. After less than two hours in the cold, they were both pale and shivering, and only warmed by the scorching rage clearly burning behind their eyes.

"How'd you get out?" Jace's teeth chattered as he stood hunched over, fingers curled around the steel-mesh sides of his cage.

"Through the window." I nudged the guard in the back with his own gun. "Let them out."

"I don't have those keys." He started to turn, but stopped when I shoved him again.

I glanced around the shed and spotted an open, rusty toolbox in one corner, holding a hammer and an assortment of wrenches. "Get the hammer and knock the locks off. One blow each." Because if anyone heard him, we wouldn't have time to waste with dainty little taps. "And if you even look like you're going to hit anything other than those locks, I will shoot you in the back." I couldn't kill as easily as Malone's men seemed to, but I could and would kill in defense of myself, or either of the men in the cages.

"What about Alex?" Marc asked, as the guard picked up the hammer and hesitated, probably trying to decide if I was serious about killing him.

"Come on!" I snapped at the guard, then glanced at Marc. "Alex is a victim of his own stupidity and arrogance."

"He's dead?" Jace asked, his voice thick with a mix of regret and relief—they fought on opposing sides, but they shared a mother.

"Just unconscious. Same with the goon outside my window. Thus the rush." I glared at the guard. "Do it. And if you have to take more than one swing, you're going to regret it."

Finally he shrugged, and I took a step back as he swung at the lock on Marc's cage. The lock popped open, and I breathed a silent sigh of relief. I hadn't been sure that would work. "Take off the chain, then do the other one."

The guard set his hammer on top of Marc's cage and unthreaded the chain as ordered. Still shivering, Marc stepped out of his pen as Malone's man moved on to free Jace.

"Here." While the guard unwound the second chain, I pulled one of the guns from my waistband and handed it to Marc. "Just in case."

When Jace was free, I handed him the cuffs, and he secured the guard's hands behind his back. "You want to put him in the cage?"

"Yeah, if either of the locks still work."

"We should gag him, too, or he'll scream until some-one shows up," Jace said. He examined the locks while Marc scrounged for something to gag him with.

Unfortunately, both of the locks were smashed, but Marc found a roll of shop towels and a roll of duct tape in an old plastic crate. He gagged the guard and taped his ankles together, then shoved him into one of the cages. Jace wound the chain around the lock hasp and the bar. Without the padlock to hold it in place, the guard would probably eventually kick his way free, but with any luck, that wouldn't be anytime soon.

With the new prisoner as quiet and secure as we could make him, we stepped outside in spite of the cold, to keep from discussing the rest of our plans in front of him—another lesson learned from TV bad guys.

Behind the shed, out of sight from the lodge, I de-briefed the guys. Figuratively. "Okay, we need to get rid of the guns before this new pile of shit hits the fan, although from the look of you both, I'd say finding a couple of coats is also a priority." I would have handed over mine, but I wasn't sure which one to offer it to. And neither of them would have taken it, anyway.

"Yes, business is obviously pressing, but first of all…" Marc looked like he wanted to hug me, even if just for my warmth, but he wouldn't let himself. "Are you okay?"

I couldn't resist a little laugh. "For once, the double standard worked in my favor. I got a warm room, hot stew, and an idiot guard. You guys were the ones freezing your butts off in cages."

"We're fine," Jace insisted through clenched his teeth, probably to keep them from chattering. "You took out three of Cal's men by yourself?"

"Brains over brawn, baby." I grinned. "If they ever stop underestimating me, I might actually feel challenged."

Jace returned my grin. "Or dead."

"So I guess this means we're moving against Malone sooner than expected?" Marc asked, arms crossed tightly over his chest for warmth, obviously unwilling to take part in the post-jailbreak levity.

"We have no other choice, unless you guys want to crawl back into those cages."

Jace's grin faltered, but couldn't be completely extinguished. "Not even if you crawled in there with me."

Marc gritted his teeth, but remained focused on the business at hand. "So…the guns. I'm guessing Malone's keeping them close. Probably in his bedroom."

I shrugged. "Actually, I'm thinking they're in the shed behind his cabin. Alex said they're locked up, and to my knowledge, none of the bedrooms have locks." At least, the ones in our cabin didn't.

"Alex told you about the guns?" Jace asked, through blue-tinted lips.

"Just that they have twenty of them, and brought ten here. But there are three fewer now." Grinning, I pulled the second gun from my waistband and handed it to him.

Jace looked impressed, but he accepted the pistol hesitantly, no doubt remembering the recovery period from his last gunshot wound. "I don't know how to shoot."

"Me, neither, but it makes a damn good threat, and I'm guessing that, up close, your aim doesn't have to be that good. Just make sure you know how to turn off the safety, or they'll figure out pretty quickly that you're bluffing." While Jace turned the gun over in his hands,

I glanced at Marc, who remained stoiç against the cold. "Okay, we need to get you guys warmed up and let Dad know we're out. Let's go through the woods." That way we'd be out of sight, and blocked from the worst of the freezing wind.

"So, this is going to go down without backup…" Marc whispered, as we picked our way carefully through the woods. The guys had both Shifted their eyes, too—they were among the first of my Pride members to master the partial Shift—and seemed much more adept hiking in their human forms than I was in mine, even with their limbs surely half-numb from the cold.

"There's no time to call in the rest of our guys, much less the thunderbirds." Who had to be contacted in person, thanks to their discourteous lack of a phone. And any other modern convenience beyond a few worn video cassettes and an old television for their children.

"We're all strong fighters," Jace said. "And getting rid of the guns will help even the odds."

But even if we managed that, war wasn't fought without casualties. We would lose someone. Maybe more than one someone. And that was not okay.

Fifteen minutes later, we peered between the trees at the back of our own cabin, listening and looking for anything out of the ordinary. If Malone knew we'd escaped, he'd have someone watching the cabin, and while we were more than ready to fight, we couldn't risk starting something big before we'd gotten rid of the guns and warned everyone else. And warmed Marc and Jace up.

"I think it's clear," Jace said finally, and I nodded. I'd neither seen nor heard anything weird, and I knew every figure who'd passed by the window. But my father

hadn't been among them. Was he still at the lodge, unwilling to leave me there alone?

My heart ached in both gratitude and frustration, and
I would have given just about anything for a cell phone
at that moment, so I could fill him in.

"Let's go." Marc stepped through the tree line, then
ran for the back steps. Jace and I raced after him. By
the time we got there, Marc was knocking on the door.
"It's locked," he explained, when I stopped on the step
below him, uncomfortable standing exposed in the porch
light.

The sheer curtain parted, and Teo Di Carlo's face appeared. His eyes nearly bugged out of his head when he
recognized Marc in the porch light, then saw me behind
him. He fumbled with the doorknob, and a moment later
ushered us inside.

"Have I ever mentioned how much I love central
heat?" Marc headed straight for the coffeepot, still dripping with fresh, hot caffeine.

"And roaring fireplaces…" Jace made a beeline for
the stone hearth. "Anyone got marshmallows?"

"How the hell did you get out?" Teo closed and
locked the door as people migrated into the kitchen,
drawn by our voices.

Marc poured coffee into two mugs, then reached for
the sugar. "Faythe broke us out."

"And who broke you out?" Vic asked, arms crossed
over his chest as he leaned against the kitchen wall. He
was still mad, and evidently rescuing Marc didn't earn
me any points in his favor, because I'd rescued Jace,
too.

"What am I, helpless?" I grinned and accepted

the mug Marc handed me, but Vic only nodded in acknowledgment of my skills. "Where's my dad?"

"He's at the lodge, questioning Malone's every word
to keep the council busy. We were just about to execute
a jailbreak."

"Yeah, I kind of have that covered." I set my mug
on the table and glanced around, trying to gather my
thoughts. "Okay, Marc and Jace need food—something
hot and heavy on the calories—and I need a phone."

Vic fingered the phone in his pocket—the phone he
was pointedly not offering me—while Teo pulled a glass
pan of something hot, cheesy, and half-devoured from
the oven.

"Here." Brian Taylor handed me his cell, and I smiled
at him in thanks. While the guys scooped big servings
of baked pasta onto plates, I texted my dad to keep the
other Alphas from overhearing our conversation.

It's F. We r out. @ the cabin.

A moment later, his reply came: On my way. And
in spite of the circumstances, I spared a moment to be
amused by the fact that my father knew how to text.
Ethan had taught him, insisting that the new skill would
come in handy. My heart ached with the realization that
he wasn't around to brag about being right.

While Jace and Marc ate, I helped myself to a plateful
of some vaguely Italian-looking combination of noodles,
cheese, and tomato sauce, and had half of it scarfed
before I noticed Vic scowling at us from the living room.
Irritated now, I made eye contact and tossed my head
toward the hall.

He nodded curtly and met me there, then followed
me silently into the first bedroom we passed.

"Okay, get it over with," I said, leaning against the closed door.

"Get what over with?"

"You're pissed at me, and everyone can see that, but our lives just might depend on each other in the next couple of hours. So grow a pair and say your peace, then get over it."

His scowl only grew. "You slept with Jace." It wasn't a question.

"Yes. And frankly, I don't have to justify that to you." He started to object, but I cut him off. "Mostly because it's unjustifiable." And suddenly I felt Ethan's absence stronger than I had since the day he'd died. I needed to talk to someone about Jace and Marc, and as awesome as my father's advice was, he was still my dad.

"Well, at least you recognize that." He huffed, but looked half-mollified by my admission.

"Will you sit?"

Vic hesitated, then pulled a desk chair away from the wall and sank into it. I let my back slide down the door and sat with my knees pulled up to my chest, looking up at him, drowning in the overload of pain and conflict that came rushing back, now that we were out of immediate danger. "I'm lost, Vic. I don't know what I'm doing."

He rolled his eyes. "And I thought this was going to be hard.… You just tell Jace thanks for the ride, you're sorry you've turned him into a panting puppy dog, but what happened was wrong and you can't live without Marc."

Tears filled my eyes and I brushed them away before they could fall.

"Shit," he whispered, and the chair groaned beneath

his shifting weight. "It's not that easy, is it?" I shook my head but refused to look up. "Do you love him?"

I nodded and wiped unshed tears on my sleeves. "I wish like hell that I didn't, but if wishes were raindrops, I'd already have drowned. The truth is that I can't stand the thought of losing either one of them."

"Fuck." Vic got up from the chair and sank to the ground a foot away. The distance he left between us said he still disapproved, but he'd put himself on my level, in full talk-it-out mode. "Marc knows it's serious?"

"Do you think he'd be this pissed if he didn't?"

"I think he'd have killed Jace already, if he didn't think he'd lose you for it."

"I know." I reached up to snatch a tissue from the desk on my right.

"You have to choose."

"I *know*."

"You have to choose Marc."

I had no answer to that. I did have to choose Marc. But I had to choose Jace, too. Yet that wasn't an option. And I couldn't hover in decision purgatory much longer.

"I'm sorry, Vic. More sorry than you could ever imagine. I just want you to know that. And to know that this isn't some stupid rebellion. I would never risk what I have with Marc over something like that. This is real, and it's the hardest thing I've ever had to do, and it's torture for all three of us. And it's all my fault."

"Well, you're right about that." Another man who wouldn't sugarcoat things for me. "But I think Jace shares more than a little of the blame."

I blinked to clear my vision and wiped the last of my tears on the tissue. "Is there anything you wouldn't have done for comfort after Sara died? If you were alone with her best friend, and you'd both just lost a huge part of your lives, and you were both hurting so bad it felt like the pain would swallow you alive?"

"Faythe, I honestly don't know. But that doesn't excuse…"

"I know. I'm not saying it excuses anything. I'm just saying that's how it happened, and afterward, I realized it didn't feel as wrong as it should have. I mean, hurting Marc felt horrible, and *still* feels horrible, but the rest of it—loving Jace—doesn't feel wrong."

Vic watched me for a moment, like he didn't know what to say, and I couldn't blame him. I knew exactly what that felt like. But before he could decide on a response, the front door of the cabin squealed open.

"Faythe?" my father called. I scrambled to my feet and threw open the door. My dad stood in the middle of the floor, winded and trying to catch his breath. "I'm fine, Dad. We're all fine."

"Not for long." He paused to suck in another deep breath. "I ran all the way here, but I could hear them behind me, about a quarter of a mile. I think they know you're gone."

"Okay." My heart pounded so hard I could barely hear anything else, and the rest of the room seemed to fade into the background as I focused on my father. "This is your call, Dad. We can surrender and wait while you guys go for the guns—we think they're in the shed behind Malone's cabin. Or we can stand and fight now."

"We're going to get the best of both worlds." He glanced over my shoulder. "Brian, go through the woods and get the guns. Take them deep into the forest and drop the whole box, then come back ready to fight. We'll destroy them later. On the way, call Aaron and Rick and tell them to get their men ready."

"I'm already on that, Greg," Bert Di Carlo said from the kitchen doorway, his cell phone at his ear.

"Good." My father looked at each of us individually, me last of all. "This time we fight."

Anticipation buzzed in my stomach like angry wasps, fear and bloodlust combining to spin my head and steel my spine. "I confiscated three guns, but there are two more in use, plus the five Malone still has locked up. Assuming he hasn't already distributed them. Colin Dean has one of those two, but anyone could have the last. So some of us should Shift, but we also need a few in human form, to disarm those last couple of 'task force' members." I pulled my shirt over my head, hopefully emphasizing the urgency.

"Agreed." My father glanced around at the room full of toms, all waiting for his orders. "Lucas, Jace, Vic, and I will stay human. The rest of you Shift. Quickly. We'll do our best to get rid of the guns, but stay out of the line of fire just in case."

Marc already had his shirt off and his pants unbuckled when I grabbed his arm and pointed toward the bedroom, where we'd be shielded from the initial onslaught. "In there." Because we were more vulnerable in mid-Shift than at any other time in our lives. At least, since infancy.

Marc headed for the bedroom and grabbed Di Carlo's other enforcer on the way.

"How many are coming?" I asked, unbuttoning my jeans in the bedroom doorway.

My father's frown deepened as his gaze settled on

mine. "I couldn't tell. But more than came for you the first time, I'm betting."

I nodded and ducked into the bedroom, leaving the door open a crack so we could get out without hands to twist the knob. I shoved my jeans and underwear to the floor, listening to my father as I dropped to my knees on the hardwood, still fumbling with the latch on my bra.

"Okay, our primary objective is to disarm and disable," our Alpha called from the front room, as the first jarring bolts of pain emanated from deep within my joints. "But because we may be facing men with guns, if it's kill or be killed, opt for the former."

On my left, Marc was in mid-Shift between the two twin beds, and suddenly I wished I'd thought to put at least one mattress between me and the door, thus between me and any potential bullets. But it was too late to move. Once my Shift began, I could only ride the waves of pain. Or let them ride me.

"Once this first group is subdued—" they were coming to rearrest me, hopefully not expecting us to actually attack "—we'll have to move quickly. We'll tape up the survivors and regroup, then head out through the woods to Malone's cabin. He's our primary target, but obviously we'll have to deal with anyone else who gets in the way. As quietly as possible, to keep from tipping him off."

My knees popped, and I groaned. Pain echoed the length of my legs, radiating outward from the center of my bones. My ribs ached fiercely as they and the accompanying muscles were reshaped to accommodate a feline layout of organs. As I stared at my hands, splayed on the floor, my palms began to plump beneath me. My fingers creaked as they shortened and thickened, growing pads suited to rough terrain.

"But above all, don't let any of them leave." My father's boots scraped the floor in the living room, and it became hard for me to simultaneously concentrate on his words and force my Shift to come faster than it would on its own. "If they warn the rest of Malone's men, we'll lose the element of surprise and be outnumbered. Got it?"

There were mumbles of assent from the men still in human form, but I couldn't help wondering if we actually had the element of surprise in the first place. Surely they weren't expecting me to just turn myself in and be hauled off quietly. Again.

"I hear them," Vic said, his voice low enough to avoid detection by the toms headed our way, but loud enough to be heard in the adjoining rooms, over the grunts and heavy breathing of so many simultaneous Shifts.

My heart rate doubled. *Moments away.* My pulse echoed in my ears, a fanfare to announce the coming attraction. We were on the brink of actual war—the first American inter-Pride brawl in decades—and I wasn't ready.

I dumped the extra adrenaline my nerves spawned into my Shift, forcing my body through the paces faster and faster. My entire head ached with pressure so severe it felt like my skull would squeeze my brain out my ears.

Instead, my face lengthened and pain exploded along the new length of my jaw. My cheekbones stretched with an odd screeching sound heard only in my head, as my ears traveled forward and all outward sound was temporarily suspended. My nose flattened and darkened, and a long, bare muzzle now took up most of the bottom half of my field of vision.

"Is everybody ready?" This time my father's voice was low, steady with a false calm.

I could only whine in answer, and I was acutely aware of Marc standing next to me now, fully Shifted. He stood between me and the door, obviously intent on protecting me until my Shift was over.

My entire body began to itch as fur sprouted over my skin, beginning along my spine, and flowing to cover every inch of me, except for my paw pads. My teeth grew so quickly they forced my mouth open, and I nearly bit off the end of my own tongue, as backward-facing barbs suddenly sprouted all over it.

Whiskers shot out of the sides of my muzzle, stark white against the dark blur of my own fur. They twitched as I sniffed the room. *Almost there. Just waiting on…*

My claws.

Even as I pictured them, my finger- and toenails grew hard and sharp, lengthening to deadly points. I sheathed them, then unsheathed them again and dug into the floor, picturing them piercing vulnerable human flesh.

And just as my tail began to swish, fully formed and twitching angrily, my father gave the "get ready!" signal from the front room: he went completely still and totally silent.

Marc and I padded silently to opposite sides of the bedroom door, where we were least likely to be shot and most likely to surprise any intruders.

Soft footsteps climbed the front steps. Malone's men were in stealth mode, too. Did they think we didn't know they were coming?

I peeked into the living room to see my father standing to one side of the front door, his back against the wall, Lucas on his left. Jace and Vic mirrored them on the other side.

The footsteps stopped. They must have realized something was wrong. How could they not, with the lights on, but no one in sight through the windows? With no voices carrying from inside.

The first man paused in front of the door. His dark silhouette spanned the entire width of the small window cut into it. His shadow turned, and I heard the faintest of whispers as he spoke to the toms behind him. I couldn't make out his words, but the message was clear: we were up to something. Or else we'd left. Run away.

My heart thumped in my ears, and suddenly I wondered if we should have. Were we making a fool's mistake, taking on men with guns while we were armed with nothing but anger, shielded by nothing but courage?

Either way, it was too late for a change of plans. The silhouette canted to one side and kicked the front door open.

I knew several of the faces, but had no names to go with them, and at a glance they all seemed to be carrying guns. Brian was too late to get rid of them. Malone's men stared into the apparently empty living room, and our men in human form held their breath. They couldn't disguise their heartbeats, but if the intruders' pulses were rushing as loudly as my own they'd never hear heartbeats, anyway.

"They ran." The first tom lowered his gun. "Bunch of cowards fucking ran away." He stepped over the threshold, and two more followed before the first one turned around.

Jace seized the nearest man's gun arm and pulled the tom in front of him, shielding himself from gunfire. Vic did the same with the second man to turn.

My father lunged with a speed I'd seldom seen from him. He grabbed the lead man's hand and forced the gun to one side, then pulled the tom to the left, out of sight from the doorway and out of the line of fire. It happened so fast I didn't even have time to worry, beyond the wordless adrenaline-laced terror already surging through me.

The tom tried to jerk free. My father squeezed his hand so hard I heard the bones crack from fifteen feet away. The tom howled and dropped his gun. Lucas bent to snatch it.

"Toss your guns inside and step forward with your hands on your heads." My father's voice carried absolute authority, a fact I'd recognized long before I took my first steps. But the three men still standing on the porch were completely unfazed.

"Not gonna happen, Councilman."

My father was seconds from losing his temper. "Drop your guns, *now!*"

"She's in here." The first tom craned his neck in my father's grip to glance around the cabin. "I can smell her. But the rest of them are Shifted. Call for backup."

Footsteps pounded on the porch as the last three toms turned and ran, two of them armed.

My father roared. His face flushed with fury, and his fist smashed into the side of the tom's head. The tom collapsed to the floor with a thud. "Get them!" my dad yelled, his throat half-Shifted, his words barely understandable.

But his meaning was clear.

I leaped into the living room and was on the porch two bounds later. I hit the grass running, frozen blades crunching beneath my paws, frigid air burning in my lungs. Marc was on my tail, and I could hear two others behind us.

My pulse raced as I ran. Each breath was a deep huffing pant, powerful in its own right, without the accompanying soft thuds of my paws on the ground.

Three men ran in front of me, clearly visible in the sad light of a cloud-covered quarter moon. One man half turned, gun haphazardly aimed. The barrel flashed. For an instant the world was too bright to bear. The bullet whizzed by several feet over my head and thunked into the frozen earth behind me.

He aimed again, and I zigged while Marc zagged. The next bullet split the air between us. Too close for comfort.

He turned to run again and I pounced. My paws slammed into his back. He screamed and fell beneath me. My muzzle closed over the back of his neck. My teeth pierced tender flesh, just enough to threaten. Blood ran into my mouth. It tasted like fear. He waved the gun at his side. I swatted it away before he could fire, dislocating his elbow. He thrashed beneath me.

A dark blur flew past us. Another thud. The second tom hit the grass with Marc on top of him. He screamed when Marc performed the same maneuver with unsheathed claws.

Wish I'd thought of that...

The third tom still pounded toward the main lodge, unarmed. Another dark blur raced past us on Marc's right—one of Di Carlo's men still in pursuit. He slammed into the last tom's back and they both hit the ground.

All three toms were down, but their screams and gunfire would surely draw more.

Teo Di Carlo slunk past me in cat form, huffing in approval of my takedown. More footsteps pounded behind us—my father, Bert Di Carlo, and at least one other tom in human form.

"You are so screwed," the man beneath me gasped. I increased the pressure on his neck and more blood trickled across my tongue and down my chin. "You're outnumbered. Malone called in a dozen extra enforcers and they're just waiting for you assholes to start some shit. Looks like they're going to get their wish."

That time my jaw clenched involuntarily. An extra dozen men? *He's right.* Even without guns, we were seriously outnumbered. They'd known we'd fight, rather than submit to an unfair trial. Or at least that there was a good possibility.

The footsteps slowed to a stop behind me. "Good work." My father knelt beside me with a roll of duct tape, and I stepped off my prisoner, but didn't release his neck until his wrists were taped.

Several feet away, other toms in human form were doing the same with the other two downed enemies— Aaron Taylor and my uncle Rick had sent their men to join the effort.

But our early victory was about to be trumped. From the other end of the complex came the unmistakable whisper-thud of cats running in feline form, sacrificing stealth for speed. Those in human form couldn't hear it yet, but when Marc and the other cat both whined, I knew they'd heard.

My father hauled my prisoner to his feet and followed my gaze into the darkness ahead. "They're coming?"

I nodded, then nudged the taped tom with the top of my head, ordering him to tell my Alpha what he'd told me. But he refused to speak, and there was no time for me to Shift and warn them.

The footsteps grew louder, and my father froze. "There are too many," he said, loud enough for the others to hear. "But on the bright side, relatively speaking, they can't carry guns in cat form." Which meant that Alex had been telling the truth about how many pistols they'd brought. By my count, we'd confiscated all but one. Colin Dean was still armed.

I tugged my father's sleeve. We should retreat. We couldn't fight that many of them, even without guns. But my dad jerked his arm free.

"It doesn't matter," he whispered. "If they want into the cabin, they'll get in. It's better to fight here, where there's room to maneuver."

I started to argue, then realized that would be futile. We were outnumbered, but we'd been outnumbered before. And if we didn't take this moment to stand up for ourselves, we might never get a second chance.

"Are you ready?" my father asked, while the last of our allies came to a stop in our midst, slick black chests heaving from their sprint, eyes flashing in the little available light.

I nodded, as the first of our enemies came into sight, a long line of snarling muzzles and fur gleaming beneath the quarter moon.

And when the first cat lunged, I leaped up to meet him.

Fourteen

We collided in midair and crashed to the ground together, the tom half crushing me. His jaw snapped shut inches from my neck. Either he didn't know who he was fighting, or he didn't care. Or Malone had finally decided I'd be easier to kill than to deal with.

I slashed with my rear feet. My claws sank into flesh and fur, then ripped through both. The tom screeched and tumbled off me. Blood poured from his thigh. I scrambled to my feet and lunged for him, jaw open and ready.

And was knocked off course in midair by another flying body.

My side hit the ground. Air whooshed from my lungs in a raspy feline grunt. I sucked in a deep breath and snorted out steam. The new tom straddled me, growling. Hesitating. He'd noticed I was female and was reluctant to kill me.

His mistake.

I lunged for his front right forepaw and crunched through bone. The tom howled and fell over. I rolled onto my feet and had only an instant to absorb what I saw.

Fighting. Brawling. Everywhere. At least three dozen toms, most in cat form, swiping, hissing, slashing, and ripping. Two of Malone's to one of ours, in most cases.

On my left, someone snarled. I turned and raised one unsheathed claw as he pounced. I slashed. My claws snagged in muscle. The tom screeched. Blood flowed, fragrant and invigorating.

Pain bit into my left rear thigh, and I inhaled the scent of my own blood. I swiped blindly and ripped through more flesh. Fresh pain tore through me as teeth sank into my right foreleg. I snapped my own muzzle around the back of the tom's neck and tasted more blood.

I clenched my jaw as hard as I could. His neck broke with a crunch I felt in my own bones. His teeth fell away from my leg. He went limp beneath me.

I stood, licking blood from my muzzle, and found myself on the edge of the fight, near the tree line. My gaze roamed the crowd, sorting through lunging bodies, bleeding appendages, and snarling faces for a familiar muzzle, the unmistakable arch of a well-known spine.

Marc. He was about fifty feet to my left, backing slowly away from two toms in cat form. He had a pronounced limp and gashes across both of his left limbs, but he was alive and still moving.

Jace was on the other side of the melee, wielding a huge hammer against a much larger tom in cat form. Brian Taylor fought near him, having returned after his unsuccessful hunt for the remaining guns.

Colin Dean and his pistol had yet to make an appearance.

I jumped back into the brawl and pounced on the back of an enemy tom before he could attack Marc. My claws raked deep ruts down his sides before he tossed me off. As I fell, I aimed one last powerful blow at his skull. He went down like a cheerleader after prom.

"Faythe, look out!"

I whirled toward my father's voice to see him pointing across the chaos at something to my left. I turned and my heart jumped into my throat. A large black blur slammed into me. I landed on my right side. Air burst from my lungs. Weight restricted my chest, and I could only suck in short, shallow pants.

An open jaw dropped toward my throat. Warm, sour blood-breath washed over my face. My pulse raced so fast I thought it would burst through my skin and into his mouth, no teeth required.

I kicked with my rear paws. One caught on his foot and pulled him off balance. The tom half fell, but recovered quickly. I swiped one forepaw over his muzzle. Blood welled in a line across his nose. He hissed. I stood. We faced off, both bleeding. Snarling.

He pounced. I dropped into a roll. A huge shadow soared between us and the little available moonlight. Something whooshed past my head. The thud of impact was almost tangible. When I stood, my foe lay on the ground, one side of his skull caved in. Liquefied brains seeped through the new cracks in his head.

"Faythe, is that you? Why can't you cats ever visit without bringin' trouble into my neck of the woods?"

Surprised beyond the capacity for rational thought, I looked up. And up. And up. There stood Elias Keller— all seven and a half feet of him. All three hundred fifty-plus pounds of him. Carrying a homemade club as big around as my waist. With his grizzled beard and incredible bulk, he even resembled a bear on two legs.

For a moment, I could only bathe in thankfulness that he recognized me on four paws. There was a time when he hadn't been able to. Fortunately, I was the only girl-cat in the Montana woods at the moment.

But then, that's what we'd thought last time—until Kaci showed up.

"What the hell are you all playin' at?" His deep voice resonated in my bones. Of course, I couldn't actually answer him, so I simply stared across the yard full of brawling cats, hoping the evidence spoke for itself.

Someone had freed the toms we'd captured, and they now fought hand to hand against our men still in human form. Jace punched one of Malone's men in the face, then followed up with a devastating blow to the kidney. He barely paused to wipe the blood dripping into his own eyes before unleashing his bloodlust on another human-form tom.

I swam in a sea of grunts, hisses, and growls. All around me, bodies thunked into the ground, then got up for more. Toms bled, and screamed, and clawed, rarely pausing over their own injuries.

I crouched to jump back into the action, but Keller grabbed a hunk of skin at the back of my neck, holding me still as no other creature on the face of the planet would have dared. But Keller had little to fear from werecats. He could easily take on several toms at once—I'd seen him do it.

I growled and tugged against him, not willing to actually hurt him, for both of our sakes.

"Hold up there, little girl. This's gotta stop." He stood,

and I noticed several things at once as he dragged a gigantic breath into his titanic lungs.

My father threw a bone-crunching punch at one of the toms who'd come to arrest us—he'd reclaimed a gun from somewhere. The tom brought his pistol up. My father knocked it away with a more nimble kick than I'd seen from him in years.

Movement on the left drew my gaze. Colin Dean stepped out of the woods holding his gun, flanked by two unarmed toms in human form.

Elias Keller roared, a deep bellow that sang in every cell in my body. I could practically see the shockwave flow over the crowd as his sound reached us.

Everyone froze, midblow. Heads swiveled his way. Obviously we weren't the only ones who could Shift one part at a time—if that sound had come from a human throat, I was a werewolf bitch in heat.

"I don't know what the hell you think you're doin', but this is my land. My home. Now you retract your claws and back down, or I'm gonna start a cat graveyard on the side of my mountain."

Jaws dropped. Fists lowered slowly. Heads—both human and feline—turned, searching out Alphas who had the authority to make the final call on a cease-fire.

Something clicked on my left, as loud as thunder against the new silence. I turned toward the sound to see Dean staring across the paused chaos, his weapon raised. I followed his line of sight to see my father standing over the tom he'd taken down, holding the repossessed gun.

I screeched.

Keller roared.

Dean's gun flashed in the dark.

I tore free from Keller's grasp and shot across the grass, leaping over prone bodies, dodging those still in motion.

I was too late.

My father lurched to one side. He staggered backward. A dark red bloom unfurled across his white shirt. My dad hit the ground. I screamed as I leaped, a horrible yowling that echoed in the shocked silence. My paws hit the grass and I collapsed next to him, nudging his head with my muzzle.

He was breathing, but the sound was wet. Labored.

Toms dropped to the ground at my side, nudging him with cat noses or asking questions he seemed unable to answer. No one seemed to know what to do.

Finally someone pushed me out of the way to tear my father's shirt open, and I looked up to find Keller holding Dean's gun. Dean lay on the ground at his feet, unmoving. When everyone not gathered around my dad warily watched the bruin instead of dispersing from the fight, he roared again. Cats scattered in all directions. As they fled, Keller stomped toward us. His huge fist clenched around the pistol and it shattered like plastic. Bits of gun fell on the grass behind him like a breadcrumb trail.

"Oh…Greg, can you talk?" Bert Di Carlo asked, leaning over my father. His hands hovered over the blood rose still blooming, and suddenly I wished I couldn't see quite so well in the dark.

Uncle Rick shook his head. "Don't make him talk."

"We have to get him inside," Jace said, while Marc rubbed his cheek along my flank, his feline gaze glued to my father. He whined in harmony with me, sharing my distress the only way he could in cat form.

"What the hell happened?" Aaron Taylor demanded. He'd been fighting on the fringes when I'd last seen him.

"That flaxen-haired pip-squeak over there shot him." Keller pointed to where Dean lay motionless on the edge of the tree line, surrounded by several of his own men. I hoped he was dead. I hoped Keller had popped his skull like a rotten pumpkin. If my father weren't bleeding and struggling to breathe, I'd have gone over to desecrate Dean's body myself, laughing hysterically at the thought of the Nordic giant being called a pip-squeak. No one but Keller could possibly consider him small.

"Let's get him inside." Keller wedged his way into the huddle and picked my father up like a baby, then followed as Di Carlo led the way to our cabin.

Marc and Jace flanked me all the way. If they hadn't, I wouldn't have known where I was going. I couldn't stop the whine leaking from my throat or the ache deep in my chest, as if I shared some echo of my father's pain, eclipsing all of my own wounds.

My father was the single most powerful person in my life. Seeing him helpless was *wrong*. So fundamentally, earthshakingly wrong that I couldn't even properly process the sight.

So I blocked it out. I busied the front of my mind with a running list of things that would need to be done— first aid, call my mom, eviscerate Colin Dean or desecrate his corpse, whichever proved necessary—while the back of my mind chanted a mantra over and over. *He'll be fine. He's not gonna die. He'll be fine. He's not gonna die. He'llbefinehe'snotgonnadie…*

He couldn't die, because my world wouldn't make sense without him. I was literally a part of my father. He'd shaped my entire life, even down to my rebellious youth, by giving me options. Challenges. Expectations. Standards. Honor. Respect. And I wasn't done with that. He had more to give, and I was ready to receive it.

He couldn't die. I wouldn't let him.

In the cabin, Keller laid him on the couch in the midst of an agonizing, respectful silence. I checked to make sure he was still breathing, then Shifted right there in the living room, while Uncle Rick carefully cut my father's shirt the rest of the way off, jaw clenched against his own pain and rage.

When I stood two minutes later, Marc was still Shifting, but Jace was there with my robe. He wrapped it around me and I tied the waist, barely noticing I was covered in goose bumps. Not to mention gashes, puncture wounds, and scratches.

"Someone call Dr. Carver." I dropped onto my knees and applied pressure to the cloth over the hole in my father's chest, taking over for my uncle, who moved to make room for me. Panic loomed within me, demanding attention, but I shoved it back and focused on the job at hand: fixing my father. Nothing else mattered.

My dad blinked up at me, and though his face was lined in agony, his eyes were dry. Mine were not.

"The doc's plane won't land for another hour." Di Carlo ran one hand through thick gray hair—no doubt what Vic's would look like in a few years.

"Okay." I blinked to clear more tears. "What can we do, then? Clean the wound? Give him something for the pain? There has to be something." My dad's breathing sounded funny. Wet, like he was sucking in each breath through a leaky straw. We had to fix that.

A hand wrapped around my arm and pulled me gently to my feet. When I turned I found myself in my uncle's arms. He held me so tight I could hardly breathe, and I fought sobs with every bit of will I had left, to keep my father from hearing me cry. Uncle Rick led me into the kitchen, but I refused to leave the doorway. Whatever he wanted to say could be said within sight of my father. I would not leave him.

"Faythe, hon, there's nothing we can do."

"I know. But Dr. Carver will know what to do, and we need to have everything ready for him." I scrubbed my face with my hands, trying desperately to get my thoughts together. "We brought a first aid kit. It's not massive, but it has the basics. We can…we can at least stop the bleeding, right?"

My uncle closed his eyes, and when his gaze met mine again, I shook my head in denial of the inevitability I saw in his. Of the grief and the growing acceptance. "We can't stop the internal bleeding. And it sounds like he has a punctured lung, Faythe, and there's nothing we can do about that."

"No…"

"Yes." He put his hands on my shoulders and made me look at him. "Faythe, your father is dying. He only has a few minutes left. So you need to decide what you want those minutes to be like. If there's anything you want him to know, you need to say it now. We'll deal with everything else later."

Tears came again. They poured down my face, and I nearly choked on sobs. I couldn't stand it. The fear burning inside me consumed all logic, devoured all hope.

This black terror threatened my faith in the very concept of justice—the idea that it was even possible. There wasn't enough pain in all of existence to make Dean pay for what he'd done.

Uncle Rick handed me a dish towel and I scrubbed my face with it. My dad couldn't be dying. He was only fifty-seven. That was too young to die. That was too young to do anything but nag his daughter for grandchildren.

But my uncle was right, and in spite of intense, insistent denial, I knew that. I felt it.

I dropped the towel on the table and took a deep breath. Then made myself take another. And another. Then I steeled my spine and walked back into the living room, suddenly aware of the murmuring and the stares. Marc knelt next to my father, talking to him quietly. My father gripped his hand and whispered something I couldn't hear, and Marc nodded. "I swear," he said, and I could see the cracks in his composed veneer. This was breaking him, like it was breaking me, and our anguish had no equal.

Jace stood near Marc, watching me. He touched Marc's shoulder, and they both moved aside.

I sank onto my knees again, and this time I saw nothing else. Nothing but my father's eyes, the same shade of green as mine. As Ethan's. More tears came, and I wiped them away.

"I love you, Daddy." The words came out broken. Halting. Wrapped around a sob that speared my heart. "Everything good in me comes from you and Mom, and I'm so sorry for all the times that weren't so good. I…"

His hand moved. More of a twitch than anything, but

I knew what he wanted. I curled my fingers around his, and tried not to notice how cold his skin was.

"Faythe…" he whispered, and I leaned closer. "I never wanted anything else in a daughter. Nothing more or less than what you are…" He coughed, and red bubbles appeared on his pale lips.

I sobbed again, and someone put a tissue in my hand. I wiped his mouth carefully, and he swallowed.

"You are stronger than you know. You're smart. You have your mother's strength and her heart, and that's all you need. I'm sorry it's come so soon, but the Pride is yours now." He squeezed my hand weakly, and I squeezed back. I didn't want to hear any more. I didn't want him to die. I didn't want to be in charge—not yet. But what I wanted had never mattered less. He coughed again, and tears trailed down my face as I blotted more blood from his lips. "Take care of our Pride. Fight for them. Lead them. They'll be counting on you."

"I'll do my best." There was nothing else I could say. I couldn't tell him I wasn't ready. Not ready was no longer an option.

"I love you," he whispered, after a moment of pained silence. "And so do they." His glance flickered over my shoulder, to where I knew Marc and Jace were standing. Watching. Waiting.

"You have to choose. You cannot make decisions for the rest of them if you can't make this one for yourself."

There was no stopping the tears then. I couldn't even slow them. I leaned down so far my cheek brushed his, and beyond the pervasive scent of his blood—so much like my own—he smelled like leather and after-shave, the scents of my childhood. "I don't know how to choose." My tears fell on his cheek, and his beard stubble scratched my chin.

"You love them both, but you'll survive the loss of one. Choose the one you can't live without."

He dragged in another painful breath, and his gaze was so intense it burned. "Tell your brothers how proud I am of them. Tell your mother she is my whole life, and has been since the moment we met. She is in my heart, and in my soul, and this will never really separate us."

He inhaled one more time. Then his grip on my hand loosened, and his fingers fell away.

My father was gone.

Fifteen

I couldn't breathe. Couldn't make myself suck in the next breath, or even force out the old one. I still sat on the floor on my knees, my forehead resting on my father's stomach, waiting in vain for it to rise beneath me. His blood stained my cheek. His hand was still damp in mine, and he still smelled alive. And as long as those things were true, I couldn't truly accept his death.

It simply hadn't happened. It couldn't have.

Yet I understood that I'd failed him.

My primary job as an enforcer was to protect my Alpha—my father—and I'd failed spectacularly. What would I tell Michael and Owen? What could I possibly tell my mother?

"Faythe?" Marc's hand landed gently on the side of my neck, the only part of me not covered by my robe. "Faythe, come on."

But I couldn't. I couldn't face them. They didn't need me. They needed my father. So did I.

Marc pulled me up and squeezed me so tight I suddenly missed that breath I didn't want to take. I sucked in fresh air and exhaled it on a sob so strong it shook us both. I cried on his shoulder, clinging to him, my eyes squeezed shut, my nose dripping. The source of my tears was a bottomless well carved out of my very soul, fed by my grief and tainted by anger so black, so charred, that it hadn't even fully penetrated my conscious mind.

But it would soon.

And when I finally opened my eyes, I saw the room full of toms through tangled strands of my own hair, while I breathed air that tasted like Marc's scent and my father's blood. Some stared at their own feet, hands shoved into pockets, tears staining usually stoic faces. Some watched me. Waiting. Expecting…something profound. Something decisive. Something worthy of an Alpha.

And that's when I truly understood, even if I hadn't totally accepted it: they needed my dad, but what they had was me. Period. Nothing would change that. And I could not fail them—not without failing my father.

I pulled in another deep breath and let go of Marc, though my arms felt unbearably, tragically empty. Jace handed me a tissue and I wiped my face, flinching when the tissue came away smeared with blood.

"Okay…" I shoved hair back from my face and glanced around the room, distantly relieved to realize that everyone was standing under his own power. There were injuries, certainly—two toms were cradling one arm apiece, and one was favoring his left leg—and cuts and bruises galore. But by some miracle, no one else was mortally wounded, or even handicapped. And they were all accounted for.

"We should assess our injuries and decide how to proceed from there. Right?" I glanced at my uncle, and he nodded.

Di Carlo stepped forward, drawing attention from me while I wiped my cheeks again. "Mateo, put together a quick report on how the other side fared. Injuries, casualties, and general disposition. Anything you can find out without actually entering any of the other cabins. Take someone with you, and be careful."

Teo nodded and headed to his room, presumably to grab a jacket and something to write with.

"Um…" I cleared my throat and started again. "Jace, can you and Vic get me an assessment of injuries on our side? What can be healed quickly by Shifting, and what can't. And what needs medical attention."

Vic nodded, and Jace gave me a small, sad smile that somehow conveyed sorrow, sympathy, and confidence, all at once. He wanted to touch me, to comfort me, to share my grief, but he wouldn't make trouble while we were in such pain, even if that meant watching Marc stand where he wanted to be.

"Uncle Rick…" Meeting his tortured gaze brought fresh tears to my eyes. He'd been crying, too. I'd never seen an Alpha cry, other than my father, when Ethan died.

"Just tell me what you need," he said.

I need my father back. I need another decade of experience. I need Calvin Malone's head mounted on a post in my front yard. I need Colin Dean staked to the ground, spread-eagle, with his stomach sliced open, so I can pull his intestines out slowly, while he screams. But my uncle couldn't give me any of that. And I intended to accomplish the last two on my own.

"I need a cease-fire." I could practically hear my brain whirring between my ears, searching for any memory of a precedent. Was the death of an Alpha enough to warrant a break in the fighting? "At least long enough to…bury my dad. Can you do that safely?"

He nodded slowly, clearly thinking. "I'll need Aaron and Bert, and I'm pretty sure Blackwell will side with us on this one. He didn't want to fight in the first place, and he won't be party to disrespecting the dead. With any luck, at least a couple of the others will feel the same way. They fought against us today, but they were led by your father for years before that."

"Good." I rubbed my forehead, fending off a monster headache as I tried to wrap my mind around everything that needed to be done. "Thank you."

The three Alphas headed for the main cabin, along with most of their enforcers, leaving me alone with Marc, Brian, and Elias Keller. Extra security was never a bad idea in the middle of a war. Fortunately, Keller showed no inclination to leave, and he wouldn't let anyone surprise us while the others were gone. He wasn't fond of Malone—who'd once called him Yogi Bear—and he'd shared a great mutual respect with my father.

"Thank you for your help, Mr. Keller." I rounded the displaced coffee table with one arm extended, though it almost physically pained me to leave my father's side. It felt like I was abandoning him.

"Call me Elias." The bruin's hand swallowed my own, up past my wrist. "There's nothing I hate more than gun-totin' Shifters. Cheaters, the lot of 'em. They got better'n human strength and speed, but they cart around guns like cowards."

"I couldn't agree more."

Keller released my hand, and I already missed its warmth.

"Um, about the guns," Brian began, hovering in the

kitchen doorway. "I couldn't find them in the shed, and once everyone ran off to fight I looked in Malone's cabin, too, but—"

"It's okay, Brian. I think we've accounted for them all now."

"Well, I hate to say it, but our gun problems may not be over," Marc began, crossing into the kitchen. "We confiscated nine of them, and you—" He glanced at Keller. "Well, you crushed the tenth, unless I was hallucinating out there. But it looks like Malone's men reclaimed the three we took from the toms who ran from our cabin before all this started."

"We didn't have a chance to get rid of them before the shit hit the fan…" I mumbled. "And they'll be looking for the rest of them." I glanced at the six pistols lined up on the breakfast table, each likely loaded and ready to fire.

"Oh, you let me worry about those," Keller's voice boomed throughout the cabin, and I got the distinct impression that if he weren't trying to respect my father's demise, he would have sounded almost giddy at the prospect. "I'll destroy the lot of 'em. May even bring the pieces back to this Malone fellow, just to see the look on his face."

I couldn't resist picturing Malone's shock and rage—especially since there was nothing he could do about it. "Can I come and watch?"

Keller chuckled softly. "I like your spunk."

That was fortunate, because at the moment, I was running on nothing but that and sheer willpower. What I really needed was a drink. And in the absence of alcohol… "Can I get you some coffee?"

"I'd love some." The bruin covered a massive yawn

with one huge hand. "I'm not normally up until…well… around April."

"I'm so sorry we interrupted your sleep." I'd completely forgotten that bruins—like natural bears—hibernated for most of the winter months.

"Oh, I suspect you have bigger things to worry about than one grumpy old bear. I'm just glad the scent of werecats prowlin' my mountain was enough to wake me up." His smile was scraggly with overgrown facial hair, but it was one of the kindest gestures I'd seen in months.

"Coffee's coming," Marc called from the kitchen. "Brian, if you want some, come fix yourself a mug."

"Thanks, Marc." I sank into the chair closest to my father and suddenly realized that I hurt. Everywhere. My jaw ached from being clenched and my throat burned from holding back tears. But beyond that, every muscle in my body ached, and I stung from cuts and throbbed from bruises all over. The fight itself had almost been eclipsed in my memory by my father's death. Had it really ended just an hour ago?

Had my father really been dead for only half that? It felt like forever already.

I stared at the couch. I couldn't stop myself. Someone had covered my father with an extra sheet from the closet, and while I knew that was the proper thing to do out of respect for the dead, I suddenly felt antsy. On edge. As if not being able to see him somehow made his death more real.

How would I ever be able to bury him?

A few minutes later, Marc came in from the kitchen carrying two mugs. He handed one to Keller, then one to me, and I stood as I accepted it. "I, uh, I need to make a phone call."

Keller's grizzly head bobbed. "Don't worry about me, now. If you don't mind, I was gonna hang around till the rest of your men get back, just to be safe. It looks to me like you guys have made yourselves a few enemies."

"More than a few, unfortunately." Marc settled onto the arm of the chair and put his arm around me, and I leaned into him, grateful for the comfort when I needed it most, in spite of all the legitimate reasons he had to withhold it. "I'm sorry we woke you up, but if we hadn't stood up to Malone tonight, he'd have had Faythe convicted and declawed tomorrow, and me and Jace executed the next day."

"What on earth for?" Keller rumbled, his ruddy cheeks flushed even redder in anger.

"For doing what we had to do to get out of the mess *he* put us in. He framed us for the murder of a thunderbird, and last week we had to turn over the real killer—one of Malone's men—to the Flight to stop the air raid on our home. And to keep them from killing Kaci."

"The kitten?" His brows drew low and his eyes narrowed. And if I wasn't mistaken, he seemed to be growling softly, deep in his throat. Keller had brought Kaci to us, during our last trip to the mountains, for my trial. He'd found her rooting through his trash for food and mistaken her for me. He could not have been more surprised to discover his mistake. Nor could we. "That weasel tried to get Kaci killed?"

"No, he tried to get her kidnapped. But the thunderbirds didn't like being lied to, and they're not the most compassionate bunch."

"Well, I'm certainly looking forward to returning his guns."

I managed a smile at the thought, but it died when I glanced at the sheet covering my father and remembered that my mother still didn't know. "I'll be back...."

I stood with my coffee and was halfway to my room when I realized I didn't have my cell phone.

"It's plugged into the charger in your dad's room." Marc stood and led the way, clearly having read either my mind or my expression. Or my very broken heart.

He closed the door behind us, and I went straight for the phone. But when I sank onto the bed to autodial, I smelled my father, and started crying again. I couldn't help it.

Marc sat next to me, our legs touching. He wrapped one arm around my waist and I leaned my head on his shoulder. "Faythe, I know this is hard. I've been there." He'd lost his mother when he was fourteen, and he'd had no other family to grieve with. If he could survive that, I could survive this. We all could. "But you have to hold it together. Your mom's going to need you...."

"I know. I'm fine." Or at least I would be. Eventually.

He squeezed me again, then stood and headed for the door, probably to give me privacy for the single most difficult call I'd ever had to make. Or hopefully ever would.

"Marc?" I wiped my eyes on the sleeve of my robe, beyond caring that my face no doubt looked like a swollen tomato. "Would you stay?"

He didn't smile, but he did nod, one hand on the doorknob. "I'll be right back." Then he slipped into the hall and closed the door softly behind him.

It took me two tries to autodial my home number, and if it hadn't been programmed into my phone's memory, I might not have been able to make the call. I wasn't thinking clearly. The endorphins from the fight had faded, along with the "spunk" Keller had admired. Now, aside from the brutal postfight aches and pains, I just felt hollow. Numb.

Very un-Alpha-like.

But the phone rang, oblivious to my distress.

"Hello?" *Michael.* My oldest brother. I almost cried in relief. Not that telling him would be easy, but it would be easier than telling my mother. Like a trial run for shredding a loved one's heart with your bare claws.

"Hey. It's me."

"Faythe? Dad said you were under house arrest. Please tell me you didn't waste your one phone call on me.…"

I could practically hear the smile in his voice, and *irony* didn't even begin to describe the fact that he was trying to cheer me up. *Tragic* was more like it.

"Um, I broke out." My next breath made my throat burn with what had to be said. "Michael…"

"You broke out of house arrest? Faythe, what's going on up there?" he asked. I sniffled, holding back tears with what felt like the very last of my strength. "What's wrong?"

"Are you alone?" I sounded nasal, like I needed to blow my nose, but perfectly intelligible. So far, so good.

"Yeah, but the office door is open."

"Close it."

He got up without a word. I heard my father's chair squeal—whose chair would it be now?—and recognized the soft click of the door. "What's wrong, Faythe. You're scaring me."

Why wouldn't the words come? Had I ever before truly been at a loss of them?

"There was a fight," I began, and pressed my fist against one eye when tears threatened again. "We had to make a stand, because they were going to try me tomorrow and take my claws. And Malone was going to have Marc and Jace executed. I know he was. We had to fight. Everyone agreed." Dad agreed.

But what if we were all wrong? If I'd known my father was going to die, I'd have been willing to lose my claws, and with them, my pride, independence, and spirit. But was his life worth Marc's? And Jace's?

There was a bigger issue. I knew it. My father knew it. We all knew it. We weren't just fighting for the immediate victory. We were fighting for the long-term. For what was right.

As difficult as that concept sometimes was to define, Calvin Malone made it easier by constantly taking the low road. By lying, and cheating, and manipulating, and kidnapping, and murdering. Right had become easier to recognize, against the backdrop of Malone's absolute *wrong*. So we'd done what was right— and paid a terrible price.

"Faythe, what are you saying?" Michael knew. I could hear it in the flat, dead quality of his voice, a defensive mechanism to keep me from hearing what he was really thinking. What he was feeling. He knew someone had died, and since our father hadn't called with the news, he probably knew who we'd lost. But he wouldn't believe it until he'd heard it. Maybe even until he'd seen for himself.

"Malone brought guns. Ten of them. We confiscated nine, but Colin Dean still had his. He…" I took a deep breath, then forced out the single most hateful words I'd ever uttered. "He shot Dad, Michael. Dean shot Daddy in the chest."

"No." That dead quality was gone. His voice now overflowed with pain, an echo of my own. "No. Is he…?"

"He died about twenty minutes ago."

He was crying now, and the sound of my oldest brother's sobs, broken by short bouts of stubborn stoicism, of strength, was more than I could take.

My own tears flowed silently, and I swiped at them as I spoke. "He said to tell you how proud he is of you. You and Owen. And to tell Mom…" My hand clenched around the phone, and I had to use my other arm to wipe my face, because the first sleeve was soaked. "I have to tell Mom. Can you get her?"

"She's going to…" He sniffled into the receiver. "Faythe, I don't know what she's going to do."

"Me, neither. Could you get her?"

"Just a minute." I heard more footsteps, then the door squealed open again. "Mom?" he called, and his nose sounded just as stuffy as mine.

She was there in an instant. "Michael? What's wrong?" The door closed again, and she came closer to the phone. "Is it Faythe?"

"She's fine. It's Dad."

"What happened? Is he okay?" she demanded, and I could hear panic building in the voice I knew by heart. If my father was my strength, she was his. A steel backbone in satin wrapping.

Instead of answering, Michael must have given her

the phone. "Faythe? What happened? Is your father okay?"

I couldn't stand the tremor in her voice. Couldn't stand being the reason it was there. I shook my head, though she couldn't see it. "I'm sorry, Mom. They had guns. There was nothing we could do...."

The phone crashed to the floor, and the impact resonated deep within my brain. But the next sound completely overpowered it.

"Nooooo...!"

Sixteen

My mother's screams cut through me like a sword through my heart, and I wanted to drop the phone. But I didn't. I would not push away her anguish. It was ours to share, and the ringing in my ears was fitting penance for failing to save him. Though it was nowhere near enough.

It would never be enough.

The phone clattered against wood, and Michael was back. "Faythe, hang on. Let me get Owen." Michael took the phone with him and though I couldn't hear the door squeal open over my mother's hysterical screaming, I heard Michael shout for Owen. As would everyone else in the house.

He was there in an instant. He'd probably started running the second he'd heard our mother scream, because our mother never screamed. Not when she was angry, not when she was hurt, not when she was excited. She was as steady as the earth's rotation, if a bit less predictable lately, and I'd just thrown her completely off her orbit.

I was hurting, too—we all were—but I knew I could

never completely understand the depth of my mother's pain until I'd lost the love of my life, my husband of thirty-three years and the father of my five children.

"What happened?" Owen's normally soft voice was almost unintelligible, and it faded into nothing as he moved away from the phone Michael still held, probably to comfort our mother.

"Michael, what the hell happened?" Owen repeated, louder this time.

My mother was still screaming, and now starting to go hoarse. I couldn't stand it. Hearing her agony—-and being unable to ease it—sent biting pain through my chest, like my heart was literally being shredded.

"Here, I'll take Mom," Michael said. "Talk to Faythe." Something scratched the receiver as the phone was passed, and my mother's cries changed when Michael held her. I wished I was there with them. We should have been able to grieve together. They should have been able to talk to my father before he died.

My father should not have died.

"Faythe?" Owen's voice was thick with dread. "It's Dad, isn't it?"

"Yeah." I'd buried my face in one hand, but looked up when the door opened. Marc came in wearing a fresh shirt but still barefoot, carrying our bright red first-aid bag. He knelt on the floor in front of me as Owen's breath hitched in my ear.

"How did it happen?"

I sighed, wishing I were anywhere else, doing anything else. I'd rather fight a dozen rogues at once than have to tell anyone else about my father's death. "Malone brought guns."

Marc tugged my robe hem open to expose one leg,

and I jumped when his hand settled on my thigh. His palm was rough and warm. I wanted to melt into his touch—into his comfort—until there was nothing else in the world. But then liquid sloshed and something cold touched my leg. Flames scorched a path through my skin, tracing gashes I'd almost forgotten about, in light of the more immediate, emotional agony.

I forced my attention back to Owen as Marc continued to clean my exposed wounds. "He arrested me, Marc, and Jace, and we had to either fight or run. We got rid of most of the guns, but Dean still had his. He… he shot Dad. In the chest."

For a moment, there was only silence over the line— Michael had quieted our mother somehow—and I refused to break it by hissing over the vicious sting in my leg.

"When?" Owen asked finally.

"Just a few minutes ago. He wanted me to tell you how proud he is of you and Michael." And Ryan? He'd said to tell "my brothers." Did Ryan even count anymore? "He gave me a message for Mom, too, but I'll wait until she's…ready to hear it."

"That may be a while…." Owen sniffled, and because he and Ryan had inherited our mother's fair coloring, I knew his face and eyes would already be red from the tears I could barely hear. "I can't believe this. It doesn't feel real."

"I know." It didn't feel real to me, either. Not yet.

"So…now what?"

Owen was the first to ask aloud the question that had been chasing its own tail in my head. "We're still figuring that out. Uncle Rick thinks he can work out a cease-fire. Then I guess we'll bring Dad home and talk about the rest of it when we're all together." I twisted to one side, wincing over the stiffness settling into my over-worked body as Marc stood to pull down one shoulder of my robe, a bottle of hydrogen peroxide in hand. "We have a lot to decide, but it can wait a couple of days, I think. Dealing with this is enough for now."

"Yeah. I guess I better go…help Michael. And tell everyone else."

"Okay. Listen, tell Kaci that if she needs to talk, she can call me. And with any luck, we'll be home tomorrow."

"I'll tell her."

In the background, my mother was crying again. Heavy, full-body sobs, which were somehow worse than the heartrending screams. Sobs spoke of the beginnings of acceptance, and I knew from experience that it was usually easier to wallow in denial.

After Owen hung up, I slid my phone into my pocket, and Marc settled onto the mattress next to me. "They'll be okay," he said, as I pulled my right arm out of my robe so he could reach the lowest gashes.

"No, they won't. None of us will. We're still not okay with Ethan dying. How the hell are we supposed to handle this?" Not that I expected an answer. Marc lifted my arm by my elbow, and this time when he pressed peroxide-soaked cotton to my cuts, I welcomed the sting. Pain was infinitely better than numbness. Pain proved that I was still alive, in spite of the gaping hole in my chest where my heart used to be.

"They're going to handle it because they have one another. And because they have you."

When I looked into his eyes, I could almost believe it, because he believed it, but when I blinked and he refocused on my arm, that confidence drained from me, leaving me cold. I couldn't escape the truth. "I'm not what they need. They need a real Alpha."

He screwed the lid on the bottle of peroxide and set it on the floor, then faced me on the bed, as grave as I'd ever seen him. "You are the Alpha now, Faythe. And that's very real."

I shook my head slowly and said to him what I couldn't have said to anyone else in the world. "I'm not ready."

"If you weren't ready, he wouldn't have named you."

I sighed and blinked back more tears. Would they never stop? "He was wrong. He didn't have any other choice." This rarely happened—an Alpha dying without a qualified son-in-law to leave in charge of his Pride.

Marc took my hand, stroking the back of it with his thumb, and I tried not to read too much into that. He was upset about my dad, too, but that didn't mean he'd forgiven me. "He had choices."

"He should have named you." Marc had more experience, as well as the respect and loyalty of the entire Pride.

"The council would never stand for that. Naming me would have caused more problems than it would solve, and more problems are the last thing this Pride needs."

"Yeah, like the council's going to be thrilled with me." No woman had ever been more hated in U.S. Pride history. But I couldn't argue with his point. It wasn't fair that my father was limited—even in the afterlife—by stupid, pointless bigotry. "So why didn't he name Michael? He's the oldest. And the smartest."

Marc actually laughed. "Michael is great at gathering information and he throws a mean punch, but he's not a leader, Faythe. And he likes the law too much to leave his practice. His heart wouldn't be in it, and an Alpha without heart is… Well, an Alpha without heart is Calvin Malone. A soulless megalomaniac who abuses his power to keep everyone else from having any."

So true, but… I stared at my lap, horrified to see that my hands were actually shaking. "What if I don't have it, either? What if my heart's not in it?" What if my heart died with Ethan and my dad? And with the part of my mother we would never get back? What if *they* were the heart of the Pride, and I was just the impulsive, stubborn bits of cardiac pulp left over in their absence?

That soft chuckle was back. "Oh, don't even start." Marc rolled his eyes, but when his gaze met mine again, his shined with sincerity. "You're *all* heart, and we both know it. You care about the people in this Pride more than you've ever cared about anything else in your life, and even when you mess up, you do it trying to defend one of them. One of *us*."

When I tried to look away, he turned my face so that I had to look at him, or make an issue of my refusal. "You're in this for the long haul, and you have been since the first time the council tried to force you into a marriage and kids before you were ready. Since you figured out they'd do the same thing to Kaci and Manx, and that neither of them would be able to fight for themselves. You belong here, Faythe. You have purpose, and you have vision, and you have exactly what it's going to take to see both of those through to the end. You know things have to change, and you know exactly what those changes should be. And the only way any of that's going to happen is with you leading the call to action."

He reached out to run his thumb over my bottom lip. "Besides, this mouth was made for shouting the truth and demanding justice. Among other things…"

I wanted to return his smile. Hell, I wanted to pull his thumb into my mouth, just to have a taste of him. But our problems now transcended our personal relationship, and I couldn't afford to lose focus.

Marc was right. He was right about all of it. But that didn't change the bottom line: the south-central Pride deserved the best, and I wasn't there. Not yet. "Marc, I can't do this on my own. I'm not ready." And it hurt to admit that, a pang of angst that echoed the trail grief had already clawed through my center. But painful or not, it was the truth—my calling, according to him.

"I know." Marc's smile was smaller now, and bittersweet, like he'd swallowed a memory that didn't taste good. "That's why he asked me to help you. He made me promise to, even if…" He closed his eyes, took a breath, and the soft smile was gone. "Even if you and I don't wind up…together."

My heart thumped so hard I was sure he could hear it, and this time I didn't even know which one of us I was hurting for. "And you did it? You said you would?"

"Yeah." He blinked again, and his jaw clenched. "I swore to a dying man. And I meant it. I'll be there for you, Faythe. No matter what happens. You can do this. He believed in you, and so do I. And if you give them half a chance, so will everyone else."

I threw my arms around his neck and held on like he might dissolve in my grip. After a moment, Marc returned my embrace, lightly at first, and though his hesitance stung, I understood it. I deserved it.

But then he hugged me for real, his chin resting on my shoulder, his stubble rough against my exposed skin. "Thank you." It came out half whisper, half sob. "I can't do this without you."

"You can once you get your feet beneath you. But you won't have to." He pulled away, but didn't get up. "And it won't be just me. I'm sure your uncle would be happy to serve as an adviser, and so will your mom, once she's had some time to deal."

I nodded, but deep inside I wondered if it would be enough. Could one young, stubborn, impulsive woman and several part-time advisers possibly fill my father's enormous shoes? Should we even try?

Yes. There was no other option.

"So, are you ready?" Jace asked, and we both whirled to see him standing in the half-open doorway, watching us. He swallowed thickly, and I understood that only part of his pain was from the loss of our Alpha. From the living room beyond came a soft background of muted voices. When had everyone gotten back? While I was on the phone?

I'd have to start paying better attention to my surroundings, or I'd be the shortest-lived Alpha in history.

"Ready for what?" I said, as Marc stood and pulled me up with him.

"For orientation." Jace shrugged apologetically, his eyes still red from his own recent tears. "Apparently Alphahood is one of those jobs where you have to hit the ground running."

"Why don't you put some clothes on…" Marc bent

for the bottle of peroxide. "And we'll get you fixed up in there."

Jace opened the door and stepped out of the way, still watching me as Marc headed into the living room. "Your allies await...."

Five minutes later, I sat on a kitchen chair someone had pulled into the living room, uncomfortably aware that every eye in the room was aimed my way. That wasn't unusual, of course, but I was pretty sure I was the first Alpha in history to address her allies and enforcers wearing nothing but a crimson halter and a matching pair of boyshorts. Marc was going to sew up my gashes during our little powwow, so I couldn't wear anything that would cover my limbs.

Lucas had laid my father on his bed, but the fresh, raw memory of his death still drew my gaze to the couch even though four enforcers now sat where he'd died, each covered in various cuts and nasty-looking bruises, as well as an assortment of bandages. Except for Elias Keller, we were a ragtag crew at best, and our Pride was now leaderless, unless I could get my act together.

"What did they say?" I asked, as my uncle sank into the chair closest to me. "Did they agree to a cease-fire?" At least long enough to arrange a funeral...

He frowned and leaned forward with his elbows on his knees, focusing his attention on me completely, as if we were the only two people in the room. That couldn't be good. "They want you to make the request yourself."

"Why? So they can try to arrest me again? Or just outright kill me?" Like I was going to willingly walk into a trap.

"It's possible, but I don't think that's what they're going for this time." Uncle Rick paused long enough to scrub both hands over his face. "I told them your dad named you as his successor, and my guess is that they want to give you enough rope to hang yourself with. Or else they want to humiliate you. This is about power. Right now, they have it...."

"And they want to see me grovel for mercy long enough to bury my father." The words tasted bitter— all of them—and I wanted to spit them out.

"Yes. But I think we can make this work for us. If you go in there with your temper in check and your feet on the ground, you have a chance to convince a couple of the other Alphas that you actually belong where your father's placed you. And that you deserve a seat on the council."

"But isn't that kind of meaningless at this point? I mean, even if I wanted to be on the council—" and I wasn't exactly eager to watch Malone pervert justice and promote himself in the name of "purification" "—they're never going to let me in. Hell, they may not even let *you guys* back in." I glanced from my uncle, to Umberto Di Carlo, to Aaron Taylor, a bit overwhelmed to be meeting with them without my father. I kept expecting him to walk in, apologize for being late, then take over. "We just started a war, and so far they're winning. Why wouldn't they want to press their advantage?"

"Because a cease-fire benefits them even more than it benefits us," Di Carlo said from across the room, holding a short glass with an inch of whiskey in the bottom. "Malone's grand scheme only works if he's in charge of the whole council, not just one battered half of it. He's going to want to put his little kingdom back together so he can wear the shiny crown. And he might even lose one or two of his own allies if he refuses to grant a re-spected fellow Alpha a proper burial. Though he prob-ably has no intention of letting the council acknowledge you as an Alpha."

"I'm having trouble understanding the part where that should matter to me." I shrugged apologetically, and in his quiet corner of the room, Keller was nodding. "I mean, if I don't belong to the council, they can't stick their collective nose into south-central Pride business, right?"

And if that was the case, maybe we should have sepa-rated ourselves from the council a long time ago. No, that wouldn't stop Malone from running our allies into the ground, but it would remove us from the immediate fallout zone, wouldn't it? And we'd need that little bit of distance, at least long enough for us to adjust to the loss of our Alpha and the emergence of the youngest, most testosterone-challenged new Alpha in history.

Yet those very benefits were my first clue that leaving the council probably wouldn't be as easy as it sounded. Malone might not want me sitting on his council, but he was never going to be willing give up his influence over the largest territory in the country.

We probably could actually have defected when my father was still Alpha, but he would never even have considered that. He wouldn't have abandoned his fellow council members to Malone's poisonous influence and emerging dictatorship.

Di Carlo's response confirmed my own conclu-sion. "Even if they were willing to let you remove your Pride from the council's collective influence—and they won't be—there's a reason the council exists. We band together because there's strength in numbers. Because in its unperverted state, the council ensures representative government and a pooling of resources and ideas that benefits everyone."

"Yes, but the operative word there is *unperverted*, and right now, you guys are operating under the thumb of the biggest power-pervert ever to swish his tail in the U.S. He's like Hitler with fur."

My uncle looked startled by the odd mental image, but then he nodded acknowledgment of my point. "Yes, but the solution to that problem is to remove Calvin Malone, not to remove the south-central Pride."

He was right. My separatist fantasy was pleasant, but fleeting. After all, the whole reason I was willing to take over leadership of the Pride in the first place was to make our hidden world a better, safer place—Marc had been right about that—and I couldn't do that if I separated us from that world.

I glanced at first Taylor, then Di Carlo, before narrowing my eyes at my uncle, searching his face for the truth. "But you don't really think he's going to let me into the boys' club…?"

"No. But I think you have to ask him to, anyway." Uncle Rick drew in a deep breath, then met my gaze with the same steel-hardened expression I'd seen on my mother—his sister—many, many times. He was about to tell me the truth, even though I wasn't going to like it. "We tried to fight our way out of this and failed. Malone's still very much alive, still very much in power, and still heavily armed, if Alex was telling the truth about the other cache of guns. And we're not ready for a second-wave attack yet. Not with your dad lying cold on the bed in there, and most of our men out of reach."

"Not to mention the severe lack of our new allies…" Marc added, kneeling next to me with the first-aid kit in hand.

I nodded slowly, as the truth sank in. "So, I have to go beg for a time-out to give us a chance to regroup. Even if that means giving Malone the opportunity to ban me from the clubhouse."

"Exactly." Di Carlo nodded firmly.

My uncle sat up straight. "Malone refusing to acknowledge you right now is a given. It doesn't matter. What matters is that you go in there and make the best possible impression on the rest of them, so that after the funeral, you stand a chance of winning them over and evening the odds against us a bit. Even after Malone's gone—assuming we can actually get rid of him—we're all going to have to work with his current allies, so the fewer enemies we make at this point in the war, the better prepared we'll be to fight later."

I considered for a moment, trying to sort through the barrage of new information and nonchoices. From the outside looking in, I'd always thought my father had a brilliant array of options spread before him—the luxury of choice—but now that I stood in his shoes, it was obvious that an Alpha had no more options than I'd had as an enforcer. And based on this first small sampling, every one of them sucked. Even worse, each choice he made carried life-or-death consequences.

I'd just stepped out of the kiddie pool and into the deep end, with no floaties. And drowning was not an option.

"Okay, I'm in. I can play nice, even if he won't." I tried not to notice Marc threading the long, curved suture needle as I forced my gaze back to my uncle. "So…what's first?"

Uncle Rick glanced at his fellow Alphas, each of whom could only shrug. Then his focus returned to me. "To my knowledge, replacing an Alpha has never gone quite like this before, so all we can really do is treat this like the ascension of any other Alpha, while acknowledging that there are necessarily going to be some differences."

Such as the new Alpha flashing the entire room a peek at her inner thighs, which couldn't be helped, with Marc preparing to sew me up. Not that the sight of flesh was new to anyone, but Alphas seldom wore sheer, lace-trimmed underwear to formal meetings.

And something told me that was just the first of many differences we'd soon discover between my father's administrative style and mine.

"Okay, I'm at your disposal." I tried not to flinch when Marc leaned over me and the needle bit into the tender skin around my largest gash. I'd opted to go without anesthesia because all we had was alcohol, and while that would have numbed more than one kind of pain, I couldn't afford fuzzy logic.

"Right." Uncle Rick stood, and his nervous pacing reminded me of my father—and of the fact that I couldn't move around to burn some of my own nervous energy. "In order to be officially acknowledged as Alpha by your Pride, the territory's enforcers must unanimously accept you by formally swearing their loyalty to you."

I'd known about the oath, of course. I'd seen it given every time my father hired a new enforcer, and I'd sworn the same oath myself when I'd been officially hired. But this was a little different, both because of the scale—*all* the enforcers would have to swear, rather than just one or two new recruits—and because without the loyalty of dedicated enforcers, an Alpha could never hope to properly lead a Pride, much less hold on to it in the face of opposition. And I'd probably break records in that last department.

If one of the enforcers refused to swear loyalty to a prospective Alpha, that Alpha had two options. First, she could fight—and beat—the opposing voter, thus expelling him from enforcer ranks. Or, she could come into the job with sworn enforcers of her own—who hadn't worked for the previous Alpha—and take the Pride by force. That hadn't happened in the U.S. Prides in more than a century, but we knew of a very recent case south of the border—that of Manx's father, who'd been executed by the Alpha challenger.

Fortunately, as in most cases, I'd been named successor by the previous Alpha, and I'd served with the other enforcers, so a hostile takeover didn't look likely, even if one of them wasn't willing to serve under me.

As if he knew what I was thinking, my uncle continued. "But being acknowledged by the council is another matter entirely—you have to be recognized by a simple majority of its existing members. But we've already agreed that that's simply not going to happen right now, so I don't want you to worry about that. When we get to the lodge, you can just make the formal request, then lose as gracefully as possible."

Well, at least there's a plan B. Which was good, because I couldn't even get a majority of the Alphas to agree to leave me breathing, much less to put me in charge of my own Pride.

"Well, let's not put the tail before the muzzle, right?

I mean, if I don't have the support of the Pride itself, the rest of this is totally moot."

I glanced down at my leg just as Marc clipped the suture thread on the first gash. About a dozen stitches, by my guess, and they weren't exactly pretty to look at. But nothing was broken or protruding from my flesh, so all in all, I counted myself lucky.

Marc must have known what I was thinking, because instead of starting on the next cut, he stood, and I stood next to him. "Before we go on, I need to know that you guys are with me." I met the eyes of the south-central enforcers one by one, wishing desperately that they were all with us. But Owen and Parker had stayed on the ranch to defend the home front, so we'd have to move forward without them for the moment.

"So this is your chance, and I want you to be honest—with yourselves, with me, and with this Pride. This'll never work if you don't trust me. If you don't truly believe that I can do this. That we can do this together. So don't worry about hurting my feelings or making me mad—I'm a big girl. But you should know that accepting me as your Alpha is going to ruffle more than a few feathers and outright piss some people off. And that the next few days and weeks—hell, maybe the next few years—will be the most difficult you've ever served as an enforcer."

I took a deep breath, concentrating on the four men who'd come to stand in a line in front of me. Marc, Jace, Vic, and Brian. It was up to them. If they all accepted me, our Pride would have an Alpha and a new starting place, no matter how rough the road might be.

But if even one of them was unwilling to put his life in my hands, well, I wasn't sure what would happen then, because I didn't want to start my leadership by having to fight one of my own oldest friends.

"So I'm asking you now, will you serve the south-central territory with me as your Alpha?" The words were old and familiar, but the fear bubbling in my stomach was not. "Will you swear loyalty to the Pride, and to me, as you did to my father?"

"You know I will." Jace dropped onto his knees in a single fluid motion so quick I barely registered the change. "I swear my loyalty and my life to the south-central Pride, and to my Alpha, Faythe Sanders."

Fresh tears came then, and I blinked them back, desperately clinging to composure. "Thank you." I took his hand when he offered it, handshake-style, and responded with the words expected of me. "I swear to lead you to the best of my ability, and to always put the Pride before myself."

When I looked up, Marc took my hand, tugging me gently to stand in front of him. "You've had me from the beginning, Faythe. Loyalty, life, heart, and soul." His hand was warm in mine, but his gaze scorched me as he knelt without ever breaking eye contact. "I swear my loyalty and my life to the south-central Pride, and to my Alpha, Faythe Sanders."

I wanted to say something. Something important and honest. Something to tell him that I understood what he was giving me, and that I would try to earn it. But before I could form a single world, Brian thumped to his knees on my left.

As badly as I wanted to cling to Marc's hand and never let him go, I could only squeeze his palm, recite the expected response, then move on to Brian.

Brian Taylor stared up at me with bright, hope-filled

eyes, and something heavy settled into my gut as he spoke the familiar oath. He didn't understand what he was getting into. Not really. He knew that most of the other Alphas wouldn't like it, but he couldn't possibly *truly* understand the fight he'd just enlisted in. The danger he'd just committed himself to.

But we needed him, and I would not deny him his chance to serve.

Only Vic still stood, and my skin prickled when I felt him watching me. Judging me, as was his right. If he had doubts, he shouldn't serve. It was that simple.

He stared into my eyes, and I stared back, hoping that he saw in me what Marc saw. What my father had seen. What I was still hoping to prove to myself. The only real truth I could claim—the only thing I knew beyond the slightest shadow of doubt—was that I would live and die for my Pride. To protect everyone in it and to try to forge much-needed change from inside the system.

"I believe you," Vic whispered at last. "I believe that you can do this. It's going to be hard. This job is going to break your heart, Faythe. It's going to bruise you from the inside out, and it may keep you from ever truly being happy. But I believe you will fight for us all with every breath in your body. I don't think you're capable of anything less."

I choked on my next breath, staggered by his profession of confidence and loyalty, knowing what he thought of my personal mistakes.

With that, he sank to his knees and took my hand. "I swear my loyalty and my life to the south-central Pride, and to my Alpha, Faythe Sanders."

I said my part, and when he let go of my hand, I stepped back and looked at them—my Pridemates. My fellow enforcers. The first brave souls to put their lives in my hands.

It didn't feel like I expected it to. There was no rush of power or glory. My first moments as Alpha felt… heavy. Somber. Like I'd just taken on a colossal debt I could never hope to repay. Being Alpha was a burden and an enormous responsibility, not a license to push people around.

And that was what Calvin Malone had never really understood.

Seventeen

A wave of shock rolled over me when the guys stood, and I realized I was no longer their coworker. I was now their boss. But the term *employer* describes an Alpha about as well the word *caretaker* defines the concept of parenthood; it is a cold, one-dimensional word that utterly fails to convey the human element.

My dad had been much more than our boss. He was our leader, guardian, adviser, landlord, counselor, sometimes a confidant, and a father figure even to those with whom he shared no blood. He was a champion and defender of those with little power and soft voices. He was a fount of wisdom and a source of never-ending patience. He was so many things I'd never even considered, and I harbored no delusion that I could fulfill all of those roles right out of the gate.

But I desperately wanted to. I wanted to be what they needed. I needed to do this right, because they deserved better than I had to offer.

"Okay, so what now?" I glanced to my uncle for advice. "We go make nice with the council?"

He nodded solemnly. "But this won't be easy."

"Nothing worth doing ever is." I took a deep breath, trying to get my thoughts in order. "How does this work?"

Marc gestured toward my chair, suture needle in hand, and I sat as my uncle stood, already pacing again. Most of the enforcers had gathered around another first-aid kit spread out on the coffee table, passing around bottles of hydrogen peroxide and bandages, a couple threading needles to sew up the worst of the gashes for fellow toms.

It was an odd sort of quiet ritual, so different from the other times they'd shared bigger bottles and passed bags of snack food. But the familiarity was there. We were family, friends, and allies, whether we were celebrating or mourning. Or preparing to face common foes.

Uncle Rick lifted a no-longer-steaming mug of coffee from an end table, and I could tell by the way he held it—making no use of the handle—that he wished it held something stronger than lukewarm caffeine.

"They're nursing their own wounds right now, just like we are." He glanced at the coffee table triage center, and I noticed that the Alphas had all already been doctored. That particular privilege of rank was born of a desire to keep our leaders alive and…well…leading. A point driven home for me when Marc began the second set of unanaesthetized stitches on the gash in my side. "And as I said, they're just as eager for a cease-fire, though Malone would never admit that."

"What do we know about their damages?" I asked, flinching when Marc's thread tugged at very tender skin.

"They have a couple of unconscious toms and a few

broken bones…" Neither of which we had. "And three casualties."

One was my kill, one Elias Keller's, and the third, if I had to guess, was Marc's. Evidently Colin Dean had lived, an oversight I would soon remedy even if it took my dying breath.

"We benefited from the element of surprise," my uncle continued. "But we've lost that now, and we won't get it back anytime soon. And they'll have the duration of the cease-fire to concentrate on healing and regrouping, but we won't."

Because we had to plan a funeral, as well as our next move.

"Did you tell them I'd come?" I asked, and Marc's sewing paused midstitch as he waited for the answer.

"Yes. And they're probably expecting you to come in guns ablaze. Literally." He turned toward the breakfast table and I followed his gaze to find the tabletop covered in the clunky black remains of six handguns, now rendered virtually unrecognizable, thanks to Keller's efforts. "Or not."

"I'll destroy the rest of them, too, if you happen ta get your hands on 'em," Keller rumbled. "I don't like guns, and it's bad enough that humans carry 'em. I can't have a bunch of cats up here, shootin' up my mountain."

"We completely agree," I said. "And hopefully Malone won't be stupid enough to actually use their few remaining guns against unarmed opposition. At least in front of the rest of the council."

"He won't," Taylor said from an armchair across the room. "He's not going to jeopardize his standing with the less loyal of his allies."

"Good." I closed my eyes, thinking as Marc clipped

the thread from the needle. "Hopefully they'll be caught off guard when I'm willing to play by their rules." I frowned up at my uncle. "What *are* their rules, exactly?"

"It's a simple formal poll. Each council member gets a chance either to recognize you as an Alpha or to refuse. You need to be recognized by five of the nine Alphas—obviously you don't get to vote, since you're not in yet."

"Okay…" My brain was racing. "I need five and I have three here." I glanced from my uncle to Bert Di Carlo, to Aaron Taylor. "So, for the long-term, I only need to start winning over two more. I think our best bets are Nick Davidson…" Because he didn't have any reason to hate me, that I knew of. "And Paul Blackwell." Because he was currently the least loyal to Malone. Though he wasn't exactly a Faythe fan.

Good thing I like a challenge.

"Faythe…" I glanced up to see Aaron Taylor watching me with a carefully guarded expression, and my stomach began to toss with dread. I saw it in his eyes before he said the words. "I'm not saying no. I think you're a hell of an enforcer, and I'm sure your father had a very good reason for leaving you in charge of his Pride. But this is a very big decision, and I'm not prepared to say yes or no just yet. So for today, I'll be declining to vote."

I could only blink. His words must not have sunk in yet, because I couldn't feel them.

He hesitated, eyes closed, then met my gaze again and continued. "You're very young, Faythe, and largely unproven. You've been an enforcer for less than a year, and while I believe your private life is your own business, I also know that there's very little about an Alpha's life that is ever truly private. All your choices will be called into question, and you'll be asked to justify every single decision you make. And without more experience, I'm just not sure you're ready to make some of those decisions yet."

I nodded, numb. Taylor was voicing my own doubts, and I couldn't even argue with them. I wouldn't have voted for me, either, in his position. But because most of the council would never even consider Marc—as evidenced by their refusal to acknowledge that he'd been reaccepted into our Pride—there was no one else to relieve me of my duty, even if I wanted to give it up.

"That's why she has us." Uncle Rick watched Taylor from the other side of the room. "She's come a long way this year, and her father knew what he was doing when he named her. She has us for guidance and advice, and frankly, we don't have time for her to gain any more experience, unless it's on the job. The south-central Pride needs an Alpha, and it needs one now."

"Councilman Taylor's right." I felt the words echo in my hollow, aching chest. I stood, facing them all, and Marc backed up to give me space. "I am inexperienced, I have made some poor choices, and sometimes I speak without thinking. I'm not going to make excuses." I looked up from the floor and met Taylor's assessing gaze. "All I can say regarding the mistakes I've made since becoming an enforcer is that I was truly trying to do the right thing. And I hope that with older, wiser, more experienced friends and allies at my back, I'll have the resources I need to make more informed, better-balanced decisions."

I smiled at my uncle to thank him for his support,

then turned to Taylor again. "But you have to make your own choices, and while obviously I wish that you had the confidence in me to decide now, I have to admit I understand your hesitation." Though it bruised some deep part of me to say those words. "But with all due respect, there's another important point I think you may be missing."

Taylor raised both brows, silently waiting for me to go on.

I took a deep breath and pressed on. "We're kind of out of options here. If I'm not going to be Alpha, who will be? Marc would get even less support in the position than I would." I glanced at Marc to see him nodding solemnly, as I repeated what he'd first told me. "And Uncle Rick is right—we can't afford to be leaderless. Especially now."

Taylor glanced from me to my uncle, then back to me, seeming to consider.

"There has to be another option. An interim leader of some sort, just until you gain a little more experience."

I shook my head slowly. "Councilman, do you have a plan for what will happen to your Pride if you were to die suddenly?"

"Yes, of course. Since Carissa hasn't chosen a husband yet, her oldest brother would take over until she's ready to settle down with a new Alpha."

That time I nodded. "My father had a contingency plan, too, and this is it. He knew—just like all of you surely do—that an Alpha could die at any time, and as much as he loves me, I know for a fact that he would never have named me as the next Alpha if he'd had a better choice. With his dying breath, he would have done what's best for the Pride. And I have to believe that's exactly what he did."

Taylor watched me in silence, obviously struggling with the decision.

"Aaron," my uncle said, breaking the tense silence. "We have to present a united front on this. If we don't, Malone *will* divide and conquer."

Taylor sighed and met my gaze again. "You speak with your father's skill and your mother's passion. If you got anything else from either of them, I guess this might not be the *worst* decision your father ever made."

I didn't dare smile. "Does that mean...?"

"You have my vote," Taylor said, nodding solemnly. "On the condition that you choose several levelheaded advisers. And that you listen to them."

"Done." I nodded, glancing at both Marc and my uncle.

"Mr. Di Carlo?" I turned toward Vic's father, well aware that Vic and Teo—and everyone else in the room—were watching us. "Do you need more time to make your decision?"

Di Carlo smiled and reached out for my hand, swallowing it in both of his. "No. I trusted your father with my life, and I trust his decision. You are a fiery little ball of fierce determination tempered by a strong moral compass and a heart as big as a bruin's. The rest will come with time and experience, if you listen to your advisers and learn from your mistakes. And I think you'll do both of those, won't you?"

I could only nod, determined not to cry again until I was alone. "Thank you." I swallowed back unshed tears of gratitude. "I'll do my best not to disappoint you."

"Oh, child, it's not my expectations you have to meet.

It's your Pride's. And something tells me your own standards are higher than even what they would expect of you."

With a sudden jolt of understanding, I realized he was right. My expectations for myself were sky-high, because they were the expectations my father had set from the beginning. And I would live up to them—or die trying.

When Di Carlo stepped back, I glanced around to find that most of the bruises had been iced, the cuts cleaned, and the gashes stitched. Marc was the last to receive medical attention, and Vic was finishing his sutures that very moment—a long but thankfully shallow cut along his right outer thigh.

"Okay, let's go." I turned toward the door, and the men stood.

"Um, Faythe?" Marc reached for my arm, and a small grin turned up one corner of his beautiful mouth. "As my first official piece of advice to the new Alpha, let me suggest that you put on some pants. And maybe a shirt." His grin grew and he pulled me closer to whisper in my ear, while Jace watched us stiffly from across the room. "While this look definitely works for me, I'm thinking the other Alphas might take you more seriously if you dress the part."

I flushed, suddenly aware that I was half-naked. And that Marc had voluntarily touched me without a needle in his hand or a grudge behind his eyes.

"Yes. Clothes. Good idea." In the bedroom, I dug through my suitcase and chose a pair of black slacks and a matching thinly pinstriped blouse. I was buttoning my blouse when the door opened. Jace stepped inside and pushed the door closed at his back.

"You okay?" he asked.

"As okay as can be expected." I tucked the tail of my blouse into my slacks and buckled my belt.

Jace leaned against the dresser facing me and his gaze searched mine. "I haven't actually had a chance to say this yet, and it feels so…inadequate. But I'm so, so sorry about your dad." He held out his arms, and I stepped into them. I let him hold me. He asked for nothing and offered only his presence, and a moment of soft, warm comfort, minutes before I'd have to show the world my steel spine and granite visage.

I put my chin on his shoulder and he rubbed my back, whispering into the hair that hid my ear. "I don't actually remember much about my dad, but there hasn't been a day since he died that I didn't wish he was still here. Hell, if he were, none of this would have happened."

"No one thing caused this, Jace. And we can't undo it. The best we can do is end it. End Colin Dean and destroy Calvin Malone."

"You know I'm with you. Whatever you need."

"I know." I sniffed back unbidden tears. "Thank you."

Before he could answer, the door creaked open, and I pulled away from him to find Marc staring at us. His jaw tightened, but he swallowed whatever he wanted to say, no doubt out of deference to the circumstances. And to the fact that Jace and I were both fully dressed. "You ready?"

"Yeah." I straightened my shirt and cleared my throat. "I just… I need a minute. With my dad."

Marc nodded, and I slipped down the hall and into my father's room, closing the door behind me, trying to block out everything else—the hushed conversation, the tension and fear roiling in waves from the living room, and the conflict and need that churned in a constant, violent cloud around both Marc and Jace.

I pushed it all back as I approached the bed, wading through the heavy silence in my head and the fresh ache my father's death had left in me, only brushing the much-sharper agony that would come when I finally had time to deal with my loss. To accept it.

The sheet someone had draped over him couldn't obscure the shape I knew so well. My father had been the single greatest strength in my life. He was the force that made the clocks tick, and the sun rise and set. In my youth, his expectations fueled my ambition and his disappointment cut deep into my heart, even when I rebelled in an attempt to forge my own path. When I grew up, making him proud still carried the same weight, even if I wouldn't admit it.

My hands shook as I folded back the sheet. He stared up at me, unseeing, and I couldn't stop fresh tears.

When I was a child, all problems had ended with a single word from my father. A smile from him was sunshine, his scowl a bolt of thunder. He was smart, and generous, and honorable without fail. He could exile a trespasser, check my math homework, and fix the leaky bathroom sink, all before dinner. For the longest time, I thought he was invincible. Above the petty problems that plagued normal people.

And now he was gone.

I sat on the edge of the mattress. "I'm going to do it, just like you wanted," I whispered, wishing desperately that he could actually hear me. "I'm going to try, anyway. I'm gonna lose, but that's not really the point, is it?" I stared at my hands in my lap, realizing for the first time that I had a narrow version of his fingernails, on my mother's long, slender fingers. How had I never noticed that before?

"I'm not going to give up just because Malone and the others refuse to acknowledge me. I'll find another way. I'm not going to let the Pride down."

Not going to let you down, either...

When I stood, I discovered that covering him up was even harder than folding the sheet back in the first place. It felt a bit like letting him go, and that was one of the scariest things I'd ever done. With my father gone—aside from the very real, very deep ache his absence left inside me—there was truly no one left to protect me if I got in over my head. I still had friends, and supporters, and advisers, but my lifelong safety net was now gone, and one wrong step would send me crashing to the ground, broken.

No amount of support or advice could fix things once I'd fallen.

Numb from the weight that had settled onto my shoulders, cold from standing out on that ledge all alone, I turned from my father to face the mirror, and I almost didn't recognize the woman who stared back at me.

She had my green eyes and it was my own long black hair I pushed back from her face. But the soul that stared out at me was bruised beyond recognition—even more damaged than the face I now wore, so different from the me in my memory, a perpetual eighteen-year-old, still shiny and excited, and convinced that education and independence were the keys to unlocking the future I'd always dreamed of.

The me in the mirror had scars on her face, fresh bruises all over her body, and serious shadows beneath her eyes. This Faythe was all dressed up in a fitted, pin-striped blouse and dark slacks, her hair a fierce nest of tangles around her face, like a wild black mane. This Faythe was ready to play her father's game, and this Faythe played for keeps.

I ran my fingers through my hair, taming it just enough to look presentable, then turned away from the mirror, satisfied with what I saw. I slipped back into the hall and stopped in my room to change into my best black boots. The heels were too high for fighting, but if this turned into a physical fight, we were screwed before we even began—Malone still outnumbered us badly, and he still had three guns.

Everyone looked up when I stepped into the living room, and more than a few eyes widened. I could tell from Marc's expression alone that I looked the part—half stone-cold businesswoman, half badass bitch.

"I'm ready. Let's get this over with." I marched toward the door, and the others hurried to follow. On the front lawn, Marc fell in on my right side, Jace on my left. Uncle Rick and his men followed behind and on the right, Di Carlo and his men behind to the left. Taylor's group brought up the rear, accompanied by the distinctive, thundering tread of the bruin, who seemed determined to stay until he knew there wouldn't be any more fighting in his territory. For which I was more than grateful.

We walked without speaking, moving briskly, and I barely noticed the cold, though I hadn't stopped for a jacket. Five minutes later, I stomped up the main lodge's front steps and pushed open the door. My men fanned out around me on the porch in standard formation.

Calvin Malone stood from the couch, struggling to

hide his surprise. I was expected, of course, but apparently I was expected to come crawling on my hands and knees, bleeding and scared, begging for mercy. But that's not how this game was going to unfold, and the sooner they understood that, the better.

"What is this?" Malone's eyes narrowed, fists clenched at his sides. Had he truly thought I'd fold beneath the pressure before they'd even had a chance to threaten me?

"This is the new player. And now it's a whole new game."

Eighteen

I stepped into the lodge and my supporters filed in after me, and I have to say, we made a pretty impressive front, even with Keller waiting on the front porch, because there just wasn't room for his bulk.

"What do you want?" Milo Mitchell demanded, standing up next to Malone, so we couldn't possibly mistake his alliances.

"A cease-fire long enough to bury my father."

"Well, look at you playing dress-up," Jerald Pierce said from the kitchen doorway, and I was pleased to see a deep, blood-crusted cut on his temple. "First you start a fight, then you want a time-out so you can lick your wounds. Is this what they mean by 'a woman's prerogative to change her mind'?" He turned to Malone and shrugged dramatically. "I guess this is the kind of hormonal impulse behavior you get when you put little girls in charge. Which is exactly why we don't do that."

Malone only watched while Pierce stalked closer and I stared at him, determined not to flinch beneath his appraisal. "You don't have the authority to ask for a cease-fire. That's an *Alpha's* prerogative."

"Well, then, it's a good thing you're looking at the new south-central Pride's Alpha." My voice came out smooth and calm, in contrast to the inferno of anger raging inside me.

"You're not an Alpha, you're a traitorous whore." Pierce's furious scowl said he was just waiting for my argument to the contrary, but it was Jace who spoke up, from my left.

"Her enforcers have accepted her and formally sworn loyalty."

"Yeah, because she's sleeping with them," Pierce spat, and I nearly bit my tongue off to keep my mouth shut. Proclaiming my private life to be private wasn't much of an option for an Alpha.

"She hasn't been recognized by the council." At the sound of the new voice, we all glanced up to see Wes Gardner enter the main room from the hall, followed by Paul Blackwell and Nick Davidson. The players had all arrived.

"Then consider this my official request to be recognized as an Alpha by the Territorial Council." I had to consciously stop myself from crossing my arms, to keep from looking closed off or confrontational.

"Faythe…" Blackwell began, and I found true sympathy in his wrinkled expression. "I'm so sorry about your father."

"Thank you." I took a subtle, deep breath, hoping I didn't look as rattled as I felt. "All I want is a chance to bury him."

"And evidently a seat on the council," Mitchell snapped.

"Only if that's what it takes to get a cease-fire." I

really hadn't expected so much resistance to that part. Maybe I wasn't groveling enough. My mistake.

"What, you can start a fight, but you can't finish it?" Colin Dean snapped from one of the bedroom doorways, and I found fury raging behind his eyes. He'd taken my father from me, stripping me of my strongest protector and drowning me in grief. He'd also single-handedly promoted me to Alpha. If and when I was officially recognized, I'd outrank him. Which explained the new-and-still-shiny rage practically glowing around the edges of his silhouette.

It took more self-control than I'd known I had to keep from pouncing on him and ripping his throat out with my bare hands, for what he'd done to my father, and to my Pride. Such a death would have been much too fast and merciful for him, but I was short on patience, and had none to waste on Colin Dean.

Unfortunately, I couldn't afford to do more than fantasize about his death for the moment. And plot it. And plan for it...

His day would come, and I would be there.

"Does she really think we're even going to *consider* confirming her as an Alpha?" Pierce was clearly talking to Malone, but his disgusted gaze never left my face.

"I think the principles you swore to uphold as a council member dictate that you at least hear my request," I returned, then shifted my attention to Malone, waiting for his response as the rest of our allies spread out into the large main room.

"She's right," Malone said finally. "She has the right to fair consideration." But we all knew that consideration was a far cry from confirmation. "Are you ready now?"

Ready to commence with the sexism and humiliation? "The sooner, the better."

Malone extended one arm toward the hallway in a grand, faux-generous gesture. "We'll convene in the dining room."

Ten minutes later, everyone was in place. Enforcers sat in folding chairs along three of the four walls. Malone sat at the head of the long table, with his allies seated on his right and my father's allies—plus Paul Blackwell—on his left, each group separated by an unseen but almost palpable political gulf, as well as the broad, slick slab of mahogany.

I'd told my newly sworn enforcers to sit directly behind me on purpose, so that I couldn't accidentally glance at them. Comfort and encouragement from loved ones could easily be seen as weakness from a potential Alpha. My uncle, Bert Di Carlo, and Aaron Taylor had my back, and Paul Blackwell had no more interest in supporting Malone than in supporting me, but I couldn't count on any of them. This was my show. My responsibility. My chance to demonstrate to not just the other Alphas, but to every tom in the room, that I had what it would take to lead and protect my Pride.

In spite of their gender bias and general distrust.

Yet when I stood at the foot of the table, facing the men who held the future of my Pride in their collective hands, my first thought was, *Damn, I really hate this room.*

Nothing good ever seemed to happen in the main lodge dining room.

"Okay, Faythe, tell us how your father died."

For one long, painful moment, I could only stare at

Malone in shock. He knew damn well what had happened to my dad; he was just trying to shake me up by making me relive the whole thing. Again.

"Dean shot him, Calvin," Di Carlo snapped, glaring at the council chair from three seats away. "I see no reason to waste time recounting something we all know."

"It's okay," I said, struggling to make my voice come out loud and firm. If I was too fragile to talk about my father's death, I wasn't strong enough to be an Alpha, and I would not give them a new reason to vote against me. They already had plenty of those. "He was shot in the chest, and he died about half an hour later, on the couch in our cabin."

"And you claim that before he died, he named you his primary heir?"

"Yes."

"In front of witnesses?" Mitchell asked, eyes gleaming with morbid curiosity better suited to a morgue tour than a formal Territorial Council meeting.

"Yes. Including three other Alphas," my uncle said, though I was almost positive none of them had actually heard what my father had said to me.

"And is it your belief that you can lead and protect the south-central Pride as well as your father did?" Malone asked, and his cold hint of a grin raised the hairs on the back of my neck. *Trick question.* There was no correct answer. If I claimed to be as good a leader, I'd be an arrogant liar, but if I admitted inferiority, I'd be unfit.

Lesser of two evils, Faythe...

"No one can run the south-central Pride as well as my father. All I can do is work hard to reach my own potential and hope that would make him proud."

"What if your potential isn't good enough?" Wes Gardner's voice was soft, but his expression was cold and even. "Do you really think it's fair of you to condemn your Pride to less than the best possible leadership if it turns out that your ambition doesn't fall in line with what they really need?"

My hands were damp with cold sweat, and I didn't know what to do with them. "Of course not. Ambition is the death of good leadership." I was unreasonably proud of myself for not glancing pointedly at Malone. "But what if I am what they really need? What if they need someone who knows them better than they know themselves? Someone who understands their strengths and weaknesses, because she's learned from her own victories and mistakes? Someone who understands the value of advice and guidance from those who have already been where she is now? Someone who loves them more than anything else in the world, and would do whatever it takes to lead and protect them?"

"Even if that means stepping down to make room for someone more qualified?" Paul Blackwell asked softly, and my next breath chilled something deep within my chest.

Always before, when I'd spoken to the council, my father was there to tell me how I was doing with a tiny nod or frown. But this time, I was flying blind, with no view of the runway. A crash landing was my greatest fear.

"Yes," I said at last. "If I found someone better qualified to lead them, then yes, I would step down. As I hope any good Alpha would. But right now, there is no one better suited for this job than I am. At least, not according to my father."

"And what if he was wrong?" Malone folded his hands on top of the table, eyeing me steadily. Daring me to answer.

A long, silent breath slipped from me while I tried to decide whether my answer would even matter. Then I blinked and met his gaze boldly. "It's my job to make sure he wasn't."

Silence met my reply. The Alphas exchanged unreadable glances, and behind me, several enforcers fidgeted in their seats.

I couldn't breathe. Was that it? No more questions?

"I think we're ready to hear from the council members." Malone stood, now facing me from the other end of the long table, and though I'd come into the meeting expecting a resounding defeat, I still found my skin prickled with goose bumps in anticipation. "Gentlemen, you will each have a chance to speak. You may recognize Ms. Sanders as Alpha, refuse to recognize her, or decline to speak."

He met my gaze then, and I stood straighter, tugging my blouse into place. "If you're recognized by five of the Alphas, you will be considered recognized by the council at large."

I nodded. Nothing new there.

Malone glanced at my uncle, who sat closest to me on the right side of the table. "Rick?"

My uncle smiled, the first friendly expression I'd seen since the meeting began. "I recognize Faythe Sanders as Alpha of the south-central Pride."

I gave him a small nod of thanks, but Malone had already moved on. "Bert?"

Di Carlo met Malone's gaze boldly. "I recognize Faythe Sanders as Alpha of the south-central Pride."

"Aaron?"

Taylor hesitated, but only for a moment. "I recognize Faythe Sanders as Alpha of the south-central Pride."

Malone frowned, but he made no comment. "Milo?"

Milo Mitchell shot me a withering glance of contempt. "I refuse to recognize Faythe Sanders as an Alpha. Hell, I ought to refuse to recognize her as a tabby, for shirking her real duty for so long."

I closed my eyes, clenching my teeth to hold back the profanity-riddled retort that wanted to spew forth.

Malone restrained a smile, but his eyes practically glittered with pleasure. "Wes?"

Wesley Gardner stared at the table. "I refuse to recognize Faythe Sanders as Alpha of the south-central Pride."

"Paul?"

Blackwell gripped his cane and sat silently for a moment. Then he looked up at me from across the table. "For the moment, I decline to speak."

I actually breathed a silent sigh of relief and managed to unclench one fist at my side. Declining to speak was infinitely better than refusing to recognize, which was what I'd expected from him. Declining to speak meant I might later be able to convince him that my father knew what he was doing. That I was right for the job.

"Nick?"

Davidson squirmed in his chair, and the resemblance to his motherless seven-year-old daughter was suddenly obvious. "I decline to speak at this time."

I'd never in my life been so thrilled with a nonanswer, and Malone's frown was like the cherry on top.

"Jerald?" Malone said, and all eyes focused on Parker's father, the final vote.

"I refuse to acknowledge Faythe Sanders as Alpha of anything but her own imagination. And frankly, I'm insulted by her arrogance."

For a long moment, Malone let Pierce's final statement hang on the air, so it could be properly absorbed, and I could do nothing but fume silently.

"That's only recognition by three Alphas," the new council chair said at last, in case anyone wasn't keeping count, and my cheeks flamed. Yes, I'd been expecting it, but that didn't make humble pie taste any better. "So my decision isn't really necessary. But I'm going to give it to you, anyway." That time, when his gaze met mine, the corner of his mouth actually twitched, obviously itching to turn up.

"Faythe Sanders, I refuse to acknowledge you as Alpha of the south-central Pride."

I nodded curtly, already turning toward the door. I couldn't get out of there fast enough. But Malone's next words brought me to a halt.

"However, out of respect for your father, I am going to grant you a cease-fire, so he can be properly buried." I started to thank him, in spite of his ironic use of the word *respect,* but Malone wasn't done talking. "And out of respect for your Pride and its tragic loss, I'm going to give you that same length of time to present an Alpha worthy of recognition by this council. If you are unable to come up with such an Alpha in the allotted time, we will appoint one."

What?

I couldn't speak. I couldn't even breathe. He couldn't do that. An Alpha had never before been appointed by anyone other than the outgoing Alpha, and even that was usually just a formality during his official retirement.

My cheeks flamed. My hands curled into fists at my sides, and I couldn't unclench them. A familiar burning began behind my eyes, and for a moment I couldn't decide whether that heat heralded more tears or a partial Shift.

"You don't have the authority for that. There's no precedent…" I began, only moderately relieved to see that Taylor, Di Carlo, Blackwell, and my uncle Rick all looked horrified.

"There's also no precedent for a Pride being unable to come up with a suitable candidate."

"I *am* a suitable candidate." I spoke through clenched jaws to keep my teeth from Shifting.

"You're not even a suitable *wife*," Dean spat from the left-hand wall. "With the way you're sleeping with half your enforcers…"

One glance from Malone silenced him, but the damage was done. Pierce and Mitchell were nodding, and even Blackwell was scowling. And it would do me no good to cry "foul."

I leaned forward with my palms flat on the table, to keep my hands from shaking. "Councilman Malone, you can't just set some random tom in place as our Alpha. This isn't your decision. People aren't chess pieces for you to move around as it suits you!"

"She's right." My uncle stood, tense muscles standing out beneath his shirtsleeves. "You can't choose another Pride's Alpha."

"And I won't have to, if Faythe does what's best for her Pride. If she steps down and chooses a suitable husband to protect them." His emphasis on "suitable" left no doubt that, in his opinion, neither Jace nor Marc qualified. "But if she won't consider her Pridemates' best interest, then I stand fully prepared to do what's best for them."

My heart pounded so hard and fast I was sure my chest would explode. "You can*not* choose my husband."

"Of course not. Nor can I make you give your poor mother a grandchild, unfortunately. Even though your family line will *die out* if you refuse to bear the next generation. But I can and will make sure your Pride has the leader it deserves, whether or not you accept him as you should. Unless you're willing to step down and do the right thing for someone else, for a change."

A growl rumbled from my throat, but my uncle's hand landed on my arm, silently warning me to choke it off. "The only way anyone else will sit as Alpha of my territory is if he wins that privilege—that *duty*—in a formal challenge. One on one, unarmed, as tradition dictates."

Malone actually laughed, glancing at his allies to see if they shared the joke. And when his gaze met mine again, it held an unbearable, bitter mirth. "You have five days to bury your father. If you don't have a new Alpha by the time he's in the ground, I *will* choose one for you. You can either fight him, or take him to bed as your husband *as tradition dictates*," he said, throwing my own words back at me as I boiled with rage that had no outlet.

"Either way, the south-central Pride will have a new Alpha by Saturday night."

Nineteen

"That mangy bastard!" I shoved my robe into the suitcase open on the bed and pushed handfuls of terry cloth into the corners, determined to make it fit. "He can't do this. Right? Malone can't just drop a new Alpha into our laps. Specifically, *mine*."

"Technically, no." My uncle sighed and sank into the chair in the corner, the dark hollows under his eyes emphasized by the weak lighting and pervasive shadows. "But then, technically, that's not what he's doing. Officially what will happen—if I have my guess—is that on Saturday night, some strong young tom will show up and formally challenge you for leadership of the Pride. That hasn't happened in living memory—at least, not that I recall—but it's definitely the historical precedent." Which I'd pointed out myself. "And the fact that Malone handpicked whoever challenges you won't be part of the official record. It'll never even be mentioned."

"So…officially, this'll all be on the up-and-up?" How the hell did Malone always manage to disguise evil manipulations as perfectly legal maneuvers?

Uncle Rick nodded reluctantly. "If a bit archaic and barbaric, yes."

"So all I can do is fight this asshole, right?" Or marry him, evidently, which wasn't going to happen. "If I beat him to a bloody pulp in front of an audience of my peers, I get to be Alpha, right?" I pushed on the top of the suitcase, but couldn't make the two halves meet, which only further pissed me off.

"I'll fight him." Marc took the robe and folded it neatly, then laid it across the open suitcase and zipped the bag closed.

"No. No way in hell." At the dresser, I shoved my hair dryer and brush into a smaller bag, fighting to keep from crushing them; my fists wanted to clench around everything I touched. "I'm *not* going to start off my tenure as Alpha by letting someone else fight my battles. What's that going to say to the other Alphas? To the entire rest of the werecat population?"

"It's going to say that you're smart. Traditionally, you're allowed to choose an enforcer to fight in your place."

"And you think you're a better fighter than I am?" Marc started to answer, but I cut him off, already rolling my eyes at myself. "Okay, you're totally better than I am, but that's not the point. I have to do this. Everyone has to *see* me do this. If I can't hold on to the Pride on my own in this first challenge, Malone will only send more challengers."

"No." My uncle shook his head slowly. "If the first one loses against you—or against Marc—Malone won't try that tactic again. He can't afford for his man to look weak, either. Instead, he'll take things up a level. Onto a broader scale."

"War?" Marc asked and Uncle Rick nodded.

"So, if that's the bottom line anyway, why don't we just skip all the bullshit—" I figured cussing *as* an Alpha was different than cussing *at* an Alpha "—and deal out a full-scale slaughter from the get-go?"

Marc frowned. "Because we'll get our asses handed to us. Again."

"Not if we work the clock to our advantage." I unzipped my toiletry bag and shoved in the shampoo and conditioner I'd only had a chance to use once. We'd landed in Montana less than thirty-six hours earlier, and since then, my entire world had crumbled. "We know when the fight's coming, and this time there's no reason we can't call in the reserves."

"What did you have in mind?" Di Carlo asked, and I looked up to find him standing in the doorway. Behind him, toms moved through the living room, packing bags and loading vehicles. Most of them would fly home, but my men and I would have to drive, with my father's body wrapped and carefully positioned in the back of the rental van.

I sat on the end of the bed, facing both Di Carlo and my uncle, and pulled Marc down to sit beside me. "Malone said we'd have five days to bury Dad and come up with a new Alpha. Today's Monday. He's planning to swoop in with his puppet Alpha on Saturday, so we just have to ramp up our own schedule and make sure he's too late."

"A preemptive attack?" Di Carlo stepped into the room and leaned against the wall beside my uncle's chair. "I see a lot of obvious risks, but we don't have a lot of options."

"Or a lot of time," Uncle Rick added.

I nodded. "And that's where the creative timeline comes in. We'll spread the word that the funeral is on Friday, but we'll actually hold a small, quiet service on Wednesday morning. Friday, we move in on Malone in his own territory. With any luck, we'll catch him off guard, while he's still getting his toy soldiers together." I glanced from Di Carlo to my uncle, trying to read their expressions. "We take out Malone and his men, and without its head, the rest of the political beast should just flop around on the ground and die."

"I like it." Marc wrapped one arm around my waist.

Jace stepped into the room with two steaming mugs, grinning at me and pointedly ignoring Marc. "Especially the part with the flopping and dying."

"Yeah, that's kind of the highlight." I accepted the coffee he offered, then I turned to the other Alphas, and the gravity of what I was planning truly sank in. "We're going to need every single tom we have. All of them." I glanced from one to the other as I spoke. "I know this isn't really your battle, so I understand if you want to bow out. But I need to know now… Are you with me on this?"

Uncle Rick frowned. "This *is* my battle, Faythe. Almost as much as it is yours. Your father was more than a friend to me, and more than an in-law. He was practically a brother, but even if he wasn't, I would never let my sister's Pride be taken over by an Alpha with no connection to the land or the people." He cleared his throat, and his eyes looked suddenly shiny. "I was born into the south-central Pride, remember? And even though I've been Alpha of my wife's Pride for more than two decades, the south-central territory still feels like home. It always will—unless Malone handpicks some strange tom with questionable motives and obvious loyalties to the Appalachian Pride or its Alpha."

He exhaled slowly and looked resolute in the dim glow of the overhead bulb. "I can't let that happen."

"Neither can I." Di Carlo looked as grave as I'd ever seen him, and he seemed to have aged ten years in the past few hours.

"Thank you." I swallowed the lump in my throat and blinked back grateful tears. "Thank you both so much." Marc's arm tightened around me and I wondered if it was okay for an Alpha to snuggle. "What about Aaron Taylor? Do you think there's any chance he'll fight with us?"

Di Carlo nodded. "Every chance in the world."

"He may not think you're ready to run the Pride on your own just yet…" My uncle began. "But there's no way he'll stand by and let Malone put someone else in charge of it. I'll talk to him and call you to confirm that he's in."

"Thanks." I closed my eyes, going over the preliminary plan for weak spots and faulty logic. "Am I missing anything? Any suggestions?"

"How are you going to make Malone believe the funeral's set for Friday?" Di Carlo asked. "If you just tell him that, he'll know you're lying."

My uncle nodded and leaned back in his chair. "I think your best bet would be to avoid all contact with the Appalachian Pride, because if you start feeding him false information directly he's going to know it."

"Yeah, I figure the only way to make him believe what we want is to make him work for the false information." I stood and had paced halfway across the room before I realized what I was doing—or that my father had often done the same thing. "So we'll actually invite everyone for a Friday funeral, including Paul Blackwell. He's the one Malone will go to for information, since none of his own allies will be invited. Blackwell won't go out of his way to help Malone, but he won't outright lie to him, either, and Malone knows that. So when Blackwell tells him the funeral is scheduled for Friday, Malone will believe it."

Marc twisted on the bed to face me. "The only problem I see with that is the rumor mill. How are you going to keep Malone from hearing about it when people leave home for the funeral a full day early? Someone, somewhere, will mention something to a friend, brother, or cousin working for Malone, and then our timeline is busted."

I shook my head slowly and turned to cross the room again before answering. "Malone won't hear about people leaving early for the funeral, because no one will be coming." I glanced from Uncle Rick to Bert Di Carlo, then back, already regretting what I would say next. "Including you guys."

"Wait, we're not invited to the funeral?" My uncle looked like I'd just slapped him, but I shook my head firmly.

"No one is—at least, not to the real one on Wednesday. Marc's right. There's no way to keep Malone from hearing about people coming from all over the country…hell, all over the *world*—" because my father knew many international Alphas "—for the funeral. Our only real option is a quiet, ranch-residents-only burial. Then, when all this is over, we'll have a proper memorial."

Uncle Rick sighed, his jaw firmly set. "Well, I can't

say I like it, but if it works, I guess the ends justify the means."

Di Carlo nodded and crossed his arms over his chest. "Of course, we'll have to tell our men something, or else they'll walk into a fight expecting a funeral."

I glanced at Marc. "Yeah, we'll have to do the same for our men." The nonenforcer Pride members, all of whom would be called in for the fight.

"Don't tell them until Thursday night," Marc said, looking from me to Di Carlo, then to my uncle. "That way they'll have all night to mentally prepare for war in Appalachia instead of a funeral in Texas, but hopefully not long enough for the inevitable rumors to spread to Malone."

And those rumors *were* inevitable, in a society where everyone had friends or family members in another Pride.

"Well, it's far from flawless, but it's certainly a plan," Di Carlo said, as my uncle rose from his chair. "I'm sorry about how all this has turned out, Faythe."

I stood and extended my hand for him to shake, but Di Carlo pulled me close instead, and kissed me on the forehead—another unusual act for two Alphas. But frankly, the way things were shaping up, history would label my term as Alpha with much stronger adjectives than *unusual*.

"You can handle this," Di Carlo said, when he stepped back to look down at me. "We can handle this together, just the way your father would have wanted it."

"Thank you," I said, and my throat felt thick again from holding back more tears.

Di Carlo nodded, then turned suddenly and headed

into the living room. I had the distinct impression that he was resisting tears, too.

"Give me a call when you guys get home," my uncle said, shaking Marc's hand. Then he turned to me. "I was only about five years older than you are when I became an Alpha, and I remember how scared I was, even with my father-in-law still around to help when I needed him. So I can't imagine how much pressure you must be under right now. But I know this—your father wouldn't have left you in charge if he wasn't completely sure you could do this. And I wouldn't be backing you up if I weren't completely sure he was right."

I couldn't stop the tears that time; the best I could do was to wipe them on my sleeve before they could fall. "Is it okay for one Alpha to hug another?"

Uncle Rick gave me a sad, slow smile. "It is now." He pulled me into a hug and squeezed me so tight I couldn't move. "You're a different kind of Alpha, Faythe. A new breed. And that difference is part of your strength. Don't try to be like the rest of us. Not even like your father. Malone's never understood you, so he doesn't know how to deal with you. And he won't know how to fight you. So long as you stay true to yourself."

I nodded, because that felt like good advice. And it might have been even more valuable, if I had any clue who the hell I really was.

We said a heartfelt, apologetic goodbye to Elias Keller, then left him Brian's phone and an extra battery. Malone and his allies were planning to stay at the complex for a couple more days, and Keller promised to let us know if they started any more trouble, or if he had a chance to destroy the rest of their guns.

The drive from Montana to the Lazy S took just over thirty hours, including bathroom breaks. We ate greasy convenience-store food in the van and took turns behind the wheel and sleeping in the back row, so we could drive without stopping for the night.

Dr. Carver's flight landed two hours before we left, so he rode back with us, next to Brian in the third row.

It was the single worst road trip of my entire life, and I spent a good six hours of it curled up in the second row, using Vic's thigh as a pillow, so that neither Marc nor Jace would feel neglected in favor of the other. But the closer we got to Texas, the harder it became for me to sleep. I couldn't stop thinking about my mother, and what I was going to say to her. Or my dad wrapped in plastic in the cargo area—such an undignified position for the most dignified person I'd ever known.

When Marc finally turned the van onto our quarter-mile-long gravel driveway on Tuesday afternoon, I was numb, inside and out. Nothing felt real anymore. My entire world had been reduced to highway sounds and the scents of grease and exhaust. And in spite of spending more than a day in the car with nothing to do, when we arrived home I realized there was nowhere near enough time to accomplish everything that needed to be done.

I was out of the van before Marc shut off the engine, and the front door opened before I made it up the steps. My mother lurched onto the porch with Michael on her heels, and she collapsed into my arms before I'd even realized her intent.

She clung to me, sobbing, and her tears soaked through the shoulder of my wrinkled blouse.

"Mom…" I glanced at Michael over her shoulder, but

he only shrugged and leaned against the door facing. His glasses sat crooked on his nose, his hair stood up funny on one side, like he'd been sleeping on it, and his eyes were ringed in dark, dark circles.

"Mom..." I tried again, and this time held her at arm's length so she'd have to look at me.

My mother looked like hell. Her slacks were wrinkled, her blouse was stained with coffee, and her straight, chin-length gray hair was tangled like she'd tried to pull it out a handful at a time. Her face was red and swollen from crying, and her gaze searched mine desperately when she stared back at me. "Is it true?"

"I'm sorry. Mom, I'm so, so sorry." I blinked through fresh tears and pushed hair back from her face, trying to find some semblance of the mother I knew. She was in there somewhere, buried beneath soul-shredding grief and denial.

"I want to see him. Bring him in—I need to see him."

"No, Mom, you don't want to..."

"Katherine Faythe Sanders, you will not argue with me." She stood up straight and tugged her blouse into place, as if that would restore her usually flawless composure and appearance. "He's my husband, and I want to see him."

"Okay, Mom..." Michael stepped forward to put his arm around her and led us both away from the door so the guys could bring the bags in. "But we can't bring him inside." He looked at me then, his expression half exhaustion, half apology. "Holly's here. She thinks it was a car wreck, so the gunshot wound is going to be hard to explain."

Great. I had to unclench my jaw to speak. "What the hell is she doing here?"

"She's trying to help," Michael snapped, while our mother stared at the van, silent tears rolling down her cheeks. "What was I supposed to do, tell her she wasn't welcome at my father's funeral?"

"You're right. I'm sorry." I closed my eyes and sucked in a deep breath before making eye contact again. "It's just that this is a colossally bad time to have a human wandering around the ranch."

He sighed. "I know."

But he didn't really know. I hadn't told any of them about Malone's threat to replace me as Alpha, because I wanted to deliver the extrabad news in person, so I'd only have to say it once.

"I need to talk to you. I need to talk to everyone who isn't Holly, actually. In the office. It's…it's bad, Michael."

He held my gaze for a moment, apparently trying to judge our placement on the disaster scale by my expression alone. Then he nodded and left our mother with me while he went to gather the rest of the household.

"Mom?" I said, and she turned away from the van to look at me. The tears had stopped and she'd composed herself. Now she just looked exhausted, and wrung out, and…*old.* "I need to talk to you, and it's important. Are you… Are you going to be able to listen?" *And understand…?* Because I knew as well as anyone what havoc grief could play on a person's comprehension.

"I'll be fine once I've seen him. I just… I have to see for myself."

"Okay. If you're sure."

She nodded and crossed her arms over her wrinkled blouse. "I'm sure."

"Just a minute." I jogged down the steps and met Marc by the van. "Hey, could you guys drive to the barn and lay him out in there? Mom wants to see him, and I can't talk her out of it." And honestly, the sooner she saw him, the sooner she could start to accept his death.

"No problem." Marc slid in behind the wheel while Vic climbed into the passenger seat, and they headed for the barn in the east field.

My mother started down the steps to follow them, but I stopped her with a hand on her arm. "Mom." I looked pointedly at her bare feet, and she followed my gaze. "Shoes."

She nodded absently and headed into the house, brushing past Jace on his way out.

"How you holdin' up?" he asked, and I let him fold me into a hug. A chaste, comforting hug, with my cheek on his shoulder, because we hadn't told those who'd missed the floor show in Montana about our relationship yet.

"My head's spinning, and there's a little nausea," I admitted softly. "There's so much to do. So much to say. It's too much all at once, for them and for me. And I honestly have no idea where to begin."

"Start with your mom," Jace suggested. "She needs you, and she shouldn't have to hear about all of this with everyone else there." I nodded, and he pulled away so he could see my face. "And as much as I hate to say it, maybe the part about you and me shouldn't be a broadcast announcement. It's not really anyone else's business, and they have more important things to focus on right now."

I scrounged up a smile. "Mr. Hammond, I believe you're getting wise in your advanced age."

He chuckled softly. "Twenty-six doesn't feel as young today as it did last month."

"Neither does twenty-three and three-quarters."

"Faythe?" my mother called, and we both looked up, startled. I stepped away from Jace and realized that if we hadn't looked suspicious before, we did then.

Smooth. So much for not telling anyone yet…

"Are you ready?" I asked, and she nodded. "I'll go with you. Jace, could you check on Kaci? Tell her I'll be there in a minute?"

He nodded and ducked into the house, pushing the door closed behind him.

My mother and I walked in silence for almost a minute, our shoes crunching first on gravel, then on the frozen, well-worn path through the east field. The main house lay behind us, long and squat, a one-story ranch house my father had designed before I was born. The barn stood ahead, much older than the house and picturesque with its peeling red paint and tall gables. I'd lived most of my life in and around those two buildings, but I'd never once imagined myself living there without my father.

I hadn't even been in the house yet, but already home didn't feel entirely like home without him. I felt like I was playing pretend, or like I'd wake up any moment from a nightmare.

"So…you and Jace?" my mother said, and I froze, then had to jog to catch up with her.

"Was it that obvious?"

"Subtlety was never your strong suit, Faythe." She stopped to look at me, and I searched her eyes for disapproval or reproach, but I found nothing I recognized, other than the fact that she was searching for something in my eyes, too. "You love him." It wasn't a question; it was a statement uttered with the confidence of long-held authority on the subject.

"Yeah. But we don't have to talk about this now. It's not really the time...."

"Faythe, there's never going to be a good time for this discussion, and I think you know that."

I nodded. Whether because she had advice to offer or because she wanted to distract herself from a reality she soon wouldn't be able to avoid, she obviously wanted to talk about my screwed-up love life. And I would have done anything she wanted in that moment, if it would help her deal with our mutual loss.

"What about Marc?"

I sighed and absently kicked a rock at my feet. "I still love Marc so much it hurts to turn around and not see him next to me. Jace is something…different. Something separate, but *strong.*"

My mother frowned, then finally nodded. "You have to choose."

Why does everyone keep saying that? "I know."

"Marc is Alpha material, Faythe, and if Jace ever starts to show any Alpha tendencies…this could get very bad."

"He already has tendencies," I said, and she nodded again, as if I'd just confirmed her suspicion. "How did you know?"

"I knew because I know you. You're strong, Faythe. Too strong for most toms. Most tomcats will either expect you to obey them, because you're a woman, or to lead them, because you're an Alpha now. But you're only ever going to love men who will be led by you, yet can hold their own with you. Men who challenge you."

I shook my head hesitantly. "But Jace doesn't challenge me." Not yet, anyway...

Her sad smile spoke volumes, and her eyes seemed to peer right into my head, and maybe my heart. "Yes, he does, or you wouldn't be interested in him. My guess is that he challenges you to be true to yourself. That he dares you to take risks you're secretly dying to take, and to feel things you're afraid to let yourself feel." She closed her eyes, and when they opened again, they shined with aching wistfulness, and some spark of excitement I couldn't comprehend. "He makes you feel alive, doesn't he? Like the entire world is one dangling live wire, just waiting for you to grab on and ride the current."

I stared at her like she'd suddenly started speaking Russian—and I understood it. "How on earth do you know that?"

Her smile grew wistful with distant memory. "I know because your father was my live wire."

Twenty

The barn doors were closed, and knowing my father's body lay beyond them made his death feel somehow even more real—more devastating—than when I'd witnessed his last breath.

"Mom, you don't have to do this." I slid one arm around her shoulders while we stared at the doors, neither of us moving to open them.

"Yes, I do." She swallowed thickly, and that spark of memory—my father as her live wire—was gone, replaced with pain and dread so thick and heavy I could practically taste them on the air. "If I don't see him, I'm never going to really believe it, because he's alive in here." She laid one trembling, gloveless hand over her chest. "He's so alive inside me that I can still hear him."

"What is he saying?" I asked, as her face blurred beneath my tears. I'd failed her more than anyone.

"He's calling me a coward." Her voice broke on the last word, and she sniffled in the cold, the wrinkles at the corners of her eyes suddenly more defined than I'd ever seen them.

"No, Mom, he would never call you a coward." Not even if it were true. He would never intentionally hurt her, and he'd never forgive himself for doing it unintentionally. "You're hearing yourself." She was the source of my frank tongue, if not the coarse language that often fell from it.

"I know." She sniffed again and stood straighter. "But it sounds like him. He's daring me to go in there and deal with this, so I can come out stronger and ready to do what has to be done. The funeral and the packing." She faced me then, eyes wide with real horror. "Faythe, I don't think I can pack up his things."

"Then don't. Who says you have to?" I tried to smile, but the best I could manage was a not-frown. "There are no rules, Mom. There's no grief timeline." Other than the five-day Alpha deadline I still hadn't told her about.

"You're right." She took a long, deep breath, then turned back to the barn. "I'm ready."

We went in through the normal-size side door, and my mother froze two feet into the barn. Marc stood beside a platform made of leftover hay bales, upon which a dark blanket covered my father's still form. I wasn't sure where they'd found the blanket, but I was grateful. It felt much less cold and sterile than sheet plastic.

When my mother finally approached, her shoulders shaking with silent sobs, he folded the top of the blanket back to my father's neck. I tried not to look, but I couldn't stop myself.

I'd seen a lot of death, of both friends and enemies, but seeing it on my father was an entirely different experience. His face had grayed since I'd last seen it, and he no longer looked alive enough for me to pretend he was only sleeping.

My mother shrugged out from under my arm and approached him slowly. Marc backed away to give her some privacy, and we joined Vic near the first long-empty horse stall, where he stared down at his own worn black hiking boots. His face was red, his eyes swollen.

Marc looked much the same. I wrapped my arms around him for a moment, then twisted in his hold to press my back against his chest.

My mom dropped onto her knees on the dirty barn floor. She put one hand on my father's cold chest and pressed the other against her own mouth, like she could stop the whole thing from being real if she could only hold back the words.

But she couldn't.

I didn't hear what she whispered, and I didn't want to. Some things are private. Some things needed to be said, even when the person who needed to hear them couldn't hear anything. Ever again.

Thoughts ran through my head so fast I couldn't truly focus on any of them. So much to be done. So little I knew how to do. So very much pain I didn't have time to deal with.

The funeral. The fight. Planning for both. Maybe I could funnel my anger over the necessity of burying my father into the plot to assassinate Malone and ruthlessly gut my father's murderer. You know, two birds, one big, bloody stone? That's an efficient use of anger motivation, right?

And Kaci. Somehow I'd have to find a way to talk to her about the fact that she'd just lost someone else.

The man who had taken her in and protected her with everything he had—including his youngest son's life—after she'd lost her own family. Kaci couldn't take much more loss, and I couldn't in good conscience tell her that my father's death would be the last.

Chances were good that we would lose someone else. Maybe several someones.

No. I went stiff in Marc's grip, and his arms tightened around me, wordlessly comforting me even though he didn't understand what had upset me.

Planning the fight was one thing, but anticipating the tragic outcome was another entirely. I couldn't think about who those potential casualties might be. Except for me. One of them might be me, and then what would happen to the Pride when I was gone?

"It doesn't feel like thirty-three years," my mother said, and I looked up from my own thoughts to see her still kneeling, still facing my father, but obviously speaking to us. "I would never have thought three decades could possibly feel so fleeting, but it feels like I slid my hand into his last week and promised to love him forever. And I've never regretted a single moment of it. Not even when he left the bathroom light on or when he fell asleep at his desk at two in the morning."

I didn't know what to say. I didn't know how to stop my silent tears, or how best to dry hers.

"We used to run together, you know. Just the two of us, out in the woods, euphoric over the wind, and the smells, and each other. We never needed anything else, but we were blessed with so very much more." She twisted to look at me then, and the pain etched into her face brought me to my knees, the ache in my heart an endless, nameless oblivion.

Marc let me go and I crossed the floor toward her.

"We were blessed with you, and with your brothers. As you grew up, I felt so helpless, like I could do little more than watch as you became your own people, all five of you. It was like witnessing a miracle, and it happened so *quickly.* One day we were fascinated by how tiny Michael's newborn feet were in those little booties, and the next, you took off for college without a backward glance. I don't know where the time went, but I spent it all with him, and it slipped away so fast."

I sat next to her on the floor, the straw scratching my back through my shirt, and pressed as close to my mother as I could get. Touch was the only comfort I knew how to give; words had abandoned me entirely.

"I don't know how to live now, Faythe," she whispered. "They say you never know what you have until it's gone, but I knew. I knew every moment, and I don't know what I'm supposed to do now, with him gone."

"You still have us," I said, well aware that we weren't enough. Having grown children wasn't the same as having the love of your life. The other half of your own soul. But I had nothing else to offer her.

Except his last words.

"He gave me a message for you," I said, and she turned to face me, her blue eyes red with tears and wide with hope. "He said to tell you that you're his whole life, and have been since the moment he met you. He said that you're in his heart, and in his soul, and even death will never really separate you."

And I believed it. If any love could transcend both time and life, it would be my parents' love.

My mother sobbed again, but this time she was

smiling, and I was glad I'd saved his message for that moment. When she truly needed it.

She sat there for several minutes, thinking. Probably remembering. Then she blinked and gave her head a little shake, and I knew she was back in the present. "We have to bury him. I have to call people…"

How could I possibly tell her that we couldn't do that? That we'd have to bury him like a criminal in the night, to keep the political fallout from making everything impossibly worse?

"I haven't even told Rick yet."

"He knows," I whispered.

She looked startled for a moment, then she nodded. "Of course he knows. He was there. I should have been there."

No, she shouldn't have.

"Mom…we have to talk about the rest of this. About what else happened."

She looked up, and I was relieved to see clarity in her eyes, even if her hand still stroked his arm, unmoving on the bale of hay. "He named you, I know." She looked suddenly worried. "That was always his plan, but it happened so soon.…"

"Yes. He left me in charge of the Pride, but, Mom, the council won't recognize me, and if we don't have an 'acceptable' Alpha by Saturday, Malone's going to try to place one of his own choosing."

My mother's eyes flashed with fury, and her entire form went stiff. "He'll have to kill me to do it."

"Us, too," Marc said, and Vic nodded.

But actually, he only had to kill *me*.

"Faythe?" Owen said, and I looked up to see him standing in the doorway with Parker. Owen held his worn cowboy hat over his chest, and as I stood, his gaze slid past me to the bales of hay where our father lay. He stepped forward, and I helped my mother to her feet, then went to meet my brother.

Owen's arms slid around me along with the scents of clean sweat and earth. There wasn't much farmwork to do on an animal-free ranch in February, but the telling scents clung to his hat and his boots, triggering a warm, familiar comfort I wouldn't find anywhere else, now that Ethan was gone.

But comfort could only do so much.

"I should have been there," he said into my hair, his chin stubble scratching my forehead.

"There's nothing you could have done." But I couldn't tell myself the same thing. I'd seen it coming. I'd seen Dean aiming his gun, and I hadn't moved fast enough. I couldn't. "We can't fight bullets." But we could rip off the hands holding the guns.

"Mom's taking it hard,"

"I know. We all are." My father's death was shock and devastation like none of us had ever felt. It changed everything. We were hacking a new path through virgin territory without him, and the backlash of branches had already left me bruised. "We'll get through it—with a healthy dose of ass kicking disguised as therapy."

"Speaking of which…" Owen let me go and stepped back, gesturing for Parker to come forward.

Parker held out his arms for a hug, and I tried to ignore the fact that he smelled like whiskey. Like a *lot* of whiskey. "I'm so sorry, Faythe," he said, when he let me go, running one hand through graying hair that suddenly seemed to be more salt than pepper.

Over his shoulder, I saw Owen wrap one arm

around our mother while they shared a private, silent viewing.

Parker cleared his throat and glanced at his feet before looking up again. "You saw my dad? How was he?"

I sighed and resisted the urge to avoid his eyes. Delivering bad news was definitely my least favorite part of the job so far. "Well, let's just say he is not my biggest fan. In fact, he may be the charter member of the 'Faythe must die a slow and messy death' club."

Parker cringed. "That bad?"

"He called me a disgrace and a whore."

"Why would he call you a whore?" Owen asked, twisting to face us without letting go of our mother.

"What, the disgrace part doesn't surprise you?" I forced a grin to let him know I was kidding—and to avoid answering his question. Behind him, Marc stiffened and crossed his arms over his chest.

Parker frowned, too distracted by his personal problems to even process Owen's question. "I just… I'm so sorry for how my dad treated you. How he's probably going to treat us all."

I shook my head and stared up at him, trying to convey import with my gaze alone. "It's not your responsibility to apologize for your father. None of this is your fault."

"Knowing that doesn't lessen the guilt."

"I know." Jace felt the same way about his stepfather's leading role in the effort to take over our Pride, and I had similar feelings about both my brother's and father's deaths. Guilt was the least rational emotion I'd ever experienced—and the most difficult to overcome.

"Hey, Brian said we missed the formal swearing,

so—" Parker shrugged, and at his words, Owen and my mother turned toward us "—we're ready to make up for lost time."

Owen forced a sad smile, one hand curling the rim of his dusty brown hat. "I think the only good thing to come out of this whole thing is the fact that my sister is now the first female Alpha in werecat history. Disgraced or not."

"She was already working hard on infamy, so I'm not sure this really makes that much difference," Marc quipped.

My mother frowned. "It makes all the difference in the world." Her warm, thin hand slipped into mine. "I'm proud of you, Faythe. Your father would be, too."

I blinked back more tears. How long would it be before we could talk about him without crying?

"I can't… I don't think I can be what he was." I swallowed thickly, and her hand squeezed mine. "At least, not yet. But Marc and Uncle Rick promised to serve as advisers, and I was hoping you would, too, when things settle down a little."

She actually managed a half smile at that. "I'm even prouder of you now."

"So, no one can come to the funeral?" Owen said, and I nodded, leaning over the back of my father's armchair. I couldn't bring myself to actually sit in it, but I had to assume some physical position of authority. It was expected. Sometimes people recognize leaders based on subconscious clues, and standing near my father's traditional seat of authority was the simplest, most seamless way I knew to reinforce the idea of me as his successor.

But since Owen and Parker had sworn their loyalty and no one present had questioned my authority yet, I couldn't help wondering if I was really trying to convince myself.

"No one who isn't already here," I qualified. "But once this is all over, we'll have a true memorial. He *will* be properly remembered."

"But not inviting people seems so…cold," Brian said, from the couch where he sat with Parker and Marc.

"Quite the opposite, really." My mother spoke softly, but had no trouble capturing everyone's attention from her perch on the love seat next to Manx. "It will be intimate. A small, closed burial will give us a chance to mourn him in private before we have to put our grief on display for everyone else he ever knew."

And just like that, it was settled. *Thank goodness.* I was in awe of my mother.

"Then we fight?" Eagerness bled through Vic's voice like spilled wine through silk.

"Yes, and we don't leave the Appalachian territory until I personally verify that Calvin Malone is no longer breathing. Colin Dean is the secondary objective, and while I'd love the chance to give him a slow, agonizing death for what he did to our Alpha, we can't afford to be that picky. I'll take him dead if taking him alive doesn't look possible." And if I knew Dean, he'd make us kill him rather than be taken prisoner.

"Is there a specific plan, beyond kill, maim, and capture?" Parker asked, looking grimmer than I'd ever seen him. He was taking the news about his father very badly, and I could smell the whiskey on his breath even from across the room. I'd have to talk to him about that.

"Yes, actually. Obviously, Patricia and Melody

Malone are completely off-limits, though you have permission to protect yourselves from them as necessary." And I was living proof that an angry tabby could be just as hard to handle as a tomcat. "As for everyone else, kill only if you have to. We're trying to whack off the enemy's head, not hack him into a million pieces, and a little mercy can go a long way."

"It can also get you killed," Parker said.

"Yeah. Let's try not to let that happen." I blinked and forced my eyes to refocus as I glanced around the room at all the faces watching me. "In addition to all that, we'll have backup from the East Coast, the Midwest, and the southeast Prides." Uncle Rick, Aaron Taylor, and Bert Di Carlo's men, of course. "As well as air support from a Flight of thunderbirds. At least, that's the plan." Though we had yet to actually secure their help, because they could only be contacted in person.

When the mumbles of surprise subsided, I continued, unable to completely bury my grim smile. "I'm hoping all of that turns out to be major overkill, but this is our last good shot at taking Malone out, and we are *not* going to mess it up."

That time, the general sentiment was approval, and a palpable surge of bloodlust-tinged anticipation.

When I'd answered the rest of the questions and outlined the basics of the private burial, I dismissed the meeting with a suggestion that everyone get some sleep. There'd be little time to rest after the funeral the next day.

"Well done," Marc said, as the last of the toms filed into the hallway.

I was exhausted, mentally and physically, and I really wanted to sit. I glanced down at my dad's chair, and Jace chuckled. "You can sit there, you know. I don't think he'd mind."

I shook my head. "I'm not ready. It feels weird." And there was nowhere else in the room to sit without looking like I was taking sides; Marc sat on the couch, and Jace sat on the love seat.

"So, are you going to stand up for every meeting?" Marc grinned like he was joking, but he wasn't. And what he really wanted to ask was if I intended to stand, rather than choose between the two of them.

"Maybe. At least until I figure out…what works best."

"Are you hungry?" Jace asked, and Marc scowled.

"No. I'm fine. Listen, guys…" I released a long exhale and finally sank onto the arm of my father's chair, one foot on the ground for balance. "You don't need to wait on me. I don't want you to. I can cook my own food and get my own coffee."

Marc actually laughed. "Faythe, you don't cook worth a damn."

"Okay, you've got me there." However, unless we were talking frozen pizza or hamburgers, neither did either of them. "But my point is that I can't be my dad, and you don't need to treat me like him. I'm still trying to figure all this out—figure out who I need to be, to be Alpha—and the last thing I need is for you two to start acting weird around me."

Jace chuckled. "At the risk of pissing Marc off, I don't think either of us has any intention of treating you like your dad."

Marc scowled again, but he couldn't argue. "I just want to take care of you, Faythe."

"I know. And I really do appreciate it. I just… I have

a lot to sort out right now. I'll get it figured out. I swear. But right now, I have to talk to Kaci."

I left them in the office, but I stopped to listen just outside the door when I heard Marc speak. "You're not making this any easier on her," he snapped, and I could practically feel Jace bristle, even with a wall separating us.

"*I'm* not making it easier on her? You're the one brooding and pouting and…"

I cleared my throat where they could hear, then headed toward the kitchen to rescue Kaci from Holly.

Twenty-one

"You're a cousin, right, Karli?" Holly said, and I pressed my back to the wall to eavesdrop for the second time in as many minutes. I'd asked Kaci to keep Michael's human wife occupied during the Shifter-only meeting in the office.

"Um... Yeah." Kaci hadn't actually had to use the identity my father had created for her with anyone but Holly so far, and I mentally crossed my fingers that she would remember it. "Why?"

"Are the other branches of this family so...weird?"

"What do you mean?" Kaci asked, and I cringed. We all knew exactly what Holly meant.

"Private funerals. Practically weekly family emergencies, usually in the middle of the night. Closed-door family meetings that include the employees, but not the daughter-in-law. Farmhands who live on the property, even though there's no livestock at all, and in the winter there isn't even any hay."

"I don't know about any of that," Kaci hedged. "My family didn't have a farm."

I almost laughed out loud.

"So, where is your family?" Holly asked, with all the sensitivity of a drunken frat boy. "Why do you live with your cousins instead of your parents?"

Aaaand, there's my cue...

I rounded the corner into the kitchen to save Kaci from having to reply, trying to look like I hadn't been listening in. Kaci sat at the breakfast bar, her long, thick brown waves pulled into a tight braid. Holly stood opposite her, measuring cocoa powder to dump into a saucepan of milk. She wore only eye makeup and had pulled her hair into a simple ponytail at the base of her skull. In jeans and a snug tee, she looked nothing like the pictures I'd seen of her on the runway, but she was still beautiful, even without all the professional hair and cosmetic artists molding her into the guise of perfection. She looked...clean and honest, if more than a little confused.

"Hey, Faythe, we're making hot chocolate." Her smile was sincere, even as her concerned gaze studied me for clues about how I was taking my father's untimely death. "You want some?"

Hot chocolate, the old-fashioned way, and unassisted beauty. No wonder Michael loved her, in spite of the obvious Shifting handicap.

"Um, sure." I slid onto the bar stool beside Kaci and gave her a subtle nod to tell her that everything was okay—as okay as it could be, considering—and that I'd fill her in soon.

"Do you have any mint extract? It's really good with chocolate...."

"Check my mom's baking cabinet." I gestured to the cabinet doors behind her, and the only human Sanders turned to look.

I probably would have liked Holly, too, if I wasn't always so busy trying to keep secrets from her. We couldn't tell her what we really were because disclosure of our existence to a human was a capital offense. Punishable by execution. Not that the Territorial Council was in any shape to enforce such a sentence at the moment, but as much of a pain as she could be at times, none of us wanted to expose either Holly or Michael to any unnecessary danger.

"Is everything okay?" Holly glanced toward the hall to indicate the meeting I'd just concluded without actually mentioning it in front of Kaci. Her intent was sweet—protect the child from all mention of tragedy—but a bit ironic, considering that Kaci knew much more about my father's death—not to mention his life—than she did.

"As okay as can be expected, considering." I ran my hand down the length of Kaci's braid, and she gave me a sad smile, accepting physical comfort on instinct, the strongest werecat impulse I'd seen in her yet.

"Good." Holly poured two drops of mint extract from the lid of the bottle into the saucepan, then opened a five-pound bag of granulated sugar and picked up a measuring cup. "I was just asking the munchkin here about her family."

Kaci went stiff, but Holly didn't notice. I rubbed Kaci's back, then started to step in for the official redirect, but Kaci beat me to it, her face caught somewhere between a scowl and a gloat. "She said we're weird."

Holly flushed instantly, and her eyes went wide. "I didn't... That's not what I meant."

"I know." I tossed my head toward the hall and Holly

frowned, then nodded and followed me with a promise to "Karli" that we'd be right back.

There was nothing Kaci liked to talk about less than the fact that she'd accidentally killed her mother and sister during her first, completely unexpected Shift. Kaci was what the experts were calling a "double recessive." She was our miracle tabby, born to two human parents who had no idea they both carried the recessive werecat "gene." Though it's actually quite a bit more complicated than the simplistic phrasing I clung to.

Kaci's human father assumed she'd died in the "animal attack" that killed his wife and older daughter in Canada, and he'd only recently given up the search for her body. But as far as I was concerned, Kaci got the worse end of the deal. She'd had no idea what was happening to her during her first Shift and she was forever haunted by the role she unintentionally played in her mother's and sister's deaths. And unlike her father, she could never achieve closure because while he could mourn her and eventually move on, she knew he was still alive, but out of reach. Because we couldn't send a teenage Shifter back to live with a human father, even if she wouldn't have had to explain her absence and her family's deaths.

In the hall, I whispered. I knew perfectly well that Kaci could hear us, but Holly did not.

"She doesn't like to talk about her family," I began, glancing into the kitchen once, as if to make sure that Kaci wasn't listening. "They died a few months ago, and we're all she has left, so she's with us for good now."

"Oh, how horrible for her!" Holly whispered, pale brows drawing low on her lineless forehead. Then she cringed, as what she'd actually said sank in. "The death part, not the part about being with you guys." She shook her head as if to reset her train of thought, while I stifled a smile. "Was it another accident?"

"Sort of. It was actually a bizarre animal attack." The key to lying effectively is to stick as close to the truth as possible. I don't *like* to lie, but when I have to do it, I want to get away with it.

On the edge of my vision, I saw Kaci stiffen again, but again Holly missed it.

"You guys have had the worst run of luck! First Karli's family, then Ethan, and now your dad… Fortunately, I don't have anywhere to be for the next two weeks, so I'm completely at your disposal. Just tell me what I can do to help."

I swallowed a groan of frustration and forced my lips into a halfhearted smile, trying to keep in mind that she had no idea she was making my job harder. Or even that I had a job. "Thanks. I'm gonna steal her away for a few minutes, but we'll be back for hot chocolate."

"Sure…" Holly went back to her cocoa and I gestured for Kaci to follow me to my room. Then I thought better of it and redirected us toward the office, which Marc and Jace had left empty. Holly didn't have supernatural hearing, but I didn't want to risk her overhearing anything, just in case.

I closed the door behind Kaci and we sat on opposite ends of the couch, facing each other with our feet tucked beneath us. "Thanks for keeping Holly occupied," I began, suddenly wishing I already had that mug of cocoa. Or better yet, coffee.

"She seems to think she was babysitting me. Are you sure she's not right?"

"I swear on my best pair of boots. I just needed an

excuse to keep her out of the meeting. I have no intention of hiding anything from you."

"Does that mean I get the boots if you're lying?"

I raised both brows at her, hoping she was kidding. "They won't fit you. And I'm not lying."

"Good," she said, and a tiny bit of the tension inside me eased. "I'd rather have my own boots, anyway." She pulled her braid over one shoulder and fingered the end of it like the bristles of a paintbrush. "So… Owen says you're the Alpha now. Does that mean you got smarter?"

I waited for some sign that she was kidding, but none came.

I sighed. "Unfortunately, no. And I'm not any older, faster, or scarier. Nor have I suddenly developed an increase in testosterone or a decrease in ovaries. In fact, just between you and me, I may be the least qualified Alpha in history."

She thought about that, then frowned. "I don't think so. I've met Calvin Malone, remember?"

"Thanks. It helps to know that, in the opinion of a thirteen-year-old, I'm better qualified than a complete megalomaniac."

She frowned. "A mega what?"

"Never mind. I just meant that Malone's a big, power-hungry nutjob."

"No arguments there."

"Mom, come on. It's too cold for you to stay out here." She'd spent most of the last day in the barn, trying to say goodbye to my father, and I was starting to worry about her physical health, as well as her emotional well-being.

"I'm not ready to go." She wiped her red, dripping nose on a tissue already soaked with tears, but didn't even look at me. "Not until it's over. All of it."

"Please, Mom." I crossed my arms over my chest, trying to stop my own shivering, but there was little point in even trying. The homemade, half-full grave at my feet was the cause of my chattering teeth and shaking limbs, rather than the cold.

Everyone else had already gone inside to mourn in quiet solitude or in somber groups. Except for Marc, Jace, Vic, and Parker, who had dug the grave, and were now refilling it in their funeral clothes, because changing into work clothes felt somehow disrespectful.

"I'm not ready, Faythe." My mother looked up that time, and great beads of moisture clung to her bare lashes and cheeks. "I need…a little more…time."

"Okay." The only real difference between my mother's mourning process and mine was that I had something important to distract me from the cold chasm growing within me with each glance at his grave, and she did not. I would lose myself in plans for the invasion of the Appalachian territory. I would focus on the burn of bloodlust in my veins rather than the agony of loss. I would pour every last drop of my pain and rage into the details, and the resulting carnage would be my father's true memorial, infinitely more heartfelt than the headstone still on order.

Shovel in hand, Marc shot me a look of sympathy that melted into concern when he saw my face. Was it that obvious?

He stabbed his shovel into the soil hard enough to make it stand up on its own. I flinched at the raw thunk, then ground my teeth in irritation over my own squeamishness. That would have to go. If it wouldn't help us beat Malone, it had no business in my head until he'd joined my father in the ground.

I took off my coat and draped it over my mother's shoulders, on top of her own, as Marc veered toward me from the side of the grave. I met him several feet away from my mom.

"You okay?" He brushed his palms together and grave dirt fell from them. The tiny clumps hit the ground and seemed to echo within my head, much louder than should have been impossible.

"I'm fine. I just need to go iron out the last few details. I have to verify the time and the number of men my uncle's bringing, then I need to leave for the airport." I was taking Vic with me to recruit the thunderbirds, because I couldn't justify taking both Marc and Jace away from the Pride when it was most in need of protection, but I couldn't choose between them.

"Maybe you should take a couple of hours off. Try to relax. Help your mom."

I shook my head slowly, trying not to stare at the ground and remember that my father was now in it. "She wants to be alone, and I don't want to relax. I want to stay pissed off, so I can finish putting this thing together with a clear head."

His frown deepened and he crossed dirty arms over the front of his dress shirt. "Anger gives you a clear head?"

I nodded. "It gives me clarity like twisting the focus knobs on a microscope."

Marc blinked, and for an instant, I read confusion in his eyes. Or maybe something darker. The hair rose on the back of my neck, though I couldn't have said precisely why.

"I take it that doesn't work for you?"

He shook his head. "Anger makes me see red, and I lose all perspective. You may recall past fits of irrationality, followed by an excess of broken stuff."

"Yeah." I frowned up at him. "That's kind of what we're going for, with Malone and Dean." And anyone who gets in the way.

"I know. Just…try to take it easy, okay?" He glanced over one shoulder and I looked up to find Jace watching us, while Parker and Vic still dug.

"There will be time to take it easy when Malone and Dean are dead."

Marc exhaled heavily. "Let's hope."

I glanced past him to the fresh, unfinished grave, and my throat suddenly felt thicker. "Thanks for…doing that."

He followed my line of sight. "It's the very least that we owe him. Seriously."

"I know." I couldn't even begin to quantify what I owed my father. My independence. The ability to defend myself. The certainty that doing the right thing was always worth it, no matter what it cost. "Come see me when you get in?"

He nodded. "Of course." Then he went back to the most hateful hole I'd ever seen, and I headed for the main house, with one more look at my mother.

Halfway there, I heard footsteps and had to drag my gaze from the ground and my thoughts out of my own head to identify the form walking toward me.

Ryan.

He hesitated when he saw me coming, then started

walking again, like he could prove his backbone by simply not running away. But it was far too late for that. He had no backbone left, and no Pride. Ryan walked in deep shadows of shame these days, and he only walked at all because in the end he'd given us the information we'd needed to capture two of his partners. Not out of the goodness of his heart, but to save his own rotten hide.

I stopped and crossed my arms over my chest, trying to look tough rather than simply cold while I waited for him. He stopped four feet away, his nose still swollen and purple. "I'm not looking for trouble, Faythe. I just came to pay my respects."

"You shouldn't be here."

Ryan scowled. "Faythe, lay off. I'm here for Mom." He tried to step around me, but I grabbed his arm and hauled him back.

"She called you, didn't she? And she called when Ethan died?"

He glanced at the ground when he spoke, and I knew nothing had changed. "Do you really want to talk about this now?" Ryan gestured over my shoulder at our mother, but I didn't turn to look at her. I couldn't, because an old question was now hammering on my nerves with all-new certainty and dread.

"She let you out, didn't she? Mom let you out of the cage...."

"Faythe, I can't do this right now."

I spoke through gritted teeth, my hands clenched around handfuls of my long black skirt. "Ryan, I swear on our father's unfinished grave that I will break every fucking bone in your face if you don't answer me right now. The council is going to start asking questions about you soon, and I'm the one who's going to have to answer them. Malone and his allies will kick her while she's down just to get to me, and *I'm* going to have to protect Mom."

Ryan's blue eyes searched mine, and I hated that I could see so much of our mother in them. "He really did it. He really named you."

"Yeah. He really did. Ryan, you need to get the hell out of here before anyone else sees you. That's all the mercy I'm ready to extend right now."

"Just let me talk to Mom. You want me to swear loyalty? I'll swear." He dropped to his knees on the frozen ground and reached for my hand, but I pulled it out of his grasp. "Please, Faythe. If you don't want to talk to me, fine. I understand. You're not ready. But I can't let her think I didn't come. Please, Faythe. For Mom."

"Get up." I pulled him up before he could move on his own. "You have one hour," I relented, against my better judgment. "If you're still here after that, I'm locking your ass back up."

He nodded stiffly. "Fair enough. Thank you." I blinked, half-convinced I'd misheard him.

He rushed past me, probably afraid I'd change my mind, and I headed for the house without looking back. I couldn't stand to see him with my mom, no matter how happy it made her to have him around, for no reason I could understand.

Inside, two groups had gathered, one in the kitchen, where there was coffee and several kinds of pie and cake, the other in the living room, where I could smell both whiskey and brandy being poured.

I passed them all and closed myself into the office alone, where I sank into the desk chair.

Twenty minutes later, I'd accomplished nothing more than staring at the back of my father's armchair when the door opened and Marc appeared in the gap. "How you doin'?" he asked.

I could still smell dirt on him; he'd come straight to me, even before showering. "I'm fine."

"They need you in the kitchen. Or the living room."

"Why? What's wrong?"

He shrugged. "Nothing, other than the fact that your father was just buried and you're ignoring everyone else who loved him."

I closed my eyes and leaned forward on the desk, my face in my hands. "I'm sorry. I was just..."

"You don't know how to be with them," he finished for me, and I looked up at him, surprised. "Because you think this is your fault."

"Yeah. I was supposed to protect him."

"We all were," Marc pointed out, as usual too rational to be argued with.

"Yeah, but he wasn't just my Alpha. He was my dad. I failed him on both counts."

Marc shook his head, but stayed put. He knew I needed space. "You didn't fail him, or anyone." He glanced at the papers and the phones on the desk in front of me. "In fact, I think he'd be proud."

I shook my head. "I haven't earned it yet. But I will."

"Come have coffee with us."

I sighed, but stood. "One cup."

He smiled. "That's a good start."

But we only got halfway down the hall before a rumble from out front froze us both in place—then jolted us into motion. We reached the door together and peered through the glass panes side by side.

Cars. I'd heard the engines, but seeing them shot fear and adrenaline through my veins like lightning through the night sky. I didn't recognize the vehicles, nor could I make out the faces behind the first dashboard from such a distance, but I knew who our uninvited guests were.

Malone. And his new Alpha wannabe.

Twenty-two

"**M**ichael!" I shouted, still peering through the sidelight to the left of the door. I whirled to find Jace jogging toward me and Marc, still in his suit, his features tense with alarm.

"What's wrong?" Jace slowed to a stop in the middle of the hall, peering over my shoulder through the glass.

"We've been preempted. Malone's out front with enough men to fill—" I turned and glanced out front again, as more people poured into the hall, Michael in front of the small crowd "—it looks like eight cars."

"Shit!" Jace swore.

"Who's Malone?" Holly asked, holding a steaming mug of coffee in front of a stylish, knee-length black dress. She was in full make-up today, in light of our formal grief.

I ignored her question and focused on my fellow tabbies. "Manx, grab your diaper bag. Kaci, throw some stuff into your backpack. Quickly!" Then I met Michael's gaze, the lines around his narrowed eyes the only sign that he was just as pissed and scared as I was.

"I want you to take Holly, Manx, Des, Kaci, and Mom out back, through the woods. Leave your car here, and call Carey Dodd for a ride on the way." Dodd was the closest nonenforcer tom in the south-central Pride, and he probably wouldn't be surprised by emergency chauffeur duty, only a week after the last call.

He nodded, tense and ready for action. "Where are we going?"

"Um, you can't go to Dodd's. They'll know his is the closest house, and when they realize Manx and Kaci are gone, they'll look for you there."

"Take them to my place," Marc said, his footsteps heavy on the hardwood as he stomped out of the kitchen carrying a huge wrench, obviously ready for battle.

"No, that's too far…" I started, my heartbeat ticking off seconds we didn't have to waste, but I stopped when Jace stepped out from behind Marc, armed with a crowbar.

"That's why they should go there," he said, as Marc dug a set of keys from the pocket of his dress pants. "And Cal's men won't follow them into the free zone. Not now that the strays know what he pulled with those tracking chips."

I thought for just a second—that's all the time I had, with the engines still growling toward us out front. "Okay. Michael, get directions from Marc. We'll call you when it's safe to come back." I turned to shout for my mother, but she was already there, standing next to a stunned-silent Holly.

"I'm not going."

I sighed, trying to keep in mind what she was going through. What we were all going through. "There's going to be a fight, Mom. *I'm* going to fight, and it won't be pretty. I don't want you involved." And I didn't want her to interfere. The one time she'd seen me fight for my life, she'd stepped in to save me, and I couldn't let her do that again. "I couldn't protect Dad, but I can damn well protect you. You're going."

"Let's not waste time arguing about this, Faythe." With that, she marched into the kitchen, shouting for Ryan. I went after her and found her talking to him by the tiled bar. "Go with them," she was saying. "You're the only one other than Marc who's familiar with the area. Keep them out of sight and keep them safe, until you get to Marc's."

"Mom, he can't—"

"Yes. He can." She frowned at me with one hand on Ryan's arm. "He's learned from his mistakes, Faythe. He won't let me down."

"And I have a car…" he offered, meeting my gaze boldly. "It'll be a tight fit, but this way you don't have to take Dodd out of the fight. And you might need him."

I had less than a second to consider. Then I grabbed Ryan by the throat and threw him against the wall while he gagged. Kaci gasped from the dining room doorway, backpack over one shoulder, and Manx put her free arm around the young tabby. I focused on my brother, on the fear floating behind his eyes. "If they don't all make it to Marc's house without a single scratch, I will person- ally rip out your throat. Understand?"

Ryan nodded, as best he could with my hand around his neck.

I let him go, and he sucked in a deep breath. "Go. Now." Ryan headed for the back door, herding Kaci ahead of him. Manx followed with Des in her arms. Owen fell into step beside her and slid the diaper bag over her shoulder, then kissed her quickly on the cheek. A moment later, they were gone, leaving a confused, terrified Holly standing next to her husband.

"I'll call when I can," I told Michael, as he tugged his wife toward the back door.

He nodded.

"What's going on?" Holly demanded. She tried to stop, but Michael only pulled harder, more concerned with getting her to safety than with explaining the details. "Who's in those cars? Are you in the mob? Oh, shit. You're a mafia lawyer. I should have known! All the late-night emergencies and secrets... Let go of me!"

Michael pulled her out the door, and when it slammed behind them, I turned to face everyone else. My men. And my mother.

There weren't enough of us. Marc, Jace, Vic, Parker, Owen, Brian, me, Dr. Carver, and my mom. Malone had a car full of toms for every able body we had, and even if we counted my mother, we were screwed. How the hell had they known about the funeral? And what the hell was I thinking, asking our allies to stay away? At least if they'd come, we'd be better defended.

Or not. If we'd had more men, Malone would no doubt have brought more to the party. His resources were endless, compared to ours.

Half a minute after the back door slammed shut behind Michael and Holly, the first car rolled to a stop in front of the house. Seven others followed in quick succession, and I was not surprised to see Malone in the front passenger seat of the first car.

I turned to face my men, dragging in a deep breath that tasted like fear and fury—but mostly fury. "We don't stand a chance in open battle. Not yet. Not like this." Suddenly I felt very vulnerable in my skirt and heels. "If Malone's brought a challenger, I'll fight him."

"Faythe…" Marc interrupted, as the first car door slammed shut at my back.

My pulse raced, and my eyes ached as a partial Shift began, unbidden, brought on by stress and bloodlust. "No. I fight for myself."

"I agree with Marc," Jace said, and neither of us could have looked more surprised. "Let one of us fight. That's what your father would want."

"That's what he would want for his daughter, if he were still here. Still Alpha. But it's not what he'd want for himself. And I'm the Alpha now. I can't afford to let someone else fight my battles. Especially this first one."

Jace frowned and Marc scowled, but neither argued.

"Besides, I can handle myself against Alex Malone. Even in a skirt."

"How do you know it's Alex?" Jace asked, and I pointed out the sidelight, through which we could now see all four occupants of the first car: Malone, Colin Dean, one of Parker's brothers, whose name escaped me at the moment, and Alex Malone.

"Oh, shit," Parker whispered, and he didn't even seem to notice that he'd cussed in front of the new Alpha. I didn't have to ask what was wrong—emerging from the second car as we watched was Jerald Pierce.

"It'll be okay, Parker," I insisted. "One way or another. Everybody ready?"

They all nodded silently, and my mother smoothed down her hair, readying her battle face. I'd never seen her look more fierce, when only moments ago she'd been ready to fall apart. No wonder my father had fallen so hard for her. How could he not?

I opened the door and stepped onto the porch, forcing my pulse to stop tripping over itself. Marc and Jace took up positions on either side of me, and the others fanned out around us, except for my mother, who stood firm to one side of the steps in front of the porch railing. It was clearer in that moment than ever before where most of my pride and obduracy had come from.

"Ms. Sanders…" Malone crossed his arms over a button-down shirt with both sleeves rolled up, in spite of the cold. Maybe hotheaded was a more accurate description of him than we'd ever really guessed.

The line of cars stretched out to his right, around the circle driveway and trailing onto the long gravel drive itself. Men were getting out, slamming doors, and I only recognized about half of them.

I crossed my arms over my chest, staring down at him from the porch. "You said we'd have until Saturday."

"No, I said you'd have until you buried your father, and there's a patch of freshly overturned earth beneath that apple tree—" he pointed toward where my father now lay alongside Ethan for all of eternity "—that says that mission's been accomplished. So…have you come up with a suitable Alpha for your Pride?"

"I am Alpha of the south-central Pride. That was my father's dying wish, and I will honor it."

"Until your last breath, no doubt," Malone mumbled, barely moving his lips as he stepped toward the porch, stopping directly in front of the bottom step.

"That's the general idea." I glanced at Alex, expecting him to join his father. But Alex wouldn't look at me. He wouldn't even look up from his shoes.

Uh-oh. That couldn't be good.

Malone half turned and nodded to one of his men, and Parker's brother stepped forward, spine stiff, gaze boring into mine. He was the oldest of the Pierce boys, and a full decade my senior. But I couldn't quite remember his name...

"I challenge your leadership of the south-central Pride. One-on-one. Winner becomes Alpha."

I opened my mouth to reply, but Parker beat me to it. "Kent, you son of a bitch, I'll kill you for this."

I glanced at Parker to find his jaws tight, his arms bulging through the material of his shirt, his hands clenched into fists at his sides. And suddenly I understood how Kenton Pierce—that was his name—had risen so quickly into Malone's good graces. And how Malone had known about the secret funeral.

Kent didn't answer his brother, so I made the only reply I could—my only option, other than handing over the Pride, my father's life's work, to a man I'd rarely ever spoken to. "I accept."

I'd never seen Kent fight, so I had no idea what his strengths and weaknesses were. But he clearly had the greater strength, size, and experience. All I had was an ironclad determination to win. To keep my Pride intact and protect my family.

Kent nodded, his expression notably absent of satisfaction, or even anticipation. He didn't look particularly happy to be challenging for Alpha status, but obviously Malone had made him an offer he couldn't refuse. At least, not if he wanted to live.

Too bad I'd have to kill him, anyway.

"This is your home turf—for the moment," Kent said, making no move to take off his jacket or prepare for the imminent ass kicking. "Do you have a forum prefer-ence? Maybe the barn?"

"No." The barn had walls. And stalls. And countless other physical elements that could be used against me. The best way to eat away at his advantages would be to deprive him of all of that. "Right there." I pointed to the circle of brown grass at the center of the driveway loop.

Kenton twisted to look, then nodded, apparently sat-isfied. "That will work. Dean?" He made a broad, one-handed gesture, and Colin Dean jogged into the center of the circle, then turned to watch me. Waiting.

It actually took me several seconds to understand. Then Kent was kind enough to state it for me. "Colin Dean will fight for the challenger."

"What?" I tore my irate gaze from Dean—who gloated at me from thirty feet away—to frown at Kenton Pierce. "You're not going to fight? And you picked Colin Dean as your...champion?" There were so many things wrong with that statement. "What, are you too scared to fight me yourself?"

Kent scowled, then glanced briefly at his father before turning back to me. "Of course not. I'm simply utilizing the resources at my disposal."

"You practiced that, didn't you?" I forced a cold smile. "I bet you have it written down on a note card in your pocket, and I bet the handwriting isn't yours. Did they make you memorize it? Did they tell you what to say after I kick your ass? Assuming you're still capable of speech?"

Behind me, Jace chuckled, but Kent glowered, his

face scarlet beneath the burn of humiliation. And if he hadn't hated me before, he might now. "Does that mean you're fighting for yourself?"

"Yeah. That's kind of this thing I do. You probably shouldn't try it, though. Cowards tend to break beneath the burden." I was trying to piss him off, practically daring him to fight me himself.

But Dean wouldn't stand for it. "We'll see who's broken in a few minutes," he called, drawing my attention from the obviously irritated Kenton Pierce. "Pick your form—fur or flesh?"

Shit. Dean was at least double my weight and had ten inches on me in height. I'd only been able to take him in human form the first time because I caught him by surprise, and the second time because I turned his own knife against him—we had yet to actually exchange blows.

But if I couldn't take him on two legs, there was no way in hell I could take him on four.

"Flesh," I replied at last, and on my right, Marc exhaled slowly. "Do I get to change, or do I have to kick your skull in wearing three-inch heels?" Not that I'd actually fight in heels; I'd go barefoot if I had to.

"Go change. But don't dawdle," Kent said, snatching the spotlight back from his "champion." "We don't have time for you to worry about what you'll be wearing when you die."

So furious I had to grit my teeth to keep them from Shifting, I turned an abrupt about-face and marched back into the house, grabbing Parker's arm on the way to haul him in with me. My mother, Marc, and Jace came on their own. Owen, Vic, and Brian stood watch on the porch.

"Faythe, you don't have to do this," my mother said, as soon as the front door closed behind us.

"Yes, I do, and we don't have time to argue about it. Call Michael and give him an update. Tell them not to stop driving until they hit the free zone."

"But…"

"Please, Mom." I unbuttoned my blouse as I walked, and they all trailed me to my bedroom. "If you really think I can handle this job, this is the time to prove it."

She stopped just inside my doorway, frowning. But she nodded and was already dialing on her way back into the hall.

"Faythe…" Marc began, but I cut him off with a one-minute finger.

"Parker…what the *fuck?*" I gave up on the buttons and ripped my shirt open, barely noticing when the shiny black disks rolled silently across my carpet.

Parker was misery given form. "I'm so sorry, Faythe. He called yesterday, all apologetic, talking about how Dad had really lost it. It just slipped out."

"Yeah, and then it slipped from him to your dad, and from your dad to Malone. And now I have to fight some giant psychopath who's only regret in this whole thing is that I'm going to die with my pants on."

"You don't have to…" Jace started, but I silenced him with one furious glance, then turned back to Parker.

"You were drinking, weren't you? You were drunk when he called?"

Parker didn't reply, but we could all see the answer in his face. "I'm so sorry."

"You sure as hell are." I unzipped my skirt and let it pool around my ankles, then stepped out of the material, wearing only my underwear and heels. "You're either with us or against us, Parker, and so far, it's not looking much like the former."

"No. I'm with you. I can make this up to you." Parker closed his eyes and sucked in a deep breath. "Please give me a chance."

I hesitated. We needed him, now more than ever. And he needed us. "You know I love you, Parker. But I love the rest of the Pride, too, and I can't let you break us. You mess up again, and you're out."

"Okay." He sniffled again. "I'm sorry."

I kicked my heels into the corner of the room. "Get yourself together and get back out there."

Parker left and Marc closed the bedroom door, as I dug through my drawer for a shirt. Something warm, but that would let me move freely. "Faythe, please don't do this," he said, and I could tell from the quiet, carefully controlled quality of his voice that he was struggling to keep from ordering me not to do it.

"We've been over this…" I pulled a snug black turtleneck from the second drawer and held it up. No holes, no stains, no defects. And blood would barely show against black.

"Faythe, look at me." Marc grabbed my arm and pulled me toward him. "You're scaring me. You are scaring the living *shit* out of me, and it kind of looks like you don't care."

I exhaled slowly and made myself meet his gaze. "I care. I really do care, and I'm sorry. But I have bigger things to worry about right now than your fear. Or even my own. If I lose, we all lose this territory. Also, I might be dead." I pulled out of his grasp and tugged the shirt over my head, then pulled my hair free from the thick, loose neck.

"Jace, help me out here," Marc said, and I froze in the act of turning down the collar, surprised into silence to hear him actually ask Jace for help. With me. "I can't deal with her when she won't listen."

"I'm listening." I selected a pair of dark jeans from the bottom drawer. They were well-worn, but still intact, so they wouldn't inhibit movement.

"But you're not hearing him," Jace insisted, as I stepped into the jeans. When I stood straight to button them, Jace wrapped a hand around each of my arms. "Faythe. We're asking you not to do this. Dean will kill you."

"Only if I don't kill him. And we all know I have a better shot at this now, in a fair fight, than on an open battlefield. When there are no rules, he'll bring a knife or a gun to the party. This is the only way I can take him. When you guys are there to make sure it's a fair fight."

Jace leaned his face down until his forehead met mine, and I could hear his heart beating too hard, his pulse rushing faster than it should. I could smell stress mixed with his personal scent, and that fueled my own anxiety. "But, Faythe, it doesn't have to be you taking him on. Let one of us fight him."

"No. It has to be me. And Marc knows why." Jace looked up, and Marc frowned, but held my gaze. "What did you say to me last week, Marc? What will happen if…someone challenges you, and you don't beat him?" That someone was Jace, and while he no doubt picked up on that fact, I wasn't going to say it out loud.

Marc sighed, but he wasn't going to lie. "If they think

I can't defend my position, they'll keep challenging me. And Malone will have reason to claim I'm not Alpha material, thus not worthy to stand at your side. To help lead the Pride."

"And that's why I have to do this. If I don't prove I can hang with the boys—even if that means taking down the biggest bully on the playground—I'm not going to be able to hold on to this Pride, now, or in the future. And you both know it." I hesitated, then sank onto the side of my bed and looked up at them both. "But beyond all that, he killed my dad. I have to do this."

Finally Marc nodded, though Jace looked less than convinced. "But I'm not going to let him kill you. I'll stop the fight if it comes down to that, and—" I stood and tried to interrupt, but he spoke over me "—and if you try to tell me not to, I swear I'll walk away right now. I can't watch him kill you."

"Me, too," Jace insisted, and I looked up to find his face lined in fear and confliction. And determination. He meant it. They both did.

"Fine. It's not like I want to die. Just make sure I'm really going to lose before you throw in my towel, okay?"

Marc nodded, and I stepped closer to him. My heart thumped so loud it echoed in my ears. I slid one hand behind his neck and Marc kissed me like he'd never have another chance. And I knew that deep down, he actually believed that. I could die in the next few minutes, and some part of him was kissing me goodbye.

When I finally pulled away from him, his jaw tensed and he closed his eyes. He glanced at Jace, then back at me, and the pain shining in his eyes had so many sources it was like looking into a kaleidoscope of anguish. "I…I'll be out there." He walked stiffly across the room and out the door, then closed it softly, and my heart ached, even in the midst of my own maelstrom of conflicting fear, rage, and dread.

But before I could decide whether or not to call him back, Jace was there, and his angst was just as real. Just as immediate. "Please don't do this, Faythe. I'm begging you. We all know you can fight, so your badass status is in no jeopardy. But you are not evenly matched against Colin Dean."

"Jace…"

"I know, you're going to do it, anyway. If Marc can't talk you out of it, what chance do I have?"

I looked up into his eyes, letting him see what all was at stake for me. "What would you do in my position? If he'd killed your father, and cut you up, and told you how he wants to make you scream before you die, and this was your one chance for a fair fight… What would you do? Honestly?"

Jace sighed, but looked far from mollified. "I'd want to rip out his insides while he watched." He wrapped both arms around me, and I wondered briefly if his warmth was the last pleasant thing I'd ever feel. "You are the single most stubborn woman I've ever met," he whispered, his lips moving against mine with the last words. Jace's kiss wasn't saying goodbye—it was begging me to stay.

When he finally stepped back, I took a moment to steady myself, then pulled my hair into a ponytail, stepped into my work boots, and headed for the door, focusing on my own devastating rage to override the fear now pulsing through me with every beat of my heart. I was neither stupid nor blind. Dean was a monster, and he was a fucking *huge* monster.

But I was smarter and faster. And I *had* to avenge my father and defend my Pride. If I couldn't accomplish two such vital tasks, what good was I, as a daughter and as an Alpha?

Outside, all eyes turned my way when I stepped onto the porch. No one spoke. I stopped to give my mother a hug and marveled at her strength—she was stubbornly resisting tears. Then I marched down the steps and into the informal ring created by our gravel driveway.

Colin Dean stood in the center of the circle. Waiting for me. Smiling crookedly, thanks to his grotesquely scarred cheek.

I glanced at Malone, expecting him—as the new council chair—to give the official signal to begin. Instead, he glanced at Dean and nodded. I turned to find a huge fist flying toward me. Pain exploded in the left side of my head, and the world spun around me. I hit the ground half-twisted, both palms flat on the grass.

But I was up in an instant, and my fury had a new face.

Colin Dean was going down.

Twenty-three

"This is what you picked to die in?" Dean sneered as I hissed at him. I wouldn't be caught off guard again. "Not that it matters. You're gonna be all red and sticky in a minute, anyway."

"This is what you get off on, right?" We circled each other slowly, my head throbbing, and I felt every single gaze on me, most of them waiting to see David stomped into the ground by Goliath. *And me without my slingshot...* "You finally have permission to beat up a girl, in front of all these witnesses, and you're just sick enough to actually believe you're doing it for a cause. The good of the entire community."

"Nah..." Dean leaned closer, risking a blow to confess his little secret where no one else would hear. "That's their cause. I'm in it for payback, which they say is a real bitch. Just like you."

He tensed in preparation to kick, but I lurched out of reach and spun for a roundhouse. His boot swung inches from my stomach. My foot slammed into his ribs. Dean grunted and stumbled to one side, but he never stopped smiling. "You're right about one thing, though—I am having fun."

My left fist smashed his nose, but he was already moving.

Dean's next kick knocked my legs out from under me. His blood seemed to drip in slow motion as I went down hard on my left hip. My injured knee screamed. My mother gasped at my back. A black blur arced toward my face. I rolled, and the world spun around me. Dean's boot hit my shoulder instead of my face.

Old pain echoed with fresh intensity in my left shoulder. Dean's foot landed beside my hip, stopping my roll. I shoved with both hands. His leg slid out from under him, and his weight crashed on top of me.

I couldn't breathe. But neither could he. Stunned, Dean gasped, and sat up to straddle my hips. I buried my right fist in his side. He grunted, then grabbed a handful of my hair and slammed my head into the ground.

My vision swam. My pulse roared in my ears, and each breath I took was a ragged gasp. Another dark blur, and pain exploded in my left side. I swung blindly and hit something soft. Hairs popped softly as they were pulled from my scalp. My skull hit the earth again, and everything started to go fuzzy. If I couldn't get him off me, I wouldn't last much longer.

I clawed at the hand curled around my hair, and the sudden scent of his blood was a fragrant pick-me-up. Actual claws would have worked better, but I was pretty sure a partial Shift would be considered cheating, since I'd opted for flesh over fur.

I dug harder into his flesh, gouging, burning with determination. Dean hissed and let go. I shoved him back and threw my weight to the right while he was off balance, tossing him to the ground. I leaped to my feet, the ranch spinning around me, and he was up an instant later, watching me warily.

Blood dripped from his broken nose. More rolled down the side of my face. My scalp burned. My brain felt like mush. My nose was dripping from the cold. But Dean looked tired and bruised, and that made it all worth it.

"You know, you don't have to make this so hard," he said, breathing heavily enough to give me hope.

"Is this the part where you try to talk me into dropping my fists and climbing into bed with Malone's marionette?" I panted, trying to slow my pulse and catch my breath.

"You're either going to lie down under your new Alpha, or next to your old one. The choice is yours."

"Well, you got that last part right." I rushed him, already swinging. Dean twisted to avoid the blow. He caught my foot and shoved me backward. I hopped, then limped on my bad knee, reclaiming my balance, But it was too late. Dean rushed me, but his hands were open. I kicked again. He swatted my foot away, spinning me halfway around. Huge hands grabbed my right arm and thigh, just above my knee. The world canted violently, and I was suddenly in the air.

The house flew past my face, a blur of bricks and mortar. I screeched. Dean grunted, and I bobbed, then lurched higher, still screaming, flailing for something to hold on to.

"No!" my mother shouted, but I couldn't see her.

Dean's grip tightened. He hurled me at the ground.

The earth slammed into me with the force of a planetary collision, and agony exploded all over my body.

My lungs wouldn't fill. My heart wouldn't beat. My head wouldn't move. I couldn't feel my limbs.

I blinked, and the colors swirled together. Something warm dripped from my ear and curled in the dip of cartilage. Distantly, someone was screaming, but I couldn't make out the words.

Something hard slammed into the side of my skull. My head rocked violently on my neck. The world went black, but distant blurs of sound still swirled around me.

Something hit my left cheek. Then my right. Something smashed into my nose, and it crunched. I tasted blood, but there was no pain. Why was there no pain? I raised one arm, but it fell away from my face with the next blow.

Someone roared, a thunder of outrage and agony.

Someone else was still screaming, but it wasn't me. I could only gurgle and choke on my own blood. Then new pain burst within my head, and the sounds disappeared, too.

There was nothing left of me but darkness and silence.

"Faythe... Please wake up, *mi vida*. Come on. Open your eyes...."

Marc. I could hear him, but I couldn't see him. I blinked, but there was only a pink haze. A one-dimensional pink haze, because my left eye wouldn't open. The air tasted like blood. I heard voices everywhere. Talking. Arguing. Shouting. Someone was laughing. And my mother was sobbing. Through it all, I heard my mother crying, and Jace whispering. He was reassuring her with words I couldn't understand, but I could tell she didn't believe them. I didn't believe them, either.

"That's it, *nena*. Wake up."

I blinked again, and some of the red cleared. Marc's face came mostly into focus, but it was oriented strangely. That's when I realized I was lying on my right side. And that the ground was freezing. And that the world was made of pain.

I gasped, and breathing hurt, so I stopped breathing, but that hurt, too. Each beat of my heart pumped agony through my abused body, throbbing in every bruise, stinging in every cut. And over it all was a background of complete anguish, like tactile white noise—if white noise could kill you.

I couldn't smell anything. Why couldn't I smell anything? My nose felt swollen, and hot, and…smashed. But that one pain was hard to separate from the general din of agony. I tried to sit up, but Marc put one gentle hand on my shoulder.

"Whoa, not yet. Give it a minute."

I sucked in a small breath through what was left of my nose—and froze. Blood. All I could smell was blood, everywhere. And most of it was mine. "Noooo…" I moaned, swallowing more of my own life force, and tears burned in my eyes. Then scalded my cheeks when they fell.

"Shhh, it's okay, *cari*. It's gonna be fine."

"It's not." I sobbed, choking on blood, and tears, and bitter pain and grief. "It's not ever gonna be okay again."

"Oh, sure it will. I know how to make her feel all better…" Colin Dean said from somewhere over me, already laughing again.

"Take one more step and I'll kill you," Marc said, talking to Dean, though his gaze never left me.

Dean laughed harder. "Why don't you pick up the pieces of your *Alpha* and get the hell out of here."

Marc stood then and growled until my mother told him to stop.

I tried to sit up again, but I couldn't. Everything hurt, and the whole world slanted when I moved my head.

"Faythe?" It was Dr. Carver. He knelt next to me in his good slacks, still dressed from the funeral. Which would be convenient if I were dying. "Can you hear me?"

I started to nod, but that hurt my head. "Yeah," I rasped instead.

"Do you know where you are? Do you remember what happened?"

"Front yard." *Bruising hands. Tilting house. Collision with the earth.* "I think I got drop-kicked."

Dean laughed again, and there was more growling, from several sources this time.

"I know you're in a lot of pain, but can you move your feet for me?" Dr. Carver asked, and panic set in, tingling like my whole body had gone to sleep. He was testing for a spinal injury.

No... I moved my right foot, flexing my calf, and the surge of relief was like aloe on a sunburn. I did the same with my left foot, and pain shot through my hip. But pain was good, right? That meant I could still feel.

Carver smiled like I'd just done a nifty trick. "Okay, now your fingers..."

I flexed both hands at once, and this time my left shoulder screamed in pain just like my hip had. And vaguely I remembered hitting the ground on my left side....

"Okay, let's get her inside. Be careful with her head."

"I've got you," Jace whispered, but I couldn't smell him. I could only smell my own blood. He lifted me, and the world pitched harder. I clung to him, terrified that I was flying again. Or falling. "Just hold on..."

"Put her in the car," Marc said, and his footsteps jogged to catch up with us. "I'll ride in back with her. We can stop for supplies on the way."

"You don't have to go," someone else said, but my eyes had closed again, and I couldn't place the voice, though it sounded familiar. "I mean it. At least let her rest in her own bed for a while first. It doesn't have to be...like this."

Marc growled, expressing more in that fierce, furious sound than I could have managed in a thousand words. "Kent, get out of my way before I rip your face right off your head."

"He's right," Jace said, squeezing me a little tighter. "Let her rest before we go."

"Go?" I murmured.

No one answered me. "She can't stay here. With them," Marc insisted, and I tried to look at him, but my eyes—my *eye,* anyway—wouldn't stay open.

"No one's going to touch her. You can stay with her. Both of you. I just feel bad putting you all out while she's still unconscious."

"I'm not..." I started, but I lost the rest of the words in a fog of pain and confusion.

"Fine. But if you come within fifteen feet of her

bedroom door, I'll feed you your own fingers, one at a time."

"He's not even coming inside," my mother insisted from somewhere nearby, and I thought I felt her cold hand on my forehead. "None of them are."

"Now, Karen, it's his house now…" Calvin Malone chided, and I flinched at the sound of his voice, though his words made little sense.

"We'll wait," Kenton said, with an impressive note of finality. "Take your time."

Jace tightened his grip, and when he jostled me, I forced my eye open to see that we were going up the steps. The porch roof came into half focus, then he turned to carry me through the front door sideways. I tried to thank him, but then everything went dark. Again.

"Faythe, you have to wake up." It was Jace this time. Something cold and wet touched my cheek, and I tried to jerk away from it. But moving hurt, and I could only moan. "Hold still," he whispered.

"I'm tired. And that's cold." I shoved at the wet rag in spite of the pain in my shoulder, and Jace laughed. But it was a relieved, half-panicked laugh, not a happy one.

The bed groaned beneath his shifting weight, and the ambient red behind my eyelids brightened when he leaned away from me. "She's making sense. Doc, she's awake and coherent." ·

"Good." Carver's decisive footsteps crossed the room toward us. "Faythe, do you feel dizzy at all? Any nausea?"

I opened my functioning eye to see his blurry,

concerned face. "A little dizzy. But mostly I just hurt. Everywhere."

"I know. Let's get a look at her ribs."

I pushed at his hands as he tried to lift my shirt. "I just want to sleep."

Jace shook his head, frowning. "You need to let the doctor check you out. You're hurt pretty bad, Faythe."

Hurt. Shit. *Malone. Kenton Pierce. Colin Dean. No-nononono!* I'd lost the Pride. The entire Pride. Everyone. I'd lost them all. Except…

I opened my eyes, and Jace came into focus in one of them. The other showed only a slit of light that was painful to look at. "Did they get away?" I demanded, clutching his arm, though my grip sent pain shooting through my left shoulder—evidently Dean had tried to rip my arm from its socket. "Manx and Kaci? And Des?"

"As far as I know, they're fine," Jace said, and my next breath sent an echo of pain throughout my body. Was it possible to literally hurt all over? "Let the doctor look at your ribs."

I laid back and let them pull my shirt up, and bit my lip to keep from screaming when the doctor touched my side. "Where's Marc?"

"He's keeping your mother occupied. She's pretty upset."

"My fault." I licked my lips and tasted more blood. "I thought I could at least hold my own."

Jace interlaced his fingers with mine. "Faythe, he picked you up over his head and threw you at the ground. There's not much you can do after that. Not much any of us could have done in your position."

"You're lucky he didn't break your back." Dr. Carver

sat on the other side of the bed and aimed a penlight at my eyes. "Or your shoulder. You have at least one cracked rib and a broken nose. Does anything else feel broken?"

I closed my eyes and tested all my joints. Most of them ached—some of them throbbed with a sharp, pins-and-needles feeling—but everything functioned. "Just my head."

"You got lucky there." Jace ran one hand softly down my arm over and over, petting me for comfort. "Marc stopped the fight before he could kick your face in. He was going to kill you. We could all see it. He was fucking high on power."

I didn't remember that. All I remembered, other than the pain was… "Marc roared."

"Yeah, and he took Dean down in a running tackle. Though to be fair, I was right behind him. And so were Vic and Parker."

"Have I ever mentioned how much I love you guys?"

Jace's eyes widened, then his lips turned up in a sly grin. "Actually, no."

"Well, I hate to break up the tender moment—" Dr. Carver said, looking anything but sorry "—but your nose is broken, and I need to set it."

I winced. "Doesn't that sound like fun…"

Jace shrugged. "It'll hurt like hell for a minute, but then it'll feel better. And if you don't do it, you're gonna look like Rocky for the rest of your life."

"Fine. Just get it over with."

Dr. Carver helped me sit up, then waited until he was sure I could stay balanced on my own. When I was sure

I wasn't going to throw up, I nodded and closed my eyes. "Okay, here we go…" he warned.

The next moment was a burst of pain in the center of my face, and the grating sound of bone against bone. I screamed. Then it was over. It still hurt, but less than before, and was easily overwhelmed by the pain in the rest of my body.

"Faythe?" The bedroom door opened and Marc came in, followed by my mother, whose face was red from crying.

My mom sniffled and wiped her tears with a damp tissue. "Is she okay?"

"She's going to live," the doc said. "But she's going to be in a lot of pain for a long time."

Jace stood so my mother could sit by me, and the moment I saw her face, I burst into tears. "I'm so sorry! I lost it. I lost the whole Pride. Everything Daddy worked for…"

"Not everything." Marc stood over her shoulder, his face carefully blank, which was my first clue that mine must look pretty bad. Well, actually, my first clue was my swollen-shut eye and the mass of puffy, sticky pain that my nose had become. "I don't think you'll lose many of the toms. But we did lose the house."

"What?" I tried to sit, and the doctor pushed me firmly back onto the pillow by one shoulder. I hissed when pain shot through the joint, and he let me go. "How can we lose the house? This is our house. Dad's house. He designed it. His company built it."

Marc sighed and my mother's eyes watered. "He paid for it in part with the Pride's money. With the tithes, just like our salaries."

"We thought that was only fair." My mom blotted

her eyes again. "We thought the property should belong to the entire Pride, rather than just the core family, so everyone would always know they were welcome."

I'd had no idea. How could I not have known? "Is that even enforceable? I'm assuming the deed doesn't list thirty-something names on it, right? Just yours and Daddy's?"

"That's right, but it still belongs in part to the Pride, and it's in the Pride's territory. We could offer to buy out the Pride's half, but I doubt the new leadership will let that happen without an actual fight. And even if they did, it would take a while to work those details out. And we still couldn't live here—inside the territory—without submitting to the new 'authority.'"

"And that's not gonna happen. So…this isn't my room anymore?" I sat up, and that time they let me. My gaze roved my shelves, my books, my dresser, and my desk. My CDs and my computer. The shelf Marc had hung for me…

"Not unless you feel like pledging loyalty to Kenton Pierce." Marc spoke through gritted teeth. His pupils were vertical slits in the glittering golden brown of his irises. "But I think in your case, that would come with certain obligations."

But pledging anything to Kent was the farthest thing from my mind.

"There are too many of them…" I still stared at my room, but what I saw was the line of cars. The dozens of men Malone—officially, Kent Pierce—had brought. "We can't take them."

"We couldn't even if we were evenly matched," Jace said, half-seated on the end of the bed. "They're armed. Ten of them, anyway."

"They're kicking us out." I said it. I understood it. But I couldn't believe it.

"The rest of us, yes." Marc's face was so flushed I was afraid his eyes would pop out of his skull from the pressure. "They're trying to keep you and the doc. The most valuable resources."

"They'd have to kill me first."

My mother huffed, and I was relieved to see anger winning out over her tears. "They very nearly did. But I have to say, this whole maneuver seems pointless They have to know you're not going to stay here with Kent. How long can he possibly expect to hold on to a territory with no tabby?"

"He probably doesn't realize he's actually lost Manx and Kaci yet," I said, sparing a moment to be grateful that they'd gotten away. "Once they figure that out, they'll probably make a move for one or both of them." And we weren't ready for that yet. I shook my head and my shoulder ached worse. "We can't wait for their next move. We'll regroup, and come back on our own terms. I have a plan." Everyone tried to talk at once, but I spoke over them. "Let's go."

My mother frowned. "Don't you want to rest first?"

"I can rest in the car. For now, I want to get out of here so I don't have to see that bastard sitting in Dad's chair. Everybody pack up quickly. Mom, can you take some more stuff for Kaci and Manx?" They hadn't had time to take much.

"Of course." She stood and helped me up, when the room threatened to slide right out from under me.

I glanced from Marc to Jace and back. "You two pack for yourselves and for the other guys. Put Vic and Brian on watch at the front door, and Parker by the back door, where he won't have to see his father or brother."

They both nodded, already heading out with my mom.

While the others carried out their tasks, I packed slowly and carefully, with Dr. Carver's help, desperately wishing for the use of both eyes. I hurt all over, but refused to take anything stronger than Tylenol until we were on the road. Carver's pills wore off quickly—damned Shifter metabolism—but, while they were in effect, tended to render me less than coherent. Or conscious.

I packed everything I could fit into the two suitcases in my closet, taking special care to empty my underwear drawer. Otherwise, I'd have nightmares about strangers riffling through my stuff while I wasn't around to defend it.

Fifteen minutes later, the guys were back, carrying three suitcases each. Jace went to help my mom with Kaci's stuff, and Marc sent the doc to pack some food and drinks. Then he closed my bedroom door and we were alone for the first time since my father had died.

I closed my eyes, suddenly nervous for no reason I could have named. "So…I guess I'm gonna look like Rocky for a while." I'd intentionally avoided more than a brief glimpse of my face while I packed, but that one glance was enough. My nose was puffy and discolored. Both of my eyes were black, one swollen almost shut. My lower lip was split and bloody. And my left cheek was purple. I wouldn't even have been able to recognize myself, if it weren't for the pain—that was getting to be pretty familiar.

"You know that doesn't matter to me."

"Good. Because if today's any indication, this may be how I spend the majority of my tenure as Alpha."

"I thought he was going to kill you," Marc whispered, leaning against the door.

"Sounds like he tried." I shoved my spare work boots into the second suitcase and forced the zipper around a tight corner, one hand pressed to my throbbing cracked rib. "Thank you for stopping it."

"Promise me you won't do this again."

"Hell, I didn't mean to do it this time. The plan was to win."

Marc crossed the room in an instant and pulled me up by my good arm. I winced, and he loosened his grip, but didn't let go. "I'm serious, Faythe. You can't win against Dean. Not even in a fair fight. This isn't what your dad had in mind when he named you. Being Alpha isn't just about fighting. Hell, most of them are too old for that, anyway. And I can't watch him kill you."

"You won't have to." I stood on my toes to kiss him, half-afraid he wouldn't kiss me back. That he'd be too mad, or...repulsed by my raw-meat face.

He kissed me like we might not for touch again for years. Like he thought he'd lost me.

I rested my forehead on his chin, glad I could breathe through my nose again, so I could inhale his scent. I hurt so badly, and I just wanted to be held. But that wasn't an option for an Alpha. Especially a disgraced Alpha.

"Are you ready?" His arms slipped around me slowly, careful of my many deep bruises.

"Yeah. Let's get out of here." I stopped in the office to grab the Pride call tree, then we met everyone else in the hallway, all seven of the guys loaded down with suitcases. My mom pulled her own wheeled bag and held a cardboard box loaded with my father's plaques, awards, and personal papers.

"Three cars," I said, when I was sure I had everyone's attention, struggling to focus through encompassing pain. "Marc and I will go with Jace. Vic, you take Owen and my mom. Protect her with your life."

Vic almost looked insulted. "As if it were in doubt."

I nodded, pleased. "Parker, take Brian and the doc. We stay together on the road, stay in touch via cell, and don't stop until we get to the free zone border. Understood?"

Everyone nodded, and I took a deep breath, then met my mother's gaze. "I'm sorry. I'm so sorry, but I swear I will fix this. *We* will fix this."

"Yes." She nodded firmly. "We will."

By then, the usurpers knew we were leaving, and they were buzzing with vicious excitement, eager to descend on the spoils of Kent and Dean's war. When I opened the front door, dozens of eyes watched me.

I ignored them all. I limped across the porch and down the steps staring straight ahead, pretending I didn't hear them. I was almost to Marc's car when Kenton Pierce stepped into my path.

"You know you don't have to go."

I tried to ignore him, but he wouldn't move, and I wasn't going to walk around him. "I'm not broken," I growled through jaws clenched shut. "I can and will drop you like bad cell service." Even if it nearly killed me.

Kent frowned. "I'm just saying you'd be safe here. I swear no one will touch you."

"If I thought you actually had the power to guarantee

that, I might… No, I wouldn't." I could hear disgust dripping from my voice. "Enjoy it while it lasts."

"Fine, if that's the way you want it." His face flushed—I'd embarrassed him. "But you know that if you won't stay and eventually accept me, we'll have to go get either Manx or Kaci. You're not leaving us much of a choice." Because without a dam, there could be no permanent Alpha.

"We won't let you take them." In fact, we'd die defending them.

Kent nodded stiffly, then glanced at Malone, and his next words sounded rehearsed. "If you, Marc Ramos, or Jace Hammond set foot in this territory without permission again, you'll be rearrested and tried on the outstanding charges."

I ignored the threat and walked on, tensing the closer we drew to Dean. Marc stiffened on my left, and I knew he wanted to put himself between me and Dean. But he didn't, and I had enormous respect for his self-control.

Dean crowded us on purpose, standing as close to the car as he could without actually touching it. When I opened the door, he leaned close. "I'm ready to finish the job whenever you are…" he whispered.

I dropped my suitcase and he lurched away from my right fist—and directly into the path of my left.

Dean stumbled back, one hand over his jaw. But he came up laughing, while I struggled not to show how much the blow had hurt my ribs and my shoulder.

The guys loaded the luggage, and as Vic held the door open for my mother, Malone approached her with his hand out, like he'd shake hers. Like they were sharing an amiable parting. "I'm sorry about the trouble,

Karen," he said, loud and clear, so everyone could hear how reasonable he was being.

She scowled up at him, eyes narrowed. Her arm flew almost faster than I could see. The smack of flesh against flesh was loud in the silence, and a small red handprint stood out starkly on his left cheek. "You have no idea how sorry you're going to be."

Twenty-four

I lay across Jace's backseat in the rapidly descending darkness, my head on a pillow, but they wouldn't let me sleep for long, because I'd lost consciousness—twice—and my pupils were dilated. Or not dilated. Whichever is bad after a head injury. Marc kept his window open at the top so the cold air would help keep me awake, and he kept checking on me. Talking to me.

But I didn't want to talk. I wanted to sleep. And I really wanted to punch something, but that train had already left the station and I wasn't on it. Evidently I'd been fucking *hit* by it.

"Faythe, it really is going to be okay, one way or another," Jace said, and I wished I could see him, but the rearview mirror was out of my line of sight.

"I know." But not anytime soon. "When can I Shift? What did the doc say?"

"He didn't. And I'm assuming that means not yet." Marc twisted in the front passenger seat to face me again, but I could hardly stand to look at him. I'd lost. I'd been humiliated, dominated, beaten, and nearly killed. And I'd let them down. All of them. All my men. Kaci.

My mother. And my father. Somehow, knowing I'd failed him hurt the worst. Even worse than my head.

"You want some more Tylenol?" Jace asked, and leather creaked as he shifted in the driver's seat. "You can't have anything stronger yet—nothing that will knock you out—but we have plenty of Tylenol."

"No, thanks." The pain was unbelievable, and as impossible as it seemed, I literally hurt everywhere. Even in my fingers. The incessant roar in my head was the worst, but my ribs and face took a close second place. But physical pain couldn't compare to the knowledge that I'd lost the Pride. The whole damn thing. Now Malone's puppet regime had settled into my father's house. They would sleep in my parents' room, go through our things, and generally rub salt into the open wound that my very existence had become.

I closed my eyes and sighed, trying to put it all away. Self-pity and self-doubt were not Alpha-worthy traits, and I did not have time to indulge them. Not if I was going to reclaim what I'd lost, either through challenging Kent—though I couldn't fight Dean again; that much was clear—or by full-scale attack.

Bracing myself for more pain, I sat up slowly, hissing when the Pathfinder hit a bump and my entire body was jostled.

Marc scowled at me. "Lie back down."

"I need the call tree and my phone." He'd held my cell while I'd fought, so it wouldn't get smashed.

"You need to rest for now. We'll start making calls when we get there."

"By then Malone will have gotten to most of them, and there's no telling what his version of the hostile takeover will sound like. Give me the phone. Please."

"We took the records," Jace insisted, as a passing highway light briefly lit the entire car. "It'll take him a while to get in touch with all the Pride members with no list and no numbers."

"Which is why we need to press our advantage. Now. They're still our toms—those who choose to stand with us—and they deserve to know what really happened." They all knew about my father, of course. We'd made those calls two days earlier. But they didn't know he'd been buried, and until Malone—or Kenton Pierce—got in touch with them, they wouldn't know about the regime change.

"Fine." Marc sighed, already digging in his bag for the member list. "But let me make the calls. If you're planning to try Shifting soon, you need to rest."

I thought about that for a moment, then nodded and laid down on my side again, my legs bent at the knee, in spite of the pain in my hips. I felt like I was shirking a big responsibility by not telling the other Pride members myself, but Marc was right. I'd be little good to them until I was healed.

However, listening to the calls was torture. Hearing my own failure and humiliation—even through Marc's blessedly biased perspective—made me feel like crawling into a hole and never coming out. At least, not until I'd redeemed myself. Which would be hard to do from my hole.

Other than Dr. Carver and Carey Dodd, I hadn't had much personal contact with the other nonenforcer toms. Most of them hadn't yet been contacted by Kent's men and they were all shocked and outraged by what we had to tell them. Most made informal vows of loyalty over the phone and promised to leave the territory immediately.

But they were not all eager to forswear the new leadership in favor of an unproven young female Alpha who'd lost a challenge—and almost lost her life—during her first week on the job. We lost about a third of our men, and the real bitch was that I couldn't blame them for having no faith in me.

After Marc made all his calls, I asked for my phone again so I could start calling our allies. Marc tried to talk me into letting him make those calls, too, but I refused. I had to be the one to call the other Alphas.

We compromised. I would call my uncle, then I'd let Uncle Rick call Di Carlo and Taylor.

Marc handed over my phone, and I sat up to autodial. I was sure Malone would have already called him, but I should have known better. Malone wouldn't be eager to advertise what he'd done until his new puppet Alpha had had a chance to recruit as many of our former Pride members as possible.

"Hello? Faythe?" my uncle said into the phone. My silence was the only reason he had to suspect trouble; I'd already spoken to him twice that morning, planning our now-defunct attack.

"Yeah, it's me." I leaned with my head on the window, letting the cold glass leach some of the heat from my utter humiliation. "Call your men back, if you've already sent them. There's been a change in plans."

"What happened?"

"Malone found out about the funeral and came in early with eight cars full of toms. Kenton Pierce challenged me, and Colin Dean fought in his place."

"What happened?" He sounded sick, and he hadn't even heard the worst yet.

"He nearly killed her," Jace called from the front seat as he steered us around a sharp curve, and I groaned, but couldn't argue.

"Marc called the fight when I lost consciousness." I closed my eyes, and realized I never wanted to open them again. "I lost, Uncle Rick. They kicked us out. We're on the way to Marc's house in the free zone now, and the only good news I have is that we got Kaci, Manx, and Des out before Malone and his men saw them. And Holly, too. She was there for the funeral."

There was silence, other than the highway wind, as my uncle considered the new information. "Are you okay?"

"No," Marc answered for me. "She has a concussion, a broken nose, two black eyes, a cracked rib, a possible skull fracture, and more bruises than I can count. She's supposed to be resting."

"I'm fine," I insisted, speaking through pain I refused to elaborate on. "And we're going to get it back. All of it. We're gonna go back in, and this time we *will* surprise them. If you're still with me." Because the third time was a charm. Right?

"You know I am. But you have to heal first. Call me tomorrow, and we'll make more concrete plans. Okay?"

"Of course."

"Guys, make sure she gets some rest, okay?"

I smiled in spite of myself as the guys answered. Uncle Rick sounded so much like my father that I was both happy and sad at the same time. I couldn't believe how much I missed him, though I knew how disappointed he'd be in me if he were still there.

By the end of a nine-hour drive spent sandwiched between the other two cars in our caravan, the least significant of my injuries had become dull throbs and most of my sore muscles had stiffened up. But my cracked rib and pummeled face hurt like Dean had come back to kick me while I was down, and my head had become the source of all earthly misery.

When we turned into Marc's driveway, my heart leaped into my throat. I didn't want to go in the house. I didn't want them to see me in my current state, and I didn't want to face them after my failure. But they already knew what had happened—my mother had called Michael from the car right after we'd left—and I couldn't avoid facing my own Pride. Not if I claimed to be their leader.

Vic pulled his car in behind Marc's—which he'd left when we'd brought him back to the ranch—and we parked beside him, behind Ryan's POS. Parker stopped right behind us.

Marc was out of the car before Jace could kill the engine. He opened the rear passenger door, but instead of helping me out, he got in next to me. "Are you okay?"

I put my head on his shoulder and let him hold me. "I have honestly never been less okay in my life."

"Yeah." He hesitated, and I knew there was more. "I only have the one bed. I want you to take it. You need to rest, and I'll…I'll just watch you sleep." They'd have to watch me for a while, because of the head trauma. "I'll have everyone else leave you alone until you feel like…being with people."

"No." I shook my head firmly, in spite of the pain. "I

appreciate the bed—I feel like I could sleep for a month. But I have to talk to them first. How can I claim to be their Alpha if I can't even face them?"

"It can wait a couple of hours," Jace said from the front seat, twisted so that he could see us both.

"No, it can't. It's already waited more than nine," I insisted. Someone knocked on the car window, and I looked up to see my mother peering anxiously at us. "Let's go. They're probably worried enough as it is."

I made it to the house under my own power, but my left hip hurt with every step, so I let Marc help me onto the porch. Jace held the door open for me, and the collective gasp when I stepped into the living room could have silenced the crowd at Texas Stadium.

Michael stood from the couch, where he'd been talking softly to Holly, and briefly, I wondered how he'd explained all this to her. We could always tell her I'd fallen out of a tree....

"Faythe...?" Kaci stood in the middle of the kitchen, holding an unopened can of Coke, staring at me as if she didn't quite recognize me. Or didn't want to.

"I'm fine. Really," I insisted. But as soon as she heard my voice—thus had to believe what she saw—she dropped the can, and it rolled under the nearest cabinet.

"Yeah." Michael came closer, studying my face in the inadequate light. "Wherein 'fine' means 'beaten to within an inch of your life.'"

"More like half an inch." I tried to smile, but the expression felt all wrong. "But I really am fine. I wouldn't mind sitting down, though."

Marc led me to the couch where I sat next to Holly, who stared at me with her mouth hanging open. Her face was tearstained, her makeup a distant memory, yet she was stunning next to me, I had no doubt.

"What…? What…? What…?" But she couldn't complete the thought.

"She keeps saying that," Kaci said, sinking onto the couch on my other side. "Pound her on the back, and she may actually finish a sentence."

The rest of the enforcers followed us in, carrying suitcases, and the minute he saw Manx, standing near one wall, rocking the sleeping baby in her arms, Owen dropped the bag he carried and made a beeline in her direction.

"You're okay?" He peeked at the baby, then stared down at her like the sun couldn't shine on a world without Manx in it. "Both of you?" The obvious fear and love in his expression broke my heart. Owen didn't have a poker face; everything he felt could be read clearly on his features and there wasn't a mean cell in his entire body. His heart could be broken so easily.

"We are fine." She smiled up at him, her features mirroring the transparent relief on his. "Now."

No, Manx wouldn't break his heart. But life just might. Owen wasn't a leader, and he was only a competent fighter. And in our world, men like that, ordinary, bighearted gentlemen, didn't get to marry and raise families, because they couldn't protect them.

At the sound of my mother's heels on the scarred hardwood, I looked up to find her watching Owen with a mixture of pride and fear, as if she were thinking the very same thing. Then she glanced around the room for Ryan, and for the first time I noticed him standing in the corner alone, watching. His gaze met mine, but I couldn't read his expression, and I didn't have the energy to deal with him at the moment.

"Dean did this?" Michael knelt in front of me for a better look. He started to tilt my face toward the light, then seemed to think better of it. "How bad is it?" But he was talking to the doctor, who'd just come in the door with his medical bag.

"Who's Dean?" Holly asked, her eyes still glazed with shock. "Some kind of mafia hit man? Why was he after Faythe? Is this some kind of…safe house?"

"You didn't tell her?" I frowned at Michael, though the movement hurt every muscle in my face.

He shrugged miserably. "No matter how I start, it sounds ridiculous. And, I have to admit, the automatic death sentence is a damn strong deterrent." He turned to Holly then, still kneeling, and put one hand on her leg, and his love shone even through his fear and frustration. "But I swear on my life that I am not in the mafia. None of us are." Before she could argue, he turned back to the doc for an answer.

"Obviously Faythe's nose is broken," Carver said. "And I suspect she has a hairline skull fracture and a cracked rib. Other than that, she's basically one big bruise. And there seems to be residual pain and soreness in her left hip and shoulder, from impact with the ground."

"Impact…?" Michael raised one brow, at me this time, but Marc beat me to it.

"The bastard picked her up like a clean and jerk, and threw her at the ground. Then he tried to kick her face in."

"Damn it, Faythe…" Michael swore, standing, and

his green eyes darkened with rage like I'd rarely seen in him. "I'll kill him."

"You'll have to wait in line," Jace said, just as Holly squeaked, "You kill people?"

"Michael. I'll be fine, and we have bigger things to worry about." I cleared my throat and summoned my Alpha voice, hoping it hadn't been revoked in light of my humiliating near-death experience. "First of all, sleeping arrangements. We're going to be here for a few days at least, and the quarters are obviously cramped. Though we are grateful for the 'safe house.'" I smiled at Marc, and he tried to smile back, but obviously my broken face kind of killed the humor. "Marc, do you still have those air mattresses from last time?"

"Yeah. Two of them. In the hall closet. And there's a hand pump, too."

"Good. Take Parker into town and buy several more. And get an electric pump, or we'll never get them all blown up. Also, blankets and pillows. Use Parker's company card." Which my father had issued to each of us, for Pride business expenses. And this definitely qualified, even if we weren't officially in the Pride anymore.

Marc nodded, though I could tell from his scowl that he didn't want to leave me here. But he wouldn't argue, because it wouldn't be safe for Parker to go into town—in the free zone—without him. The local stray population knew Marc's scent from the time he'd spent here, and most of them would know what he'd suffered to help them, after Malone's plot to tag them all with GPS tracking chips.

"Mom…" I turned, holding my sore side, to find her watching me, one arm linked through Ryan's. "You, Kaci, and Manx can stay in the front bedroom. Michael, you and Holly take the middle room. It's small, but you'll have it to yourselves." For at least some semblance of privacy, though we'd be able to hear anything they said. "The guys can camp out in here.

"Ryan…" I started, then stopped. I wanted to kick him out. Driving the refugees into the free zone didn't absolve him of past crimes, and I still couldn't look at him without remembering that he'd set me up to be kidnapped and sold. But we needed him, and I couldn't let my personal grudges stand in the way of the Pride's well-being. *The greater good, Faythe.*

"Are you staying?" I finally asked. "Can we trust you?"

"Yes, on both counts." Ryan nodded calmly. "I want to make up for—"

"No. You can't." I wanted there to be no mistake about that. "But you do owe me," I said, and he nodded again. "Take Vic into town and get food. Lots of food. Manx, will you show them what kind of diapers you need?" I asked, and she nodded, but before she could move, Owen was already digging in her diaper bag for samples.

I looked around the room, taking it all in. Meeting each pair of eyes. Wishing desperately that my father were there. Had we buried him only that morning? It already felt like an eternity had passed since I'd seen him.

Marc hovered near the door, holding his car keys, ready for action as usual. Jace stood in the doorway to the hall, watching me carefully, his expression a mixture of concern for me and…restlessness. He looked like he wanted to do something about our current situation, and standing still was about to kill him.

Most of the other guys looked pissed off and a little disoriented, but not truly traumatized by our forced relocation, because the burden wasn't theirs, and neither was the responsibility. They had the luxury of following orders, and evidently the confidence that I would know what to do soon, if I didn't already. That I could lead them.

If only I had that same confidence in myself.

My mother looked exhausted, plain and simple. I caught Ryan's attention and nodded subtly toward an empty armchair, then pointedly at our mother. He led her to sit.

Kaci sat glued to my side, oblivious to the many bruises my clothes hid, clinging to the only thing she understood, the only thing she still had, when the rest of her world had been ripped out from under her. She was homeless and on the run—again—and the only difference this time was that she wasn't alone. And for the moment, that was all I had to offer her.

Holly… My biggest regret of the day—other than not being able to pound Dean into a large puddle of pureed tomcat—was that Holly had been with us when the proverbial shit hit the fan. But truthfully, I wasn't sure how safe the south-central territory would be for her now, without us there, and the only alternative would mean separating her from her husband.

At the moment, she looked confused and scared, but mostly mad, and my opinion of her went up another notch at the steady spark of anger in her eyes.

"As of now, we are officially in exile," I began, when I was sure I had everyone's attention. "However, I have a plan. We will take our territory back. But it's going to take a few days to organize, which is actually kind of convenient, because it's probably going to take a few days for me to heal. Right, Doc?" I forced a good-humored smile his way, and he tried to return it.

"At least."

"Until then," I continued. "This is home. I want everyone to get plenty of rest tonight, because tomorrow, we make plans to bury the new council chair. And don't worry about the shovel shortage," I said, glancing from face to determined face. "Because Calvin Malone has just dug his own grave."

Twenty-five

"Holly, would you like a drink?" I asked, eyeing Michael, wondering why he hadn't thought of that already. But he only shook his head, and I caught a flare of annoyance in his frown.

"She doesn't drink. Alcohol has too many calories."

And homemade cocoa doesn't? I glanced from my brother to his wife, whose hands were actually shaking in her lap. "I think she'd make an exception today."

Holly nodded, crossing her legs beneath her funeral skirt. "Something strong." Maybe some of my clothes would fit her, until we could take her shopping.

Michael stood, and I called after him as he headed for the kitchen. "There should be several bottles left under the sink, and with any luck, the ice tray's full. But I doubt there's anything to mix with, other than Coke."

While he poured, I glanced around the living room, assessing the general level of despair while I tried to decide how best to help my brother tell his wife that he wasn't entirely human. And neither was his family.

We had a little more breathing room, with four of the

toms gone on errands, but Marc's small house was still a tight fit for a group our size. I'd sent my mother to lie down, and Jace had blown up one of the air mattresses in the front bedroom for Manx and Des, who were both already asleep. He'd blown the other one up for Kaci, but so far she'd refused to leave my side, and I couldn't really blame her.

Owen, Brian, Carver, and Jace were playing poker at the card table in the kitchen, but had only made it through two hands so far, because Owen kept leaving to check on Manx, and Jace kept staring at me rather than at his hand.

Michael returned with a drink for his wife—whiskey and Coke, based on the scent—and sank onto the couch next to her, drawing in a long, tense breath. He was ready. But I couldn't let him do it.

Disclosure of our existence to a human was a capital offense, punishable by an automatic death sentence. In this particular case, we had no choice—Holly obviously knew something was very, very wrong, and even her mafia fixation would cease to make sense once we started planning for the renaissance of the south-central Pride.

But I couldn't give Malone a chance to take another brother from me or a husband from Holly. And if they didn't want to kill me for handing Lance Pierce over to the thunderbirds, then disclosing our secret to Holly wouldn't change that.

"Michael. Let me."

He frowned. "Faythe…"

I shrugged. My Pride. My responsibility. "What are they going to do? Kill me twice?"

"You sure?" Michael asked, eyeing me closely.

"Yeah."

"Okay, what the hell are you talking about?" Holly drained her short glass and coughed, then clutched it like nothing else in the world made sense at that moment. "If you're not some kind of mob family, who were the men in those cars and how can they kick you out of your own home? And if we had to run away to protect the women and children, why did we leave Faythe behind?"

Michael put a hand on her arm, trying to calm her. "Faythe isn't a woman—she's an Alpha."

I frowned at Michael, warning him not to say anything else. All the important facts needed to come from me, or he'd be opening himself up to serious trouble.

"Um, point of fact," Jace chimed in from the card table, flaunting an actual grin—the first I'd seen in a while. "That's not an either/or. She's very definitely a woman, too."

Michael's eyes narrowed in irritation, but he refrained from replying, probably because his own personal life was in a bit of a shambles at the moment. He knew about me and Jace—we'd made a detail-less disclosure to the adult members of the household, out of necessity—but Kaci did not, so I shot Jace a censorious glance.

He shrugged in apology, but didn't look very sorry.

"I'm not following any of this," Holly snapped, and I had to respect her spirit. "Look, I know something's wrong, and you guys have always been a little weird— sorry, but it's true—and I'm sitting here scared to death that someone's going to bust down the door with an automatic weapon and *equalize* us. So I wish you'd just spit it out. Whatever you have to say can't be worse than what I'm imagining."

"Don't bet on that…" Kaci mumbled, and I put a hand on her arm to quiet her.

"You're right." I tried to smile at Holly to reassure her, but I couldn't make my mouth cooperate. I was not in a smiley kind of place. "I'm sorry for what you've been through today, and I know it must be scary. But I need you to be patient. And as openminded as you can possibly manage."

Holly only nodded, splitting her focus between me and Michael.

"We're not in any kind of mob or gang, though I can understand how it might look like that, from the outside." I took a deep breath, uncomfortably aware that I was about to intentionally break one of our three most important laws. "We're shape-shifters. Specifically, feline. We're werecats. All of us."

Holly blinked. Then she blinked again. Her mouth opened, then snapped shut. Then she turned to Michael, brows raised in question. "I'm seriously traumatized here, and she's making jokes. This isn't funny. Tell me what the hell is going on, or I'm out of here. For good, Michael."

"She's not joking. I know it sounds impossible. Crazy—" he began, but she cut him off.

"You think! I hope the men in those cars had a year's supply of straitjackets and Thorazine, because you're all insane. All of you. I'm leaving…" She tried to stand, and my hand closed over her wrist. Michael stood with her, moving smoothly between his wife and the front door.

"Let go of me!" She snatched her arm from my grip, and I let her go. Everyone was watching Holly now, except for Jace, who watched me expectantly.

"Michael…" I warned, hoping he could calm her without…extreme measures.

"Holly, you can't go. It's not safe—"

"The hell I can't." She tried to step around him, and he took her by both arms, pleading with her silently to cooperate.

I stood. "Look, I'd show you myself, but in case you haven't noticed, I'm not exactly at my best tonight." And Dr. Carver had forbidden Shifting until morning, at least.

Jace stood and dropped his cards on the table. "I'll show her."

"No." I wasn't going to put anyone else at risk.

Jace rolled his eyes. "Cal wants me dead, anyway. What's he gonna do, kill me twice?" He flashed another grin at having thrown my own words back at me, and I could only scowl. "Besides, you already told her. She's fully disclosed. I'm just offering a demonstration."

I thought for a moment, then finally nodded.

Jace stepped into the middle of the living room, already pulling his shirt over his head. His arms bulged in the light from the dusty fixture overhead.

"What is he doing?" Holly demanded, and she actually took a step back when he unbuttoned his pants. "Why is he taking off his clothes?" She glanced at Kaci, then at Michael, silently demanding that he put a stop to what must have seemed like absolute insanity, for the sake of the child, if for nothing else.

Kaci cleared her throat, drawing Holly's attention as Jace stepped out of his jeans and underwear and dropped onto his hands and knees. "It's weird at first. Especially all the nudity. I know, 'cause I used to be like you. But Shifting with clothes on just doesn't make any sense.

I tried it once. My shirt tore and I got all tangled up in my jeans."

Holly only gaped at her until Michael took his wife's hand. When she turned back to him, he gestured to where Jace was now on the floor on all fours, in the first phase of his Shift. His skin began to ripple, and Holly gasped. Her hands shook, the tremors so violent she nearly dropped her empty glass. When his wrists and ankles lengthened, she took a step back, ripping her hand from Michael's grip. "No. No, this isn't real. You…you put something in that drink. What did you do to me?"

Michael faced his wife and took her chin gently in both hands, forcing her to look at him. He leaned down so that their foreheads met and whispered to her, crooning almost like he would to a child. "It's real, Holly. It's all real. I'm sorry I never told you, and I'm even sorrier that I have to now. But you need to see this. This is who I am. This is who we all are, and if you can't live with that after you truly understand it, then you can go. No one will stop you."

Though that was up for debate. We couldn't risk her telling anyone else, and frankly, that hadn't truly seemed like a credible threat until that very moment.

"But first you have to see," Michael finished. Then he stepped to the side, revealing Jace again.

Jace's hands and feet had become paws, his digits already plumping into toe pads. His fingernails lengthened and hardened into claws, even as his head began to bulge and shift with the formation of his new muzzle.

Holly's pulse raced. Each breath came faster than the last. She was hyperventilating, and based on her physiological signs of stress, *she* could have been the one Shifting.

"It's okay…" Michael whispered, his arms around her waist for comfort, his chin resting on her shoulder. I'd rarely seen him like that, as the gentle, concerned husband, and even though she was clearly near total breakdown, she didn't push him away. He could still comfort her, even when he was part of what she feared. It was achingly sweet, in the most surreal way imaginable.

In the middle of the floor, Jace looked like a giant, bald cat. His spine was a knobby ridge trailing over his back, ending in a long, flesh-colored tail. And as I watched, thick black fur began to sprout at his spine, spreading rapidly to cover his entire body.

Holly gasped again, but she now looked more awed than anything, though there were still clear lines of fear and disbelief around her eyes. Seconds later, the show was over. Jace stood tall on four legs, arching his spine dramatically as he stretched to get comfortable in his new form, like a giant Halloween cat. Then he stuck his rump in the air and waved his tail in greeting.

Fortunately, he refrained from showing off either his sharp new teeth or his wickedly curved, retractable claws. Either of which might have been too much for Holly, at least this early in the game.

Jace stepped toward her, and Holly yelped and nearly backed over her husband.

Kaci laughed, and her genuine amusement sounded strange to my ears—I hadn't heard it in such a long time. She crossed the floor toward Jace boldly and sank to her knees in front of him, running one hand over his head to scratch behind his ears.

"Karli, don't!" Holly breathed, but Kaci only laughed again.

"It's okay. I can do that, too. Wanna see?"

But though she looked fascinated, Holly clearly did not want to see any more Shifting just yet.

Jace purred and rubbed his cheek against Kaci's, marking her with his scent, reassuring her that they were still good friends—a typical cat greeting. Kaci trailed her hand over his back, as far as she could reach without getting up. Then she looked up at Holly, and the calm I saw on her face—some small bit of peace, in spite of so much recent trauma—eased part of the guilt weighing so heavily on my heart and mind. Kaci was okay. Somehow, in spite of all she'd been through with us and before she'd found us, Kaci was going to be just fine. And if anyone could help Holly adjust, it was our own little human-born tabby.

"You wanna pet him?" Kaci asked, encouraging Holly with her unspoken display of trust. Her comfort with the huge cat did more to convince Holly than anything we could have said to her. "He'll let you. If I ask him to," Kaci added as an afterthought, and I smiled at her small, instinctive attempt to establish her rank in the Pride—over Holly. That meant that she considered herself to have come first, but also that she recognized Holly as one of us. Part of the family, finally. For better or for worse.

"Um, I don't…" Holly started, and Michael rubbed her arm.

"Go ahead. It's okay. He's still Jace. In fact, he's almost more Jace now than he was in human form."

Holly frowned at that, but when Michael tugged her forward, she let him.

She wouldn't kneel next to the giant cat—proving that humans aren't completely devoid of a self-preservation instinct—but she did bend over and tentatively touch the fur on his back, once Jace had given her permission with a soft purr.

The moment she touched him, she believed. I saw the difference in her face. It was one thing to see—we truly could have spiked her drink, or she could have been dreaming. But she couldn't deny the physical reality beneath her hand.

Holly's eyes widened, and she stroked Jace's back again. "It's soft, but kind of coarse…" she whispered, as if speaking out loud might anger the cat and get her eaten. "Not like a house cat."

"We're not house cats," Michael said softly, and Holly stood to look at him.

"You can…? You can do this?"

He nodded, studying her reaction carefully. "I *have* to do this at least every few weeks, or I get sick. But I usually do it a lot more often than that. It's part of who I am."

"That's where you go…" Holly was studying her husband now. "That's why you're always on the ranch. So you can do this. So you can *be* this."

I shrugged. "Well, that, and because we've kind of had a bad patch lately, politically speaking."

"What does that mean?" Holly asked, and Michael promised to explain it later, insisting that she'd probably heard enough for the moment. Half an hour later, they retired to their room, and I could hear Michael whispering to her, explaining about territories, and Prides, and the council, in spite of his proclamation that sleep ought to come before further trauma.

I liked Holly even more for her persistence.

While we waited for the other toms to return, Dr. Carver gave me another once-over on the couch. My eyes were dilating properly by then and I had no more dizziness or nausea, though I still looked like I'd fallen face-first into a meat grinder. And felt like it, too.

The doc said that if nothing went wrong in the night—a possibility which evidently included a stroke from a blood clot in my brain— I would be clear to start Shifting to heal in the morning. But for the moment, he insisted I take several Tylenol and go to sleep.

I tried. I really did. But I couldn't find a comfortable position on the couch—I still hurt all over and could hardly see out of my left eye—and I wasn't willing to oust my mother from the only bed. And every time I closed my eyes, Dean was waiting behind my eyelids to kick me in the head, or to cut me again, or to slice my clothes open. After about an hour, Jace curled up on the floor in front of the couch, and I let one hand trail over his fur. He purred, and that sound and his scent made me feel safe enough to fall asleep, in spite of myriad pains Tylenol couldn't touch, and I didn't wake up until the other toms returned with our supplies.

When my mother heard them unloading the cars, she came out of the bedroom to help and insisted I get in the bed. Jace tried to follow me, but Marc snarled, and as I took off my jeans and climbed beneath the covers, I heard his footsteps clomp down the hall after us.

"*Hell,* no. This is still my house, and you're not going in my bedroom. Not with her. Not even in cat form."

Jace growled, but Marc must have held his ground, because Dr. Carver stepped in then and said he'd watch me for a while. Which was good, because I honestly didn't have the energy to break up another fight at the moment.

I fell asleep again and, that time, I didn't wake up for twelve straight hours.

Twenty-six

When I woke up, the room was bright with natural light, and Marc's alarm clock read 1:44. Thursday afternoon. *Shit.* I sat up too fast and gasped over the pain in my…everything, as the room seemed to swim around me.

"Whoa, slow down," Marc said from the desk chair, and I jumped, then flinched at the second flare of pain. I hadn't smelled him because the entire room already smelled like him. The chair creaked as he stood, then the bed squealed as he sat next to me. "How do you feel?"

"Like I should have Shifted five hours ago. Why did you let me sleep so long? I need to call my uncle." I threw back the covers and was surprised to discover that I was still wearing the shirt I'd fought in the day before, still stiff with my own dried blood. I stood—and almost screamed when my left foot hit the floor. My sore hip had stiffened while I slept, and a test movement from my left arm revealed that the same had happened with my shoulder.

"He already called. I told him you were still recuperating, and he's expecting a call from you this afternoon."

"Marc, you have to tell me when one of our allies calls! We have a lot to do, and we need their help. I'm the Alpha now!"

"You're going to be a dead Alpha if you don't take time to rest and heal."

"Consider me rested. And healing's on the agenda for today, too. But first I need to talk to Uncle Rick. Where's my phone?" When my heart stopped trying to pound its way out of my chest, I headed for my suitcase, in spite of the sharp pain in my side and my left hip.

"It's on the charger in the living room. What's the plan?"

"I'm going to talk to my uncle, then I'm going to Shift until I'm healed. Didn't I just say that?"

Marc huffed. "I was talking long-term. Yesterday you said you had an idea."

"Oh." I rummaged through the bag on Marc's dresser for a pair of exercise shorts and a T-shirt, since I wouldn't shower until after I'd Shifted enough to be presentable in human society. "Yeah. We're going to fight, and we're going to do it the right way. With the element of surprise on our side, and all our allies and men in place. Including the thunderbirds. Malone and his men can't defend against them any better than we could. The birds are going to be the determining factor in his war. We're gonna take back the ranch and the Pride. Permanently."

"So…road trip?" Jace asked from the doorway, and I nodded.

"Yeah. Once I'm healed enough to be seen in public." I started to pull my arms from the bloody turtleneck, but stopped when the pain in my side shot through my entire torso.

"Here, let me." Marc was at my side before I could answer, and I could hear Jace's teeth grind together from across the room as Marc ran his hands lightly up my sides beneath my shirt, holding it up so I could pull my arms free. He even stretched out the neck so it wouldn't brush my broken nose when he lifted it over my head. Jace stomped out of the room when Marc helped me into the shorts and clean T-shirt, still careful with my damaged face, but I hurt too badly to care whose feelings were bruised and who'd just used me to assert his dominance. Again.

Dressed, I limped into the front of the house for my phone.

The living room looked like a sleepaway camp. Someone had propped the air mattresses against one wall, but there wasn't enough furniture for everyone to have a seat, so most of the guys sat on the floor, playing cards in the middle of the living room. Manx was nursing Des on the couch, and Owen sat next to her, reassuring her softly that everything would be okay. They wouldn't be homeless for long. That I'd find a way to get us back home, or to start a new home. That she and the baby would be safe.

My mother was rattling around the kitchen, clanging pans, openly lamenting Marc's utter lack of a twenty-quart stockpot.

Kaci sat at the card table with Holly and Michael, playing the Shifters home version of Fact or Fiction. "So…what about allergies?" Holly asked, as I stepped around a pillow someone had left on the floor and narrowly missed an open suitcase. "Is anyone ever allergic to you guys? Because of cat dander?"

I rolled my eyes, glad she seemed to be adjusting, and Kaci laughed. Michael chuckled softly. "I think our dander is mostly human."

"Hey, how do you feel?" my mother asked, as I pulled my phone free of its cord on the kitchen counter. "You don't look much better."

"Thanks." I forced a smile. She was right. The bruises around my eyes were darker than they'd been the day before, the side of my head was swollen and horrifically tender to the touch, and my rib felt like it was being recracked with every step I took. But my poor nose... The bridge was very puffy and discolored, and the only bright side I could find, after an extensive search, was that thanks to Dr. Carver, it wouldn't heal crooked. "I feel like I got trampled by a bruin stampede, but I'll be better after I've had a chance to Shift and shower."

My mother opened her mouth, probably to tell me to be careful. But then she only closed her mouth and gave me a sad smile, and I could see in it everything she'd left unsaid—every consuming fear for me—and I loved her for both her concern and her restraint.

"I'll be careful," I said, and her smile developed, like one of those old Polaroids, suddenly brighter, where it had been gray before.

I dialed on the way back to the bedroom, waving a silent greeting to Kaci. She called my name, but before I could answer, my uncle was speaking into my ear. "Faythe?" I gave Kaci a one-minute finger, then ducked into the bedroom and closed the door on Marc and Jace before I realized they'd followed me down the hall.

"Did you get some rest?" Uncle Rick asked, as I

sank gingerly into the desk chair and pressed the power button on Marc's computer.

"More than I wanted. But I'm up and running now. I'm leaving tomorrow to recruit the thunderbirds, and I was thinking we could hit Kenton and his little toy soldiers on Monday morning. Before dawn, when they're least expecting it. If you're still with me."

"I'm in. And so are Bert Di Carlo and Aaron Taylor. They're standing by, waiting for word."

"Awesome."

"But, Faythe, Marc made it sound like you'd need a while to recuperate. Aren't you moving a little too fast?"

"We're running short on time and long on enemies, Uncle Rick," I said, then glanced up when the bedroom door opened. "I'll be fine by Monday." Marc stepped in with a steaming mug of coffee, flavoring the air with French vanilla creamer. Jace was right behind him, carrying several turkey sandwiches on a paper plate.

My uncle sighed into my ear. "Okay. But we need to know for sure that Malone and the bulk of his men are still on the ranch before we move in. Otherwise, even if we remove Kenton from the picture, what's to stop Malone from setting someone else up in his place?"

"I agree. Malone is the objective. We could send scouts in advance of—"

"Won't work," Marc said, setting the full mug carefully on his desktop. "You think he'd go to all the trouble of kicking us out, then not patrol his new territory? If he's still there, one of his men will smell us the minute we set foot on the property."

Damn. Marc was right, of course. And there was no way we could disguise our scents well enough to fool a fellow werecat, and no way we could avoid leaving them with every step we took.

But what if we didn't have to set *foot* on the property...?

"I have an idea." Marc's brows rose in question, but I shook my head to say I'd tell him later. "It's not a sure thing, but it's worth a shot."

"Okay, then, I'll leave that up to you unless I hear otherwise," my uncle said. "Do we know yet how Malone found out about the early funeral?"

I bit back a groan and picked up the mug. "The leak was on my team, but it's been taken care of. But just in case, I think all the men need to know exactly how much is riding on this. We can't afford to tip Malone off again."

"Agreed. I'm not planning to fill my men in until Sunday, and the penalty for discussing the maneuver to anyone outside the Pride—including family members— is expulsion."

"Good. It'll be the same on my end." I sipped from the mug, enjoying the warmth of it in my hand. "I'll call you after I speak to the Flight."

"Be careful, Faythe."

"You know I will." When I'd hung up, I raised the mug toward Marc like I'd toast him. "Thanks. You didn't have to do that." I was uncomfortable with the thought of either him or Jace waiting on me, but I wasn't going to turn down their help out of pride, especially when I was only twenty-four hours past the worst beating of my life.

Besides, how often had I taken coffee to my father?

But that thought didn't help. I wasn't my father. I wasn't even *like* my father. If I were, I wouldn't have lost—spectacularly—to Colin Dean. We wouldn't be hiding in the free zone, abusing Marc's generosity and taking over his small house. I wouldn't be planning a covert trip to another werecat free zone to solicit help from another species, whose only previous contact with us could hardly be described as "friendly." So I certainly didn't deserve to be treated like they'd treated my father. I had yet to earn that privilege.

"What's your idea about recon on the ranch?" Marc asked.

I set the mug down and jiggled his computer mouse, irritated by how long the computer was taking to boot up. "This is going to sound crazy, but thunderbirds can do much better reconnaissance than we can, from much farther away. From any decent distance, Malone and his men would have no idea they weren't regular birds, because there's nothing to judge scale against in the sky."

"You want the birds to do recon for us?" Jace sat with his hip on the edge of the desk until Marc scowled at him. He stood, but didn't move away.

"Yeah. It'd be safer and faster."

"And you think they're so bored they'll offer to spy on Malone for entertainment value?" Marc asked. "Because we can't afford to absolve their debt on anything less than full-scale combat."

"I know." I frowned. "Maybe I can present it as a package deal…"

Jace shrugged, drawing my attention. "You only need one bird for this job, right?"

"Yeah, I guess."

"What about Kai?" The thunderbird Owen had captured during their raid on our property. "We spared his life. According to their law, doesn't that mean he owes us?"

My smile developed slowly, and it was all for Jace. "That just might work. Thanks."

"So, we're leaving tomorrow?" Jace set the plate on the desk in front of me, then leaned against the wall where he could see both me and Marc.

"Yeah. I'm trying to book the flights, but the site's taking forever to load...."

"Here, let me do it," Marc said, already reaching for the mouse.

"Thanks." I set my credit card on the desk, then carried my plate and mug slowly to the side of the bed, where I used his old nightstand as a table. But even sitting up hurt my ribs, and it took most of my concentration to ignore the pain. "We need three seats on the earliest flight to Roswell tomorrow morning." Because Roswell was the nearest airport to the thunderbirds' nest. Seriously.

"So we're just gonna, what?" Jace frowned, as I bit into the first sandwich, wincing over the pain in my nose when I chewed. "Storm in on the ranch and start throwing punches? Don't you think they'll be expecting that?"

"Probably." I shrugged, then swallowed. "But the classics never die. And hopefully they won't be expecting air support." And I was just as bothered as the next guy by the fact that we needed help from another species to even our own odds. "We go in when they're not expecting us and we target Malone and Dean. And we fight anyone who stands between us and them."

"We might have to kill Kent," Marc said, as his computer hummed and beeped, the outdated dial-up modem protesting its involvement in the day's work.

"Kent's already made his choice, and he'll have to live with the consequences. Or not." Jace frowned again, and I knew what he was thinking. I didn't want Parker to lose another brother, and I certainly didn't want to be the one who made that happen. Especially after Kent had offered me what he naively considered to be safe asylum in my own former home. But there were bigger issues at stake, and I'd do what I had to do to protect my men.

And to earn their trust back.

I'd just finished the third and final sandwich when Marc finally spun in his desk chair to face me. "Okay, we take off from Jackson at 9:38 in the morning. We need to be there an hour early, minimum, and it's a two-hour drive. So we'll have to leave here around 6:00 a.m."

"Great. Thanks." I finished my now-lukewarm coffee, then handed both dishes to Jace. "I'm going to Shift a couple of times, and hopefully start to put this head trauma behind me. Not to mention the broken nose. I can hardly stand to look in the mirror at the moment." And the lower arc of my field of vision was a bluish purple haze of bruises I could barely see.

"You'll have to eat again between Shifts," Jace said, heading slowly, reluctantly, toward the hall. "I'll bring some more sandwiches in about half an hour. Do you need anything else?"

"A meat mallet and one more shot at Dean's head," I said, carefully pulling the T-shirt over my head all on my own. If I couldn't take the pain of changing clothes, how the hell was I going to Shift?

Jace forced a grin, but beneath the effort, he looked tense. Disappointed. "Soon, hopefully. Yell if you need anything else."

I tried on a smile, but it didn't work. "Thanks, but I just need to Shift." And to heal. And to think. And to become a competent, respectable Alpha overnight. I met Marc's gaze. "Can you get the guys up to speed on the plan? And smell Parker's breath? He's officially cut off from the bar until further notice."

"Sure." Marc selected Shut Down from the start menu on his desktop, then turned off the monitor and stood to push his desk chair in. "Do you want me to bring you more coffee? Or some water?"

"I'm fine for now, guys. Really." I glanced over Marc's shoulder into the hallway. "Could you close the door? I don't think Holly needs another demonstration quite so soon."

Marc nodded and disappeared into the hall, and the door clicked shut behind him. And I was alone enough that I didn't have to wear the Alpha face I hadn't yet perfected. Or the enforcer's poker face I wore all too often. Or any other face that would hopefully hide how scared, and furious, and unsure, I was. How convinced some deep, dark part of me was that this new plan, this latest reincarnation of the fight-or-die routine, would fail spectacularly and kill not just me, but everyone I loved.

I couldn't let that happen. I couldn't afford to lose again.

I shoved my shorts down and stepped out of them, then carefully lowered myself to my knees on the rough carpet. My side felt like I'd been stabbed. My left hip protested sharply and my shoulder sang in harmony with it. Even my nose throbbed harder from my change of position—or maybe altitude—and it felt like someone had driven a hammer through the left side of my skull.

I embraced the pain as both penance and consolation. It was the consequence of losing the most important fight of my life, as well as proof that I'd survived. Pain was a reminder of my arrogance and weakness, and if I ever forgot that lesson, Dean would kill me. I had no doubt of that.

So instead of ignoring the pain, I called out to it, reaching for more. Pain is part of who I am. It's the defining characteristic of a Shifter's transformation. Pain is what I suffer from my enemies. It is what I deal out to those who break our laws. It is what I protect my charges from. Pain is what I inherited from fate, that fickle bitch who gave me a mouth and fists, then put me in a world that wanted only my womb and my cradled arms.

Pain is what I feed from when nothing else will nourish the noxious fury in my heart. It's what I cling to when everything else—every*one* else—slips right between my grasping fingers.

And pain was what I clung to that afternoon, with my brother and father murdered, my Pride stolen, my body beaten, and my responsibility crushing me like the weight of the world resting firmly on my chest.

I closed my eyes and called out to pain—in all its glorious forms—and rode it like a runaway horse.

Miguel pins me to the floor of a commercial van, while I fight nylon rope and try to scoot away. His grip bruises my thigh, his invasion bruises my soul....
In my present hell, fueled by remembered rage and pain, my hands and feet thickened into paws.

Miguel straddles me on a bare mattress in a filthy basement cell. He punches my face, but that doesn't shut me up, so he punches me again....

On Marc's bedroom floor, my nails hardened into claws, digging into the carpet in lieu of enemy flesh.

In my own basement, Luiz kicks me, snapping two of my ribs....

My spine lengthened beyond my tailbone, already swishing angrily before my tail had even fully formed.

On a forested hillside in Montana, Zeke Radley stabs my right hip, plunging white-hot agony all the way to the bone....

That echo of pain sang deep in my marrow, and my face began to elongate, a muzzle forming where there had been only chin and broken nose before.

And finally the pain swept everything else away in a blinding wash of agony that incinerated thought, obliterated memory.

I'd Shifted for the first time since becoming an Alpha.

My cat form felt different this time, in no way that could be explained simply by my new rank. I felt powerful, and lethal, and barely restrained. My new body was born of pain and rage, and had both to unleash.

But I had nowhere to put the power. Nothing to unleash it on, without hurting someone I loved. I had no way to expend that vicious power, except in more pain for myself. So I Shifted back, less than two minutes after I'd first stood on four paws.

The pain was worse that time instead of better, in spite of the small wounds I could feel healing. As if pain was this violent power's purpose. *My* purpose...

I needed power, and I deserved pain, so I took them both. Again, and again.

I Shifted back into human form while bitter memories played behind my eyes like old filmstrips, jumpy and out of focus, and almost too fast to truly understand.

Andrew straddles me on the glass-strewn floor, punching me, over and over. Kevin Mitchell backhands me in a suburban living room, then the memory stutters and he jerks my arm hard enough to crack the bone. In the Montana woods, a big black cat pounces on me, his rear claws rip into my stomach.

I collapsed on Marc's bedroom floor, covered in sweat, yet shivering. My pulse raced. My breathing was too fast and too shallow.

I rolled onto my hands and knees, and the room spun around me. I clutched the footboard, and when the earth stilled, I pulled myself up slowly and turned to the mirror, mentally cataloging my aches and pains. My bruised ribs had gone from black and purple to bluish-green, but the cracked one still screamed every time I moved. My shoulder no longer hurt, so I swung my left arm to test it. All good. Holding the edge of the dresser for balance, I dropped into a deep squat. My left hip felt limber, my motion smooth.

The bruises around my eyes had faded and yellowed, but they weren't any smaller. The side of my head still looked lumpy, and it still throbbed without being touched. The swelling in my nose had decreased, but when I touched the bridge, it still hurt. Gritting my teeth, I pushed on my nose until my eyes watered from the pain, then I clutched the edge of the dresser and studied my reflection. Frowning. It wasn't enough.

Again. I had to do it again.

I turned and dropped onto my knees. The carpet blurred with my tears while reality blurred with my pain. *Again…*

The old deer stand gives beneath me, and my arm is shredded from wrist to elbow.

Colin Dean pins me to the wall by my neck. My feet dangle. I can't breathe. The memory stutters, and he's cutting my face, threatening worse….

I stood in cat form again, stretching. The buzz of power still burned beneath my skin, and my side still hurt, but I felt like I could jump out a five-story window and land on all four feet. I was *strong*. Starving, and hurting, and exhausted, but so incredibly strong…

I closed my eyes and my whiskers twitched. Warm, metallic-scented air brushed my fur from the vent overhead. And I called to the memories again…

Ryan turns out the light and closes the door, leaving me alone with Abby. I've never been so scared….

The thunderbird swoops, snatching Kaci from the front yard. Her legs dangle above my hand. I can't reach her. Terror and despair wash over me and I know I've lost her….

Human form again, and I could hardly move. My hair hung in my face, stringy with sweat. My arms shook. I pulled myself up using the edge of the dresser for support. I looked wild. The bruises were gone, but the flesh beneath my eyes was still dark. My cheekbones stood out sharply, and my face was pale. My head no longer looked puffy, but it was tender, and when I touched the bridge of my nose, my eyes still watered.

I dropped to the floor again. I needed to Shift, but I could hardly remember why. My tongue felt thick and dry when I swallowed, so I bit it until I tasted blood.

A black cat drops out of the branches and knocks Ethan to the ground. His unsheathed claws slash Ethan's throat. Ethan reaches for me. He dies with my name on his lips....

Cat form again, and that time I couldn't stand. I fell onto my stomach, panting, and the room refused to come into focus. The pain echoed inside me, filling the emptiness, sucking at the cold with blazing agony. My stomach was eating me alive, demanding fuel, but I wanted only the blaze. The fire.

Colin Dean aims his gun, and the flash is blinding in the dark. My father falls. Blood blooms on his shirt like a midnight rose. And then he is gone, and I'm being sucked into darkness the size of a pinprick, and the pain is...

The Shifts began to run together. Memories of loss and triumph—because Shifting was my glory; it enabled justice and was my sword and my shield—fueled them long after my energy waned, long after the buzz of power faded. The pain was all a blur—past and present, physical, and psychological. And for the past two cycles, I couldn't even stand. Could only force my body through its paces one final time, wondering if that would be enough.

When it was over, I couldn't sit up. I lay on the floor panting, huffing, sweating, boiling with agony. My ribs had healed. My knee had healed. My cheek looked normal at the bottom of my vision. And still there was pain. Deep, deep pain, in places I couldn't reach.

My weight on the floor bruised my hip. My neck creaked when I lifted my head. I tried to get up, but my legs wouldn't cooperate. How many times? It was too much. Too fast.

Tears poured down my face, silent, because I didn't have the energy to sob. The buzz of power had abandoned me, and part of me had gone with it. I didn't deserve the power. Not yet. But I deserved the pain.

"Faythe?" The door creaked open, and I smelled Marc. "Faythe!" He was at my side in an instant, lifting me, and even his gentle touch bruised. A second later, Jace was there, too. "Get her some water," Marc whispered. "And something to eat. But don't say anything."

"What happened?" Jace took his cue to whisper from Marc.

"I think she Shifted. Look at her face."

"But…one Shift can't heal like that. Hell, four Shifts can't heal like that."

"I know. Get the water. And close the door behind you."

Marc laid me on the bed, and I blinked up at him, but his face wouldn't come into focus. My eyes were so dry it hurt to blink.

"What the hell are you doing? Trying to kill yourself?" His voice was thick with emotion, and his eyes were damp. "You're stronger than that. Suicide is the coward's way out. People are depending on you!"

"Don't want to die," I whispered. "I needed the pain."

"What the hell are you talking about?" His eyes narrowed, like he wanted to understand, but he couldn't. It wasn't in him. Everything was black and white for Marc. Right and wrong. Good and bad. He understood the spectrum of pain—he'd certainly been through enough of it—but not what it meant to me. He didn't understand how making myself suffer and relive so many bad memories could possibly lead to catharsis, a psychological release of emotional poison. "You weren't in enough pain already?"

"It clears my head. I needed more."

The door creaked open, and Jace came in with a sweating bottle of chilled water and a box of protein bars. He cracked open the bottle and handed it to me.

It took all of my concentration to manage the bottle, to keep from dribbling water all over myself, but I drained half of it before coming up for a breath.

"What the hell were you *thinking?*" Marc took the bottle when I lowered it, while Jace ripped open the snack box. "Even under the best of circumstances, you should eat between Shifts, and this is hardly the best of circumstances. How many times did you Shift?"

"I don't know. Lost count."

"In half an hour?" Marc cursed in Spanish, and I flinched. "What are you, brain-dead?"

"I'm sorry." I swallowed thickly and took the protein bar Jace handed me. "I didn't mean to go so far. I just… I needed to heal, and I needed it to hurt. That's the only way I could make sense out of any of this."

"What the hell does that even mean?" Marc demanded, forgetting to whisper that time.

I couldn't answer. I couldn't make him understand what I could hardly understand myself.

Jace sighed. "She was punishing herself."

"No, I…" I shook my head. That wasn't it. That sounded crazy. Yet he was right, though I would never have put it in those words. "It just… It seemed like a failure on so massive a scale should involve more pain. Like I shouldn't have been able to just walk away from a loss that cost *everything* for so many people. Like if I wasn't hurting, I wasn't paying for what I cost us."

"You didn't walk away from it," Marc pointed out, ever helpful with the literal interpretation. "Jace carried you. And damn, Faythe, Dean nearly killed you. How is that not enough pain?"

"It just…wasn't."

"You're not making any sense. You did the best you could, and what happened wasn't your fault."

"Yes, it was." I bit into the snack bar and avoided his eyes. "My best wasn't good enough, and that's not an option for an Alpha."

Marc stared at me for nearly a minute, and I could almost hear the gears whirring in his head. Grinding. But he didn't really get it, and he hated that. Finally he stood and stomped toward the door. "Make sure she eats the whole box," he growled. Then the door closed behind him, and I was alone with Jace.

I should have called out to Marc. I should have called him back and figured out a way to explain myself to him. But I was too tired to think, and beyond frustrated.

"He doesn't get it," I whispered, wadding the first empty wrapper into a cellophane ball. "Why can't he get it?"

Jace laid back on the bed next to me, one arm propping up the pillow beneath his head. "Because he's never failed to measure up. Failure has never ripped a hole in his gut so deep and wide that physical pain is a mercy and a punishment all at the same time."

"But you have?"

Jace sat up and met my eyes with a gaze so intense my next breath caught in my throat and refused to budge. "I left Ethan in the woods, and he died. We were partners, and I left him, Faythe." He glanced down at his hands, and I started to argue. He'd only left because Ethan told him to get Kaci to safety. He hadn't abandoned his partner. But before I could put my argument into words, he looked up again, and something deep in my stomach clenched. "And every time Cal hurts you, and I can't kill him, I feel the same way. Like I'm not worth the air I breathe if I can't protect you."

Twenty-seven

"Wow. It feels insane to be coming back here so soon." I pulled my duffel higher on my shoulders and glanced around the Roswell airport and the small crowd of morning commuters.

Marc veered toward a row of waiting-room chairs within sight of the car rental place, where Jace was at the front of a short line. Marc sank into the first chair, dropping his bag at his feet. "Considering what happened last time, and everything that's happened since then, I'd say 'insane' is putting it mildly."

I collapsed onto the seat beside him and stared at my bag in my lap. I had no idea what to say. Things had gotten quiet between us since he'd walked out after my frenetic Shifting extravaganza, and every time I looked at him, it felt like someone was sinking claws through my chest. It felt even worse when he looked at me, and yet worse still when he didn't.

But I was thankful for my mostly healed body, even after what it had cost me, physically—I'd been practically comatose for nearly another twelve hours after I'd fallen asleep.

"You okay?" he asked, and in my peripheral vision, I could see him watching me.

"Are you?" I wanted to take his hand. I stared at it, lying all alone on the chair arm between us. But I was afraid that would make me look needy. Weak.

"Right now? Yeah." He twisted in his chair to look at me with unbearable, heartbreaking longing in his eyes. "Because it's just the two of us." He glanced around at the harried morning commuters and shrugged. "Relatively speaking. But in a few minutes, it'll be me, you, and *him*..." He nodded to the rental counter, where Jace was now talking to a clerk with really poofy hair. "And there's only so much of that I can take."

"Marc..."

"Just let me finish," he said, and I nodded. I didn't know how to complete my aborted thought, anyway, and I welcomed words from him, when he spoke so often with his fists lately. "I can see how connected you are to each other, and I know that it's not just physical, which means it's not just going to blow over. But sharing you with him is like being asked to cut out my own heart and hand half of it over to someone else. It fucking hurts, Faythe. Like I'm dying."

"So...I'm killing you." It wasn't a question; I already recognized it as the truth. Marc wasn't himself because he couldn't have all of me, and that was killing both of us.

"And every cat instinct I have is telling me to kill Jace, but I can't. My human half knows that if I try to rush you into a decision, or do anything to dissuade you from picking him, it'll backfire on me."

I blinked, confused. "Why would it backfire?"

He frowned, as if he knew me better than I knew

myself. "If I make Jace into the underdog, you'll fight for him out of instinct. You always fight for the oppressed. That's just who you are, and that's one of the reasons I love you. Even if that isn't working out in my favor this time."

My next breath felt almost too thick to drag in. "He's not the underdog, Marc." I exhaled heavily and fought the urge to drop my gaze. "There is no underdog."

"That's the whole problem. You and I have a real history, Faythe. By rights, I should be the front-runner, and he should be the underdog."

"I know." But I couldn't make myself not love Jace any more than he could make himself not love me. And that's when the reality of the situation truly sank in. I was going to have to walk away from one man who truly loved me in favor of another. And choosing one didn't mean I'd quit caring about the other.

But did they both understand that? Hell, did *either* of them?

Yes. Jace understood. He knew that loving Marc didn't make me love him any less. But Marc couldn't compromise. It just wasn't in his skill set.

"And the worst part of this?" He hesitated, rolling his eyes at his own statement. "Well, it's not the *worst* part, but it's bad enough. The thing is, as much as it kills me to see you with him, when I'm not there, he's the best qualified to protect you. So even if I thought either of you would listen, I couldn't ask you to stay away from each other right now. I'm not going to stand in the way of your safety, even if it means losing you to him."

Tears filled my eyes, and I blinked them away.

"Just..." When I didn't look up, he stopped and tilted my chin until my gaze met his. His eyes were swimming with pain. "Faythe, just tell me you two are being careful. Don't give him what you won't give me."

At first, I didn't understand. Then I did, and I knew what it cost him to ask me that.

"Marc, I'm not... We're not..." I took a deep breath and started over. "It was just that once. And yeah. We were careful," I whispered, the ache in my heart threatening to swallow me whole. He let go of my chin, and I stared down at my hands. "More careful than you and I are." Because sometimes Marc and I just...got distracted and forgot. I reached for his hand, but he pulled away from me, and my chest hurt so bad I could hardly breathe.

"Hey, what's wrong?" Jace asked, and I looked up to see him walking toward us with a set of keys in one hand and a folder full of paperwork in the other.

"Nothing."

Everything.

I swiped one sleeve across my eyes and stood, throwing my bag over one shoulder. "Let's go."

Jace frowned, but knew better than to press the issue.

He'd rented a domestic compact car that got great gas mileage, but came with few extras. Marc drove, because his control issues were in overdrive and he couldn't take a backseat to Jace.

I didn't want to drive. My control issues were reserved for people who tried to tell me when and whom to marry.

"Too bad they don't have phones. I can't help thinking this would go much more smoothly if we could've called ahead to warn them that we're coming," Jace said from the backseat.

I twisted in the passenger seat to face him. "And say what? 'Hey, we're coming. Please don't eat us'?"

"Well, that certainly beats, 'Dinner's on, come and get it!'"

I smiled, but Jace's joke had its basis in truth. Thunderbirds were birds of prey, and they preferred raw meat. And when indulging wouldn't put them in imminent danger of being discovered, they had no qualms about consuming human flesh. In fact, while cannibalism is one of the greatest taboos for werecats, thunderbirds ritualistically consumed the flesh of their enemies and of their own dead.

Also in the con column for dropping in unexpectedly at a thunderbird nest was the fact that they didn't like visitors. Or surprises. Or werecats. All things considered, we'd been on few riskier missions. And very few that were more important.

After an hour-long drive from the Roswell airport, we pulled off the highway onto a narrow, uneven gravel road, surrounded on both sides by steep hills and rock facings. Nothing made me feel more insignificant than being surrounded by mountains. Except maybe dangling one hundred fifty feet in the air, with nothing between me and death-by-gravity but a pair of sharp, hostile thunderbird talons.

Either way, I was totally out of my element in New Mexico, and more grateful than ever that Marc and Jace had both come, even if riding with the two of them was like riding in a funeral procession. On the way to my own grave.

About four miles down the road, we came to the first obstacle: an old abandoned vehicle positioned sideways in the middle of the road. If we hadn't been driving a compact, we'd have had to either push the old steel-framed car out of the way on four flat, rotting tires—doable, but unpleasant even for three werecats—or leave the rental car and walk the rest of the way. A mile and a half later, the road was blocked again, this time by two even older stalled cars and a large boulder. The thunderbirds were serious about discouraging salesmen. And trick-or-treaters. And Thin Mint–bearing Girl Scouts.

We had to walk from that point on, armed only with cell phones and protein bars. By the time we came to the pile of huge rocks, likely intentionally tumbled into the middle of the road, the nest was within sight. It sat at the end of the valley, built on an outcropping jutting from the juncture of two hills. The huge lodge-type structure was at least six stories high, by my best guess, and more than two hundred feet in the air. With nary a staircase in sight.

The broad front porch looked out over the sheer drop like a safety-featureless balcony and doubled as a landing pad for the several dozen giant birds housed within.

Marc stopped to stare up at the structure, mouth slack in what could only be awe. "I've seen it before, but it's no less impressive the second time around."

"Impressive, scary as hell. Opinions vary," I muttered.

He shook his head. "You can't argue that that's not an incredible piece of craftsmanship. I bet they built the whole thing themselves."

I shoved my hands in my pockets and trudged ahead so the guys had no choice but to follow. "I know they did. But you wouldn't be so impressed by it if you'd ever been flown up there, dangling like a worm to a nest full of giant chicks."

"I guess." But he couldn't tear his gaze from the nest, and I realized this was the first time he'd seen it in daylight. Middle-of-the-day sunlight, in fact.

"So, how are we supposed to get their attention?" Is there a doorbell hidden in tree bark around here somewhere?" Jace glanced at the tree-covered hills encroaching steadily on the narrow road, which was starting to make me feel claustrophobic. "I don't think I can hit the window with a pebble from here...."

Something squealed faintly overhead, and I glanced up as the front door swung open. "I don't think getting their attention is gonna be an issue...." But suddenly I wasn't sure I wanted their attention.

I knew exactly what kind of damage an angry cat could inflict—hell, I'd nearly been killed by several of them. I'd even seen a pissed-off bruin throw a full-grown tom into a tree hard enough to break the cat's spine. But I'd never in my life seen anything scarier than a flight of enraged thunderbirds, and suddenly, coming to demand that they repay their debt seemed like a colossally bad idea. What if they didn't remember their promise to me, or they'd changed their minds? What if coming unannounced—not that we'd had any choice— was considered bad form, punishable by being ceremonially pecked to death, then eaten?

But we were out of options. If we couldn't recruit them to unleash that awesome dive-'n'-slash fury against our enemies, we could wave goodbye to the south-central Pride forever. And to our freedom, not long after that, because I had no doubt that once Malone's grip on his new puppet regime was secure, he'd come after us, and all three of us would rather die fighting than be taken prisoner. Then what would happen to Kaci, Manx, and my mother?

Overhead, two forms appeared at the edge of the front porch, staring down at us. From at least three hundred feet away and two hundred feet up, all I could make out was the typical short, extremely stocky build of two male thunderbirds. I couldn't even tell for sure whether or not they wore clothes.

They could see us much more clearly—a bird can spot a mouse running through a field from the air, and for the thunderbirds, it didn't seem to matter whether they were in human or avian form. Not that I'd seen many of them in exclusively one form or another; they tended to prefer endless odd combinations, similar to my own face during a partial Shift. Only their best-of-both-worlds routine was infinitely more useful than mine.

"Do you know them?" Jace squinted into the morning sun, glaring just above the roof of the nest/lodge.

"I don't *know* any of them. They don't think like normal..." I whispered, then sputtered to a stop as the two forms suddenly leaped from the porch in sync. And completely wingless.

Marc and Jace both gasped at the abrupt—and apparently suicidal—jump, and it took most of my self-control not to do the same thing.

Upon takeoff, one wingless bird veered left while the other veered right, fully human arms spread wide. Less than a second later, when they'd put enough distance between their artfully falling bodies, both thunderbirds seem to ripple in the air, and suddenly both sets of arms doubled in length and sprouted feathers. Just like that. What had been normal—if heavily muscled—human arms were suddenly six foot long, darkly feathered wings, in the span of less than two seconds.

Their midair Shift was the single most amazing thing I'd ever seen. Bar none. Shifting for the birds didn't work the same way it worked for us, or presumably for the bruins. Their transformation was neither slow nor awkward, and I could see no sign that it hurt. And—obviously—they could do it in midflight.

That was the equivalent of a werecat Shifting in midstep. Midleap, even. I couldn't imagine undergoing such a miracle of transformation, or how different our lives might have been if it were possible, and I spared one moment to be both stunned and impressed. But then common sense took over, and I returned to a healthy state of caution.

The birds swooped toward us in sync, wingtips less than a foot apart. Marc and Jace backpedaled, and after an instant's hesitation, I decided to stand my ground. Still, my heart beat in terrified syncopation for a moment before the birds dropped onto the ground in front of me, even as the avian-scented wind from their last powerful flap blew hair back from my face. Their feathers receded and their limbs shrank to normal size in the time it took for them to fold their huge wings at their sides.

And only once they'd landed did I realize that they were indeed naked, apparently unaffected by the bitter cold. Well, *almost* unaffected…

I blinked and forced my pulse to slow as Marc and Jace took up protective stances on my left and right, towering over the emissaries. For thunderbirds, these were pretty tall—only an inch or so shorter than my own five-foot-seven frame. But thunderbirds were walking—or flying—proof that size isn't everything. Inch for inch, they were the single most ruthless predators I'd ever encountered, and they were built for both flight and fight.

Their spindly legs and narrow waists enabled them to build weight, and thus power, where it was really needed for flight—in their thick arms and powerful chests. I'd never seen pecs so well-defined, biceps and triceps so chiseled. They could have been carved from granite. As could their cold, decidedly unwelcoming expressions.

For a moment, we all stared at one another, the cats in wary amazement, the birds in outright suspicion. And when their faces gained human features, I realized I knew them by both face and name.

"Cade and Coyt, right?" I said, hoping my smile looked more confident than it felt.

"Girl-cat," the one on the left returned in his odd, multitonal voice, nodding in imitation of an actual greeting. And considering that I didn't know which of them was which, I couldn't work up any irritation over the fact that they'd obviously forgotten my name. Or saw no reason to use it. "You've come to claim what we owe you?"

"Yes. But first I want to speak to Kai. He owes us his life, and I'm calling in his personal debt first."

Twenty-eight

"You think he'll go for that?" Marc asked, as Cade and Coyt dropped onto the porch overhead, one right after the other.

I shrugged and turned to face them both, hunching deeper into my coat. "I give it a fifty-fifty chance of total failure. If Kai refuses to repay a debt he legitimately owes, he'll be dishonored in front of his entire Flight. Thunderbirds always avenge their dead, honor their word, and pay their debts. Those seem to be the only laws they have." Based on what little time I'd spent with them.

Marc frowned. "It's that 'legitimately owes' part that worries me."

"Thus the fifty-fifty shot of failure." I stared up at the nest, watching for any sign of activity. "It all depends on whether or not I'm able to bullshit him into thinking he owes us."

"The odds are always in your favor when bullshit's involved." Jace grinned, and I couldn't help returning his smile.

"It's not bull," Marc insisted. "We could have killed

him when we caught him. Probably should have, considering how little information he actually gave us. So by their way of thinking, Kai owes us his life."

"Let's hope you're right." The door overhead squealed open again, and Cade and Coyt stepped to the edge of the porch, this time followed by a third, slightly smaller form. Kai. It had to be.

Cade and Coyt leaped off the porch in opposite directions—evidently standard operating procedure for jumping from tall buildings—and when they were far enough away to avoid collision, the third bird followed, already sprouting feathers all over his rapidly lengthening arms.

The two larger birds landed directly in front of us with bold, heavy thumps, and seconds later their companion dropped to the ground a few feet behind them, showing off an odd combination of a bird's upper body and a human's lower half. His face Shifted as he stomped toward us, his curved, pointed beak melting into his face as his feathers retreated like magic. Or at least like movie-magic.

Cade and Coyt stepped aside as Kai approached, wings spread aggressively, bare human feet evidently unbothered by the rough, cold gravel.

"What debt do you claim from me?" he demanded, his weird, dual-tone voice scraping down my inner chalkboard. Kai's black eyes flashed in anger, but I got the distinct impression that part of that was to cover up…embarrassment? Yeah. Something in his bearing—overkill on the menacing posture?—told me he was humiliated at having been called out by a trio of werecats claiming he owed an as-yet-unpaid debt.

Good. Maybe this'll work, after all….

"It's really not complicated. We spared your life, ergo, you owe us." I crossed my arms over my chest, neglecting my frozen fingers in favor of the most confident look I could muster.

His jaw clenched visibly, beady black eyes narrowing. "I was ready and willing to die honorably, as a prisoner of war."

I huffed, showcasing legitimate skepticism. "Yet, here you stand. A fully healed, functional member of society." Wherein *society* was defined as a Flight of giant, ruthless, cannibalistic birds of prey.

Kai's arms suddenly sprouted long, dark brown feathers, and his hands arced into wickedly curved talons, three digits in front, and a fully opposable, needle-sharp thumb-digit. "Only because you wouldn't kill me."

I grinned and tossed my hair over one shoulder. "Which brings us back to the part where you owe us."

"I owe you nothing but a lesson in honor." He stepped forward threateningly, puffing up like an angry rooster. Marc and Jace bristled at my sides, prepared to fight if necessary. "I was perfectly willing to die for my Flight," Kai insisted, and I forced my racing pulse to calm.

"You didn't sound too willing to die for your cause when you were begging me not to leave you alone in the deep, dark basement, walled in by the earth itself. To leave a window open so you could see your precious sky. And what did I do? I opened that window. We not only spared your life, we gave you comfort. And water, and shelter. Do you provide similar accommodations to prisoners of war?"

He opened his mouth to protest, and I interrupted before he could, remembering how well they'd treated

Kaci when she was their hostage. "Without previous negotiations, or the hope of some reward in return?"

The thunderbird's eyes narrowed. "Are you not here in search of just such a reward?"

My eyebrows rose. "Clever, aren't you? And again, we're back to the fact that you owe us. Are you going to quibble like a spoiled child, or are you going to stand up like a man—er, bird—and settle the debt you've incurred?"

Kai seemed to deflate a bit, but didn't unclench his jaw. He glanced from side to side, and though I couldn't read much in either of the other birds' expressions, evidently Kai could. He huffed, then turned back to me, spine straight and stiff.

"I will not dishonor my Flight by shirking my duty. You granted me some small measure of comfort when I was at your mercy, therefore I owe you some small manner of gratitude."

Uh-oh. "Small manner of gratitude" didn't sound quite big enough to cover what we needed.

"You don't sound very grateful. We saved your life."

"No." Kai shook his head firmly, jaw set. "You merely refrained from taking it. Those are two entirely different things. What do you want?"

"We need you to do some reconnaissance. A simple flyby over our ranch. All you have to do is count the cars and tell us how many men you see hanging around the property."

Kai shook his head without a moment's hesitation. "Not even if you fed me your firstborn, still wet and screaming."

I blinked, but for a long moment, his words made no

sense. Not the refusal. The part about cannibalizing my theoretical future child. "Well, isn't that…gruesome? Who are you, Rumpelstiltskin?"

Kai frowned, as if *I* made no sense to *him*. "No thunderbird would claim a name so senselessly flamboyant."

Or any sign of a sense of humor, for that matter. What was I thinking?

"Never mind." I rubbed my temples with half-frozen fingers, and when I licked my lips, I tasted blood. They'd cracked open from the cold. "Are you prepared to pay your debt or what?"

"Yes. But failing to take my life when I was willing to lose it is not worth such a task."

"You wouldn't be in any danger—" I started.

"Of course not. I have nothing to fear from creatures who can't even leave the surface of the planet under their own power," Kai insisted, though he probably still bore the scars Owen had given him.

Grrr… I'd forgotten what a pain in the ass thunderbirds were. Inevitably.

"Okay, I get it. You're scared. But maybe you could talk to one of your friends for me. Get someone else to—"

"No one else will do it. No member of our Flight would debase himself as your errand boy."

I swallowed a growl of frustration. "You can't answer for them. You guys may have this weird hive-mentality thing going on, but you don't actually share a brain, right?"

Kai's eyes narrowed as he frowned, obviously as impatient as I was. "They will say no. I know that like I know exactly how you'd taste, just from smelling you, but…"

Marc's growl ripped through the air. Jace snarled and lunged at Kai. I threw myself between them, chest to chest with Jace. Cade and Coyt sprouted insta-feathers and beaks, facing off against Marc, two on one.

"Stop!" I shouted, desperate to avoid a confrontation we could not win. I wedged my arms between my body and Jace's and shoved him as hard as I could, then held out one hand to stop his rebound. Only once he stayed back—eyes and canines already Shifted—did I dare take my gaze from him to glance at Marc. Marc stood with his legs spread wide for balance, eyes glittering with rage, fists high and close to his body. He was ready to throw down, and that could only end in death. Whose, I was afraid to speculate.

I stood with my arms spread in the universal signal for Stop! "There will be no tasting of any kind. Right?"

"Damn right," Marc snapped, while Jace only growled.

When Kai made no reply, I glared at him. "Will you guys play nice if we do?"

He narrowed dark, small bird eyes at my phrasing. "We will not attack unprovoked. That would be dishonorable. But with provocation… Well, I've never actually tasted fresh cat, and while I typically find carnivore flesh distasteful, I'm feeling like something a little exotic tonight."

Great. Somebody was obviously still bitter over his time underground.…

"No provocation. Just take us up there so I can present a rational request to someone who isn't looking to peck my eyes out."

Kai made a high-pitched screeching sound in the back of his throat, and it took me a moment to realize he was laughing. "You won't find that in the nest. But if I get you an audience…you will consider my debt paid?"

I hesitated just long enough to decide that was the best deal we'd get out of them. Unless they had another infant I could rescue. Finally I nodded. "Paid in full. Should we shake on it?" I stuck my hand out, but Kai only frowned.

"Is your word worth so little you must offer pointless physical gestures?"

I huffed and crossed my arms over my chest. "Fine. Never mind. Safe passage to your nest and an audience with someone more useful than you obviously are. Passage for all three of us," I added as an afterthought.

Marc mumbled something behind me, and I twisted to hear him better. "What?"

He rolled his eyes. "Safe return passage, too. Don't get us stranded up there."

Oh, yeah. I turned back to the birds, trying to hide my embarrassment. "And safe return passage for all three of us. If you promise all of that, I'll consider your debt absolved."

Kai nodded quickly, looking so relieved that I wondered if I should have pressed for more. "Fine. You're first."

"Okay. Just one minute." Already dreading the short, safety net–less flight, I turned to Marc and Jace and motioned them into an impromptu huddle. "Do *not* lose your temper in there. We'll be safe as long as we don't start anything. Got it?"

They both nodded reluctantly, and I turned to find all

three thunderbirds already in full avian form—one of the scariest sights I'd ever seen in my life. Much scarier than either a bruin or a werecat in animal form, because we looked very much like our natural-born counterparts. But there was no bird in the world as big as a thunderbird, and by all the laws of physics—what little I understood of it, anyway—that meant they shouldn't have been able to fly. They were too heavy. But then, they shouldn't have been able to Shift so quickly, either. No wonder they held themselves apart from us.

The world had never seen anything like the thunderbirds, and with any luck, neither had our enemies on the council, other than Malone. They'd never know what hit them.

"Okay, let's get this over with." I held my arms out, and at my signal, Cade and Coyt rose into the air with several flaps of their huge, powerful wings. The air they moved blew hair back from my face and froze my already-dripping nose, but I barely had time to notice that before Cade—or Coyt—wrapped his thick talons around my upper arms in a bruising grip.

I closed my eyes as the earth abandoned my feet, and several seconds later, the other ferry-bird grabbed my ankles.

Don'tlookdon'tlookdon'tlook…

I didn't exhale in relief until the weather-worn wooden porch boards came into sight beneath me. One bird dropped my ankles, and my shoulders were wrenched mercilessly when my body swung free beneath me. Then the other bird let me go, and I crashed to my knees on the porch, eye to eye with a sizable knothole, through which I could see the ground, two hundred feet below.

Heart racing, I lurched to my feet and scrambled

away from the edge, pressing my back against the side of the building, irrationally afraid of being blown off the porch by the gust of wind beneath the approaching thunderbirds' wings.

A minute later, Jace landed where I'd fallen, and I helped him up. "You okay?"

"Hell, no." He actually wobbled on his feet and clung to me, his face whiter than a sun-bleached Texas sidewalk. "There's a reason cats don't have wings."

"Yeah, but at least we always land on our feet."

"Then why did I land on my ass?"

I didn't have an answer for that one, so I just pulled him against the wall while we waited for Marc.

Marc's arrival was no better, and clearly no less traumatic. "Never. Again," were his only words, as we followed Kai into the nest. I could not have agreed more.

Inside, my gaze was drawn upward, though I'd seen it all before. Twice. It was still impressive, in a how-many-ways-are-there-to-die kind of way. Most of the first floor was taken up by a large, open living space, scattered with worn but comfy-looking chairs and couches, all piled high with old, faded pillows, like little mininests. Along three sides of the room were several closed doors leading to other rooms, and directly across from the entrance stood the staircase.

There was no ceiling. The room was open all the way to the roof, six stories up, and along the way, platforms and long, thick beams jutted from the walls, each occupied with one or more birds in various stages of mid-Shift. And they all stared down at us.

The second and third floors were arranged like hotel rooms ringing a large, open lobby. Most of the doors were closed, and in the far corner I could see the room where Kaci and I had woken up on our previous trip.

"Kai!" We all whirled at the sharp, disharmonic screech, and I flinched as Kai soared over our heads in response to the summons. He landed in front of a nude elderly female thunderbird with a human face and long white hair.

"I've granted them an audience, to absolve myself of debt and uphold the honor of my word."

The old bird turned from Kai to face us. "Come forward and state your business, then be gone. We want no contact with your species beyond removing ourselves from your debt."

"Fair enough." I wasn't exactly tickled to be there, either. "Is anyone among you willing go on a reconnaissance mission for us?"

"Will this mission absolve us of our debt to you?" a softer but equally creepy dual-tone voice asked, and I turned to find a dark-haired mostly human man waiting for my answer.

"Not alone, no. This mission is simple and safe—hardly worth Wren's life." At a shuffling sound behind me, I turned to see the toddler safe in her mother's arms. I smiled at them both, then continued. "I have something else in mind to erase that debt. This recon is...separate." I hesitated, reluctant to say the next part, but I was out of options. "A favor, of sorts. Which I will gladly repay."

"No. You are of no use to us," the old crone half shrieked. "Now we are done. You will go." With that, she turned her back and spread her wings, preparing to take to the air. We had been dismissed.

Twenty-nine

"Wait!" I shouted, and the crone lowered her wings, then pivoted slowly to face me again, cocking her head in that weird avian manner. Like she was curious, but not in a good way. Curious like a child examining a dying bug. "Don't you want to see justice done?" I demanded, trying to ignore the fact that everyone was staring at me now, and that the only two sets of eyes that didn't look hostile were both feline. "If you do this, Calvin Malone will pay for what he did to you!"

The old woman stepped closer, and vague shuffling movements began all around us. Talons scraped the floor with each step. Feathers made a soft, eerie rustling sound. Several beaks snapped together in menacing, hollow clacks. The birds were closing in. Gathering to watch the show, with us at the center of their circle. We were prey, surrounded by several dozen full-grown thunderbirds.

And in that moment, Kai's promise of a safe return trip no longer seemed so ironclad. Would he still honor our deal if they told us to leave, and we refused?

"We've had justice for Finn." The male bird crossed

still-human arms over his bare chest. "You brought us his killer, and we feasted on every edible part of his body." At his words, the inarticulate din around us grew stronger, like the birds were all fidgeting in anticipation, and my pulse raced uncontrollably. "We have no further business with you until you claim the debt we still owe. And we have no further business with Calvin Malone at all."

"But he lied to you. He used you! He nearly robbed Finn of justice and he certainly made fools of you all!" I couldn't understand their ambivalence. How could they not be *burning* to see Malone pay?

The male bird drew closer, and as I watched, the slightest ripple crawled over the skin on his crossed forearms, as if feathers wanted to sprout there, but he was holding them back. Along with his temper? Did that work the same way the partial Shift did for us? The angrier a bird got, the more likely to burst into feathers and claws?

"Our egos are not so fragile that they are bruised over every insult," he insisted. "Malone lied to us, and for that, he has lost all credibility. But in the end, we suffered nothing from his lie. On the contrary, ill-meant though his manipulation was, it afforded us much needed recreation."

Recreation? Slaughtering members of our Pride was recreation?

But I probably shouldn't have been so surprised. The thunderbirds were hardly our brother-species. More like distant cousins. Once or twice removed. *Far* removed.

"So, you don't care that Malone's just going to get away with this?"

"No." Kai stepped up to his Flightmate's side. "Do

not bother us with this matter again, or you will find yourself less warmly welcomed."

Yeah. Their warm reception made my mother's deep freeze look nice and toasty.

"Faythe…" Marc put a hand on my shoulder, and I nodded without looking at him.

"I get it. They aren't going to help with the recon," I mumbled. "Now if they refuse to help rip the living shit out of our enemies, we'll be oh for two."

"What's that?" Kai's head tilted in interest this time. "You want us to defecate on your enemies? We're eager to repay what we owe, but we aren't pigeons, leaving droppings when- and wherever the urge strikes."

I fought inappropriate laughter at the very idea. "Sorry. My colloquialisms seem to lose clarity in the translation. No defecation. No bodily fluids of any sort, except for blood, hopefully."

The older female bird spoke up from somewhere to my left, and the crowd parted to reveal her. "You have caught our attention, Faythe Sanders. What blood can we spill for you, to absolve our debt?" Their obvious eagerness looked a little too much like feline bloodlust to me, but so long as it was working for us, rather than against us, I was willing to deal.

But first, a precaution… "So, this is a definite no on the reconnaissance?"

"Unequivocally." Kai's feathers had receded, but he opened and closed his wing-claws like fists in anticipation of a fight.

"Fine." Though it was actually far from fine. But not unexpected. "Then I'm ready to call in your debt. We've tried to deal with Malone through political means, and that was a spectacular failure. So we're going to remove him from power by force…"

"The only proper way…" The crone's head bobbed eagerly, her beady eyes gleaming.

"… and you're going to fight on our side."

"Fight…"

The whispers echoed throughout the cavernous room, accompanied by more rustling of feathers, scratching of talons against the floor, and excited clacking of beaks. And after several seconds of that, the questions came hard and fast.

From above: "To kill or maim?"

"Whichever proves necessary." I glanced up, but was too late to spot the speaker. "But you can only fight our enemies. Don't touch our allies."

From my left: "How will we tell you apart? You all look the same to us in cat form."

"I don't know." I whirled, but again found myself speaking to the entire crowd. "We'll mark ourselves somehow." I rubbed my forehead, already overwhelmed by the number of details I hadn't even considered.

"When do we leave?"

"Can we eat what we kill?"

"No!" I shouted, horrified by the images now forming in my head—birds perched on a field of corpses, tearing furry flesh from broken bones. "Even our worst enemies deserve a decent burial." Except Luiz. We'd scattered his ashes to be trampled regularly. But that was another story…

Screeched from the back of the room, as I spun again, and Jace reached to steady me: "Will there be enough to go around, or must we compete for our kills?"

"Unfortunately, I suspect there will be plenty, but

that really depends on how many of you are willing to come." And that's when I lost track of who was speaking. They called out from everywhere, having apparently forgotten I was even there.

"All of us!"

"We will all go…"

"It's only fair…"

"Someone must stay with the children…"

"Some must stay to hunt…"

"Then we'll draw quills. Feathers into the pile! The twenty drawn will go and fight!"

"Wait!" I had to shout to be heard. "Don't you want the details?"

Kai frowned, one of the few birds still paying me any attention. "No. We want the fight, and the feast."

"No! I said there will be no feasting! It's a war, not a fucking dinner banquet!" I threw my hands up in exasperation. Mentioning war to a Flight of thunderbirds was evidently like dangling candy in front of a class full of children! Ruthless, deadly children… "Listen, please!" And finally the din began to die as several dozen sets of small, black eyes focused on me.

"I'm glad you're all so eager." And even more glad that they'd be fighting on our side. "But there are important details. This isn't a free-for-all, and I won't consider your debt paid if you don't play by the rules."

"Faythe, I don't think they're interested in our rules," Jace whispered, inches from my ear.

"Well, that's too damn bad," I muttered, as the huge crowd of birds reassembled around us. Then I raised my voice to address the crowd. "Okay, here's the deal. When we're ready, we'll give you a time and place. You show up and wait for the signal. Then you attack. You can only attack the enemy—again, we'll make sure we're clearly marked—and you can*not* eat what you kill." The fact that I even had to repeat that particular warning gave me chills. "If you're hungry when it's all over, pizza's on me. But no snacking while you work!"

Marc chuckled, but most of the birds only looked confused.

"If someone surrenders to you, knock him unconscious, but let him or her live," I insisted. We'd discovered that during large-scale fighting it was easier to knock out surrendering enemies, rather than risk tying them up, which could lead to escape, betrayal, or both. We'd sort the bodies—both living and dead—after the action was over.

"Everyone understand?"

"Why not simply kill them all?" a familiar voice asked, and when I glanced to my left for the source, I came eye to eye with Neve, the she-bird my father had shot during the onslaught against our Pride. She'd obviously fully recovered.

"For the same reason we didn't kill you when we could have. Or Kai. We're interested in winning—in removing Malone from power and dealing out justice. But we're not in this for the slaughter." At least, not once Malone's blood was soaking into the ground and Colin Dean's innards had been exposed to the rest of the world.

"Then you're fools." The old woman watched me in blatant disgust now. "You suffer abuse from a rival, yet you would cut that rival's head off but let its body live. Your rival will grow a new head and rise again, and again you will make a pitiful effort to stop it, but never truly eliminate it. Mercy is a weakness, child. It is a trait of your human half, and you indulge it like a spoiled child. Just as the wolves did. I assume you know what happened to the wolves."

Um, yeah. "Extinction. But they were killed by human hunters."

"Yes, and by the bruins, and by us, and by some of your own ancestors, no doubt. Because the wolves bred weakness as if it were a virtue. If one group had risen to control the rest—or eliminate them—they wouldn't have made such easy prey."

"Malone's allies comprise fully half of the Pride cat population. And you seriously think we should just…kill them all?" I could barely even conceive of such large-scale death, and so much of it pointless! "I don't know about you guys, but our numbers aren't exactly swelling. We're doing well to maintain our current population, and killing off half of us is not going to help that."

The crone shook her head, as if she pitied my ignorance. "But those who remain will be stronger, and the next generation will be stronger still, from having cleansed the gene pool."

She did *not* just say that. I glanced at Marc to see him scowling.

"Is that what happened to you guys? Until last week, our most recent thunderbird sighting was more than fifteen years ago. We assumed that was because you keep to yourselves, but maybe that's not it. Maybe you've scrubbed your own gene pool so vigorously there's little of it left. Maybe *you'll* be next to follow the wolves."

For a moment, the crone looked like she'd either burst into feathers or flames, and my heart pounded so hard the front of my shirt jiggled. Had I just insulted the entire thunderbird way of life, surrounded by several dozen of their best specimens?

But then the old lady burst into harsh, cackling, dual-toned laughter, black eyes shining. "You are soft with foolish, sentimental ideologies, but that comes with youth. You will grow harder and smarter, if you are not ground beneath your enemy's boot. But if your people fight half as fiercely as you speak, your species might yet have a shot at survival."

I exhaled heavily and felt both Jace and Marc relax on either side of me. Thank goodness my youth and foolish idealism amused her. They just pissed most people off.

"Let's wrap this up," Marc suggested softly, and I could not have agreed more.

"Okay, so that's basically it. Only kill the enemy, and only if he doesn't surrender. And *no eating the casualties.* We'll let you know when we're ready to go. It won't be long, but you have to wait for word from us."

Speaking of which…

While the birds protested the rules with reactions ranging from strong frowns to angry clucking, I dug my cell from my pocket and held it up. "Does anyone here know how to work a cell phone?" *Or even what one is…?*

Beck stepped out of the crowd, and I recognized him from the assault on our ranch as the bird who'd come to help Neve after she was shot. "I spoke on your father's phone. Is yours like his?"

"Yeah." Fortunately, I hadn't yet upgraded to a smart-phone, and with fewer options on the device, there were fewer ways for the thunderbirds to mess this up. "Okay,

I'm going to leave my phone here with you guys, and we'll call you when we have a concrete plan."

"Faythe, you can't leave your phone here," Marc said, angling me away from the crowd.

Jace nodded before I could reply. "It isn't safe for any of us to be out of communication right now."

I rolled my eyes at them both, already digging in my other pocket. "Relax." I held up my father's phone, trying to swallow the lump in my throat. I felt guilty for claiming it—like I was taking another right I hadn't earned—but we couldn't afford the time for another flight to New Mexico just to tell the birds we were ready for them.

Jace grinned. "Good thinkin'."

Even Marc looked impressed. Mostly. "What about the charger?"

I smiled and pulled it from my jacket pocket, unreasonably pleased with myself for having thought that far ahead. Fortunately, generators—and thus outlets—were among the few modern conveniences the birds used, mostly to provide light and heat.

I showed Beck how to use the phone—just the basics—then gave him a list of names that might appear on the screen when I called, just in case something went wrong with my dad's phone.

"Okay, keep it plugged in somewhere where the children can't reach it—" fortunately, most of the small ones couldn't fly very well yet "—and don't answer it unless the call is from someone on that list." I'd left a very comprehensive list, but knowing my luck, some college friend I hadn't heard from all year would pick this week to try to get reacquainted, and wind up talking to a thunderbird in New Mexico instead.

That would be fun to explain.

"How long will it take you to get to the ranch?" Marc asked, as one of the other birds carried the phone through an open doorway.

"We will need twenty-four hours' notice, to account for rests in flight and recuperation before the fight," the old woman said, and I wondered if she'd be fighting alongside her younger relatives.

I nodded. A day's notice. We could do that.

When everything was settled, I took one last longing glance at my phone, now plugged into an outlet in a badly outdated kitchen, then let Cade—or maybe Coyt—ferry me to the road. The return trip was no less pleasant than the flight up to the nest, but when we'd all three landed on the ground safe and sound, I decided to count our blessings. No one got maimed or killed, and we'd secured air support for the upcoming fight. Which, with any luck, would give us the advantage we needed, even if Malone's men outnumbered us. And they surely would.

We froze all the way back to the car, but once we had the heater going full blast, I called my uncle to make a report.

"Hello?" he said, by way of a greeting, his voice leery with suspicion. And that's when I realized that his caller ID had probably showed my father's name.

"It's me. Sorry. I had to leave my phone with the thunderbirds, so I'm using my dad's. I have good news and bad news. Which do you want first?"

My uncle chuckled, obviously relieved, and his laugh sounded eerily like my mother's. "I'll take them in order of importance."

But even that was tough to determine, so he got

chronological order. "The bad news is that the thunderbirds won't do recon for us, as I'd hoped."

"That's too bad. It was a good thought, though. What's the good news? They've committed to the fight?"

"Enthusiastically," I said, as Jace turned off the birds' gravel road and onto the highway. "They're scary-eager."

"Wow. Okay." His surprise was obvious, as was his relief. "So, how many are coming?"

I grinned at both of the guys in the rearview mirror. "Twenty. They're drawing quills to see who gets the honor. And every last one of them is eager to shed tyrannical blood for us."

I was ready to shed more than a little of it myself.

Thirty

"I could try Alex," Jace said, reclining on the motel bed with his arms crossed behind his head. "But honestly, I think you'd have better luck with that than I would."

"Not after I took his gun and left him tied up under the bed." The memory made me smile as I leaned back in the chair and propped my feet on the rickety breakfast table. "I think the only other possible source we have on the inside is Kenton. He seemed less than thrilled to be playing his part, and I think he's feeling guilty. Parker might be able to work that to our favor."

"I think—" Marc paused, rolling his eyes while an airplane engine roared overhead, momentarily drowning out all other sound.

Our return flight didn't leave until nearly six in the morning, which left us with a good eight hours to kill. Not enough time to drive instead, but too much to waste in an airport bar when we could be resting and mentally preparing for the coming battle.

When the plane had passed, Marc shoved my feet off the table and dropped into the chair next to me. "I think we're missing the most obvious possibility. Maybe we shouldn't be looking for a source on the inside, but a source on the outside."

"Meaning...?" I was tired from all the travel and stiff from my recent beating, even after the Shifting marathon, and would have loved to lie down—but the room had two beds. Jace had claimed one, and Marc's duffel lay on the end of the other. I couldn't take a nap without making an all caps DECLARATION, and they both knew it. At this rate, I'd wind up sleeping in the bathtub.

"Meaning we don't have to talk to someone on the ranch to find out whether or not Malone's there. Wouldn't it be easier for Jace to just call his mother?"

I raised an eyebrow at Marc. "That's not a bad idea." I twisted toward Jace in the hard chair, wishing for a pillow. "You think she'll fall for that again?"

"I don't know. She's in denial, but she's not brain-dead. She knows I used her last time, and she knows the basics about what happened to Lance Pierce. She may not know the whole story behind Dean's pretty new face, but she probably knows I was involved."

"None of that matters," Marc insisted. "She's your mother, and she's already lost one son. She's not going to give up the chance to reconnect with her firstborn, even knowing he's using her. Look at Ryan and your mom." Marc glanced at me briefly, then turned back to Jace. "Karen's one of the smartest, most insightful women I've ever met, but she has a total blind spot where Ryan's concerned, even knowing what he did. Your mom has to know deep down that whatever Malone told her about you isn't true. She'll talk to you."

Jace sat up on the bed, frowning, and I could practically taste his reluctance. "Even if she does, she's not going to give up sensitive information."

I leaned forward, catching his gaze and holding it. "We don't need to know what Malone sleeps in. We just need to know whether or not he's on the ranch. And you don't have to actually ask her. Just steer the conversation around to him. Ask if he's mad that you called. If he can hear what you're saying. That way if he's not there, she'll tell you."

Jace nodded slowly. "Okay. That sounds like almost as much fun as being stoned to death, but I'm in." He shrugged, and his gaze met mine boldly. "You know I'll do whatever you need done."

Marc's growl was almost low enough to go unnoticed. But I noticed. "Just make sure your mom's not running the same scam on you," he snapped. "The last thing we need is for you to tip our hand, so she can call Malone with the details."

Jace bristled and sat up straight. "Back off. I'm not an idiot."

Marc's brows furrowed into a hard, dark line. "No, you're just an opportunistic bastard who slept with a friend's girlfriend before her brother's body was even cold!"

Anger flared deep in my chest, but before I could yell at Marc for bringing Ethan into this, Jace launched himself from the bed. If he'd had fur, it would have been standing on end. "You are *way* over the line, and you better step back while you still can."

Marc started to stand, but I beat him to it, and when I begged him silently to stay seated, he leaned back in his chair, but still gripped the armrests. I nodded in grateful acknowledgment of his cooperation, then turned to Jace. "Sit. Please."

Jace glared at us for a second, then sank fluidly onto the edge of the bed.

I angled my own chair to face them both, then sat, fighting the urge to bury my head in my hands. Or in the sand. "Guys, I know what I've put you through, and I can't even tell you how sorry I am. I've made a lot of mistakes, and for the past few days, I've been too busy figuring out how to take care of the Pride to concentrate on more personal matters. And I know that's not fair to either of you. But I owe it to the Pride—to all of you—to give the fight my full attention right now. After that, though, I swear…"

"You just lost your dad and your brother." Jace scooted closer across the bed, his brows furrowed in sympathy. "And two days ago you were nearly beaten to death, then got kicked out of your home. That's enough to deal with. Take your time."

"Thank you." I gave Jace a tense smile, then turned to Marc.

He sighed heavily and leaned forward with his elbows on his knees, heartache dulling the brilliance of his eyes. "There's nothing I can say right now that isn't going to make this worse. I can't pretend I'm okay with watching you two together, or waiting for you to make up your mind."

Marc glanced at the floor, then met my gaze again, letting me see the brutal misery my indecision was causing him. "It's easy for Jace to tell you to take your time, because he stands to lose nothing from this—a month ago, he wasn't even on your radar, and now he's at the center of the screen. But I stand to lose everything." He swallowed thickly, like the words were getting caught in his throat, and suddenly my heart felt bruised and heavy. "I lose a little more every day I have to see you with him. And I can't watch that anymore, Faythe. I need to know what I mean to you."

Vertigo washed over me, like I'd just plunged downhill on a roller coaster and left my stomach behind. "Are you asking me to choose? Right now?"

Marc stared at his hands in his lap. Then he looked up at me, his gaze equal parts dread and determination. "Yeah. I am. I have to, for my own sanity. So make up your mind, Faythe. Me or him. For better or worse. Right now."

"Marc, please don't do this…" I clutched the edge of the table, panic building in my chest. The pressure was so great I could hardly breathe.

"Damn it, Faythe!" Marc stood and stomped across the room, then turned to face me, pain and frustration lining his strong features. "I hate knowing you want him to touch you. And I hate it even worse knowing that there's more to it than that. If you want him more than you want me, just fucking tell me and get it over with. We don't even know if we're all going to live through the fight, and I don't want to die without knowing whether you love me as much as I love you."

I met Marc's gaze, and my heart hurt so badly I wanted it to stop beating just to end the pain. "Marc, you know I love you…"

His eyes searched mine, his focus shifting from one to the other. Then he exhaled, and his anguish stole my breath. "I know that better than *you* seem to know it. We belong together, Faythe. I've known that since the moment you realized you could piss me off and make me smile in the same sentence, when you were fifteen years old. I know you better than anyone else ever will. I know what nightmares wake you up in the middle of the night. I know where you go to be alone when you sneak off during a group run. I know that you're every bit as tough as the face you show the world, but that underneath that, you're scared. And I also know that fear has never stopped you from doing a damn thing you put your heart into. So why can't you put your heart into *us?*"

"Marc…" I started, and his face blurred with my tears.

"He loves you." Marc glanced at Jace over my shoulder, then refocused on me. "But I love you more. He could walk away from you with a broken heart, if he had to, and live to love another day. But I can't. Since the first time we kissed, there's never been anyone for me but you. Not in my bed, not in my life, and not in my heart. And there never will be. And that's what I need to hear from you. Now." His hope, and fear, and desperation, were so thick in the room that I could hardly breathe. "Purgatory's just another kind of hell, Faythe."

"I…" I curled my hands into fists to keep them from shaking. On the edge of my vision, Jace stiffened, waiting for my answer, every bit as tense as Marc was, and my heart throbbed within the vise of my chest. "I can't… I can't do this right now." I could only juggle so many crises at a time, and I couldn't afford to be rushed into a decision that would determine the course of the rest of my life. And both of theirs. I had to be sure, beyond any possibility of a doubt.

Otherwise, I'd be ruining us all.

Marc blinked. Reactions passed over his face too quickly for me to focus on, but the kaleidoscope of emotions ended in pain and anger. Then, suddenly, his face was blank. He'd locked me out, and that realization bruised me deep in my soul.

"Fine." His voice cracked on that one syllable, and he backed slowly across the room toward the door, jaw clenched. "But I can't hang around and wait for you to make up your mind. I'm done with this." One hand on the doorknob, he turned to Jace and spoke through clenched teeth. "Don't let her follow me. Do you understand?"

Jace nodded, mute. Obviously stunned beyond words.

Then the door slammed, and Marc was gone.

"No!" The closing door—a sight I would forever associate with devastating loss—shook my very foundation, triggering a tsunami of remorse and anguish I could not surface from. The pain inside was like nothing I'd ever felt. Dean could beat me to death an inch at a time and it wouldn't compare to having my heart ripped out and shredded in front of me.

Was this how Marc felt when he found out about Jace…?

"Marc!" I raced across the room, but Jace beat me to the door. "Move! I have to catch him."

"No. Faythe, no…" Jace held me back, and when I tried to push him away from the door, he picked me up and held me. I reached around him, clawing the wooden door frame when I couldn't reach the knob. My nails broke. Blood streaked the door, but I hardly felt that pain—my fingers couldn't compare to my heart. To the other half of my soul that had gone missing.

"Let me go!" I didn't realize I was crying until I saw teardrops soaking into Jace's shirt. "Put me down!"

He set me down, but stood firm in front of the door, and I hardly recognized the pained lines spanning his forehead.

I took a deep breath. "Jace, get the hell out of my way."

He exhaled slowly and stared straight into my eyes, holding me by both arms. "He doesn't want to see you right now. I'm sorry. I didn't want it to go down like this, but you heard him."

Yeah, I'd heard him. But I didn't believe him. He'd dumped me once before, but that hadn't lasted. This wouldn't, either, so long as I could find him before he'd gone too far to follow... "Last warning, Jace. Move."

"I can't. I'm sorry..."

My fist slammed into his cheek, and Jace's head smacked the door. "Damn it!" He rubbed his face and the angry line of his jaw rivaled the devastation behind his eyes. "You fucking hit me!" His blue eyes narrowed and he crossed his arms over his chest like a nightclub bouncer. "He doesn't want to see you, Faythe. And I don't blame him. You have a right to make your choice, but he has a right to his, too, and he made it."

I shook all over; the room blurred beneath tears I couldn't stop.

Jace sighed and uncrossed his arms. "Faythe." I looked up to find him staring down at me, his blue eyes dark like the sky before a storm. "He's gone."

"No..." I fell onto my knees, clutching at my stomach, trying to fight the hollow feeling growing inside me. "He can't be. He promised..." I sniffled, and pain flared to life in my still-kind-of-broken nose.

Jace sank to the floor in front of me, his back against the door. He pulled me into his lap and I wrapped myself around him, my chin on his shoulder, his pale stubble rough against my wet cheek. I put one palm against the cold metal door, willing it to open. Willing Marc to be standing there.

But Jace was right. He was gone, and the closed door wasn't going to deliver my miracle.

"What am I going to do without him?" I whispered, as Jace's hand smoothed my hair down my back and slow tears trailed toward my chin.

He inhaled, and his chest expanded beneath mine, solid and warm. "You're going to cry, then you're going to pick yourself up and keep going, because there are a lot of other people depending on you now, with or without Marc."

Even beneath the weight of this new catastrophe, I knew Jace was right. I held him tighter. "But I get to cry first?"

In reply, he guided my head onto his shoulder and stroked my hair again as I sobbed.

Later, when my tears were spent and his legs were probably half-dead from lack of circulation, I sat up and leaned my forehead against his. "Thank you."

He rubbed my back with both hands. "Anytime."

"I'm sorry I hit you."

Jace frowned. "Me, too. Did it bruise?"

"Yeah. Does it hurt?"

"Hell, yeah, but probably less than your nose." He set me on the floor so he could stretch his legs. "You want something to eat?"

"No." Maybe never again. "I just want to sleep." Forever and ever.

"No problem," Jace said, but his familiar grin was noticeably missing. This wasn't how he wanted to win. I knew that. But I didn't have anything else in me at the moment.

I cleaned up in the bathroom and changed into the tee and boyshorts I'd brought to sleep in, and when I came out, Jace sat in a chair at the table, fully dressed. Both of the beds had been turned down. His bag lay on the floor beside the one nearest the door, and he'd put my duffel in the middle of the rug between the beds. "Take your pick," he said, and I wanted to cry all over again. Though I'd never thought it possible, I was tired of making choices.

When I just stared at both beds, he went into the bathroom and closed the door.

I turned out the light and climbed into the bed farthest from the door, turning to put the bathroom at my back. When Jace came out, he stood silent for a minute, and my heart ached for us both. I knew what he was doing. He was watching me not-sleep in the bed Marc had left cold and empty, instead of the one he'd be warming.

My eyes watered again, and I hated myself. I'd lost Marc, and it hurt *so much*. But turning away from Jace out of guilt wouldn't make any of us feel any better. Yet I couldn't make myself say his name.

Finally he sighed, and his footsteps headed for the other bed. Cloth rustled behind me as Jace got undressed. A moment later, the bedsprings creaked and the lamp clicked off.

I closed my eyes, and the tears ran over.

We lay there in the dark, but for the glow from the

alarm clock, together, yet alone. Suffering similar brands of misery. I could hear him breathe. I heard his mattress creak every time he moved, and I knew he was listening to me not-sleep, too. But I couldn't get his words out of my head.

Could he be right? Was Marc gone for good? It hardly seemed possible. I could still smell his scent on the duffel he'd left behind. Had he left it on purpose, because he was coming back? Or had he abandoned it, like he'd abandoned us? When I closed my eyes, I saw his face, so hurt, so angry. Would it be any easier to live without him, knowing he was still out there somewhere? Or was he as lost to me as my father was to my mother?

Would I lose Jace, too, if I shut him out? If I didn't give him what was left of my heart, now that no one else wanted it? Would I be betraying Marc again by taking the only option left to me? Or would I be saving us all from further misery by finally making my decision— even if I no longer had much of a choice?

Marc had made his decision. He'd left me with Jace. And I felt wretchedly cold and empty, lying in bed alone, when someone I loved—someone who loved me—was doing the same thing six feet away.

I rolled over and Jace blinked at me from his bed, lying on top of the covers like he was impervious to the cold. He wore black boxer briefs and a frown. I swallowed, then took a deep breath. "You said I wouldn't have to sleep alone—that you wouldn't ask for anything. Did you mean it?"

Something passed over his face. Something like relief, only deeper. Something that hurt but felt good at the same time. "Yeah. I'm good for whatever you need me for, Faythe. Just don't push me away."

"I need company." Warmth. Consolation by touch— the human-form version of werecats sleeping in big piles for comfort.

He blinked again, and I barely saw him move. A second later, the mattress sank and Jace was warm beside me. The red glow from the alarm clock showed me half of his face and one deep blue eye. I kissed him, then turned over and snuggled into his chest. He draped one arm over my waist, his hand splayed across my stomach. His next breath was deep, and slow, and shaky, but true to his word, he just held me.

I stared into the near dark and tried not to think about the war, and the men that we'd lose. Marc, whom I'd already lost. Jace, whom I wanted so desperately to keep, but couldn't let touch me.

I'd lost Marc because I loved Jace, but I couldn't truly be with Jace, because I loved Marc. And it all hurt so deeply I could hardly breathe.

"Are you okay?" Jace asked, and his arm tightened around me, pulling me closer. His bare chest was warm against my back, even through my shirt. His foot slid between my ankles, an oddly intimate contact that some- how demanded nothing.

"He promised he'd stay," I whispered, hating myself for letting Marc go, and for not being able to let go of him. "He promised my dying father that he'd stay and help me. He didn't just leave me, Jace. He left us all."

"I'm so sorry," Jace said, and I believed him. He knew what the loss meant to the Pride, as well as to me personally.

"I don't understand. He loves the Pride more than

anything in the world. More than he loves me. I wanted to skip out on our wedding and elope, but he wouldn't go, so I went without him. He chose you guys over me when I was eighteen. How could he leave us all now?"

Jace had no answer. At least, none he wanted to say out loud. But we both knew I'd broken Marc's heart.

Jace sighed and brushed my hair over my neck. "He's gone, and I can't replace him, Faythe. But I love you as much as he does. And I'm still here. Doesn't that mean anything?"

I closed my eyes, and more tears fell on the pillow. I rolled over and kissed him, and when I finally pulled away, I met his tortured gaze so he could see the truth in mine. "It means everything."

That night, I fell asleep breathing Jace, still tasting him from our last kiss.

But I dreamed about Marc.

Thirty-one

We got up early to make our flight and arrived at the gate with half an hour to spare. Marc wasn't there, and it took every bit of self-control I had to keep from looking devastated by his absence. He still had his ticket—it wasn't in the duffel he'd left behind, which I'd checked as my luggage—and we were headed back to his house. Where else would he go?

What kind of massive bitch must I have been to run a man out of his own life?

"He'll be fine," Jace whispered, pulling me close to drop a kiss on my temple. "He always is."

"I know."

While Jace took one last trip to the restroom, I called Michael. I'd already given him the thunderbird update, so when he answered, my unprecedented lack of an opening line was a dead giveaway that something was wrong.

"Faythe?"

"Yeah." I fidgeted in the plastic airport chair, but couldn't get comfortable.

"What's wrong? Did the thunderbirds back out?"

Yeah, right. "Um, I think they'd move forward even if *we* backed out."

"Then what is it?" In the background, I heard pots clanging, though it was only five-thirty in the morning, their time. Obviously I wasn't the only one having trouble sleeping.

"Have you…?" I leaned back in my chair and covered my eyes with one hand, as if that would shield me from the questions he would surely follow mine with. "I don't suppose you've heard from Marc, have you?"

"Not since you left." Michael hesitated, and I heard footsteps. Then a door closed, and the background noise disappeared. When he spoke again, his voice was soft. *Bless my oldest brother and his flawless sense of propriety….* "Why? What happened?"

"He left. I lost him." And the admission hurt just as much aloud as it did rattling around in my hollow chest.

"Because of Jace?"

"Because I couldn't choose."

Silence, except for my fellow travelers, chatting and sipping predawn coffee. Then my brother sighed. "I'm sorry Faythe."

I sighed and let my hand fall into my lap. The light from the airport was bright after my self-imposed darkness. "I'm just glad there'll be plenty of ass to kick soon."

"How soon were you thinking?"

"The day after tomorrow. That should give everyone time to converge. Could you call Uncle Rick for me? I'm about to get on a plane. If he's good with the timing, I'll call the thunderbirds when we land and tell them where to meet us."

"No problem." But he exhaled heavily, and I knew that if Marc didn't come back, his absence would be hard on more than just me.

"Hey, Michael?"

"Yeah?"

"Don't tell anyone else about Marc. I'll tell them when I get there. It'll be better coming from me."

"You sure?"

I sighed, anything but. "Yeah."

Jace returned about a minute after I hung up, and we boarded the plane five minutes after that. He dozed during the flight, his fingers intertwined with mine. I stared at the empty seat on my other side.

"Wait, he just *left?*" Kaci frowned at me from the couch and pulled her earbuds out of her ears, as if she may have heard me wrong. "He wouldn't do that. Marc would never just leave."

My mother put one arm around her, but Kaci's accusing gaze never left me, and it grew colder with each second. "What did you do?"

"Kar—" Holly shook her head and started over, still trying to get used to the tabby's real name. "Kaci, I'm sure it was nothing Faythe did." Obviously looking for support, she glanced across the breakfast table at Manx, who sat nursing her baby, then up at Michael, who stood behind his wife, sipping a steaming mug of coffee. Neither of them spoke.

"Yes, it was," Kaci insisted, and no one argued with her. Except for Holly and Ryan, the rest of them knew about Jace and had no doubt already figured out the basics of how it went down. "The only reason he'd leave us is if he had to leave *you*. You dumped him again, didn't you?"

"Kaci, that's none of our business," my mother admonished softly, but her gaze held mine, equal parts sympathy and curiosity. She'd been in my shoes, and no doubt she hadn't tripped all over the place in them, like I had.

"It's okay. She has a right to know." I crossed my arms over my chest and leaned against the wall by the door, wishing for some of Michael's coffee. "You all do." Because Aaron Taylor was right—there was no such thing as privacy for an Alpha. Everything I did affected them all. "He dumped me."

"Why?" Kaci didn't miss a heartbeat, and I wished I'd been half as perceptive at her age. "What did you do?"

I glanced at Jace, who mirrored my stance on the other side of the door, and I was suddenly glad we'd both showered before our flight. Otherwise, they would all have smelled us on each other—except for Holly.

Ryan followed my gaze to Jace, and his eyes widened. Kaci caught on a second later, and the hurt in her eyes ripped right through me. "Do you have to take *everything* for yourself?" Without waiting for an answer, she stood and ran for the hallway. An instant later, a door slammed.

I started to go after her—with no clue how to start that particular conversation—but my mother stood. "I'll talk to her." I hesitated, then finally nodded. Kaci probably didn't want to hear from me, anyway. At least, not for a little while.

I headed for the kitchen and the lure of fresh coffee, but when I passed by Ryan, his mouth opened, his brows

high in what could only be amusement over my catastrophic personal life. I didn't even slow. "One word,
and I'll rebreak your nose."

Ryan's mouth snapped shut. Though his nose had
been broken several days longer than mine, his looked
much worse. He obviously hadn't Shifted as much as
I had. I wasn't sure which one of us that said the most
about, considering that my last Shifting binge nearly
left me unconscious.

I drank two cups of coffee alone in the kitchen, trying
to concentrate on the upcoming fight. Our allies had all
RSVP'd, and I'd given the birds the pertinent details,
including the fact that all the good guys—the ones they
weren't allowed to slaughter—would be wearing a strip
of bright orange construction tape tied somewhere on
their bodies, be they human or cat.

But my thoughts kept wandering to Marc, and to
my fervent wish that I'd thought to tell Kaci about Jace
without an audience. I'd completely forgotten about her
crush on him, with all the other life-and-death drama
going on around me. But to her, that crush probably *was*
life-or-death, and I'd just given her a double scoop of
bad news.

My father would never have been so thoughtless.

"So…Faythe was with Marc, but then she slept with
Jace?" Holly said, drawing my attention to the card
table, where Michael and Owen had joined her and
Manx. "And when Marc found out, he left you all high
and dry without your major source of muscle?"

"Um, yeah, I guess that sums it up." Michael shrugged
at me in apology, but I could only roll my eyes. My life had
become an open book. Evidently a very *adult* book.

"This place is like a scary, furry soap opera," Holly opined, evidently oblivious to the fact that I could hear her. And see her.

"I could not agree more." I set my empty mug on the counter and headed into the living room without waiting to watch Holly flush. But when I saw my mother on the couch with Ryan, I frowned.

"She didn't want to talk," Mom explained, and I sighed. I didn't want to go to war with Kaci hating me.

In the hall, I started to open the door to the room she was sharing with Manx and my mother, but stopped when I heard Jace's voice from inside.

"Hey, kiddo, don't be mad at Faythe. She didn't mean to hurt your feelings, and neither did I."

"I'm not a kid," Kaci insisted, and I could tell from the nasal sound of her voice that she'd been crying.

"I know. Sorry. People called me 'kid' until after I turned twenty. And now that I've said that, I remember how much I hated it, too."

"I'm not mad at Faythe. I'm just… I knew you liked her—*everybody* knew that," Kaci said, and the air mattress squeaked as Jace squirmed. "And I guess I kinda knew she liked you back. But…what about Marc?"

However, what she really meant—but wouldn't say— was: *What about me?*

"Kaci, sometimes things just happen," Jace said softly. "And it's nobody's fault. Or it's everybody's fault. Sometimes people connect when they don't mean to. When it isn't convenient, or even fair. Sometimes it doesn't mean anything, and they can both go their separate ways afterward. But sometimes it changes things for them both, and for a lot of other people."

Kaci was silent for a minute, presumably thinking that over, and I held my breath in anticipation of her response. When it came, I nearly laughed out loud. "When you say 'connect,' you're not talking about some sappy, deep eye gazing, are you? You mean you and Faythe hooked up, and things got messy—figuratively speaking—so Marc walked. Right?"

"Um, yeah. That's the short version."

And suddenly I felt sorry for Jace. He wasn't prepared for Kaci's birds-and-bees routine, or her uncanny ability to boil down any complicated situation into two sentences or less. Nor was he prepared for her complete lack of a verbal filter.

"But she still loves Marc," Kaci said, as if she weren't gutting us both and laying our dripping emotional innards on the floor for all to see.

"I know," Jace admitted, and my heart ached for us both. For us *all*. "That's her business."

"Is he coming back?"

"I don't know. I hope he will. He'll always have a place in the Pride. But he's really mad and hurt right now."

"He might get over it. If you stay away from Faythe for a while."

Oooh, clever girl, working her own angle! I was almost proud.

Jace cleared his throat, and I knew he'd gotten serious. "I can't do that, Kaci."

"I know." She sighed, but no longer sounded like she was fighting tears. "But it was worth a shot."

I snuck back into the living room before I could be caught eavesdropping, but the place was packed, and every gaze seemed to be trained on me. There was no room to breathe. So I stomped out the front door and sank onto the top concrete step with my elbows on my knees, staring at the driveway, where Marc's car still sat, unclaimed. A minute later, the door squealed open, and Vic sat down next to me. "Well, you really fucked up this time."

I choked on the absurdity of his understatement and probably would have been irritated by his delivery, coming from anyone but Vic. "Does the term 'Alpha' mean nothing to you?"

"You know I'm right."

"Doesn't matter now. He left." And just saying the words made the bloody hole in my heart gape wider.

"Do you blame him?"

"No." I turned on Vic, and the back of my throat burned with words I needed to say, but probably shouldn't. "I blame myself. It's all my fault—I've never denied that. But he just got up and walked out, in the middle of the night! Without even taking his stuff."

"Maybe it hurts too bad for him to see you and know he can't truly have you. It's the same reason he never took a shift watching you at school, only it's worse now, because this isn't just physical betrayal—you let someone else into your heart, and until now, that's been Marc's exclusive territory. But he doesn't have that anymore."

"But I can't help that!" I scrubbed my face with both frozen hands. "I can't help loving Jace."

"Maybe not," Vic conceded. "But you didn't even try. You didn't love Marc enough to even *try* living without Jace."

I frowned, my head spinning, my stomach churning, my heart aching and empty. "This is the worse pep talk ever."

"This isn't a pep talk. This is the truth."

I had no answer for that. Vic was right—again. "But this is about more than our relationship. He broke a promise. He didn't just leave me. He left you guys, too, when we need him most. People are going to die—some of whom he's known half his life—and he's not going to be there to see it. To prevent it. How could he do that to…the Pride?" Because no matter how badly Jace and I had hurt him, the rest of them hadn't done a damn thing, and *they* didn't deserve to be deserted.

Vic frowned, but held my gaze, and my stomach pitched harder. "What?" I demanded, when he didn't say whatever he was thinking.

"He's not breaking his promise, Faythe. He'll be there for the fight."

"You talked to him?" My heart thumped hard enough to bruise my chest. I'd tried calling him twice, and didn't even get his voice mail. "When did you talk to him?"

"This morning, before your flight landed."

"And he's coming back?"

Vic nodded and met my gaze, and the truth shining in his burned. "He promised your dad he'd help you, even if you two didn't wind up together. And that's what's happened, Faythe. He's coming back for your father and for the Pride. Not to be with you."

"Are you sure you want to do this?" I asked, watching Jace stare at his phone. Moonlight shone bright on his face, and his eyes seemed to glow. He was beautiful, without a doubt.

"Hell, no." He gave me a nervous grin and leaned next to me against the trunk of a massive oak tree in Marc's backyard. "But we do what we have to do, right?"

"Whatever it takes." That had become my mantra. I'd do whatever it took to get the Pride back, and I'd sort out the carnage later. And Jace was in it with me, one hundred percent.

"Can I get a kiss for luck?"

I went up on my toes. "You can get a kiss for whatever you want." Because Marc had washed his hands of me, so there was no reason not to kiss Jace now. So why did I still feel half-empty inside? Why was I sure my chill would last long after I went in from the cold?

"Well, at least there's a perk." Jace kissed me, and though my heart ached, my body responded. Remembered. But it wasn't the right time. There hadn't *been* a right time, because there was no privacy in such a small house.

But privacy wasn't the real problem. The problem was that being with Jace could only make me feel better for a few minutes at a time. Marc was always there in the background, just out of reach, while my hands ached to touch him. I couldn't tell Jace that, and eventually I would learn to deal with my loss, but getting over Marc wasn't as easy as jumping into Jace's bed. It would take time, and denying that would be doing us both a disservice.

A car door closed in the front yard, pulling me from my private agony. In the house, they were waiting for us, all packed and ready to go. We just needed official word from Patricia Malone that her husband and his men were on the ranch. Once we had that, we could leave. We'd eat dinner on the road and arrive in time to attack before dawn, when our invaders were hopefully still asleep.

Uncle Rick, Aaron Taylor, and Bert Di Carlo were all

standing by with their men, within a few hours' drive of the ranch. Waiting for word. The thunderbirds had assembled a couple of hours' flight from the property, ready and eager to swoop in on command.

"I guess it's time," Jace whispered against my ear, and I tightened my arms around his neck.

"Yeah. Let's just get it over with." I understood his dread and respected his willingness to work through it.

He stepped back and autodialed.

"Jace?" His mother answered on the first ring. "Is that really you?"

"Yeah. It's me." He turned away from me, and I stared at the back of his head, brown waves shining in the moonlight.

"You shouldn't be calling here. Cal says you… Do you know what they think you did?" Over the line a door opened, and her light footsteps rushed quickly over a hard-surface floor.

"No, but I know what I actually did, and I know why I did it."

"They said you turned Lance Parker over to the thunderbirds and let them kill him. Cal says you tried to kill Alex, and that you cut up Colin's face. Is…is any of it true?"

Jace sighed. "I never tried to kill Alex. I was just defending myself and Faythe."

"But you did the rest of it?"

He leaned against the tree again, and I could see his frustration in profile. "I don't know what all Cal's told you, or what you believe, but you're my mother, and I was kind of hoping you'd take me at my word, even if my version doesn't line up with his. Cal framed us,

Mom. Lance killed a thunderbird, and Cal set us up to take the fall. We had to turn Lance in to keep them from slaughtering the rest of our Pride and killing Kaci Dillon. We did what we thought was right. And I stand by that."

Patricia was quiet for a long moment. Almost half a minute. "I'm sorry you were put in such a difficult position."

"I'm *still* in that position. Cal's put Kenton Pierce in charge of the south-central Pride and kicked us out. We're living in the free zone, Mom. All of us. Women and children included."

Her sharp inhale spoke volumes. "That can't… That's not safe, Jace. You have to send the women back. Kent will take them. I know he will. Or we will. Send them here."

I rolled my eyes and leaned against the tree trunk, but Jace answered without even glancing at me. "They won't go. I need to talk to Cal, Mom. I have to work something out. Can you put him on the phone?"

"He's…" Springs creaked as she sat on what sounded like a bed. "He's not here. He's still helping Kent get everything set up in Texas. But don't call him there, Jace. Not unless you're going to send the women to us. If you come back into the territory, they're going to arrest you, and Cal says… Jace, he doesn't think he can keep the other Alphas from giving you the death sentence. Treason is a very serious charge, and they don't seem inclined toward mercy."

I nearly laughed out loud. *Cal* couldn't convince the *others* to go easy on us? Patricia Malone was either in serious denial or completely brain-dead.

"I…" Jace faked a hesitant pause. "Thanks for the warning. I guess I better lay low for a while."

"Yes. But thank you for calling. It's good to know you're okay."

"Thanks. Can I call you again, just to check in?"

Brilliant! If Patricia were inclined to tell Malone that we called, he'd be ready to take advantage of another call later, but hopefully completely unprepared for the imminent attack.

"Please do. I love you, Jace."

"Love you, too, Mom." He flipped his phone closed and shoved it in his pocket before turning back to me, and when he did, his fists were clenched at his sides. "I hate what he's done to my mother. To my father's Pride. And he's completely warped Melody."

"I know. I'm sorry." I shoved my hands in my pockets, wishing I knew how to comfort him.

"Let's hit the road. I don't want to lose any of this anger before I see Calvin."

My anger was in no danger of fading. In fact, I was confident I'd still be marinating in rage until Calvin Malone spat out his bitter last breath.

Thirty-two

I was a bundle of raw nerves, buzzing with bloodlust, drowning in impatience, and cranky from spending nine hours stuffed in a car. Again. Jace and I were in the lead, with Michael and Holly in the backseat. Behind us, Owen drove with Ryan, Manx, Kaci, Des, and Mom. Parker, Vic, Dr. Carver, and Brian rounded out our caravan in Vic's car.

We'd considered leaving the women in the free zone, to keep them as far from Malone as possible. But the truth was that they'd be no safer there—largely unprotected and surrounded by strays, most of whom had never even seen a female of their own species— than they would be inside the south-central territory. So long as Malone died without ever finding out they were there.

I wondered if the others were all as restless as I was. So far, Jace and Michael seemed to be taking everything in stride, though I knew from the tension in Jace's arms that he couldn't be as calm as he looked.

"So, you guys do this all the time, right?" Holly asked,

leaning forward with a hand on the back of my seat. "This fight is no big deal? It's not really dangerous?"

I glanced from her to Michael and decided to let him field that one.

He sighed. "We fight a lot, yeah, but this isn't a normal fight. It's more like a war. Or at least a battle. Calvin Malone and his men kicked us out of our home and our territory, and we have to take it back by force."

"But you're just going to beat some guys up, right? No one's going to get…killed?" When Michael didn't answer, she turned on him, and I saw the horror on her face in the rearview mirror. "Michael, have you killed people?"

"Not by choice," he finally answered, and Holly's mouth opened and closed, without producing any sound. "We do what has to be done to protect ourselves and the rest of our Pride. That's just the way it is. I'll explain it better when I get back, but I don't have time right now."

Because Carey Dodd's house had just come into sight at the end of the street.

"But what if you don't come back?" Holly demanded, as Jace turned into the driveway. "Who's going to explain that to me?"

Michael took her by the shoulders, as Jace turned off the engine. "I will come back," he said. "I haven't told you the truth after all these years just to…" But he clearly didn't know how to finish.

I twisted in my seat to face them as Owen pulled into the driveway behind us. "Holly, try not to worry. Glasses notwithstanding, your husband's kind of a badass."

"Really?" She looked both hopeful and skeptical.

"Yeah. Did you think all those muscles come from

pushing paperwork at judges? He's done this a time or two, and he always comes out on top." Which was more than I could say for myself lately.

Thanks, Michael mouthed to me, as he helped his wife from the car. I nodded, and wordlessly accepted another layer of guilt for having given her false hope. I couldn't guarantee Michael's safe return any more than I could guarantee my own. But neither could I justify letting her worry, when there was nothing she could do to change things.

Dodd met us at the door and ushered us inside. The other toms were waiting for us in his living room, having parked elsewhere and walked the rest of the way in the dark. His house was so packed with large men it looked like the Dallas Cowboys had stopped in for a visit. At my count, nineteen toms waited for orders, all either watching me or eyeing Manx, Des, and Kaci in awe and curiosity.

While Michael and Owen said their goodbyes to Holly and Manx, I found my mother and Kaci in the kitchen.

"Who are all these guys?" Kaci asked, peering nervously through the doorway into the packed living room.

"They're the Pride members who've remained loyal. Most of them are going to fight with us, but we're leaving Carey and Ryan here with you. You remember Carey Dodd, right?" He'd been driving the getaway car when one of the thunderbirds dropped a huge bolder on it during their siege on our ranch.

Kaci nodded, and though her eyes were shiny, she seemed to be denying true tears an exit. "I'm not mad at you, Faythe. I just wanted you to know that before you go fight. Just in case…. I know Marc's supposed to meet you there, but Jace is pretty good, too, isn't he? And Vic and the others?"

"Yeah. They're all great fighters. And with any luck, when this is over, we can all move back home." Four days away from the ranch felt like forever, when I wasn't gone by choice. "You and Mom try to keep Holly calm, okay? She's new to this." Even newer than Kaci.

"I'm not staying," my mother said softly. I had to process that for a moment before her intent truly sank in.

"Oh, yes, you are." I planted one hand firmly on the counter separating us. "I can't take you into this fight, Mom. Dad would never forgive me. Hell, I'd never forgive myself if something happened to you."

She propped her hands on the hips of her gray slacks and eyed me like I'd just threatened to ruin my dinner with cookies. "Katherine Faythe Sanders, I've spent my entire life in this territory, and I've lived on that ranch since before you were born. I will be there when its fate is decided, and if you try to keep me from it, I will never, ever forgive you."

I gaped at my mother, speechless. "But…" I pulled her to the side so we could argue in whispers, well aware that Kaci was straining to hear. "Mom, this is a war. People are going to die. I can't let you become one of them."

She frowned fiercely. "I know my limits, Faythe. I haven't seriously fought anyone since before Michael was born, and I'm not going to take on more than I can handle. And no one's going to be gunning for an old dam, anyway. I just want to be there. I *need* to be there."

I scowled at her, but she only rolled her eyes. "I'm not asking permission. I'm stating my intent. You may be my Alpha, but I'm still your mother. Let's go." And with that, she crossed the kitchen to kiss Kaci on the forehead, then stalked into the living room and out of sight. Leaving me speechless.

Jace pulled me aside when I stepped into the main room to issue the final orders. "Did I hear that right? Your mother's coming?"

I huffed. "Yeah, and if you try to stop her, she'll ground you till you're thirty." Before Jace could argue, I stepped into the center of the room and cleared my throat. And almost dropped dead of shock when silence descended and every head in the room turned my way.

There were no whispers, no jokes, and no stupid questions. They were wearing their game faces, and they'd all come to fight. And they were prepared to die for our cause.

A chill of awe ran through me at the power we represented. The potential we held. The future was in our hands—not just the future of our Pride, but of our entire species, because with Malone disposed of and me reinstated as Alpha, things would change. They would have to. And the men surrounding me believed in that change, or they wouldn't have been there. They believed with every cell in their robust bodies, with every thrum of restrained power and bloodlust humming through them.

The only thing wrong was Marc's absence, and I felt that like I would have felt a missing limb. He was supposed to meet us in the woods behind the ranch, but I kept turning to spot him, expecting to find him with us already, watching me from the corner or standing by with advice. And every time I couldn't find him—every time I remembered that he'd left me—the wound broke open all over again.

And the worst part was that I had opened that wound in the first place.

Jace stepped up behind me and wrapped one arm around my waist, whispering in my ear. "You okay?"

"Yeah." I shook my head, trying in vain to concentrate on the task at hand. "Just…thinking."

"I think it's time for a little talking, then a lot of fighting."

I nodded, and Jace stepped back. When I looked up, I found everyone watching the two of us in one combination or another of confusion and surprise. I cleared my throat again. "First, thank you all for showing up today. Your loyalty will not be forgotten."

Several toms nodded, but no one interrupted.

"Second of all, the Midwest, East Coast, and southeast Prides have all sent men to fight with us, and we'll be meeting them in the woods behind the ranch in just a few minutes. Also, I've cashed in a favor from a Flight of thunderbirds in New Mexico, and when we leave here, I'll call them in."

They all already knew about our air support, but a murmur of general fear and skepticism ran through the crowd, anyway.

"Our main objective is to take out Calvin Malone. Not capture him. Not spank him and send him home crying. I want him dead. If you have a shot, take it. If not, fight for that shot. Kill if necessary, but show mercy if it won't get you killed. If someone surrenders, knock him unconscious and move on."

There were a couple of grumbles, but no one openly objected.

"Because the thunderbirds can't tell us apart in cat form—and you're all going in cat form—everyone will get a strip of orange construction tape." I gestured to Jace, and he held up the three rolls we'd bought on the way. Di Carlo, Taylor, and my uncle were all similarly equipped. "One of us will tie it to one of your front legs, so the birds know you're off-limits. Do not lose that tape. Hopefully I don't have to tell you how dangerous thunderbirds are, and we can't afford to take hits from friendly fire. Any questions?"

"Where's Marc?" One of the older toms—from somewhere near the Oklahoma panhandle—asked.

I answered without hesitating, but no one was fooled. "He's coming separately, but he'll be there." But they all heard what I hadn't said, and glances flicked toward Jace, who stood tall against the wall to my left, neither acknowledging nor denying. "Anything else?"

"When do we get started?" Holden Pierce called out from the far corner of the room. Parker's youngest brother was our newest Pride member, and he'd remained loyal to us, rather than his father. He was only a sophomore in college, and I felt another strong pang of guilt at the knowledge that I might be sending him to his death before he'd really lived.

But he'd made his choice. We all had.

I smiled. "Right now. Load up."

My pulse raced as I picked my way carefully through the woods, aiming for silence in spite of my awkward human form. I wouldn't get to Shift. Someone had to call all the allies together and tie a bunch of orange flaps around feline legs. But I was armed. I had cat eyes, and I carried a crowbar in my left hand and a folding knife in my left pocket. And once the fight began, I'd have cat teeth, and claws on one hand.

That was the best compromise I could find between Faythe-the-Alpha and Faythe-the-fighter.

Jace was in human form, too, at least so far, to help me tie.

We'd gone about half a mile with me in the lead when brush rustled on my left, and I froze. My heart raced and I raised my crowbar. All movement behind me stopped, as our toms followed my lead, instantly on alert.

A dark blur soared over the brush to land in front of me, huge and tensed for action. I sniffed the air and relaxed. My cousin Lucas. He seemed to recognize me at the same time, and he stalked forward to run his head under my waiting palm. A moment later, more toms leaped over the brush, and my uncle stepped into sight from around a thick pine tree. Bert Di Carlo and Aaron Taylor were right behind him.

They'd contributed six men apiece—seven, including themselves—to the effort, which put our ground troops at a staggering forty-two toms, all ready and willing to kill—or die—for the cause. It was the largest offensive in living memory, even without counting the thunderbirds.

"Faythe..." My uncle stepped forward for a quick hug, then held me at arm's length to study my face. "Are you ready for this?"

I gave him a firm nod, then a small smile. "I was about to ask you the same thing."

"Ready and willing," Di Carlo answered for them

all, hugging my mother in greeting, and my heart beat so hard my chest ached. It was time.

But Marc wasn't there. I pulled Vic aside for a moment and asked if he'd heard from Marc again, but he could only shake his feline head.

What if he'd gotten caught on the way in? What if he'd gotten killed? What if he'd simply changed his mind—decided not to come because he couldn't stand to be near me?

"He's probably just running late," Jace said, rubbing one hand along my back. "He'll be here."

I nodded, then pulled out my father's phone and called myself. Beck answered on the second ring. "It's Faythe Sanders," I said, half whispering, even though we were still a mile and a half from the ranch. "Are you ready?"

"We are always ready," the thunderbird answered, his dual-tone voice screeching softly into my ear.

"Good. Move in and perch nearby. When you see the fight begin, have at it. But remember the rules…"

"We know. Do not kill anyone wearing an orange flag, and do not partake of our kills."

"Right."

When I hung up, Jace, my mother, and the Alphas were already tying orange strips to the toms' legs. I shoved the phone into my pocket and joined them, then tied a short strip to Jace's upper arm.

"You can do this," he whispered, as he tied a matching length to my left arm. "And I'll be right there with you."

I tried for a smile, but failed.

"With any luck, this is overkill." We were attacking in the middle of the night for a reason. Hopefully,

Rachel Vincent

everyone would be asleep in human form, and we would give them no time to Shift. Baring catastrophe, getting to Malone should be easy, and I was fervently hoping that the biggest problem we'd have would be consoling the thunderbirds over the small scale of the promised slaughter.

Well, that and the guns. But hopefully Malone and his men weren't hard core enough to sleep with their pistols.

When everyone was ready, we started forward again, and as we crossed the creek I'd played in my whole life, the thunder of giant wings roared overhead, beating the air as the thunderbirds overtook us.

Nearly two dozen of them.

My pulse surged again. We had the power, we had the numbers, and we had the home-field advantage. How could this go wrong?

Twenty minutes later, I peeked between two trunks on the edge of the tree line, staring at the back of my own house like a thief in the night. And that's exactly what I felt like—I'd come to steal my life back, and heaven help anyone who got in my way.

Jace and my mother stood to my right, my Alpha allies to my left. Spread out behind us were our toms— including my brothers and lifelong friends—scattered among the trees.

I took a deep breath. Then I stepped into the yard.

The men followed me, cats moving much more stealthily than I could on two legs, and I caught my uncle's gaze, then pointed toward the guesthouse. Our allies and their men were going to guard the guesthouse, front and back, to keep as many of Malone's men off us as possible, while we attempted a relatively peaceful assassination in the main house. Then we'd deal with the fallout.

At least, that was the plan.

But as our allies spread out around the guesthouse, Mateo Di Carlo and my cousin Lucas among them, I started to get a very bad feeling.

Jace and I headed for the back porch of the main house, with Michael on my left and Owen on his other side, both in cat form. On Jace's other side, Vic and Parker stalked silently, their white, warm puffs of breath the only sign that they were living, breathing beings, and not cold, efficient emissaries of death, come to help me send Malone on his way.

I tucked my crowbar under my Shifted left arm as I climbed the back porch steps, glad concrete didn't creak. I wasn't sure whether or not Kenton would have thought to change the locks, so I had my keys, just in case. And if they didn't work, I'd kick the door in. Not exactly stealthy, but definitely expedient.

However, before I could test the knob, it turned on its own, and my heart jumped into my throat. The back door swung open slowly and Colin Dean leered at me, his gun aimed at my chest, his mutilated cheek stretching beneath deep shadows in the dark hallway.

"Back for more already?" He glanced at Jace then and arched one brow, like they shared some intimate secret. "We just can't keep this little puss satisfied for long, can we?"

Thirty-three

"Dean." My pulse tripped, and I tried futilely to slow it as a shiny set of cat eyes blinked at me from deeper in the hallway. Then a second pair of eyes. Then a third, fourth, fifth… Too many to count

They'd already Shifted. Which meant they'd known we were coming. I stepped back. Jace's hand steadied me when I almost missed the bottom step, and my mind raced. How had they known? How *long* had they known? Long enough to bring in more men?

I opened my mouth to demand to talk to Malone— I couldn't kill him if I couldn't see him—but before I could, the guesthouse door squealed open behind me, and somebody snarled.

I turned to find more toms in cat form pouring out of the guesthouse, flowing like a river of black fur to surround our allies. At least another dozen. We weren't outnumbered yet, but it was much closer than I'd hoped for. And they definitely were not caught off guard.

"Surprise!" Dean stepped onto the porch, and I took another step back. "When we heard you were coming, we thought we'd throw a party in your honor. Hope you don't mind, but we invited a few extra guests."

"How did you know?" I demanded, trying to control the slight tremor in my voice.

"Well, it turns out that little Melody Malone is definitely her father's daughter. She overheard her mother telling loverboy here where her daddy was, then called Cal directly to report the suspicious phone call. Cal called in every tom within driving distance, and told us to sleep in cat form, just in case. Though I have to say, we didn't think you'd show up quite so soon.…"

"Where's Malone?" I demanded, seething.

"He's around. Pulling the strings from behind the curtain. Smart Alphas don't expose themselves to the melee. After all, who's going to run things if the Alpha dies?" Dean stepped onto the middle of the top step, and cats poured out of the house behind him and leaped to the ground, face-to-face with my own men. At my rough estimate, I counted nearly a dozen. Some of them I knew, some I didn't, but none of them looked surprised.

Jace tugged my right arm, and I started to back up with him, but Dean shook his head. "Don't move, pussycat. Or I *will* shoot you."

Michael snarled at my side, and Jace was growling deep in his mostly human throat, but there was nothing they could do. We were fast, but bullets were faster. Fortunately, so far Dean was the only one in human form, thus the only one carrying a gun.

"What's the matter, Faythe?" Dean taunted, as his toms slunk closer. Two of them faced Jace, snarling softly, trying to steer him away from me. "I thought you liked being outnumbered by men. This is like your dream date, right?"

I slid my keys into my pocket and took the crowbar in my right hand, determined not to rise to the bait. "Why don't you put down the gun and fight fair?"

"We already tried it that way, and I mopped up the floor with your tight little ass. Not to mention your face. Now put down the crowbar, or your boy takes a bullet." He swung his gun toward Jace, and my heart clawed its way into my throat.

"Faythe, he's bluffing…" Jace mumbled.

"No, he's not." And the truth was that he might shoot Jace even if I cooperated. I dropped the crowbar, my gaze locked on Dean's sneer.

"Good girl." He jogged down the steps, his aim steadily trained on the center of Jace's chest. His shadow stretched across the grass beneath the porch light, not quite hiding the vicious grin he aimed at Jace. "I bet she takes the top, doesn't she? A girl like that has to be in control all the time, or she just can't have any fun, right?" Dean's sneer found me again, his gaze tracing the scar he'd left on my cheek, then wandering lower. "But once I put her down, she's damn well gonna stay there."

He reached for my arm, but I jerked away. My fist slammed into his jaw. Dean growled. He backhanded me with his empty left hand, and I staggered backward, determined not to fall. "I *will* kill you."

Dean laughed, and his gaze never left mine. He reached for my arm again, and when I started to step back, he raised the gun, aiming at Jace's face. "Think very carefully."

"Faythe, *no*…" Jace growled, right fist clenched at his side, the claws on his left paw sheathing and unsheathing over and over again.

"It's okay," I said, and when Dean grabbed my arm that time, I let him, even though my skin crawled. "I'll kill him, then meet you right back here." Because Jace couldn't fight with a gun trained on him, and I stood a better shot of taking Dean out without the rest of his men around. "No worries."

Dean laughed and glanced at Jace. "Oh, no, you can totally worry. And in a few minutes, and you can all hear her scream."

Owen growled and Michael snarled, advancing on the toms who faced them.

Dean pulled me up the first step, still aiming at Jace. "Kill the toms. Leave the bitch to me."

Cats all over the yard burst into motion. Snarls and hisses rang out like a violent chorus, a fitting soundtrack to accompany my waking nightmare. The scent of blood blossomed on the air, and I clenched my jaw against a scream as Dean hauled me up the steps by one arm.

"No!" Jace shouted, as two toms advanced on him.

Dean shoved the gun into my spine, and Jace burst into action. He swung at the tom on his right, swiping his clawed hand across an exposed flank. The tom howled, and Jace dropped into a roll. He came up with my crowbar, but then Dean dragged me over the threshold and kicked the door shut behind us. I could still hear the fight, but I couldn't see it. Couldn't see who was winning, or who might be dying.

And I couldn't fight Dean while he still had the pistol.

"Walk, bitch." He shoved his gun into my side and pulled me down the hall with him. "What's with the tape?" He flicked the orange flagging tied to my arm, but I only glared at him. The thunderbirds were our

proverbial ace in the hole, and I wasn't going to tip
him off.

Not that it mattered. Before I could come up with a
believable lie—or even a smart-ass, obvious one—an
avian screech split the night outside, and Dean's head
jerked up. He shoved the gun harder into my ribs and I
flinched while he glanced down the hall.

"Kent, take your group outside. The bitch brought
air support."

My father's office door swung open—it had already
been ajar—and Kenton Pierce stepped into the hall, followed by five toms in human form, all carrying guns.
The shock of seeing them in my father's private space
was so traumatic that I almost didn't notice how strange
the pistols looked. How long…

Silencers. Shit! The birds would never know what
hit them if they couldn't hear the guns being fired.

The men raced past us toward the back door, all
armed except for Kent, who probably hadn't had time for
target practice yet. The moment the back door opened,
I shouted, "Jace, they have silencers!" Then all I could
do was listen as Dean pushed me toward my own room,
boiling with rage on the inside. I had to get the gun out
of his hands.

Kent hung back when he saw where we were headed,
and a spark of hope blazed through my mounting fear.

"Don't you bad guys ever get tired of the same old
routine? You threaten rape, I kick your ass, and evil
is defeated again. Couldn't we shake things up? How
'bout you try to smother me with my fluffy pink pillow
instead?"

Kent froze the minute he heard the R-word.
"Colin…"

Dean ignored him. "Sounds like fun. Unfortunately, Malone wants you alive."

Kent jogged toward us as Dean shoved me through my own doorway. I went down on my knees, but was up in an instant and spun to face him again, frozen with the gun still aimed at my chest.

My stomach churned, and bile rose into my throat. "You're sick." I backed away from him, desperate for a chance to draw my knife. But I couldn't do that until he either turned around or got really close.

"Colin." Kent Pierce stepped into the doorway, looking almost as sick as I felt. "Don't do this."

Dean shrugged, without ever taking his attention or his aim from me. "She brought this on herself, and no one's going to care if I break her in."

"I care," Kent said. That made two of us. Kent glanced from me to Dean, and I held my breath, waiting for Dean to succumb to the distraction. "I'm ordering you to...not do this."

Oh, yeah. Malone picked a real badass to run his puppet regime.... But I'd take what I could get.

"I don't work for you," Dean said, and I nearly screamed in frustration when he stalked slowly toward me, evidently unbothered by the fly in his ointment.

"Fine. We'll see what Cal has to say about it."

And finally Dean froze. His forehead furrowed, and his empty hand clenched into a fist. "Cal's gonna say this!" Dean whirled in a scary-fast roundhouse. His foot hit Kent's head. I shoved my hand into my pocket and pulled out the folding knife. Kent flew back and smacked his skull on my door frame. I pressed the button and the blade popped out of the handle. Kent went down like a sandbag, out for the count.

Damn.

I lunged for Dean as he turned. He swung the gun up. I sliced his right biceps with the knife. He yelled and slapped his free hand over the wound.

I kicked, high and fast, and the gun flew from his hand. I let go of the knife, dropped to my knees, and lunged for the pistol with my one human hand. Dean stepped on my Shifted paw and kicked the gun under my bed, putting his full weight on my arm. I screamed and jerked my paw free. He kicked me in the stomach, cutting off my air for several precious seconds.

Before I could suck in my next breath, he was on me, crushing me. He pinned my Shifted arm to the floor and ripped my shirt half-open. My human fist slammed into his ribs. His smashed into my cheek. Pain exploded in my face. I thrashed, trying to throw him off, but he was too heavy. I couldn't move my legs.

Dean ripped the rest of my shirt. I stretched for the knife I'd dropped, trying to scoot sideways while the room swam around me. I made it several inches before he reached for the waistband of my jeans.

"No!" I threw another punch at his face. Blood dripped from his split lip. My pulse whooshed in my ears and I clawed at his fingers with my human hand, trying to free my Shifted paw. His blood ran, slick beneath my nails. I grabbed his thumb and pulled. The digit snapped backward.

Dean howled, and let go of my paw to cradle his injured hand. I sucked in air, and the room surged back into focus, colors so crisp they were almost painful. Dean punched me with his good hand. I raked my cat paw across his stomach, ripping through cotton and flesh at the same time, silently dedicating the blow to my father.

Dean screeched and clutched his stomach. Blood soaked us both, hot and sticky. I slashed him again. He shrieked and fell off me. I rolled onto my knees and shoved my paw into the gore his stomach had become, tearing loose great chunks of soft tissue.

Dean screamed beneath me. His eyes glazed with pain, and still I tore at him, rupturing soft bits I couldn't identify. There was nothing else in that moment. No war. No pain. No loss. There was only Dean, and blinding rage, and the blessed numbness that came with the bloodlust I'd succumbed to. The room was *made* of his blood, and I was made to spill it.

"Faythe?"

Snarling, I whirled at the sound of my name. Kent stood in the doorway, clutching the frame for support. I leaped up, hissing. He blinked. Then he was gone. His footsteps thundered as he screamed down the hallway.

I turned back to Dean and surveyed the damage with an odd detachment, part survival instinct, part bloodlust afterglow. His torso was shredded. The carpet was soaked in his blood. It squished beneath my shoes. A loop of his intestines stretched across the floor, where I'd thrown it.

I backed away slowly, and bloody footprints followed me, pressed into clean carpet by my own boots. Dean would never touch me again. He'd never fire another gun.

One down, one to go…

I turned toward the door and caught my reflection in the mirror above my dresser. My face was splattered with blood, my hair tangled with it. My bra and torn shirt were soaked, my bare skin slick and red with it. Bits of gore clung to my jeans.

But a horrible, atonal shriek from outside ripped through my encroaching shock, and reality slammed into place, so sharp it could not be denied.

War. My war. My friends and family fighting for their lives.

I wiped my hands on my jeans, then snatched my knife from the floor, closed it, and shoved it into my pocket, then ran into the hall. I slid a bit on the tile, my boot soles still slick with blood. Then I raced for the back door and shoved the screen open.

Thirty-four

For a second, I could only stare. I'd stepped out of my childhood home and into hell.

All around me, claws flew and cats howled. Blood splattered, and birds dove screeching from the air. Bodies thunked to the ground, bones crunched, and dark forms soared, snarling toward their targets. The backyard was a cacophony of pain and rage, a stunning mosaic of violence unrivaled in my lifetime. In living memory. In U.S. Pride history…

From my left came a soft thwuk—mechanical, cold, and discordant enough among the more visceral brutality to pull me from encroaching shock. I turned to find a tom on two legs cowering in the corner formed by the back porch, aiming a silenced pistol at the air. He fired again, and overhead, a thunderbird screeched, wobbling in midflight.

I raced down the steps and grabbed the crowbar I'd dropped earlier, then rounded the porch toward the coward, glad he couldn't hear me over the general din or see me in the shadows. I rammed the straight end of my crowbar deep into his gut. The coward screamed and dropped his gun. I yanked my crowbar free, then kicked the gun beneath the porch and moved on, flexing my sore, sticky paw as I went.

I skirted the backyard battlefield, on the lookout for my mother, Calvin Malone, and other men with guns. On my left, Michael yowled, and I dashed forward to help him, then stopped when he clamped his muzzle over his opponent's throat. He could handle himself.

"Faythe!"

I whirled around to find Jace racing toward me from near the guesthouse. I took several steps in his direction, then stopped when another thwuk sounded on my right. The shooter missed, but took aim again immediately. I swung my crowbar at his gun hand and his arm broke with a satisfying crunch. While he screamed, I bent for his gun and threw it as far away from the fight as I could.

Jace darted left around a rolling, snarling pair of cats and pulled me farther from the melee. "Are you okay?"

"Sticky. And pissed."

He sniffed, and seemed satisfied to smell only enemy blood. "Dean?"

"Dead. The hard way."

"Are you…" He fingered the edge of my torn shirt. "Did he…?"

"Not even close. Where's my mom?"

"I told her to stay near the guesthouse, but…" Jace suddenly shoved me over and rolled out of the way as a dark form flew toward us. The cat thumped gracefully to the ground and swatted at Jace, claws unsheathed. I swung the crowbar at his left shoulder, and the cat hissed at me, ears flattened against his head. Jace's Shifted paw arced down, and the cat howled. "Go find your mom!" he shouted, as he and the cat faced off.

"Thanks. Here!" I tossed him the crowbar—the bad guys were less likely to kill me than they were him— and took off toward the guesthouse with my folding knife in hand, dodging snarling bodies and assessing the carnage as I went.

We'd attacked before dawn so the night would cover our approach, but that had turned out to be a mixed blessing. The dark was working against the shooters, but it wasn't helping the thunderbirds, either. They could only clearly see the bodies within the sphere of the porch lights, and when they swooped in, silenced guns thwuked.

We were outnumbered on the ground, and several of the fallen bodies wore orange tape around their front legs. And those who were left fighting now faced two and three enemy cats apiece, and many had been backed into corners and against walls.

The three allied Alphas had grouped near the side of the guesthouse, their backs to the walls, swinging makeshift weapons while a couple of allied enforcers fought alongside them, trying to protect them and being shredded for their efforts.

I veered toward them, knife held ready. "Uncle Rick!" I shouted, and he looked up.

"Faythe!" Then his eyes went wide. "Look out!"

Something heavy hit me from behind. I landed face-down in the freezing grass. Hot cat breath puffed against the back of my neck, and my attacker snarled. His claws sank through the remnants of my shirt and pierced my skin.

I froze. My breath stuck in my throat and refused to

budge. My pulse raced. This was it. I was going to die, facedown in my own backyard, killed by some faceless, nameless enemy grunt.

Something thudded over me—flesh hitting flesh. Pain pricked several points on my back as the claws were ripped loose. Someone snarled. Someone else whined. The whine ended in a gurgle, and the scent of fresh blood thickened on the air.

I sat up, my pulse roaring in my ears. Ryan stood over the body of my attacker, blinking at me. He licked blood from his muzzle. The other guy gurgled, then breathed his last, blood pouring from his ruined throat.

Ryan nudged my hand with his head, then clamped his teeth closed over the tail of my torn shirt and tugged me away from the action.

"What the hell are you doing here?" I demanded. But I knew the answer, even if he couldn't say it. Mom had come, so he'd followed to protect her. And saved my life in the process. "Thank you." I whispered, giving his head a quick scratch. "Now find Mom."

His head bobbed, then Ryan was gone, off on the only mission he'd probably ever accept from me.

I knelt, groping for my knife in the dark. My fingers closed around cold steel just as a new growl rumbled behind me. I turned slowly, backing away in an awkward crab crawl. The cat followed me, snarling, baring his teeth. I didn't know him. I didn't know half these cats, and of those I did recognize, few of them were Malone's men. His allies had sent toms, too.

"You want me?" I whispered, and the tom's head bobbed. "What are you waiting for?"

He pounced, and I dropped onto my back. His paws landed on my shoulders. I shoved my knife into his stomach and dragged it through his flesh until it snagged on his sternum. Blood poured over me. He fell over sideways without another sound.

I stood and glanced around, counting the orange strips flapping in the predawn wind. Eight. There were only eight of us left in cat form. The others were all down, and though some were still breathing, they weren't getting up. And Malone was nowhere to be found.

On my left, Michael was backing away from three toms. Halfway across the yard, Owen limped away from two more. Teo Di Carlo stood guard in front of his father, bleeding from countless gashes, yet snarling and swiping at four toms.

We've lost....

My heart ached, and fresh tears rolled down my cheeks, unbidden. I'd led them all into the slaughter.

Then, suddenly, a thunderbird swooped out of the air, blowing my hair back with the wind he created. He soared toward Owen and raked deadly talons into the side of one of the enemy cats, digging into the flesh at the last minute. His powerful wings flapped, and both bird and squalling, kicking cat rose into the air. Twenty feet up, the thunderbird release his prey. The enemy tom crashed to the ground, unmoving, a fur-covered bag of broken bones and torn flesh.

I felt like cheering. If the thunderbirds weren't giving up, even as they were slowly shot from the sky for a fight that wasn't even theirs, we couldn't, either.

We hadn't lost until I'd bled my last.

I rushed the toms growling at Michael and shoved my knife between the ribs of the nearest, then swiped my claws across the back of a second. The third jumped Michael, and the other two turned on me, hurt, but not out. I backed away slowly, and suddenly Jace was there.

He swung the crowbar. The curved end smashed through the first cat's skull. But before I could swing my blade, a sudden surge of light caught my eye. I glanced up to find my mother standing in the guesthouse doorway, backlit from inside. She stumbled onto the porch, and Malone came out behind her, holding her by one arm.

The bastard had taken a hostage!

I pressed my knife into Jace's palm and had gone two steps when my mother whirled on Malone and punched him in the face. Malone let her go to hold his cheek, then stormed after her.

My mom ran down the steps. In my peripheral vision, Jace slashed the knife across our opponent's throat. A dark blur flew out of the shadows toward my mother. A second blur intercepted it, and both bodies fell to the ground.

Ryan roared. The other cat slashed. His claws raked over Ryan's abdomen, and my brother collapsed.

No!

My mother fell to the ground at his side. Malone tried to pull her up. Jace raced toward them. I ran after them all, then froze when a deep, unearthly roar ripped through the air.

I turned, and something burst through the tree line. I stared across the yard in confusion as a second huge, dark form emerged from the woods, shoving an entire tree out of the ground in the process.

"What the hell?" Jace asked, from ten feet away, and I smiled, suddenly warm all over.

"Bruins. It's Keller." And someone else. Hopefully

someone else friendly. And as I watched, several smaller forms poured out of the woods behind them. Toms, in cat form. Fresh, and uninjured. Who the hell were they? Where on earth had they come from?

One stopped in front of the crowd, looking over the carnage. Searching for something. He planted his feet firmly, and roared.

And my heart plummeted into my stomach.

"Marc!" I shouted, euphoric, in spite of the bloodbath all around me.

Jace hesitated. He looked at me, then at Marc. Then he raced toward Malone.

Marc twisted my way and the other cats surged around him, and absently I noticed that they all wore orange bands around their front legs. And suddenly I understood. Strays. He'd recruited strays to fight for us. And they'd arrived just in time.

Marc met my glance briefly and bobbed his muzzle. Then he leaped into the fray.

I picked up the crowbar and wiped it on my torn shirt. Then I jumped back into the fight.

I swung metal at everything that didn't have orange tape flapping around its leg. The newcomers were fresh and uninjured. They tore into our enemies like dogs into fresh meat, and the screams that accompanied their involvement gave me a giddy smile.

Something swiped at my leg, but I barely noticed. I lived for the crunch of bone, the flow of blood. I fed on the screams and the whimpers, working my way through the carnage toward Malone. He was the whole point.

When I was twenty feet away, Malone screamed. I looked up from the body at my feet to see him backing away from Jace. But he was out of room, and out of options. Malone's back hit the porch rail. Jace's fist slammed into his stepfather's gut. Malone flinched all over, and suddenly I understood. Jace still held my knife. He hadn't punched Malone; Jace had stabbed him.

"This is for my mother!" Jace shouted, and his fist flew again. "And for Brett!" He shoved the knife home again, and by then I could smell Malone's blood. Jace pulled the knife out and pinned Malone to the porch rail by one shoulder. "And this is for my father..." He looked straight into his stepfather's eyes, and slid the blade across Malone's throat.

Jace stepped back and dropped the knife. The body fell to the ground. He turned to face me, and Malone twitched at his back. Jace made it three steps, then he fell to his knees.

I ran for him and dropped to the ground at his side. I wrapped my arms around him, and he shook in my grip. Jace clung to me, and I let him. Feet away, my mother knelt over Ryan's body, crying, oblivious to the slaughter around her. I stared out at the yard over Jace's head, and exhaled silently. Then I blinked.

It was over. The strays had made short work of the remaining opposition.

In the new quiet, the rush of air overhead caught my attention, and I looked up as the remaining birds dropped onto the ground, already Shifting into mostly human form.

"Faythe Sanders?" Beck called, and I let go of Jace to stand. The bird approached me, almost fully human, and bleeding from a bullet wound to the side. "It seems you have won your war, and it was a glorious battle indeed. Unless you have changed your mind about feasting on the bodies of your enemies, we will take our leave."

I nodded, shocked beyond logic for the moment, then shook my head abruptly. "No. No feasting. But thank you all."

He tilted his head to one side, like he didn't understand gratitude. "We will consider our debt paid, and we look for no further contact with you or your species." He reached up for something hanging from a cord around his neck, and I only recognized my phone when he handed it to me.

I nodded. "Fair enough." Especially considering that half a dozen bird bodies lay scattered about the battlefield.

With that, the birds lifted into the air almost as one. Several swooped in pairs to pick up the bodies of their fallen Flightmates, then they took off together toward the west.

I stared after them, in awe and in gratitude.

The sun was just peeking over the trees to our east when I turned to look over the battlefield. Bodies lay all around me, many still breathing, but seriously injured. Our losses were grave. Our victory was bittersweet. And our road to recovery would be rockier than the tumble we'd taken to get to this point, I had no doubt.

But the war was over. We had won.

And Marc had come back.

Thirty-five

"I called Holly," Michael said, coming to a stop at my side with his hands in his pockets. "I asked her to take Manx, Des, and Kaci to our house. I don't think they should come back here just yet."

"Agreed." It would take hours to dispose of the bodies, and hours more to hose down the grass to wash away the blood. "Maybe they can stay for a week or so? Until I can…get this place put back together?" My carpet would have to be replaced before Kaci could come back inside, even once we'd cleaned up the yard. The smell of Dean's blood in the house would traumatize her.

Hell, it would traumatize me, too.

"Of course."

"How's Mom?" I asked, watching as she knelt beside an injured tom, aiding Dr. Carver on autopilot. Her movements were stiff, her eyes glazed with shock. "How is she really?"

"She's dealing, for the moment, but it's going to hit her the minute she stops moving long enough to get a deep breath. He saved her life, Faythe," Michael said, and I knew he was talking about Ryan. "She wants to put him next to Ethan. And I think you should let her."

I nodded slowly, crossing my arms over the clean shirt and jacket I'd changed into. "Yeah. He saved my life, too." If he'd lived to be one hundred, Ryan could never have made up for what he let happen to me, Abby, and Sara. Even by saving my life. But in dying for our mother, he'd done it in a single instant. In the end, he'd died protecting someone he loved. It wasn't quite like Ethan, but I wasn't going to dishonor his sacrifice. Nor was I willing to break my mother's heart. Not after all she'd been through already.

"Do you have the count?" I asked, already dreading his answer.

"Yeah. Eighteen dead on their side, and there may be a couple more in a few hours. Everyone who's left is hurt pretty badly, but most of them will live."

I struggled to keep my horror hidden. So many lives. So much loss. So much death. But revolution comes with a price, and the best we could do now was try to deserve it. "On our side?"

Michael swallowed thickly, and I made myself look at him. "Ten dead, not counting Ryan. Three of Uncle Rick's, two of Di Carlo's, and two of Aaron Taylor's."

"Lucas?" I asked, my heart thumping painfully.

"No. He broke an arm, and got a pretty good gash on his thigh, but he's going to be fine. Teo, too. He dropped six toms on his own."

I didn't doubt that. Teo Di Carlo was one hell of a fighter.

"And our three, other than Ryan?" I asked, dreading the answer like I'd never dreaded anything in my life.

"Tom Hagarty and William Wright." Two of our

nonenforcer volunteers, who'd believed in me enough to die for our cause. But that left one more.

I turned slowly to the sheet-covered body I'd avoided looking at for the past hour. And to the tom who sat on the ground next to it, head in his hands, crying steadily.

"You're going to have to deal with him soon," my brother insisted.

"I know." I sighed and uncrossed my arms. Michael put one hand on my shoulder and I squeezed it, then crossed the ten feet of bloodstained grass between me and our greatest battlefield loss. I knelt on the ground next to Kenton Pierce, heedless of my blood-soaked jeans, and carefully pulled back the sheet to expose Parker's face, so cold and pale in death.

He looked peaceful, in spite of his violent end, and I couldn't stop more tears, in spite of all I'd already cried.

"I don't know how all this happened..." Kent sobbed. "A month ago, everything was fine, and now I have two dead brothers, and one barely breathing." He glanced across the yard, to where a gravely injured Holden Pierce was being treated by Dr. Carver.

"We all have choices, Kent," I said, running one finger down Parker's cold cheek. His chin stubble was rough on my skin, and somehow that characteristic of growth—of life—made his death seem more real than it should have without more time for it to sink in. He'd evidently shifted to try to heal mortal wounds, but it wasn't enough. "You and Lance dug your graves, and now Parker's lying in his."

Kent sobbed harder, and I wanted to hit him for whining and feeling sorry for himself over the destruction he'd helped bring about. But I didn't, because of what he'd tried to do for me. Kent wasn't a bad guy—he was just weak enough to be used by his father and Calvin Malone. But weakness wasn't a killing offense. Not in the south-central Pride. Not under my command.

"Get yourself together." I pulled the sheet gently over Parker's face and stood, tugging Kent up with me. "You're going home today."

"You're going to let me go?" He scrubbed tears from his face and stared at me like he'd heard me wrong.

"I'm going to *make* you go. You're not welcome here, Kent. Ever again. And Parker stays with us. The rest of your family can come to the funeral, but you keep your father at home. Do you understand?" Because I couldn't afford to let him close enough to launch a counterattack with what men he had left.

Kent bobbed his head. "Thank you."

I nodded curtly, then left him to mourn his brother in relative solitude, while I made my way toward Owen. He sat on the grass at the end of the triage line, a makeshift bandage wrapped around his thigh, cell phone cradled in his lap.

I sank onto the ground next to him. "How you doing?"

"I'm scared," he said, and I could tell from his expression that his fear had nothing to do with the battle, and everything to do with the phone call he'd just finished. "I talked to Manx, but Teo had already called her. He brought down six toms, Faythe, and he said he did it for her. To protect her freedom. He can protect her better than I can. But…"

"But she loves you," I finished, when he couldn't.

"Yeah." However, his obvious despair belied such

good news. "I know it's crazy, but she does. She swore she did. But we don't have a Pride, and even if we did, I'm not Alpha material. I know that. But I love her, and I love Des, and I want him to be mine. I want to give her more, if she wants, to make up for what she lost."

I put one arm on his shoulder. "Owe, that's not crazy. That's love, and love doesn't always make sense." It didn't *ever* make sense, in my experience. "And you *do* have a Pride. You have this one. And you both always will."

"But we already have a tabby," he pointed out, obviously meaning me.

"No, you have an Alpha bitch. And even if I become a dam someday, so what? We're already the weird Pride. Why can't we have two tabbies? Or three? This is a brave new territory now, Owen. Manx and her children will be safe here. We'll all protect them. And you will love them."

And maybe someday, if Bert Di Carlo was willing to institute a similar compromise, depending on her own romantic interests, Kaci might see fit to give his territory a second chance at life. At a new generation.

"You're serious?" Owen's expression hovered on the edge of a smile, as if he didn't dare make that leap.

I grinned. "Are you questioning your Alpha?"

"Hell, no."

"Good. Make your phone call."

Owen was grinning from ear to ear, already dialing when I stood to make my way back to Jace, my heart thumping painfully. I dreaded the next moment with every cell in my body. But the universe had delivered my miracle—given me a second chance—and I could not mess this up again. Not and live with myself.

Jace leaned against the back porch rail, alone, and I stood close enough that my arm touched his. "Are you okay?" I asked, and he only hesitated an instant before nodding.

"Calvin's dead. I'm better than I've ever been. With one exception." He looked up, and I followed his gaze toward the woods. To where the strays and the bruins had congregated. With Marc.

I sighed, and my heart felt so bitterly, unbearably bruised. "He came."

"Yeah. He did." Jace stared at the ground and crossed his arms over his chest.

"Jace…"

"Don't." He turned to face me and ran one hand down my arm slowly, as if to make the contact last. "I know. I knew the moment you saw him. You were happier that he came back than you were that I stayed. I know when I've lost."

I sniffed back tears and reached up to hug him. "I'm so sorry, Jace," I whispered, as his arms wound around me for the last time, squeezing me hard enough to hold my fractured heart together, even if just for the moment.

"Don't be." His cheek scratched mine, and I breathed in his scent, trying to memorize it. "We do what we have to do."

"This doesn't mean I don't—"

"Stop." He pulled away from me, and the pain in his eyes echoed deep inside me. "Don't say you still love me. That'll just make this harder."

I nodded, swallowing the words that wanted to be said. "What are you going to do?"

He sighed. "I'm going to take Cal's body home to

my mother. Then I'm going to kick Alex's ass and take back my father's Pride. Someone's going to have to run things until Melody eventually has a husband qualified to take over. Who knows, maybe I can undo some of what Cal did to her. Show her that she has options."

I smiled. "If anyone can do that, it's you. Is there anything I can do to help? "

Jace glanced at the ground, then met my gaze again. "Yeah, if you believe in me, recognize me. As Alpha. I'll have to be confirmed, even for temporary control, and I could use a few votes…"

"You'll have mine." And I was sure my own allies would help too. We could all use the extra support a Jace-controlled Appalachian Pride would represent.

Jace's smile faded, and his gaze intensified. "Thank you, Faythe."

"For what?"

"For giving me a chance. It was all worth it. Every single minute. Even this one."

I couldn't stop tears then, even when Jace kissed me, for the last time. When he pulled away, he leaned with his forehead against mine. "Damn, this is harder than I thought, and that doesn't seem possible."

"I know." I was shivering, and not from the cold.

He let me go, and I stepped back. "Go on. He's waited long enough."

I nodded and made myself turn away from him, my shoulders shaking. I'd only gone a few feet when the back door squealed shut behind me, and Jace was gone.

I took a deep breath and headed toward the tree line.

There were six toms, other than Marc, and two bruins—Elias Keller had brought a friend.

I owed them my life. My Pride. My eternal gratitude. And I had no idea how to say that.

Marc saw me coming and met me halfway. My heart thumped as I watched him walking toward me, wearing nothing but jeans, in spite of the cold. He had a gash in his left arm and blood had soaked through the material over his right calf, but other than that, he looked good. Very, very good.

"Hey," I said, when he stopped less than a foot in front of me.

"Hey." He shoved his hands into his pockets, and his glittering brown gaze bored into mine.

"Thank you." I sniffled and blinked away tears, but my eyes just filled again. "If you hadn't shown up…"

He crossed both arms over his bare chest, half covering the clawmark scars. "I made a promise."

"How did you know about the orange tape?"

Marc shrugged. "I called the Flight and made them swear not to tell you. My name was on the list of approved phone calls, remember?"

I did remember.

He hesitated, then glanced at the men he'd brought. "You want to talk to them?"

"Please."

"Come on…" He led me to the others without taking my hand or my arm. Without touching me at all.

"Hey, kitten," Elias Keller said as soon as I was within hearing range. The trees at his back swayed beneath a frigid breeze, including the one he'd knocked over during his grand entrance.

"Elias…I can't thank you enough." I cleared my throat, choking back a sob of gratitude, so I could at

least aim for composedly appreciative. "You guys…
you're all amazing. I don't even have the words…"

"And you don't need them." Keller's massive, warm
hand swallowed mine, and he squeezed gently. "Cat or
bear—or evidently bird—we fight for what's right."

I didn't think the birds really gave a damn about our
ideas of right and wrong, but I wasn't going to argue.
"Who's this?" I asked, glancing at the other bruin, who
was every bit as big as Keller, though not quite so tall.

"This is Evert." Keller slapped one massive hand on
the other bear's broad shoulder. "I needed a ride, and he
said he'd only drive me if he could get in on the action.
Worked out well for everyone, don't you think?"

"Very well." My smile could not have been wider.
"It's wonderful to meet you, Mr. Evert."

"Likewise," the new bruin boomed, pushing long,
pale hair from his face. "I haven't had exercise like that
in years, even if it did interrupt my nap."

I smiled and turned to the only stray I recognized:
John Feldman. "Mr. Feldman, I am in your debt. If
there's any way I can return the favor, please don't hesitate to ask."

"I won't." His voice was hard, but still as smooth,
and dark, and gorgeous, as his skin. "Marc assures us
that any Pride run by you will be stray-friendly, and we
figured it can't hurt to establish a good relationship with
our neighbors."

"I completely agree." And my relief had no limit. I'd
been afraid that after what Malone had done to several
members of the stray population, they would think the
rest of us beyond redemption. "And you're all welcome
here as our guests. I can't thank you enough for what
you've done for us."

We chatted for a few more minutes and I invited them all to stay over. Then I said goodbye and Marc followed me across the yard for a little privacy.

"I don't…I don't know what to say, Marc." The guest-house cast its early-morning shadow over us both, and the winter air was several degrees chillier there than in the sun.

"Yeah, me, neither." He glanced at the berry-laden holly bushes, then back up at me. "I couldn't let you down. Couldn't let the Pride down. But nothing's changed. You don't owe me anything. But if you *want* me…I can't share you, Faythe. I won't. It's all or nothing, for me. You've always known that."

"I know." The tears wouldn't stop, and I felt like a fool, because I had nothing to wipe them on. "I want you. I want you so badly I can't stand it. When you left, it felt like the world got darker. Like I couldn't truly see anything. Couldn't feel anything."

"Faythe…" His frown was dark enough to eclipse the sun, and I realized he'd seen me kiss Jace. "This doesn't matter, if you still love him. So please stop—"

"I do love Jace," I said, and Marc's face crumpled. He started to turn, but I grabbed his arm and wouldn't let him pull away. "I can't help that. I love him, but I can live without him. I can't live without you, Marc. Please don't ask me to."

"You…? You're serious?"

I nodded. "As a broken heart. I want you to stay. The Pride needs you, but I'd be lying if I said that has anything to do with this. Stay for me. Stay *with* me. There will never be anyone else. Not in my bed. Not in my life. And not in my heart."

Marc smiled, hesitantly at first. Then he smiled for

real, and the gold in his eyes glittered with light from within. I'd never been able to resist those eyes.

I glanced down and pulled the chain from beneath my shirt, so that the ring he'd given me months ago hung in full sight. "Marry me, Marc."

His eyes widened. His gaze snapped from my face to the ring, then back again.

"Is that a yes?" I grinned.

His smile lit up the whole world.

And Marc kissed me.

I held on to him, hardly daring to believe he was real. That he'd truly come back.

My struggles with the council weren't over—hell, my *fight* with them might not even be over—and something told me that my Alpha growing pains had just begun. But this first hard-won victory proved that anything was possible. Jace could be an Alpha. Manx could marry for love. Owen could be a husband and father. My mother could welcome Angela into our lives and openly spoil a human grandchild. Abby, and Melody, and Kaci, and all the other young tabbies, could have options, and both the privilege and responsibility to fight for them.

And I could handle anything life saw fit to throw at me with my men at my back and Marc at my side.

Together, we represented a new page in werecat history: a stray and a tabby, leading the country's largest Pride. The next generation might label us rebels, or—if we were lucky—revolutionaries. But however we'd be described down the road, looking forward, I was content to know that from that moment on, we'd be running things our way. The *right* way, politics be damned.

And by doing that, maybe I could make my father— forever my own Alpha—proud.

* * * * *

ACKNOWLEDGMENTS

Thanks to Kim, who first saw potential in me and in Faythe. Yours was the first real vote of confidence in me, and I will never forget it.

Thanks to my agent, Miriam Kriss, who made it all happen.

Thanks to my editor, Mary-Theresa Hussey, for kick-starting this project and seeing it through. I appreciate both your gentle nudges and the occasional neon flashing arrow. ;-)

And thanks to Number 1, who takes care of so many practical concerns, so I can spend so much time in my fantasy world. This series would not have been the same without you.

Look for all 3 books in the brand-new trilogy
from *New York Times* and *USA TODAY*
bestselling author

HEATHER GRAHAM

Available wherever
books are sold!

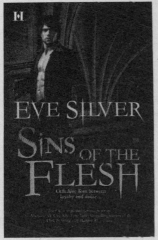

RACHEL VINCENT

32913	PREY	___ $7.99 U.S.	___ $9.99 CAN.
32908	PRIDE	___ $7.99 U.S.	___ $9.99 CAN.
32914	ROGUE	___ $7.99 U.S.	___ $9.99 CAN.
32907	STRAY	___ $7.99 U.S.	___ $9.99 CAN.
32760	SHIFT	___ $7.99 U.S.	___ $9.99 CAN.

(limited quantities available)

TOTAL AMOUNT $ _____
POSTAGE & HANDLING $ _____
($1.00 for 1 book, 50¢ for each additional)
APPLICABLE TAXES* $ _____
TOTAL PAYABLE $ _____
(check or money order—please do not send cash)

To order, complete this form and send it, along with a check or money order for the total above, payable to MIRA Books, to: **In the U.S.:** 3010 Walden Avenue, P.O. Box 9077, Buffalo, NY 14269-9077; **In Canada:** P.O. Box 636, Fort Erie, Ontario, L2A 5X3.

Name: _____
Address: _____ City: _____
State/Prov.: _____ Zip/Postal Code: _____
Account Number (if applicable): _____
075 CSAS

*New York residents remit applicable sales taxes.
*Canadian residents remit applicable GST and provincial taxes.

MIRA®

www.MIRABooks.com

MRV1010BL